A *Book Of*

FINANCIAL ANALYSIS AND CONTROL

M.Com. Part - I : Semester - II
As Per New Syllabus
Effective from June 2013

Dr. Suhas Mahajan
B.A., M.Com., Ph.D. (Finance)
Research Guide, University of Pune and YCMOU
Nashik

Dr. Mahesh Kulkarni
M.Com., M. Phil., L.L.B., D.T.L., Ph.D. (Management)
Research Guide, University of Pune and YCMOU
Nashik

NIRALI PRAKASHAN
ADVANCEMENT OF KNOWLEDGE

N0248

Financial Analysis And Control (M.Com. Part I : Sem. II)   **ISBN : 978-93-83971-36-7**

Third Edition   :   January 2016

©   :   Authors

Published By :
NIRALI PRAKASHAN
Abhyudaya Pragati, 1312, Shivaji Nagar
Off J.M. Road, Pune – 411005
Tel - (020) 25512336/37/39, Fax - (020) 25511379
Email : niralipune@pragationline.com

✦ DISTRIBUTION CENTRES

PUNE

Nirali Prakashan : 119, Budhwar Peth, Jogeshwari Mandir Lane, Pune 411002, Maharashtra
Tel : (020) 2445 2044, 66022708, Fax : (020) 2445 1538
Email : bookorder@pragationline.com, niralilocal@pragationline.com

Nirali Prakashan : S. No. 28/27, Dhyari, Near Pari Company, Pune 411041
Tel : (020) 24690204 Fax : (020) 24690316
Email : dhyari@pragationline.com, bookorder@pragationline.com

MUMBAI

Nirali Prakashan : 385, S.V.P. Road, Rasdhara Co-op. Hsg. Society Ltd.,
Girgaum, Mumbai 400004, Maharashtra
Tel : (022) 2385 6339 / 2386 9976, Fax : (022) 2386 9976
Email : niralimumbai@pragationline.com

✦ DISTRIBUTION BRANCHES

JALGAON

Nirali Prakashan : 34, V. V. Golani Market, Navi Peth, Jalgaon 425001,
Maharashtra, Tel : (0257) 222 0395, Mob : 94234 91860

KOLHAPUR

Nirali Prakashan : New Mahadvar Road, Kedar Plaza, 1st Floor Opp. IDBI Bank
Kolhapur 416 012, Maharashtra. Mob : 9850046155

NAGPUR

Pratibha Book Distributors : Above Maratha Mandir, Shop No. 3, First Floor,
Rani Jhanshi Square, Sitabuldi, Nagpur 440012, Maharashtra
Tel : (0712) 254 7129

DELHI

Nirali Prakashan : 4593/21, Basement, Aggarwal Lane 15, Ansari Road, Daryaganj
Near Times of India Building, New Delhi 110002
Mob : 08505972553

BENGALURU

Pragati Book House : House No. 1, Sanjeevappa Lane, Avenue Road Cross,
Opp. Rice Church, Bengaluru – 560002.
Tel : (080) 64513344, 64513355,Mob : 9880582331, 9845021552
Email:bharatsavla@yahoo.com

CHENNAI

Pragati Books : 9/1, Montieth Road, Behind Taas Mahal, Egmore,
Chennai 600008 Tamil Nadu, Tel : (044) 6518 3535,
Mob : 94440 01782 / 98450 21552 / 98805 82331,
Email : bharatsavla@yahoo.com

niralipune@pragationline.com | www.pragationline.com
Also find us on f www.facebook.com/niralibooks

Preface ...

There are a number of books on the subject of Financial Analysis and Control available in the learners market but they do not meet the basic requirements of M.Com. students of University of Pune. This book is written as per the revised syllabus prescribed for M.Com. Semester-II students from June, 2013. We do hope that this book will definitely help to meet the growing requirements of the students of management accounting from the faculty of Commerce and Management. This book adopts a modern and novel approach towards the study of Financial Analysis and Control keeping in mind the specific requirements of the readers and practitioners of this subject.

All the topics included in the syllabus are explained in simple but apt language. Equal stress is also given to necessary accounting theories and a wide variety of practical problems. We have taken appropriate care to incorporate basic accounting concepts, accounting standards and tabular representation of techniques of financial analysis and control. Proper emphasis is also given to charts and graphs to simplify the accounting theories and practices. This book has been designed to serve as a self sufficient text for M.Com. students. It will definitely add to our satisfaction if this book would be more useful as a guide for practicing accountants, professional managers, dynamic entrepreneurs and enthusiastic teachers of the subject of management accounting.

We sincerely thank the senior faculty members from various Colleges, Management Institutes and Accounting Associations for guiding and constantly encouraging us in our enterprise and the ever challenging students community who inspired us to write this book as per their requirement.

We are also thankful to Shri. Dineshbhai Furia, Shri. Jignesh Furia, and Shri. Akbar Shaikh, Mrs. Nirja Sharma, Mr. Prasad Chintakindi and the entire staff of Nirali Prakashan, Pune for their earnest help in bringing out this book with vigour and accuracy. We have taken utmost care to make the text error free. Nevertheless, we do not rule out the possibility of certain shortcomings or misprints still remaining, we will be grateful to the reader if such errors are pointed out and brought to our notice.

We must concede that this book would never have been written without the support, encouragement and inspiration of our family members; many, many thanks to them.

Any criticism or valuable suggestions for further improvement of this book will be gratefully acknowledged and highly appreciated.

January, 2014   **Dr. Mahesh Kulkarni**

Pune 411021   **Dr. Suhas Mahajan**

Syllabus ...

University of Pune
M.Com. Part I : Semester II

Financial Analysis and Control

Course Code 201

Unit 1 - Long Term Investment Decisions   (10 L)

Capital Budgeting – Meaning – Importance – Evaluation Technique and Methods – Pay Back, Rate of Return, Discounted Pay Back Period – Discounted Cash Flow – Net Present Value – Internal Rate of Return, Modified Internal Rate of Return – Profitability Index, Relationship between Risk and Returns.

Unit 2 - Cost of Capital   (10 L)

Meaning – Definition and Assumptions – Explicit and Implicit Cost – Measurement of Specific Cost – Cost of Debt – Preference Shares – Equity Shares – Retained Earnings – Weighted Average Cost of Capital.

Unit 3 - Marginal Costing   (08 L)

Meaning of Marginal Cost and Marginal Costing – Advantages – Limitations – Fixed and Variable Cost – Contribution – Break–even Analysis – Profit Volume Ratio – Limiting Factor.

Unit 4 - Short Run Managerial Decision Analysis   (08 L)

Introduction – Analytical Framework. Decision Situations : Sales Volume Related Decisions – Sell or Further Process – Make or Buy – Product Line / Divisions / Departments – Short Run Use of Scare Resources – Operate or Shut Down.

Unit 5 - Budget and Budgetary Control   (06 L)

Meaning – Definition and Scope of Budget and Budgetary Control – Types of Budgets – Financial Budget – Master Budget – Flexible Budget – Capital Budget.

Unit 6 - Standard Costing   (06 L)

Concept, Advantages; Types of Standards – Variance Analysis : Materials, Labour, Overhead – Managerial Uses of Variances.

Contents ...

List of Figures, Graphs and Charts ...

Chapter **1**...

Long-Term Investment Decisions

Synopsis...

1.1 CAPITAL BUDGETING

Management Decisions on the commitment of funds to long-term uses within the business are among the most critical for its continued success, while also being among the most difficult to make. Such decisions are critical because they deals with the large amount of funds over long periods and there is very little chance of reversing the decision once made and put into effect. The commitment of huge amounts to highly specialised machinery, for the manufacture of a product which loses popular favour shortly afterwards, cannot be reversed quickly. **Capital Investment Decisions,** therefore have long lasting influence for good or evil on the profitability of the business enterprise.

The **Investment Decision** is a very difficult decision because it requires an accurate assessment of future events. The longer ahead that it is necessary to forecast, the more difficult the process becomes. The uncertainties surrounding the future are caused by technological, economic and social changes, competitive forces and the actions of governments.

Methods of investment project selection are techniques which can be used to assist management; they are not substitutes for management. Unless the techniques are set within the proper framework of management decisions and policy, disappointment in the outcome is certain.

The major management policy decisions are necessary before any capital investment appraisal technique can be fully effective, if they are,

- Setting the objective and long-term goals of the business.
- Deciding on the balance to be maintained between owners funds and borrowed funds in the capital structure.
- Setting parameters for risk and profitability which will be acceptable.

The success and growth of any commercial enterprise depends upon efficient utilisation of available resources. This is particularly true in case of acquisition of fixed assets where the quantum of investment and risks involved are reasonably very high. Therefore, such decisions are subject to a systematic evaluation process which is known as **'Capital Budgeting'**.

1.1.1 MEANING

Capital Budgeting refers to planning the deployment of available capital for the purpose of maximising the long-term profitability of a firm. It is the firm's decision to invest its current funds most efficiently in long-term activities and in anticipation of flow of future benefits over a number of years. The term **Capital Budgeting** is used interchangeably with "capital expenditure management", "long-term investment decision" and "management of fixed assets". This represents planning in advance to secure additional funds required for implementation of specific projects.

According to **'G. D. Quirin',** the **Capital Budgeting** decision, involves a current outlay or series of outlays of cash resources in return for an anticipated flow of future benefits. Capital Budgeting is adopted to evaluate expenditure decision relating to current outlay the benefits of which are likely to spread over a period of longer time than one year. The real distinction between capital expenditure and revenue expenditure lies not in the immediate charging of expenditure to income, but in the duration of the period taken for its recovery in cash. Precisely, capital expenditure recoveries are made over a long period of time.

Capital Budgeting is the process by which companies allocate funds to various investment projects designed to ensure profitability and growth. Evaluation of such project involves estimating their future benefits to the company and comparing these with their costs.

Thus, Capital Budgeting involves:

- the search for new and more profitable investment proposals, and
- the making of an economic analysis to determine the profit potential of each investment proposal.

It is a process by which available cash and credit resources are allocated among competitive long-term investment opportunities so as to promote the greatest profitability of company over a period of time. It refers to the total process of generating, evaluating and following up on capital expenditure alternatives.

Definitions

Capital Budgeting may be defined as the firm's formal process for the acquisition and investment of capital. It involves firm's decision to invest its current funds for addition, disposition, modification and replacement of fixed assets. The importance of fixed assets management could be marked out for the following purposes:

- Risk associated with their longer life (some time with perpetual life).
- High cost factor.
- Problems of acquisitions and replacement.
- The use of efficient machinery and equipment is necessary for economies of scale, especially, in the present competitive world. Because of technological changes, the investment in fixed assets is likely to increase, old assets become outdated and many have to be replaced. Planning for long-term capital expenditure is the most important function of every business because substantial amounts are involved and investment of funds is spread over a considerable period of time and returns flow back at different intervals in unknowing amounts.

Some of the important definitions given by certain eminent authorities on the subject concerned are as follows:

i) *Weston and Brigham*:

"**Capital Budgeting** involves the entire process of planning expenditures whose returns are expected to extend beyond one year. The choice of one year is arbitrary, of course, but it is a convenient cut off point for distinguishing kind of expenditure."

ii) *John J. Hampton*:

"**Capital Budgeting** describes the firm's formal planning process for the acquisition and investment of capital and results in capital budget that is the firm's formal plan for the expenditure of money to purchase fixed assets."

iii) *G. C. Philippatos*:

"**Capital Budgeting** is concerned with the allocation of firm's scare financial resources among the available market opportunities. The consideration of investment opportunities involves the comparison of the expected future streams of earning from a project, with the immediate and subsequent stream of expenditures for it."

iv) *Sidney Davidson*:

"**Capital Budgeting** as, the process of choosing investment projects for an enterprise by considering the present value of cash flows and deciding how to raise the funds required by the investment."

Thus, Capital Budgeting is primarily concerned with the planning and control of expenditure for tangible fixed assets, such as :

- Replacement of machinery and equipment that are over-utilised to its full capacity.

- Acquisition of new facilities that have higher productive or labour - saving capacities than to existing facilities and removal of old facilities.

- Acquisition of new buildings, and the enlargement and improvement of existing building.

- Acquisition of additional machines and other facilities of the kinds already owned in anticipation of increased sales of present product lines.

- Acquisition of new kinds of facilities needed for new product lines to be taken on.

Features

Capital Budgeting have the following important features :

i) It involves exchange of current funds for future benefits, funds once invested in long-term activities. They benefit future period, they have the effect of increasing the capacity, efficiency, span of life or economy of operation of an existing fixed assets.

ii) Capital Budgeting decisions have long-term implications for a firm. The effects of capital budgeting decision extend into the future and have to be endured for a longer period than the consequences of current operating expenditure.

iii) Capital Budgeting is an important function of management because it is one of the critical determinations of the success or failure of the company. It advised how excessive capital spending may create excessive capacity and increase operating costs and reduce its profit earning capacity.

iv) Capital Budgeting decisions are irreversible because we could seldom find ready markets for the disposing of capital assets. The only option available to the firm is to scrap the capital assets, leading to selling them at a substantial loss in the event of decision being proved wrong.

v) Decisions relating to capital investment are among the difficult and at the same time, the most critical a management has a make. These decisions require an assessment of future events which are uncertain. It is really a complex problem to estimate the future benefits and costs correctly in quantitative terms because of economic, political, technological and social factors.

The examples of Capital Budgeting Decisions are as follows:

- Expansion of business by investment in plant and machinery.
- Introduction of a new product.
- Replacing and modernizing a process.
- Mechanisation of process.
- Decision regarding choice between alternative machines.

The Specimen of Capital Budget is as follows:

ATLAS CO. LTD. ANDHERI
CAPITAL BUDGET

Date : _____   Proposal No. : _____

To   :   Capital Expenditure Committee

From :   _____   Division/Section : _____

Request to the Committee

i)   Introduction

ii)   Need and importance of the project

iii) Duration of the project

iv)   Timing

    a)   Commencement

    b)   Completion

v)   Proposed Expenditure

    • Cost Assets ₹ ....

    • Freight and Delivery charge ₹ ....

    • Cost of Installation ₹ ....

    • Miscellaneous Expenses   (+) ₹ ....   ₹ ....

    • Total Cost

vi)   Increase in Earnings (Estimated)

vii) Scheduled Profitability

    a)   Internal rate of return

    b)   Payback period

    c)   Discounted payback period

    d)   Accounting Rate of Return

Remarks of Capital Expenditure Committee

No. .... Chairman of the Committee

1.1.2 IMPORTANCE

Capital Budgeting refers to the practice of allocating on a regular periodic basis money to be used for assets including building, machinery, plant and equipment etc. Thus it is the process of planning and controlling major expenditure on projects with extended lives. For a big commercial enterprise it may entail millions of rupees spent annually on complex facilities. For a smaller commercial concern it might entail the occasional purchase for one machine costing several thousand rupees.

Capital Budgeting decision is of paramount importance in financial decision making because:

i) Capital budgeting decision vitally affects the profitability of a business concern. An appropriate investment decision can give spectacular returns. But ill-advised and incorrect investment decision will affect the very survival of even large sized concerns.

ii) A capital expenditure decision has its own impact over a long-period of time, and it invariably affects company's future cost structure. For instance, if a new plant is acquired to introduce a new product into the market, a company firmly commits itself thereby to additional fixed costs towards labour, insurance, rent. etc. It should also be noted that even if the investment turns out to be unsuccessful, the company has to bear the additional fixed costs.

iii) Capital project decisions are irreversible, such decisions once made, cannot be easily reversed without considerable financial loss to the company.

iv) Capital project decision involves huge capital outlay. When majority of the companies have only scarce resources, capital project decision becomes a complicated task. This necessitates very careful and correct investment decision as otherwise, it would not only result in losses but also deprive the company from earning profits other investment which could not be effected due to lack of funds.

1.2 EVALUATION TECHNIQUES AND METHODS

In view of the utmost importance of capital budgeting decisions, a sound appraisal method should be adopted to measure the economic worth of each investment project.The investment evaluation criterion should possess the following characteristics :

i) It should distinguish between acceptable and non-acceptable projects.

ii) It should have an inbuilt quality of ranking project in order of their desirability.

iii) It should solve the problem of choosing from among several alternative project.

iv) It should be a suitable criterion which is applicable to any conceivable capital investment project.

v) It should recognise the fact that bigger benefits are preferable to smaller ones and the early benefits are preferable to the later ones.

There are various methods for evaluating and ranking the capital investment proposals. In all these methods, the basic approach is to compare the investments in the project to the benefits derived therefrom.

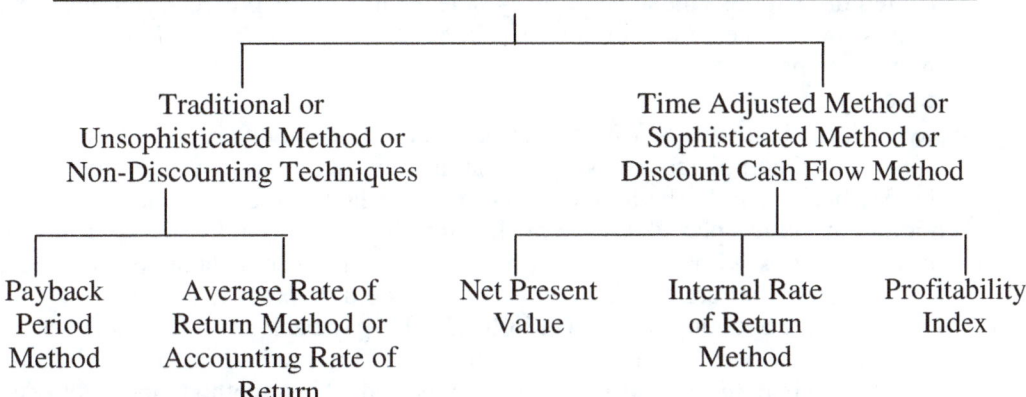

These methods of investment evaluation are summarised as follows:

1.2.1 PAY BACK

One of the traditional method of capital budgeting is the **pay back method**. The pay back period method examines the worth of an investment proposal by the time taken to recoup the investment. The term pay back period refers to the period which the project will generate the necessary cash to recover the initial investment. The pay back period is defined as, the number of years required for the proposal's cumulative cash inflows to be equal to its cash outflows. In other words, the pay back period is the length of time required to recover the initial cost of the project.

Pay back period reciprocal = (1 / Pay back period) × 100.

If the project generates constant annual cash inflows, the pay back period can be computed by the following formula :

$$\text{Pay back Period} \ = \ \frac{\text{Initial Investment (cash outlay)}}{\text{Annual Cash Inflow}}$$

Advantages :

The **advantages** of the pay back method are as follows :

i) The pay back method is undoubtedly an improvement over the criterion of urgency.

ii) It is easy to understand and simple to adopt in any concern. It is used as an effective tool for evaluating investment proposals such that the investment with the shorter pay back period is preferred to investment with longer pay back period.

iii) The short-term approach involved in the pay back method greatly minimises the possibility of losses through obsolescence.

iv) The method enables a firm to choose an investment which yields a quick return on cash funds.

v) The method considers the liquidity as well as solvency of a firm as a guiding principle in the capital budgeting decisions.

vi) The use of pay back method is preferred for the simple reason like the returns beyond three or four years are quite uncertain and the same is disregarded in any planning decision.

vii) A company which is running short of funds and with no other sources of raising the required funds, must necessarily select only those projects yielding quick returns and hence, more importance is attached to this method of evaluating investment proposals.

Disadvantages :

The pay back method suffers from certain **shortcomings** which are as follows :

i) This method completely ignores all cash inflows accruing from the project after the pay back period. The application of this method in the case of a project with a longer gestation period will be misleading. From this point of view, heavy and basic industries with longer gestation periods can never be launched since they begin to yield the returns after a lapse of considerable period of time.

ii) It fails to take account of the cash inflows after pay back period. Projects having long gestation period will not be taken up, if this method is followed though they may yield high returns for a long period. This method does not value projects of different spans of economic life. The economic life of a project is the life beyond the pay back period.

iii) It is not an appropriate method of measuring the profitability of an investment project, as it does not consider the entire cash inflows generated by the project.

iv) It fails to consider the pattern of cash inflows - magnitude and timing of cash inflows. In other words, it gives equal weight to returns of equal amounts even though they occur in different periods.

v) The pay back period method is not consistent with the objective of maximising the market value of firm's shares.

vi) Another limitation of pay back method is that it does not measure precisely even the cashflows expected to be received within the pay back period, in the sense that it does not differentiate between the projects in terms of the timing or magnitude of cashflows. It takes into consideration only the recovery period. This happens because it does not discount the future cashflows and treats a rupee received in the second or third year as equivalent to a rupee received in the first year. In short, this method ignores the time value of money as shown in the following example.

ILLUSTRATIONS

ILLUSTRATION 1

Ashoka Ltd., Agra considering for the purchase of a machine. Two machines A and B each costing ₹ 1,50,000 are available.

Cash inflows are expected to be as under.

Year	Machine A ₹	Machine B ₹
1	45,000	15,000
2	60,000	45,000
3	75,000	60,000
4	45,000	90,000
5	30,000	60,000

Calculate pay back period.

SOLUTION

Pay back period of Machine A $= ₹\ 45,000 + ₹\ 60,000 + \dfrac{₹\ 45,000}{₹\ 75,000}$

$= 2.6$ years

i.e. 2 years and 7.2 months i.e. 2 years 7 months and 6 days

Pay back period of Machine B $= ₹\ 15,000 + ₹\ 45,000 + 60,000 + \dfrac{₹\ 30,000}{₹\ 90,000}$

$= 3.3$ years

i.e. $3\frac{1}{3}$ years i.e. 3 years 4 months.

ILLUSTRATION 2

Balaji Co. Baroda is considering to expand its production. It can go in either for a computerised machine costing ₹ 2,24,000 with an estimated life of $5\frac{1}{2}$ years or an ordinary machine costing ₹ 60,000 having an estimated life of 8 years. The annual sales and costs are estimated as follows :

	Computerised Machine ₹	Ordinary Machine ₹
Sales	1,50,000	1,50,000
Costs :		
• Materials	50,000	50,000
• Labour	12,000	60,000
• Variable Overheads	24,000	20,000

Calculate the pay back period and advise the company.

SOLUTION

Calculation of Contribution

Particulars	Computerised Machine ₹	Ordinary Machine ₹
Cost Price	2,24,000	60,000
Sales	1,50,000	1,50,000
Less : Variable Cost	86,000	1,30,000
(Materials + Labour + Variable overheads)　(−)		
∴　Contribution	64,000	20,000

$$\text{Pay back Period} = \frac{\text{Original Cost}}{\text{Annual Cash Inflows}} = \underset{\text{CM}}{\frac{₹\ 2,24,000}{₹\ 64,000}} = \underset{\text{OM}}{\frac{₹\ 60,000}{₹\ 20,000}}$$

$$= 3.5 \text{ years} \qquad = 3 \text{ years}$$

The pay back period in case of ordinary machine is shorter, hence ordinary machine is preferable.

ILLUSTRATION 3

Crystal Ltd., Chembur is considering for investing in a project requiring a capital outlay of ₹ 4,00,000. Forecast of annual income after depreciation but before tax is as follows :

Year	₹
1	2,00,000
2	2,00,000
3	1,60,000
4	1,60,000
5	80,000

Depreciation may be taken at 20% on original cost and income tax at 50% of net income. Evaluate the project using pay back method.

SOLUTION

$$\text{Annual Depreciation} = \frac{₹\ 4,00,000 \times 20}{100}$$

$$= ₹\ 80,000$$

Statement of Net Cash Inflows

Years	Profit after Depreciation (A) ₹	Tax at 50% (B) ₹	Cash Inflow A – B + Depreciation ₹
1	2,00,000	1,00,000	1,80,000
2	2,00,000	1,00,000	1,80,000
3	1,60,000	80,000	1,60,000
4	1,60,000	80,000	1,60,000
5	80,000	40,000	1,20,000

Payback period = ₹ 1,80,000 + ₹ 1,80,000 + ₹ 40,000 = 0.25 years (means – 3 months)

₹ 1,60,000 = 2.25 years (i.e. 2 years and 3 months)

2 years

ILLUSTRATION 4

Domino Ltd., Delhi proposes to increase the production of the company. They are willing to purchase a new machine. There are three types in the market. The following are the details regarding them :

Particulars	Type A ₹	Type B ₹	Type C ₹
Cost of machine	17,500	12,500	9,000
Estimated savings in scrap	400	750	250
Wages per operator	250	300	250
Cost of indirect materials	–	400	–
Expected savings in indirect material	100	–	250
Additional cost of maintenance	750	550	500
Additional cost of supervision	–	800	–
Operators not required (number)	11	20	9
Estimated life of machine	10 years	6 years	5 years
Taxation at 50% of the profit			

You are required to advise the management which type of the machine should be purchased.

SOLUTION

Profitability Statement

Particulars	Type A ₹	Type B ₹	Type C ₹
Machine cost	17,500	12,500	9,000
Life of the machine	10 years	6 years	5 years
Saving (per year) in costs :			
• Wages	2,750	6,000	2,250
• Scrap	400	750	250
• Indirect materials (+)	100	–	250
Total (A)	3,250	6,750	2,750
Additional Expenditure			
• Indirect material	–	400	–
• Supervision	–	800	–
• Maintenance (+)	750	550	500
Total (B)	750	1,750	500
Marginal Profit (A – B)	2,500	5,000	2,250
Net Savings after tax of 50%	1,250	2,500	1,125
Pay back period	14 years	5 years	8 years
Pay back profitability	Nil	2,500	Nil

The company is advised to purchase machine Type B since it ranks first both in pay back as well as pay back profitability criteria. In the case of Type A and Type C, the life of each machine is shorter than the pay back period.

ILLUSTRATION 5

In Escorts Ltd., Edalabad a project costs ₹ 20,00,000 and yield annually a profit of ₹ 3,00,000 after depreciation at $12\frac{1}{2}\%$ but before tax at 50%.

Calculate pay back period.

SOLUTION

Particulars	Amount ₹
Annual Profit	3,00,000
Less : Income Tax (−)	1,50,000
	1,50,000
Add : Depreciation $\frac{12\frac{1}{2}}{100}$ × ₹ 20,00,000 (+)	2,50,000
Annual Cash Inflow	4,00,000
Payback Period = $\frac{₹\ 20,00,000}{₹\ 4,00,000}$	5 years

1.2.2 RATE OF RETURN

Average Rate of Return is defined as the annualised net income earned on the average funds invested in a project. In other words, the annual returns of a project are expressed as a percentage of the net investment in the project. This method is mainly based on accounting approach rather than cashflow approach. The Average Rate of Return method, consists of aggregating all the earnings after depreciation and dividing them by the project's useful life-span. The resultant average earning over the period is divided by the average investment over the period. The average investment in a project represents the simple arithmetic mean of the values of the asset at the beginning and the end of the useful lifespan of the asset, which is always zero at the latter point of time. Under these circumstances the average investment in a project is always one-half of the original investment. For calculating the average rate of return, sometimes the value of the initial investment is used in the place of average investment. However, it should be remembered that the use of the average investment is more logical. For the calculation of average rate of return the following formula can be adopted.

$$\text{ARR} = \frac{\text{Average annual earnings after taxes and depreciation}}{\text{Average Investment}} \times 100$$

$$\text{ARR} = \frac{\text{Average annual income after taxes and depreciation}}{\text{Initial Investment}} \times 100$$

Calculation of an Average Investment :

As said earlier, there is no common understanding regarding the consideration of outlay or investment. Some may take the initial investment and some consider average investment. Average investment is normally considered as half of the depreciated investment and the other half of the non-depreciated investment. This may be expressed as follows :

$$= \frac{\text{Original Investment}}{\frac{1}{2}\text{ depreciation} + \frac{1}{2}\text{ non-depreciated outlay}} \quad \text{OR} \quad \frac{\text{Original Investment}}{2}$$

Another formula is adopted with or without the consideration of scrap value of the asset, particularly in case of machinery.

The accountants use half the outlay as average investment under the presumption that the asset utilisation in the project life period is only partial. Because, a portion of outlay will be recovered from depreciation.

$$\text{Average Investment} = \frac{\begin{array}{c}\text{Net Working Capital + Salvage Value +}\end{array}}{}\ \frac{1}{2}\,(\text{Initial Cost of the machine} - \text{Salvage value})$$

Accept or Reject Criterion :

The average rate of return method facilitates the decision-maker to decide whether to accept or reject an investment proposal. Based on this method as an accept-reject criterion, the actual average rate of return is compared with a predetermined or a minimum required rate of return or cut-off rate. A project is accepted, when the actual average rate of return is higher than the minimum desired rate of return. Otherwise, the project is rejected. Alternatively, the ranking method can be employed to decide on the capital investment proposals.

Advantages :

The **advantages** of average rate of return are as follows :
i)   The average rate of return method is also simple to understand and easy to adopt. What is required is only the accounting profits in a project after providing for taxes. This figure can be easily obtained.
ii) This method is considered superior to the payback method in the sense that it takes into consideration the earnings over the lifespan of project and hence, facilitates the comparison of the values of different projects.
iii) This method takes into consideration only the net earnings after providing for depreciation, as it is of vital importance in the appraisal of investment proposals.
iv) It can readily be calculated using the accounting data.

Disadvantages :

The average rate of return method suffers from the some **shortcomings** as that of the payback method and they are given below :   .
i)   It ignores the time value of money. Profits earned in different accounting periods are valued equally.
ii) It does not consider the length of life of projects.
iii) It is not consistent with the firm's objective of maximising the market value of shares.
iv) It ignores the fact that the profits earned can be reinvested.
v)   It does not consider the benefits accruing to the company as a result of sale.

ILLUSTRATIONS

ILLUSTRATION 1

Frammy Ltd. Faizpur is considering the purchase of a machine. Two machines are available X and Y. The cost of each machine is ₹ 60,000. Each machine has an expected life of 5 years. Net profit before tax during the expected life of the machine are given below :

Year		Machine X ₹	Machine Y ₹
1		15,000	5,000
2		20,000	15,000
3		25,000	20,000
4		15,000	30,000
5	(+)	10,000	20,000
Total		85,000	90,000

Following the method of return on investment ascertain which of the alternatives will be more profitable. The average rate of tax may be taken at 50%.

SOLUTION

Statement of Profitability

Year	Machine X			Machine Y		
	Profit before Tax ₹	Tax at 50% ₹	Profit after Tax ₹	Profit before Tax ₹	Tax at 50% ₹	Profit after Tax ₹
1	15,000	7,500	7,500	5,000	2,500	2,500
2	20,000	10,000	10,000	15,000	7,500	7,500
3	25,000	12,500	12,500	20,000	10,000	10,000
4	15,000	7,500	7,500	30,000	15,000	15,000
5	10,000	5,000	5,000	20,000	10,000	10,000
Total	**85,000**	**42,500**	**42,500**	**90,000**	**45,000**	**45,000**

Average Profit	₹ 42,500 ÷ 5 = ₹ 8,500	₹ 45,000 ÷ 5 = ₹ 9,000
(After tax)	₹ 60,000 ÷ 2 = ₹ 30,000	₹ 60,000 ÷ 2 = ₹ 30,000
Investment	(₹ 8,500 ÷ ₹ 30,000) × 100	(₹ 9,000 ÷ ₹ 30,000) × 100 = 30%
Rate of Return	= 28.33%	

Machine Y is more profitable where it is presumed that net profit is arrived after providing for depreciation.

ILLUSTRATION 2

Determine the accounting rate of return from the following information of the two machines A and B relating to Gemini Ltd. Gangapur.

Particulars	Machine A	Machine B
Original Cost	₹ 56,125	₹ 56,125
Additional Investment in Net Working Capital	₹ 5,000	₹ 6,000
Estimated life in years	5 years	5 years
Estimated Salvage Value	₹ 3,000	₹ 3,000
Income tax rate	55%	55%

Annual Estimated Income after depreciation and tax.

Particulars	₹	₹
1st Year	3,375	11,375
2nd Year	5,375	9,375
3rd Year	7,375	7,375
4th Year	9,375	5,375
5th Year	11,375	3,375
Total	**36,875**	**36,875**

Depreciation has been charged on straight line basis.

SOLUTION

$$\text{Average investment} = \frac{\text{Original Investment} - \text{Scrap Value}}{2}$$

$$+ \text{ Additional Networking Capital} + \text{Scrap Value}$$

$$\text{Machine A} = \frac{(₹\,56,125 - ₹\,3,000)}{2} + ₹\,5,000 + ₹\,3,000$$

$$= ₹\,26,563 + ₹\,8,000$$

$$= ₹\,34,563$$

$$\text{Machine B} = \frac{(₹\,56,125 - ₹\,3,000)}{2} + ₹\,6,000 + ₹\,3,000$$

$$= ₹\,26,563 + ₹\,9,000 = ₹\,35,563$$

$$\text{Annual Average Net Earnings} = \frac{\text{Total income after depreciation and tax}}{\text{Estimated life of Machine}}$$

$$\text{Machine A} = \frac{₹\,36,875}{5\text{ years}} = ₹\,7,375$$

$$\text{Machine B} = \frac{₹\,36,875}{5\text{ years}} = ₹\,7,375$$

$$\text{ARR} = \frac{\text{Annual Average Net Earnings}}{\text{Average Investment}} \times 100$$

$$\text{Machine A} = \frac{₹\,7,375}{₹\,34,563} \times 100 = 21.34\%$$

$$\text{Machine B} = \frac{₹\,7,375}{₹\,35,563} \times 100 = 20.74\%$$

ILLUSTRATION 3

In Hindalco Ltd., Himmatpur the yearly working results of two machines are given below :

Particulars	Machine I ₹	Machine II ₹
Cost	45,000	45,000
Sales	1,00,000	80,000
Total Cost per year (Excluding Depreciation)	36,000	30,000
Expected Life	2 years	3 years

Which of the two should be preferred ?

SOLUTION

Calculation of Annual Average Earnings

Particulars		Machine I ₹	Machine II ₹
Sales		1,00,000	80,000
Less : Cost	(−)	36,000	30,000
		64,000	50,000
Less : Depreciation	(−)	22,500	15,000
Net Profit		41,500	35,000
Annual Average Earnings		41,500	35,000
Annual Investment		22,500	22,500
Average Rate of Return		$=\dfrac{₹\,41,500}{₹\,22,500} \times 100$ $= 184\%$	$=\dfrac{₹\,35,000}{₹\,22,500} \times 100$ $= 156\%$

Machine I has higher average rate of return, hence Machine I should be preferred.

ILLUSTRATION 4

Indiana Ltd. Indore is proposing to expand its production can go in either for an computerised machine costing ₹ 2,24,000 with a estimated life of $5\frac{1}{2}$ years or an ordinary machine costing ₹ 60,000 having an estimated life of 8 years. The annual sale and costs are estimated as follows :

Particulars	Computerised Machine ₹	Ordinary Machine ₹
Sales Costs	1,50,000	1,50,000
Material	50,000	50,000
Labour	12,000	60,000
Variable overheads	24,000	20,000

Compute the comparative profitability of the proposals under the 'payback period' and return on investments methods. Explain the difference in the results obtained under the two methods.

SOLUTION

Computation of Payback Period.

Particulars		Computerised Machine	Ordinary Machine
Cost of the machine	₹	2,24,000	60,000
Sales	₹	1,50,000	1,50,000
Variable costs	₹	86,000	1,30,000
Contribution	₹	64,000	20,000
Number of years to recover cost	Yrs.	$3\frac{1}{2}$ years	3 years

After paying back the capital, the former will work for 2 years whereas the latter machine will work for 5 years more. Hence ordinary machine is preferable.

Calculation of Return on Investment :

Particulars		Computerised Machine	Ordinary Machine
Contribution per year	₹	64,000	20,000
Average investment in machinery	₹	1,12,000	30,000
Rate of Return	%	$= \dfrac{₹\ 64,000 \times 100}{₹\ 1,12,000}$ $= 57.14\%$	$= \dfrac{₹\ 20,000 \times 100}{₹\ 30,000}$ $= 66.67\%$

Ordinary machine gives higher return so ordinary machine is preferable to the computerized machine.

ILLUSTRATION 5

Jolly Ltd., Jaipur is proposing to take up a project which requires an investment of ₹ 40,000. The net income before depreciation and tax is estimated as follows :

Year	Net Income before Depreciation and Tax ₹
1	10,000
2	12,000
3	14,000
4	16,000
5	20,000

Depreciation is to be charged on straight line basis. Tax rate is 50%.

Calculate Average Rate of Return.

SOLUTION

Calculation of Annual Average Net Earnings :

Particulars		₹
Total Net Income for 5 years before depreciation and tax		72,000
Less : Depreciation for 5 years	(−)	40,000
		32,000
Less : Income Tax at 50%	(−)	16,000
Net Profit after depreciation and tax for five years		16,000

$$\text{Annual Average Net Earnings} = \frac{₹\ 16,000}{5\ \text{Yrs.}}$$
$$= ₹\ 3,200$$

$$\text{Average Investment} = \frac{\text{Original Investment} - \text{Scrap Value}}{2}$$

$$= \frac{₹\,40,000 - \text{Nil}}{2} = ₹\,20,000$$

$$\text{Average Rate of Return} = \frac{\text{Annual Average Net Earnings}}{\text{Average Investment}} \times 100$$

$$= \frac{₹\,3,200}{₹\,20,000} \times 100 = 16\%$$

ILLUSTRATION 6

In Kalyani Ltd., Kalyan project requires an investment of ₹ 10,00,000. The plant and machinery required for the project will have a scrap value of ₹ 80,000 at the end of its useful life of 5 years. The profits after tax and depreciation are estimated as under :

Year	₹
1	50,000
2	75,000
3	1,25,000
4	1,30,000
5	80,000

Calculate Average Rate of Return.

SOLUTION

Calculation of Average Investment:

$$\text{Average Investment} = \frac{\text{Original Investment} - \text{Scrap Value}}{2}$$

$$= \frac{₹\,10,00,000 - ₹\,80,000}{2} = \frac{₹\,9,20,000}{2}$$

$$= ₹\,4,60,000$$

Calculation of annual average net earnings:

Profit after depreciation and tax

Year		₹
1		50,000
2		75,000
3		1,25,000
4		1,30,000
5	(+)	80,000
Total		4,60,000

$$\text{Average} = \frac{₹\,4,60,000}{5\ \text{yrs.}} = ₹\,92,000$$

$$\text{Average Rate of Return} = \frac{\text{Annual Average Net Earnings}}{\text{Average Investment}} \times 100$$

$$= \frac{₹\,92,000}{₹\,4,60,000} \times 100 = 20\%$$

1.2.3 DISCOUNTED PAY BACK PERIOD

Discounted Payback is an improvement over payback method. This method has been developed to overcome the time value drawback of the payback approach. Discounted Payback Period is defined as the length of time that elapses before the present value of the cumulative cash inflow is at least as large as the initial cash outlay. The payback period is computed after discounting the net cash benefits of the project at the company's cut-off rate to their present values. The discounted payback period does give same recognition to the time value of funds that flow before payback is accomplished. The following illustration will explain the mechanics of computation of' discounted payback period.

1.2.4 DISCOUNTED CASH FLOW

As investments are effected in anticipation of future returns, the time value of money is basically considered while evaluating investments. Time is always crucial for the investment such that the sum received today is worth more than the same sum to be received tomorrow. Thus, in evaluating investment proposals, it is essential to consider the timing of return on investment.

Discounted Cash Flow Method or Time Adjusted Technique is an improvement over payback method and average rate of return. An investment is essentially outlay of funds in anticipation of future returns. The presence of time as a factor in investment is fundamental for the purpose of evaluating investment. Time is always crucial for the investor so that ₹ 1 received today is worth more than ₹ 1 to be received tomorrow. In evaluating investment project, it is important to consider the timing of returns on investment. Discounted cash flow technique takes into account both the interest factor and the return after the payback period.

The discounted cash flow method considers the net cash flows as representing the recovery of original investment plus a return on capital invested. Another characteristic feature of this method is that it takes into consideration all benefits and costs of the project during the entire period. The discounting cash flow methods are mainly divided into two types and they are the Net Present Value Method (NPV) and the Internal Rate Of Return Method (IRR). Two variations of the NPV method, i.e. terminal value and profitability index are also considered. As a group, all these methods are often referred to as time adjusted or present value or discounted cashflow methods.

1.2.5 NET PRESENT VALUE

The net present value method is one of the discounted cash flow techniques explicitly recognising the time value of money. It is considered to be the best method for evaluating the capital investment projects. It correctly admits that cash flow arising at different time periods differ in value and are comparable only when their present values are found out.

The net present value method can be also defined as the summation of the present values of cash proceeds in each year minus the summation of the present values of net cash outflows in each year. The equation for the net present value, assuming that all cash outflows are made in the initial year (t = 0), will be :

$$NPV = \frac{A_1}{(1+K)} + \frac{A_2}{(1+K)^2} + \frac{A_3}{(1+K)^3} + \ldots + \frac{A_n}{(1+K)^n} - C = \sum_{t=1}^{n} \frac{A_t}{(1+K)^t} - C$$

Where A_1, A_2 ... represent cash inflows, K is the firm's cost of capital, C is cost of the investment proposal and n is the expected life of the proposal. It should be noted that the cost of capital, K, is assumed to be known; otherwise, the net present value cannot be determined.

The acceptance rule as applicable to net present value method is, to accept the investment project if its net present value is positive, (i.e. the present value of cash inflows is less than the present value of cash outflows). The rule of thumb symbolically represented is as follows :

- NPV > zero - Accept
- NPV < zero - Reject

Steps involved in the Net Present Value Method

- An appropriate rate of interest should be selected to discount cash flows. Generally, the appropriate role of interest is in the firm's cost of capital.
- The present value of cash inflows and the present value of investment outlay (i.e. cash outflows) should be calculated using the discount rate.
- The Net Present Value should be found out by subtracting the present value of cash outflows from the present value of cash inflows.

Thus, net present value method is a process of calculating the present value of flows (inflows and outflows) of an investment proposal, using cost of capital as the appropriate discount rate, and finding the net present value by subtracting the present value of cash outflows from the present value of cash inflows.

The net present value method can be used to select between mutually exclusive projects by considering whether the incremental investment generates a positive net present value.

Using the net present value method, projects can be ranked in order of net present values i.e. first rank will be given to the project with the highest positive net present value.

Advantages :

The net present value technique of evaluating investment proposals has the following **merits**.

i) The most significant advantage of the NPV method is that is it recognises the time value of money.

ii) The concept of the present value of series of cash flows is an important feature of the analysis of different investment potentialities. The net present value technique analyses the merit of relative capital investments. It estimates the present value of their cash flows by using a discount rate equal to the cost of capital.

iii) It considers all cash flows over the entire life of the project in its calculation.

iv) If one wishes to maximise profits, the use of NPV always finds the correct collection of projects.

v) It is consistent with the objective of maximising the welfare of owners. (i.e. wealth of the shareholders of the company).

Disadvantages :

The net present value method also suffers from the following **limitations**.

i) This method is difficult to understand as well as to use, when compared to the payback method or even the ARR method.

ii) The NPV method assumes that the discount rate i.e. firms cost of capital is known. But, the cost of capital is difficult to understand and measure in practice.

iii) It may not give reliable answers when dealing with alternative projects under the conditions of unequal lives of project.

iv) Decisions arrived at may not be satisfactory when the projects being compared involve different amounts of investment.

ILLUSTRATIONS

ILLUSTRATION 1

Find out the net present value for the project undertaken in Lotus Ltd., Lonavala which requires an initial investment of ₹ 20,000 and which involves a net cash inflow of ₹ 6,000 each year of for 6 years. The cost of funds are 8%. These are no scrap value (present value of an annuity of ₹ 1 for 6 years per annum in ₹ 4,623).

SOLUTION

Particulars		₹
Present value of Cash Inflow ₹ 6,000 × ₹ 4.623		27,738
Less : Initial Cash Outlay	(–)	20,000
∴ Net Present Value		7,738

ILLUSTRATION 2

In Mayuri Ltd., Mysore choice is to be made between two competing proposals, which require an equal investment of ₹ 50,000 and are expected to generate net cash flows as under the cost of capital of the company is 10%.

Particulars	Project X ₹	Project Y ₹
1st Year end	25,000	10,000
2nd Year end	15,000	12,000
3rd Year end	10,000	18,000
4th Year end	Nil	25,000
5th Year end	12,000	8,000
6th Year end	6,000	4,000

The following are the present value factors at 10% per annum.

Year	₹
1	0.909
2	0.826
3	0.751
4	0.683
5	0.621
6	0.564

Which proposal should be selected ? Using NPV method suggest the best project.

SOLUTION

Comparative Statement of Net Present Values

Year	PV Factor at 10%	Project X Cash Inflows ₹	Project X Present Values ₹	Project Y Cash Inflows ₹	Project Y Present Values ₹
1	0.909	25,000	22,725	10,000	9,090
2	0.826	15,000	12,390	12,000	9,912
3	0.751	10,000	7,510	18,000	13,518
4	0.683	NIL	NIL	25,000	17,075
5	0.621	12,000	7,452	8,000	4,968
6	0.564	6,000	3,384	4,000	2,256
Total Present value of Cash Inflows		(+)	53,461	(+)	56,819
Initial Investments (Cash Outlay)		(−)	50,000	(−)	50,000
Net Present Value			₹ 3,461		₹ 6,819

It is suggested that, since Project Y has the highest net present value, Project Y should be selected.

ILLUSTRATION 3

Nelco Ltd. Nagpur is willing to purchase a machine for the expansion of their existing factory. With this end in view they seek your advise as to which one of the following machines would be more profitable. For this you are supplied with the following data :

i)   Cost of each type of machine amounts to ₹ 1,00,000

ii)   Discount rate for all types of investment is 10%.

Cash Flow

Years	Machine A ₹	Machine B ₹	Machine C ₹	Machine D ₹
1	30,000	10,000	20,000	20,000
2	40,000	30,000	40,000	30,000
3	50,000	40,000	50,000	35,000
4	30,000	60,000	35,000	40,000
5	20,000	40,000	30,000	40,000

SOLUTION

Profitability Statement

Machine A		Machine B		Machine C		Machine D		Dis-count factor (10%)
Cash inflow ₹	Present value ₹	Cash inflow ₹	Present value ₹	Cash inflow ₹	Present value ₹	Cash inflow ₹	Present value ₹	
30,000	27,270	10,000	9,090	20,000	18,180	20,000	18,180	0.909
40,000	33,040	30,000	24,780	40,000	34,040	30,000	24,780	0.826
50,000	37,550	40,000	30,040	50,000	37,550	35,000	26,285	0.751
30,000	20,490	60,000	40,980	35,000	23,905	40,000	27,320	0.683
20,000	12,420	40,000	24,840	30,000	18,630	40,000	24,840	0.621
1,70,000	1,30,770	1,80,000	1,29,730	1,75,000	1,32,305	1,65,000	1,21,405	

This statement indicates that Machine C would be more profitable investment, though cash inflow in this machine is less than Machine B. Machine C has more or less standard cash inflow early in its working life. Hence, present value in case of C is relatively higher.

ILLUSTRATION 4

Ojus Ltd., Osmanabad firm has two investment opportunities, each costing ₹ 1,00,000 and each having the expected profit as shown below :

Year	Expected Cash Profits	
	Project A ₹	Project B ₹
1	50,000	20,000
2	40,000	40,000
3	30,000	50,000
4	10,000	60,000

After giving due consideration to the risk criteria in each project, the management has decided that projects should be evaluated at a 10% cost of capital and project B, a risky project with a 15% cost of capital.

Compare the NPVs and suggest the course of action for the management if,

a) Both the project are independent.

b) Both are mutually exclusive.

Following are the present value factors :

Year	PV factor at 10%	PV factor at 15%
1	0.909	0.870
2	0.826	0.756
3	0.751	0.657
4	0.683	0.572

SOLUTION

Comparative Statement of Net Present Values

Year	Project A			Project B		
	PV Factor at 10%	Expected Profit (Cash inflows) ₹	Present Values of (Cash Inflows) ₹	PV Factor at 15%	Expected Profit (Cash inflows) ₹	Present Values of Cash Inflows ₹
1	0.909	50,000	45,450	0.870	20,000	17,400
2	0.826	40,000	33,040	0.756	40,000	30,240
3	0.751	30,000	22,530	0.657	50,000	32,850
4	0.683	10,000	6,830	0.572	60,000	34,320
Total Present value of Cash Inflows		(+)	1,07,850			1,14,810
Initial Investments (Cash Outlay)		(−)	1,00,000		(−)	1,00,000
∴ Net Present Value			₹ 7,850			₹ 14,810

It is suggested that,

a) if both the projects are independent, accept both the project, as net present value of both are positive.

b) if both the projects are mutually exclusive, accept project B as its net present value is higher than that of A.

ILLUSTRATION 5

In Porwal Ltd., Pune a project undertaken initially costs ₹ 25,000. It generates the following cash flows :

Year	Cash Inflows ₹	Discount Factor at 10% ₹
1	9,000	0.909
2	8,000	0.826
3	7,000	0.751
4	6,000	0.683
5	5,000	0.621

Taking the cut-off rate as 10% suggest whether the project should be accepted or not.

SOLUTION

Statement of Net Present Value

Year	Cash Inflows ₹	P.V. Factor at 10% ₹	Present Value of Cash Inflows ₹
1	9,000	0.909	8,181
2	8,000	0.826	6,608
3	7,000	0.751	5,257
4	6,000	0.683	4,098
5	5,000	0.621	3,105
Total Present Value of Cash inflows		(+)	27,249
Less : Initial Outlay		(−)	25,000
∴ Net Present Value			2,249

It is suggested that, the project should be accepted since net present value is positive.

ILLUSTRATION 6

Given below is information regarding six mutually exclusive investment proposals undertaken in Qualis Ltd., Ratlam :

Proposal	Outlay ₹	Cash Inflow (after all current expenses and taxation)		
		I Year ₹	II Year ₹	III Year ₹
A	10,000	10,000	Nil	Nil
B	10,000	5,000	5,000	5,000
C	10,000	12,000	4,000	2,000
D	10,000	8,000	6,000	2,000
E	10,000	2,000	4,000	12,000
F	10,000	6,000	2,000	8,000

The salvage value at the end of three years is nil in all cases. You are required to rank these alternative proposals based upon,

a) Payback Period

b) Average Rate of Return

c) Net Present Value (discounting Rate – 10%)

Briefly explain the reason for any difference in the rankings.

SOLUTION

a) Payback Period

Proposals	Outlay ₹	Payback period	Rank
A	10,000	1 year	2
B	10,000	2 years	4
C	10,000	$10,000 + 12,000 \times 12 = 10$ months i.e. $5/6^{th}$ year	1
D	10,000	$1^{1}/3$ year	3
E	10,000	$2^{1}/3$ year	6
F	10,000	$2^{1}/4$ year	5

b) Average Rate of Return

Proposal	Outlay ₹	Total inflow for 3 years ₹	Total savings ₹	Average return for 1 year ₹	Average rate of return (%)	Rank
A	10,000	10,000	Nil	–	–	6
B	10,000	15,000	5,000	1,667	16.67	5
C	10,000	18,000	8,000	2,667	26.67	1
D	10,000	16,000	6,000	2,000	20.00	3
E	10,000	18,000	8,000	2,667	26.67	2
F	10,000	16,000	6,000	2,000	20.00	4

c) Net Present Value at 10%

Proposal	Year Cash inflow ₹	Discount factor at 10%	Present value ₹	Net Present value ₹	Rank
A	I^{st} 10,000	0.90909	9,091		
	Less : outlay		10,000	(–) 909	6
B	1st 5,000	0.90909	4,545		
	IInd 5,000	0.82645	4,133		
	IIIrd 5,000	0.75131 (+)	3,757		
	Total		**12,435**		
	Less : Outlay (–)		10,000	2,435	5
C	1st 12,000	0.90909	10,909		
	IInd 4,000	0.82645	3,306		
	IIIrd 2,000	0.75131 (+)	1,503		
	Total		**15,718**		
	Less : Outlay (–)		10,000	5,718	1

D	1st 8,000	0.90909	7,273		
	IInd 6,000	0.82645	4,959		
	IIIrd 2,000	0.75131 (+)	1,503		
	Total		**13,735**		
	Less : Outlay	(−)	10,000	3,735	3
E	1st 2,000	0.90909	1,819		
	IInd 4,000	0.82645	3,306		
	IIIrd 12,000	0.75131 (+)	9,016		
	Total		**14,141**		
	Less : Outlay	(−)	10,000	4,141	2
F	1st 6,000	0.90909	5,455		
	IInd 2,000	0.82645	1,653		
	IIIrd 8,000	0.75131 (+)	6,010		
	Total		**13,118**		
	Less : Outlay	(−)	10,000	3,118	4

ILLUSTRATION 7

Rotex Ltd., Raipur which has a 50% tax rate and 10% after tax cost of capital, is evaluating a project which will cost ₹ 1,00,000 and will require an increase in the level of inventories and receivables of ₹ 50,000 over its effective life.

The project will generate additional sales of ₹ 1,00,000 and will require cash expenses of ₹ 30,000 in each year of its 5 year life. It will depreciate on straight line basis. What is the Net Present Value ? The discount factor at 10% is,

1st year	0.9091
2nd year	0.8264
3rd year	0.7513
4th year	0.6830
5th year (+)	0.6209
Total	**3.7907**

SOLUTION

Calculation of Cash Inflows :

Particulars		₹
Sales		1,00,000
Less : Cash Expenses	(−)	30,000
		70,000
Less : Depreciation	(−)	20,000
		50,000
Less : Income Tax @ 50%	(−)	25,000
Profit after tax		25,000
Add : Depreciation	(+)	20,000
∴ Annual Cash Inflows		45,000

Calculation of Net Present Value :

a) Present Value of Cash Inflows :　　　　　　　　　　　　　　　　　　　₹

i)	Annual Cash Inflows	(₹ 45,000 × 3.7907)	1,70,581.50
ii)	Inflow of working capital in the fifth year	(₹ 50,000 × 0.6209)	31,045.00
	Total Present Value of Cash Inflows		2,01,626.50

b) Initial Cash Outlay :

i)	Fixed Assets	₹ 1,00,000		
ii)	Working Capital	(+) ₹ 50,000	(−)	1,50,000.00
∴	Net Present Value (A − B)			₹ 51,626.50

1.2.6 INTERNAL RATE OF RETURN

The Internal Rate of Return method is yet another discounted cash flow technique which takes into consideration the magnitude and timing of cash flows. It is also known as time adjusted rate of return, marginal efficiency of capital, marginal productivity of capital, yield on investment and so on. It is employed when the cost of investment and the annual cash inflows are known while the unknown rate of earning is to be ascertained.

The internal rate of return can be defined as that rate which equates the present value of cash inflows with the present value of cash outflows of an investment. In other words, the internal rate of return will be that rate at which the present value of cash inflows and outflows set off each other or the net present value of the investment is zero.

Internal rate of return is that rate at which the sum of discounted cash inflows equals the sum of discounted cash outflows. It is the rate at which the net present value of the investment is zero. It is called internal rate because it depends mainly on the outlay and proceeds associated with the project and not on any rate determined outside the investment. This method advocated by **Joel Dean**, takes into account the magnitude and timing of cash flows.

The internal rate of return method like the net present value method considers the time value of money by discounting the cash streams. But the determination of the discount factor is different in both cases. In the case of the net present value method, the discount rate is the required rate of return which is equivalent to the cost of capital and its determinants are external to the investment proposal under consideration. In the case of internal rate of return method, the discount rate depends entirely on the initial outlay and cash proceeds of the investment project under consideration. In other words, the internal rate of return is based on facts which are internal to the proposal and hence named as such.

The internal rate of return is determined by solving the following equation.

$$C = \frac{E_1}{(I+r)} + \frac{E_2}{(I+r)^2} + \frac{E_3}{(I+r)^3} \ldots\ldots + \frac{E_n}{(I+r)^n}$$

Where E_1, E_2, E_3, represent the net cash earnings from years 1, 2, 3 etc. C represents the required investment and 'r' the rate return.

While using the discounted cash flow method, the analyst must determine the amount of required investment and estimate the net cashflow over the lifespan of the investment project in order to solve the unknown rate of return. Though the algebraic formulas appears to be difficult, the time adjusted rate of return can be easily calculated in all cases where cashflow is uniformly the same during the lifespan of the project, with the help of Annuity Table (No. II) showing the present value of ₹ 1 received annually over 'n' years by adopting the following two steps :

i)   The factor to be located in the relevant annuity table (No. II) is calculated by using the following simple equation.

$$F = \frac{I}{C}$$

Where 'F' represents the factor to be located, 'I' represents the original investment and 'C' the cash inflow per year. This factor indicates the same relationship of the investment and cash inflows as do the payback calculations.

ii) The factor thus calculated is located in Table II on the line representing the number of years corresponding to the estimated useful life of the asset and the relevant percentage of the discount which represents the rate of return.

This method is also known as : Marginal efficiency of capital, Rate of return over cost, Time adjusted rate of return, and Yield of an investment.

Accept or Reject Criterion : Accept the project if the internal rate of return is higher than or equal to the minimum required rate of return. The minimum required rate of return is also known as cut off rate or firm's cost of capital.

A project shall be rejected if its IRR, is lower than the cut-off rate. While evaluating two or more projects, project giving a higher internal rate of return would be preferred.

Calculation of Internal Rate of Return :

a)   **Where cash inflows are uniform :**
     Internal Rate of Return can be calculated by locating the Factor in Annuity table (Annuity Table of Present Value of ₹ 1 Received Annually for N years).

$$\text{Factor} = \frac{\text{Original Investment}}{\text{Cash Flow Per Year}}$$

Advantages :

The internal rate of return method is a sound technique or evaluating investment projects which has the following **merits** :

i)   This method considers the time value of money like the net present value method.

ii) It takes into consideration the cashflows over the entire life span of the project.

iii) Business executives and non-technical people understand the concept of internal rate of return much better than that of net present value. Even if they do not follow the definition of internal rate of return in terms of the equation, they are well aware of the used meaning in terms of the rate of return on investment.

iv) The calculation of the cost of capital is not a prerequisite for using the IRR method of evaluating investment projects, unlike the NPV method. In fact the

IRR suggests, the maximum rate of return and gives a true picture of the profitability of the project, even in the absence of the cost of capital of the company.

v)   It is consistent with the overall objective of maximising shareholder's wealth.

Disadvantages :

The internal rate of return method suffers from following **disadvantages**.

i)   This method is difficult to understand as well as to apply in practice as it involves tedious and complicated calculations. As stated earlier, it involves a trial and error procedure and cumbersome computation problems especially in the case of projects with uneven cashflow streams.

ii)   Secondly, this method does not give unique answers in all situations. It yields negative rate or multiple rate under certain circumstances which is rather confusing.

iii)   It implies that intermediate cash inflows generated by the project are reinvested at the internal rate of the project, whereas the net present value method implies that the cash inflows are reinvested at the company's cost of capital. The reinvestment rate assumption under the internal rate of return method appears to be more unrealistic.

ILLUSTRATIONS

ILLUSTRATION 1

In Sony Ltd. Sangali equipment involves an initial investment of ₹ 60,000. The annual cash flow is estimated at ₹ 20,000 for 5 years.

You are required to calculate internal rate of return of the project.

SOLUTION

In this case cash inflow is uniform for five years.

$$\text{Factor} = \frac{\text{Initial Investment}}{\text{Cash Inflow Per Year}}$$

$$= \frac{₹\ 60,000}{₹\ 20,000}$$

$$= 3$$

Referring to the Annuity Table in the line of 5 years, the discount percentage would be between 18% (₹ 3.127 present value of annuity of ₹ 1) and 20% (₹ 2.99 present value of annuity of ₹ 1).

ILLUSTRATION 2

In Texmo Ltd. Tatanagar, Project X involves an initial outlay of ₹ 1,60,000. Its lifespan is expected to be three years. The cash streams generated by it are expected to be as follows :

Year	Cash Inflow ₹
1	80,000
2	70,000
3	60,000

Calculate the internal rate of return.

SOLUTION

Year	Cash inflow ₹	Rate of Discount (14%)	Present value ₹	Rate of Discount (16%)	Present value ₹	Rate of Discount (15%)	Present value ₹
1	80,000	0.877	70,160	0.862	68,960	0.870	69,600
2	70,000	0.769	53,830	0.743	52,010	0.756	52,920
3	60,000	0.675	40,500	0.641	38,460	0.658	39,480
		(+)	1,64,490	(+)	1,59,430	(+)	1,62,000
Less : Initial Cash Outlay	(−)		1,62,000	(−)	1,62,000	(−)	1,62,000
∴ Net Present Value			(+) 2,490		(−) 2.570		Nil

It is clear from the above that the net present value = zero, with the discount rate of 15%, This is the IRR. When the rate is higher than this (16%) the net present value is negative and a rate lower than this (14%) gives a positive net present value.

The accept or reject rule, using the internal rate of return method is to accept the project if its internal rate of return is higher than or equal to the minimum rate of return representing the cost of capital or cut-off rate or more precisely r > k. The project is rejected when its internal rate of return is lower than the cost of capital or more precisely r < k.

ILLUSTRATION 3

In United Ltd. Ujjain A project costs ₹ 16,000 and is expected to generate cash inflows of ₹ 4,000 each for 5 years.

Present value of ₹ 1 at varying discount rates for a period of 5 years.

Year	7%	8%	9%
1	0.9346	0.9259	0.9174
2	0.8734	0.8573	0.8417
3	0.8163	0.7938	0.7722
4	0.7629	0.7350	0.7084
5	0.7130	0.6806	0.6499
Total	**4.1002**	**3.9926**	**3.8896**

Calculate internal rate of return.

SOLUTION

The annual cash inflow is uniform for 5 years.

Calculation of Factor :

$$\text{Factor} = \frac{\text{Original Investment}}{\text{Annual Cash Inflow}}$$

$$= \frac{₹\ 16,000}{₹\ 4,000}$$

$$= 4$$

Referring to the Row of Total given under the heading "present value of ₹ 1 at varying discount rates for a period of 5 years", Factor 4 lies between 3.9926 and 4.1002. Therefore, internal rate of return lies between 7% and 8%.

Present value of Cash Inflow at 7% PV Factor $= 4{,}000 \times 4.1002 = 16400.8$

Present value of Cash Inflow at 8% PV Factor $= 4{,}000 \times 3.9926 = 15970.4$

By interpolation IRR will be,

$$IRR = A + \frac{C-O}{C-D}(B-A)$$

$$= 7 + \frac{PV \text{ at } 7\% - \text{Original Investment}}{PV \text{ at } 7\% - PV \text{ at } 8\%} \times \text{Differences in rates}$$

$$= 7 + \frac{(16{,}400.8 - 16{,}000)}{16{,}400.8 - 1{,}5970.4} \times (8-7)$$

$$= 7 + \frac{400.8}{430.4} \times 1$$

$$= 7 + 0.931$$

$$= 7.931\%$$

ILLUSTRATION 4

Voltas Ltd., Vashi installs a plant and machinery in rented premises for the production of a component part, the demand for which is expected to last for only 5 years. The total capital put in by the sole trader is as under :

Particulars	₹
Plant and Machinery	2,70,500
Working Capital (+)	40,000
Total	**3,10,500**

The working capital will be fully realised at the end of 5th year. The scrap value of the plant expected to be realised at the end of the 5th year is only ₹ 5,500. The trader's earnings are expected to be as under. Present value factors of various rates of interest are as follows :

11%	12%	13%	14%	15%
0.9009	0.8929	0.8850	0.8850	0.8696
0.8116	0.7972	0.7831	0.7695	0.7561
0.7312	0.7118	0.6931	0.6750	0.6575
0.6587	0.6155	0.6133	0.5921	0.5718
0.5935	0.5674	0.5428	0.5194	0.3972

You are required to compute the present value of cash flows discounted at the various rates of interests given above and state the return from the project.

SOLUTION

Year	Cash Flows ₹	Present Discount Value (at)				
		11%	12%	13%	14%	15%
1	70,000	63,063	62,503	61,950	61,404	60,872
2	1,00,000	81,116	79,720	78,310	76,950	75,610
3	1,30,000	95,056	92,534	90,105	87,750	85,475
4	90,000	59,283	57,195	55,195	53,289	51,452
5	60,000	35,610	34,044	32,568	31,164	29,832
Total		3,34,128	3,25,996	3,18,128	3,10,557	3,03,251

Cash Flow in years 1 to 4 is profit as given less tax. In the fifth year, the amount also includes ₹ 5,500 the expected scrap value and ₹ 40,000 the working capital to be released. At 14% the inflow are almost equal to the outflow i.e. project therefore yields 14%.

1.2.7 MODIFIED INTERNAL RATE OF RETURN

If the cash flow stream shows a multiple reversal sign in cashflow stream with poor size of cash flows, the internal rate of return can be modified i.e. multiple. Here a meaningful single rate has to be calculated, based on the size of positive cash flows size in the period immediately after initial investment.

In actual practice, internal rate of return is usually found by the frustrating method of trial and error, picking a rate from the present value table and discount the streams of earnings at the rate. If the present value of total benefits is greater than the investment outlay, a higher rate should be tried and if the present value of the total benefits is less than the investment outlay, lower rate is applied. Where present value of cash benefits and investment outlay is equal the choice proves to be correct and the discount rate is considered as internal rate of return of the project.

a) **Internal Rate of Return for Even Cash Flow :**

When all cash inflows are equal, then the project's internal rate of return can be found by a relatively simple process. Steps involved in the process of calculation are:

i)   Divide the investment outlay by the annual cash earnings and obtain a quotient.
ii) Go across the four-year (life of the project) row of the annuity table.
iii) Proceed to the right along the correct row until the number is reached that is closest to the quotient. .
iv) Proceed to the top of the table and find out the interest rate that heads the column in which factor is located.

ILLUSTRATION

ILLUSTRATION 1

Wimco Ltd., Warangal is considering to buy a machine today for ₹ 6,340 and the project will yield an annual net cash return of ₹ 2,000 for a four-year period. After the fourth year, the company receives nothing.

What rate of interest is being earned on this commitment'?

SOLUTION

Using the above process:

i) $\dfrac{\text{Investment Outlay}}{\text{(Annuity)}} = \dfrac{₹\,6,340}{₹\,2,000} = ₹\,3.170.$

ii) Go across the four year row of the annuity table.

iii) Proceed to the right along the correct row until the number, which is closest to the quotient, is reached.

iv) Proceed to the top of the table and find out the interest rate that heads the column in which the factor is located. In this way, we get 10 per cent as discount rate.

b) Internal Rate of Return for Uneven Cash Flows :

When cashflows are uneven, they cannot be treated as an annuity and the present value of each year's cash inflow must be calculated. The following illustration will explain how the appropriate discount should be calculated through trial and error method.

ILLUSTRATIONS

ILLUSTRATION 1

Zenith Ltd., Zanshi has two alternative under consideration, the acquisition of 'Machine A' for use in the office and the acquisition of 'Machine B' in production department. Information on two proposed capital expenditure are given below :

Particulars	Machine 'A' ₹	Machine 'B' ₹
Cost of 'Machine A' (Scrap value of ₹ 100)	10,000	–
Cost of 'Machine B'	–	15,000
(No scrap value)	–	500
Installation cost	–	4,000
Additional Current Assets	5,000	10,000
Cash Benefits before Depreciation and Tax	3,000	4,000
Depreciation	(Depreciation Annually for three years)	(Depreciation Annually for four years)

Which of the two projects should be given priority, presuming corporate tax rate of 50 per cent ?

SOLUTION

Before ranking projects, the investment outlay of the two projects and their cash benefits will have to be worked out as below :

Particulars	Machine 'A' ₹	Machine 'B' ₹
Investment Outlay	10,000	19,500
Net Cash Benefits		
Before Depreciation and Tax	5,000	10,000
Less : Depreciation (–)	(3,000	4,000
Cash Gains before Tax	2,000	6,000
Less : Tax @50% (–)	1,000	3,000
Cash Gains after Tax	1,000	3,000
Add : Depreciation (–)	3,000	4,000
∴ Cash Inflow	4,000	7,000

Thus, 'Machine A' will result in a net cashflow of ₹ 4,000 a year for three years and salvage value of ₹ 1,000 in the third year. On the other hand, 'Machine B' will result in cashflow of ₹ 7,000 a year for four years and there will be an additional cash inflow of ₹ 4,000 at the end of fourth year as a result of recovery of working capital.

Finding the interest rates of projects and ranking them by trail and error process :

By a trial and error process, we have to experiment with different interest rates until the one is found that comes closest to equating the streams of net annual cash flow to a present value that is equal to the cash outlay of the project.

Table 1 shows the computation of internal rate of return of the projects with uneven cash inflows.

Table 1

'Machine A'	'Machine B'
First guess at 15%	First guess at 21%
₹ ₹	₹ ₹
$4,000 \times 0.86957 = 3,478$	$7,000 \times 0.82645 = 5,785$
$4,000 \times 0.75614 = 3,025$	$7,000 \times 0.68301 = 4,781$
$4,000 \times 0.65752 = 2,630$	$7,000 \times 0.56400 = 3,948$
$1,000 \times 0.65752 = (+) 652$	$7,000 \times 0.46651 = 3,269$
$\underline{9,791}$	$4,000 \times 0.46651 = (+) 1,866$
	$\underline{19,649}$
Second guess at 13%	Second guess at 19%
₹ ₹	₹ ₹
$4,000 \times 0.88496 = 3,540$	$7,000 \times 0.84034 = 5,882$
$4,000 \times 0.78315 = 3,133$	$7,000 \times 0.70616 = 4,943$
$4,000 \times 0.65752 = 2,778$	$7,000 \times 0.59300 = 4,151$
$1,000 \times 0.69305 = (+) 693$	$7,000 \times 0.49867 = 3,491$
$\underline{10,138}$	$4,000 \times 0.49867 = (+) 1,991$
	$\underline{20,458}$

Third guess at 14%			Third guess at 19%		
₹	₹		₹	₹	
4,000 × 0.87719 =	3,509		7,000 × 0.83333 =	5,833	
4,000 × 0.78315 =	3,078		7,000 × 0.69444 =	4,861	
4,000 × 0.67497 =	2,700		7,000 × 0.57900 =	4,053	
1,000 × 0.67497 = (+)	675		7,000 × 0.48225 =	3,376	
	9,962		4,000 × 0.48225 = (+)	1,929	
				20,052	

The calculation of the three situations shown in Table I reveals that rates of return in the case of 'Machine A' and 'Machine B' will be respectively 14% and 20% because at these rates if the projects cash earnings are discounted, total of discounted value of streams of earning will be equal to the amount of investment outlay. Since the 'Machine B' fetches higher return than the 'Machine A' the company should accord priority to 'Machine B' over the 'Machine A'.

ILLUSTRATION 2

Amino Ltd., Anand wants to add a new product line marketable for 5 years after which the product would be discontinued. The following costs and revenues data are produced :

	₹
Cost of equipment required	40,000
Working capital additionally required due to increased business	35,000
Annual sales revenue	38,000
Salvage value of equipment in 5 years	5,000
Annual out of pocket costs for salaries, advertising etc.	23,000
Overhaul of the equipment required in 4 years	2,000

The cost of capital is 12%. Would you recommended that the new product line be introduced ?

SOLUTION

There are several cash outflows and several cash inflows. Further, the additional working capital required initially was ₹ 35,000. But after 5 years the productive life is finished. Hence, after 5 years additional working capital which was required as cash outflow will now stand released and will act as cash inflow.

Cash Inflow	₹
1. Sales revenue	38,000
Less out of pocket cash	23,000
Annual net cash flow	15,000

Items	Years	Amount of cash flow ₹	12% factor	P.V. ₹
Cash Inflow :				
i) From sale	1 – 5	15,000	3.6	54,000
ii) Salvage value	5	5,000	0.56	2,800
iii) Working capital released	5	35,000	0.56 (+)	19,600
∴ Total				76,400
Annual Cash Outflow (P.V.):				
i) Equipment	Now	40,000	1.00	40,000
ii) Working capacity needed	Now	35,000	1.00	35,000
iii) Overhaul of equipment	4	2,000	0.63 (+)	1,260
∴ Total				76,260

Net present value :   Cash Inflow (Annual) –   Cash Outflow (Annual)

76,400   –   ₹ 76,260   = ₹ 140

Therefore, new product line to be added.

1.2.8 PROFITABILITY INDEX

The Profitability Index is yet another method of evaluating the investment proposals. It is also known as the Benefit Cost Ratio. It represents a ratio of the present value of future cost benefit at the required rate of return to the initial cash outflow of the investment. This is similar to net present value approach. The profitability index approach measures present value of returns per rupee invested. While the net present value is based on the difference between the present value of future cash inflows and the present value of cash outlays. Where projects with different initial investments are to be evaluated the profitability index method proves to be the best technique. The formula to calculate the profitability index is as follows :

$$\text{Profitability Index} \quad = \frac{\text{Present value of Cash Inflows}}{\text{Present value of Cash Outlay}}$$

This method is also known as benefit-cost ratio because the numerator measures the benefits and the denominator the costs.

This rule of acceptance or otherwise of the project, using the profitability index method, is to accept the project if its profitability index is greater than one and reject it if its profitability index is less than one. In other words, the net present value will be positive when the profitability index is greater than 1 and it will be negative when the profitability index is less than 1. Thus, the net present value and profitability index approaches give identical results regarding investment proposals.

The selection of the projects with help of profitability index method can be effected on the basis of ranking. The project with the highest profitability index is given the first rank followed by others in the descending order.

Accept or Reject Criterion

Like net present value and internal rate of return methods, profitability index is a conceptually sound method of appraising investment projects. It provides ready comparison between investment proposals of different magnitudes. Projects can be ranked on the basis of profitability index. Highest rank will be assigned to the project with highest profitability index, while the lowest rank will be given to the project having lowest profitability index.

Net present value method and profitability index yield the same "accept or reject" rules because, profitability index can be greater than one only when the projects net present value is positive. In case of marginal projects, net present value will be zero and profitability index equal to one. However, a conflict may arise between the two methods if a choice between mutually exclusive projects has to be made.

Advantages:

The profitability index method has the following advantages :

i) This method takes into consideration the time value of money as also the total benefits spread throughout the lifespan of the project. It can be employed safely as a sound investment criteria.

ii) This method is a better evaluation technique than the net present value method in a situation of capital rationing. For example, two project may have the same net present value of ₹ 15,000. But project X requires an initial investment of ₹ 1,20,000 where as Y requires only ₹ 60,000. Project Y should be preferred on the basis of profitability index method. But the net present value method will give identical ranking to both the projects. Thus, the profitability index method is superior to the net present value method as the former evaluates the worth of the projects in terms of the relative rather than absolute magnitudes.

Disadvantages:

This method suffers from the following serious drawbacks or disadvantages :

i) This method is not easy to understand, and difficult to use in practice.

ii) It involves more tedious calculations than the traditional method.

ILLUSTRATIONS

ILLUSTRATION 1

The initial outlay of the project is ₹ 1,00,000 and it generates cash inflows of ₹ 50,000, ₹ 40,000, ₹ 30,000 and ₹ 20,000 in the four years of its lifespan. You are required to calculate the net present value and profitability index of the project assuming 10% rate of discount.

SOLUTION

Year	Cash Inflows ₹	Discount Factor at 10%	Present Values (2 × 3) ₹
1	50,000	0.909	45,450
2	40,000	0.826	33,040
3	30,000	0.751	22,530
4	20,000	0.683 (+)	13,660
		Total	1,14,680
		Less : Cash Outlay ∴	1,00,000
		Net Present Value	14,680

$$\therefore \quad \text{Profitability Index (Gross)} \ = \ \frac{₹ \ 1,14,680}{₹ \ 1,00,000}$$

$$= 1.1468 \text{ profitability index (Net)}$$

$$= 1.1468 - 1$$

$$= 0.1468$$

Alternative Methods:

All discounted cash flow techniques, have one ingredient in common i.e. that all these techniques are based upon the discounting procedure by which the further cash flows are discounted to find out their present economic worth.

Net Present Value:

The Net Present Value of an investment proposal may be defined as the sum of the present values of all the cash flows less the sum of present values of all the cash out flows associated with a proposal.

- Calculation of Net Present Value :

  On the basis of the definition of NPV, it may defined as :

  $$NPV = \frac{CF_0}{(1+K)^0} + \frac{CF_1}{(1+K)^1} + \frac{CF_2}{(1+K)^2} + \frac{CF_3}{(1+K)^3} + \frac{CF_n}{(1+K)^n}$$

  $$NPV = \sum_{i=1}^{n} \frac{CF_i}{(1+k)^i}$$

where,   NPV = Net Present Value

         CF = Cash flow occurring at time 0, 1, 2, 3 ...n

         K = The Discount Rate and

         n = Life of the project in years

OR

$$NPV = \sum_{i=1}^{n} \frac{CFi}{(1+k)^i} - Co$$

         = Initial cost of the proposal time T_0, T_1, T_2, T_3 ......

ILLUSTRATION 2

A firm is considering a capital budgeting proposal having initial cost of ₹ 15,000 (including installation, charges) besides requiring additional working capital of ₹ 20000. The project is expected to generate annual cash flows of ₹ 20,000, ₹ 50,000, ₹ 60,000, ₹ 40,000 and ₹ 30,000, respectively during the next five years. Thereafter project is expected to be scrapped away for ₹ 25000. The discount rate is given 10%. Find out the net present value.

SOLUTION

Calculation of Net Present Value		PVP = Present Value Factors	
Time	Cash flows ₹	PVF (10% CFT)	Present values ₹
To	− 1,70,000	1.000	(−) 1,70,000
T1	20,000	0.909	18,180
T2	50,000	0.826	41,300
T3	60,000	0.751	45,060
T4	40,000	0.683	27,320
T5	75,000*	0.621	46,575
		Total	(+) 8,435

The total cash flow for the year T5 is ₹ 75,000 (i.e. ₹ 30,000 + working capital release ₹ 20,000 + salvage value of ₹ 25,000).

Profitability Index:

This technique which is a variant (alternative form) of NPV technique, is also known as Benefit Cost Ratio or Present Value Index. The PI is calculated by dividing the former by latter.

Calculation : The PI is calculated as follows :

$$PI = \frac{\text{Total Present value of cash inflows}}{\text{Total Present value of cash outflows}}$$

$$PI = \sum_{i=1}^{n} \frac{CF_i}{(1 + k)^i} \div Co$$

ILLUSTRATION 3

A firm is evaluating a proposal which requires a cash outlay of ₹ 40,000 at present and of ₹ 20,000 and at the end of HOW. It is expected to generate cash inflow of ₹ 20,000, ₹ 40,000 and ₹ 20,000 at the end of 1st year, 2nd year and 4th year respectively. Given the rate of discount of 10% the calculation of profitability index is expected from you.

SOLUTION

Calculation of the profitability Index.

Year	Cash flow ₹	PV (10% n)	Present value ₹
0	(−) 40,000	1.000	(−) 40,000
1	20,000	0.909	18,180
2	40,000	− 0.826	33,040
3	(−) 20,000	0.756	(−) 15,020
4	20,000	0.683	13,660

Present value of cash out flows = ₹ 40,000 + ₹ 15,020 = ₹ 55,020
Present value of cash inflows = ₹ 18,180 + ₹ 33,040 + ₹ 13,660
                             = ₹ 64,880

$$PI = \frac{\text{Total Beseut value of cash inflows}}{\text{Total Beseut value of cash outflows}}$$

$$= \frac{₹ 64,880}{₹ 55,020}$$

$$= 1.18$$

Internal Rate of Return:

The internal rate of return of a proposal is defined as a discount rate which produces a zero net present value i.e. the internal rate of return is the discount rate which will equate the present value of cash inflows with the present value of cash outflows. Internal rate of return is also known as Marginal Rate of Return or Time adjusted Rate of Return. Calculation - Symbolically the internal rate of return is equal to the value of "r" in the equation as follows :

$$CO_0 = \frac{CF_0}{(1 + r)^0} + \frac{CF_1}{(1 + r)^1} + \frac{CF_2}{(1 + r)_o^2} + \frac{CF_n}{(1 + r)^n} + \frac{Sv + Wc}{(1 + r)^n}$$

where, CO_0 = Cash outlays or outflows at time
            CF = Cash inflow at different point of time

n = Life of the project and

r = Rate of discount (yet to be calculated)

Sv & Wc = Salvage value and working capital at the end of the year

$$CO_0 = \sum_{i=1}^{n} \frac{CFi}{(1+r)^i} + \frac{S+W}{(1+r)^n}$$

or

$$O = \sum_{i=1}^{n} \frac{CFi}{(1+r)^i} + \frac{S+W}{(1+r)^n} - CO_0$$

It may be noted in the above equation that this equations to be solved to ascertain the value of "r". Unfortunately the value of "r" can only be ascertained by the trial and error procedure together with linear interpolation.

The detailed procedure for calculation of internal rate of return can be explained in two different situations, i.e.

a) When future cash flows are equal.

b) When future cash flows are unequal.

a) When future cash flows are equal :

In case, the proposal has only one cash outflow in the beginning and a stream of equal cash inflows in future. The calculation of internal rate of return is rather simple. This can be explained with the help of following example.

ILLUSTRATION 4

A firm is evaluating a proposal costing ₹ 1,00,000 and having annual inflow of ₹ 25,000, occurring at the end of each of next 6 years. There is no salvage value.

SOLUTION

The IRR of the proposal may be calculated as follows :

Step I : Make approximation of internal rate of return on the basis of each cash flow data. A rough approximation may be made with reference to the payback period. The payback period in the given example is 4 years (i.e. annual cash inflow, 25,000, 1,00,000 ÷ 25,000 = 4 years). Now, search for a value nearest to 4 in the 6th years row of the PVAF table. (Present value of a future (annuity) table. The closest figures are given in the rate 12% (4.11 annuity) and the rate 13% (3.998). This means the IRR of the proposal is expected to lie between 12% and 13%.

Step II : In order to make a precise estimate of the IRR, find out the NPV of the project for both these rates as follows :

At 12% NPV = (₹ 25,000 × PVAF) – ₹ 1,00,000

= (₹ 25,000 × 4.111) – 1,00,000

= 1,02,775 – 1,00,000

= ₹ 2,775 (12% 6 years)

At 13% NPV = (₹ 25,000 × PVAF) – ₹ 1,00,000

= (₹ 25,000 × 3.998) – ₹ 1,00,000

= (12 (–) 50)

(13% 6 years) = ₹ 99,950 – ₹ 10,000 = (–50)

Step III : Find out the exact IRR by interpolating between 12% and 13%. It may be noted that IRR is the rate discount at which NPV is zero. At 12% NPV is ₹ 2750 and at 13% the NPV is ₹ 50. Therefore, the rate at which the NPV is zero will be higher than 12% but less than 13%. By interpolating difference of 1% (i.e. 13% − 12%) over NPV difference of ₹ 2,825 (i.e. 2,775 + 50 = 2,825).

$$IRR = 12\%, (+)\frac{1,02,775 - 10,000}{1,02,775 - 99,950}$$

$$= \frac{2,775}{2,825} = 12.98\%$$

The IRR can also calculated by starting from 13% as follows :

$$IRR = 13\% (-)\frac{₹\,1,00,000 - ₹\,99,950}{₹\,1,02,775 - ₹\,99,950}$$

$$= \frac{50}{2825}\ 0.2\ (Approx)$$

$$= 13 - 0.2$$

$$= 12.98\%$$

b) When future cash flows are not equal :

This can be explained with the help of following example.

ILLUSTRATION 5

A firm is evaluating proposal costing ₹ 16,000 and expected to generate cash inflows of ₹ 40,000, ₹ 60,000, ₹ 50,000, ₹ 40,000 and ₹ 40,000 at the end of each of next 5 years respectively. There is no salvage value thereafter. In this case, there is an uneven stream of cash flows and the internal rate of return can be approximated as follows.

SOLUTION

Step I : Find out the weighted average of cash flows :

Year	Cash flow (CF) ₹	Weight (W)	(F × W) ₹
1	40,000	5	2,00,000
2	60,000	4	2,40,000
3	50,000	3	1,50,000
4	50,000	2	1,00,000
5	40,000	1	40,000
	Total	**15**	**7,30,000**

Weighted Average = ₹ 7,30,000 ÷ 15 = ₹ 48,667.

Step II : Considered the weighted average as the annuity of cash inflows and find out the pay back period.

For the above case payback period is ₹ 1,60,000 ÷ 48,667 = 3.288.

Step III : Now search for a value nearest to 3.288 is 5 years row of the "PVAF" table. The closest figure given in the table are 15% (3.352) and 16% (3.274). This means that the IRR of the proposal is expected to lie between 15% and 16%.

Step IV : Find out the NPV of the proposal for the both these approximate rates as follows :

Year	Cash inflow	PVF (16% n)	PVF (15% n)	PV (16% n)	PV (15%)
01	40,000	0.862	0.870	34,480	34,800
02	60,000	0.743	0.756	44,580	45,360
03	50,000	0.641	0.658	32,050	32,900
04	50,000	0.512	0.672	27,600	28,600
05	40,000	0.476	0.497	19,040	19,880
			Total	**1,57,750**	**1,61,540**

$$\text{At 16\% NPV} = ₹\ 1,57,750 - ₹\ 1,60,000$$
$$= ₹\ (-)\ 2,250.$$
$$\text{At 15\% NPV} = ₹\ 1,61,540 - ₹\ 1,60,000$$
$$= \text{Rs } (+)\ 1540.$$

Step V : Find out the exact IRR by interpolating between 15% and 16%. At 15% the NPV is ₹ 1540 and at 16% the NPV is ₹ (−) 2250. Therefore the rate at which NPV is zero will be more than 15% but less than 16%. By interpolating the difference of 1% (i.e. 16% - 15%) over the NPV difference is ₹ 3790. (i.e. ₹ 2250 − (−)1540).

$$IRR = 15\%\ (+)\ \frac{₹\ 1,61,540 - ₹\ 1,60,000}{₹\ 1,61,540 - ₹\ 1,57,750}$$

$$= \frac{1,540}{3,790} = 0.40\ (\text{approx}) = 15 + 0.40$$

$$= 15.40\%$$

$$IRR = 16\%\ (+)\ \frac{₹\ 1,60,000 - ₹\ 1,57,750}{₹\ 1,61,540 - 1,57,750}$$

$$= \frac{2,250}{3,790} = 0.60\ (\text{approx.})$$

$$= 16\ (-)\ 0.60$$

$$= 15.40\%$$

ILLUSTRATION 6

Bhargav Ltd. Bangalore has to replace one of its machine for which it has following options :

a) Installation of equipment "Best" having cost of ₹ 75,000 which is expected to a generate a cash inflow of ₹ 20,000 per annum for next 6 years.

b) Installation of equipment "Better" having cost of ₹ 50,000 which is expected to generate a cash inflow of ₹ 18,000 per annum for next 4 years.

Which equipment should be preferred if the company adopts method of,

i)   Payback Period

ii)   Internal Rate of Return.

SOLUTION

Payback Period Method :

Payback period of equipment "Best" is ₹ 75,000 ÷ 20,000 = 3.75 years

Payback period of equipment "Better" is ₹ 50,000 ÷ 18,000 = 2.78 years

So, equipment "Better" having lower payback period of 2.78 years may be preferred.

Internal Rate of Return Method :

Equipment "Best" :

Initial outlay   =   ₹ 75,000

Inflows   =   ₹ 20,000 per year for 6 years

$PVAF_{(\%6)}$ =   ₹ 75,000 ÷ 20,000 = 3.75

In the PVAF Table, the values nearest to 3.75 in the 6 year row are found in 15% (3.784) and 16% (3.685) column. Now, the IRR may be found by interpolating between 15% and 16% as follows :

$$= \ 15\% + \frac{3.784 - 3.750}{3.784 - 3.685} = \ 15\% + 0.34$$

$$= \ 15.34\%$$

Equipment "Better" :

Initial outlay   =   ₹ 50,000

Inflows   =   ₹ 18,000 per year for 4 years

$PVAF_{(\%4)}$ =   ₹ 50,000 ÷ 18,000 = 2.778

In the PVAF Table, the value nearest to 2.778 in the 4 year row are found in 16% (2.798) and 17% (2.743) column. Now, the IRR may be found by interpolating between 16% and 17% as follows :

$$= \ 16\% + \frac{2.798 - 2.778}{2.798 - 2.743}$$

$$= \ 16.36\%$$

The equipment "Better", having IRR of 16.36% may be preferred over the equipment "Best".

ILLUSTRATION 7

Chandra Ltd., Chennai is considering a new project for which the investment data are as follows :

Capital Outlay   ₹ 2,00,000   Depreciation @   20% p.a.

Forecasted annual income before changing depreciation, but after all other charges are as follows :

Year	₹
1	1,00,000
2	1,00,000
3	80,000
4	80,000
5	40,000
∴ Total	4,00,000

On the basis of the available data, set out calculations, illustrating and comparing the following methods of evaluating the return :

a) Payback method,

b) Rate of return on original investment, and

c) Internal Rate of Return.

SOLUTION

Since there is no tax, the annual income before depreciation and after other charges is equivalent to Cash flows.

a) Capital outlay of ₹ 2,00,000 is recovered in the first two years (₹ 1,00,000 (year 1) + ₹ 1,00,000 (year 2), therefore, the payback period is two years.

b) Rate of return on original investment :

Year	Cash flow (CF) ₹	Depreciation ₹	Net income ₹
1	1,00,000	40,000	60,000
2	1,00,000	40,000	60,000
3	80,000	40,000	40,000
4	80,000	40,000	40,000
5	40,000	40,000	–
			2,00,000

$$\text{Average income} \ = \ \frac{₹\ 2,00,000}{5} = ₹\ 40,000$$

$$\text{Rate of Return} \ = \ \frac{\text{Average income}}{\text{Original Investment}} \times 100$$

$$= \ \frac{₹\ 40,000}{₹\ 2,00,000} \times 100 \ = \ 20\%$$

c)   Calculation of Internal Rate of Return :

$$\text{Average cash flows} = \frac{\text{Total cash flow}}{\text{Number of years}}$$

$$= \frac{₹\,40,00,000}{5}$$

$$= ₹\,80,000$$

$$\text{Pay back value} = \frac{\text{Cash out flows}}{\text{Average cash flows}}$$

$$= \frac{₹\,2,00,000}{₹\,80,000}$$

$$= 2.5 \text{ years}$$

Factors closest to pay back value of 2.5 corresponding to 5 years (life of the project) are 2.532 (28%) and 2.436 (30%). Since the actual cash flow stream is higher in initial years than average cash flows, higher discount rate of 33% may also be tried along with 30%.

Year	CF	PVF at		Total PV ₹	
	₹	20%	33%	30%	33%
1	1,00,000	0.769	0.752	76,900	75,200
2	1,00,000	0.592	0.565	59,200	56,500
3	80,000	0.455	0.425	36,400	34,000
4	80,000	0.350	0.320	28,000	25,600
5	40,000	0.269	0.240	10,760	9,600
				2,11,260	2,00,900

The internal rate of return of a project is the rate of discount at which the net present value is 0. Since the net present value at 33% is ₹ 900 only (i.e. ₹ 2,00,900 – ₹ 2,00,000), the internal rate of return is 33% (approx.)

ILLUSTRATION 8

Dora Ltd., Delhi requires an initial investment of ₹ 40,000. The estimated net cash flow are as follows (figures in ₹).

Year	1	2	3	4	5	6	7	8	9	10
Net cash flow	7,000	7,000	7,000	7,000	7,000	8,000	10,000	15,000	10,000	4,000

Using 10% as the cost of capital (rate of discount), determine the following :

i)   Payback period,

ii)   Net Present Value, and

iii)   Internal Rate of Return.

SOLUTION

i) **Pay back period :**

Initial Outlay	₹ 40,000
Cashflows for 5 years	₹ 7,000 + 7,000 + 7,000 + 7,000 + 7,000
	= ₹ 35,000
Balance outlay	= ₹ 40,000 – 35,000
	= 5,000
Cashflow for year 6	= ₹ 8,000

Therefore, Payback period $= 5 \text{ years} + \dfrac{₹ 5,000}{₹ 8,000}$

$= 5.62 \text{ years}$

ii) **Net Present Value (at 10% of cost of capital)**

Year	Cash flow ₹	$PVF_{(10\% n)}$	PV ₹
1	7,000	0.909	6,363
2	7,000	0.826	5,782
3	7,000	0.751	5,257
4	7,000	0.683	4,781
5	7,000	0.621	4,347
6	8,000	0.564	4,512
7	10,000	0.513	5,130
8	15,000	0.467	7,005
9	10,000	0.424	4,240
10	4,000	0.386	1,544
	Total inflows	(+)	48,961
	Less Initial outlay	(−)	40,000
	Net Present Value		8,961

iii) **Internal Rate of Return :**

The net present value at 10% has been found to be ₹ 8,961. So, in order to find out IRR, the cashflows may now be discounted at say 14% and 15% as follows :

Year	Cashflows ₹	$PVF_{(14\%n)}$	PV ₹	$PVF_{(15\%n)}$	PV ₹
1	7,000	0.877	6,139	0.870	₹ 6,090
2	7,000	0.769	5,383	0.756	5,292
3	7,000	0.675	4,725	0.658	4,606
4	7,000	0.592	4,144	0.572	4,004
5	7,000	0.519	3,633	0.497	3,479

6	8,000	0.456	3,648	0.432	3,456
7	10,000	0.400	4,000	0.376	3,760
8	15,000	0.351	5,265	0.326	4,905
9	10,000	0.308	3,080	0.284	2,840
10	4,000	0.270	1,080	0.247	988
	Total inflows		41,097		39,420
	Less Initial outlay		40,000		40,000
	Net Present Value		1,097		− 580

At 14% NPV is ₹ 1097   At 15% NPV is ₹ − 580

The IRR may be found by interpolating between 14% and 15% as follows :

$$IRR = 14\% + \frac{₹\ 1,097}{₹\ 1,097 + ₹\ 580}$$

$$= 14\% + 0.65$$

$$= 14.65\%$$

ILLUSTRATION 9

Essar Ltd., Edalabad is considering the replacement of its existing machine which is obsolete and unable to meet the rapidly rising demand for its product. The company is faced with two alternatives :

i)   To buy machine A which is similar to the existing machine or

ii)   To go in for Machine B which is more expensive and has much greater capacity.

The cash flows at the present level of operations under the two alternatives are as follows :

Cash flows (in lakhs of ₹) at the end of year :

Particulars	0	1	2	3	4	5
Machine A	(−) 25	–	5	20	14	14
Machine B	(−) 40	10	14	16	17	15

The company's cost of capital is 10%. The finance manager tries to evaluate the machine by calculating the following :

i)   Net Present Value

ii) Profitability Index

iii) Payback Period

At the end of his calculations, however, the finance manager is unable to make up his mind as to which machine to recommend. You are required to make these calculation and in the light thereof to advise the finance manager about the proposed investment.

Note : Present value of ₹ 1 at 10% discount rate are as follows :

Year	0	1	2	3	4	5
P.V.	1.00	0.91	0.83	0.75	0.68	0.62

SOLUTION

Calculation of Net Present Value :

Year	CF (₹ in lakhs)		$PV_{(10\%n)}$	Total PV (₹ in lakhs)	
	Machine A	Machine B		Machine A	Machine B
0	(−) 25	(−) 40	1.00	(−) 25.00	(−) 40.00
1	–	10	0.91	–	9.10
2	5	14	0.83	4.15	11.62
3	20	16	0.75	15.00	12.00
4	14	17	0.68	9.52	11.56
5	14	15	0.62	8.68	9.30
			NPV	12.35	13.58

Calculation of Profitability Index :

Particulars	Machine A (₹ in lakhs)	Machine B (₹ in lakhs)
$\dfrac{\text{P/V of cash inflow}}{\text{P/V of cash outflow}}$	$= \dfrac{37.35}{25.00}$ $= ₹\ 1.494$	$= \dfrac{53.58}{40.00}$ $= ₹\ 1.339$

Calculation of Payback Period :
(₹ in lakhs)

Year	Cash inflows		Cumulative cash inflows	
	Machine A	Machine B	Machine A	Machine B
0	(−) 25	(−) 40	–	–
1	–	10	–	10
2	5	14	5	24
3	20	16	25	40
4	14	17	39	57
5	14	15	53	72

In both cases, the Pay Back Period is 3 years.

Conclusion :

Particulars	Machine A	Machine B	Choice
i) Net Present Value	12.35	13.58	B
ii) Profitability Index	1.494	1.339	A
iii) Payback Period	3 years	3 years	Indifferent

ILLUSTRATION 10

In Foxy Ltd., Fattepur the cash flows from two mutually exclusive Projects A and B are as under :

Years		Project A	Project B
0	₹	(−) 22,000	(−) 27,000
1 − 7 (Annual)	₹	6,000	7,000
Project Life	(Years)	7	7

i)   Calculate net present value of the proposals at different discount rates of 15%, 16%, 17%, 18%, 19% and 20%.

ii) Advise on the project on the basis of internal rate of return method.

SOLUTION

Computation of Present Value of Cash Inflows of Different Projects.

Discount Rate	Cash Flow		PVAF	Present Value Cash flows	
	Project A ₹	Project B ₹		Project A ₹	Project B ₹
15%	6,000	7,000	4,160	24,960	29,120
16%	6,000	7,000	4,040	24,240	28,280
17%	6,000	7,000	3,922	23,532	27,454
18%	6,000	7,000	3,812	22,872	26,684
19%	6,000	7,000	3,706	22,235	25,942
20%	6,000	7,000	3,605	21,630	25,235

Calculation of Net Present Value:

Discount Rate	Present Value of Inflows (A) ₹	Net Present Value (A) ₹	Present Value of Inflows (B) ₹	Net Present Value (B) ₹
15%	24,960	2,960	29,120	2,120
16%	24,240	2,240	28,280	1,280
17%	23,532	1,532	27,454	454
18%	22,872	872	26,784	(−) 216
19%	22,235	235	25,942	(−) 1,058
20%	21,630	(−) 370	25,235	(−) 1,765

Calculation of Internal Rate of Return:

Project A : Since outflow of ₹ 22,000 is falling between ₹ 22,235 and ₹ 21,630, the IRR must be between 19% to 20%. So, interpolating the difference of ₹ 605 between 19% and 20%, the IRR comes to 19.39%.

$$= 19\% + \frac{₹ 22,235 - 22,000}{₹ 22,235 - 21,630}$$

$$= \frac{₹ 235}{₹ 605} + 19\%$$

$$= 19.39\%$$

Project B : Since outflow of ₹ 27,000 is falling between ₹ 27,454 and ₹ 26,684, the IRR must be between 17% to 18%. So, interpolating the difference of ₹ 770 between 17% and 18%, the IRR comes to 17.59%.

$$= \frac{₹ 27,454 - 27,000}{₹ 27,454 - 26,686}$$

$$= \frac{₹ 454}{₹ 770} + 17\%$$

$$= 17.59\%$$

Conclusion : As per the NPV technique, the Project A acceptable even if the discount rate is as high as 19%, whereas, the Project B becomes unviable even at 18%. As per IRR technique, the Project A is acceptable and is having an IRR of 19.39% against the IRR of 17.59% of Project B.

1.3 RELATIONSHIP BETWEEN RISK AND RETURNS

In business firms, the investment is made with certain expectations. One such expectation is that there will be regular inflow of cash. But the cash inflow will not be there as expected. This situation of difference of variation in the inflow is called **risk**. In certain investment there will be definite and expected **returns**, say a deposit in a bank or a company. These deposits are time deposits and yield a definite return. If you deposit ₹ 1,00,000 in a bank at an agreed rate of 10% p.a., you will be getting periodical interest on the amount deposited as agreed upto the date of maturity of the deposit. In this investment there is no element of risk involved.

But when you invest the same amount in business or in corporate securities i.e. equity shares, the return on such investment is indefinite. You may or may not get profit or dividend out of it. Even if there is inflow of income it cannot be measured as it is precisely expected in case of bank deposits. 'Thus, **risk** is a term, which explains the difference between the expectation of returns on investment and the actual realisation. In capital budgeting, several alternatives of investment are examined before an investment decision is taken and then the firm invests in project, which is found feasible.

But when the project is implemented it may not work to the expectation if environmental factor change. This will have an impact on **returns** and there may be an irregular inflow of cash. This irregular and variation in inflow is what is called risk. If the variation is too much, then the risk will be more and if the variation is less, the projects will be less risky,

There are three situation invovled in returns in capital budgeting, which are Certainty, Uncertainty and Risk. **Certainty** here refers to a situation where the actual returns on investment will be equal to the estimated returns and this is symbolically expressed as "1". **Risk** is an element, which falls nearer to zero. This means there is an impossibility of return in an investment. **Uncertainty** falls in between certainty and risk. It means the absence of a perfect foresight about future events. It is exclusive and non-measurable concept and characterised by incomplete information about, alternative courses of action. It prevails when an experiment is not replaceable and in reality, it cannot be defined in a clear and unequivocal manner. The probable accurance of an event is not known. The future loss cannot be foreseen. Hence the management cannot employ planning process to deal with such a situation,

Fixing Parameter of Risk and Return:

If management has included its long-term goals, the achievement of an after-tax rate of return on capital employed of 15 per cent, there is little merit in accepting new investment proposals which yield only 8 percent, even though this may be more than the cost of capital. In such a case, management should set the minimum target return that will be approved after considering the likely mix of projects and returns that would provide the required 15%.

Most firms are obliged to invest a part of their capital in uses, which provide no returns, or one too intangible to measure. The provision of recreational facilities for staff, and expenditure on fire and burglary prevention required by the insurance company, fall into this category. Since the cost of capital has to be exceeded by new investment as a whole, it is necessary for the earning projects to make up the deficiency.

In setting the parameters, the board should also consider inflation, risk and uncertainty. Inflation seems to be approved by most governments with little chance if its being arrested in the foreseeable future. Management fails in its duty to shareholders, if it does not take inflation into account in its financing and investment decisions.

Risks and uncertainty are always present in the investment decisions, more so in some investments than in others. When the risks are high, management may well set a higher minimum rate of returns than for when they are low. This may be formalised by classifying investments by degree of risk or type, and setting different minimum rate of return criteria for each. Typical categories could include :

Cost Saving Investment	Low Risk
Financing Investments	Low Risk
Leasing or Buying	Low Risk
Replacement Machines	Medium Risk
Extension of Existing Capacity	Medium Risk
Marketing New Products	High Risk

Risk is a characteristics interest in all business. Both external and internal characteristics create varying degree of uncertainty. According to Willsmore, business decisions are generally made under conditions of uncertainty rather than under conditions approaching certainty. In fact, both risk and uncertainty are the extreme ends of the same spectrum and most classes of business risk come somewhere between the two. Probability is usually measured as a fraction or decimal between zero and unity or one.

QUESTIONS FOR SELF-STUDY

I. Theory Questions:
   i)   What is capital budgeting? Why is it significant for a firm?
   ii)   Critically examine the various steps involved in capital budgeting process.
   iii) Outline the financial management techniques of evaluation of capital investment in fixed assets.
   iv)   What are the features of discounted cash flow method of evaluating on investment proposal. Is it a reliable techniques?
   v)   Define the term "capital budgeting". Give the features of capital budgeting decisions.
   vi)   Explain the merits and demerits of the pay back method.
   vii) How do you calculate the account rate of return? Give example.
   viii) Explain the merits and demerits of ARR methods.
   ix)   Explain the various steps involved in NPV method.
   x)   Explains the merits and demerits bf NPV method.
   xi)   **Write short note on :**
         a) Capital budgeting, b) Payback method, c) ARR method and d) IRR method.
   xii) Explain the merits and demerits of IRR methods.
   xiii) Explain the merits and demerits of PI method.
   xiv) Write a short note on Risk and return.

II. Practical Problems:

i) Machine A costs ₹ 1,00,000 payable immediately. Machine B costs ₹ 1,20,000 half payable immediately and half payable in one year's time. The cash receipts expected are as follows:

Year (at end)	Machine A ₹	Machine B ₹
1	20,000	–
2	60,000	60,000
3	40,000	60,000
4	30,000	80,000
5	20,000	–

At 7% opportunity cost, which machine should be selected on the basis of NPV?

ii) A company has to consider the following project :

Cost ₹ 10,000, Cash Inflows are as follows :

Years	₹ 10,000
1	1,000
2	1,000
3	2,000
4	10,000

Compute the internal rate of return and comment on the project if the opportunity cost is 14%.

iii) Bajaj Ltd., Belapur is considering two different investment proposals A and B. The details are as under :

		Proposal A ₹	Proposal B ₹
Investment Cost		**9,500**	**20,000**
Estimated Income	Year 1	4,000	8,000
	Year 2	4,000	8,000
	Year 3	4,500	12,000

Suggest the most attractive proposal on the basis of the NPV method considering that the future incomes are discounted at 12%. Also find out the IRR of the two proposals.

iv) Dixy Ltd., Deolali wants to replace the manual operations by new machine. There are two alternative models X and Y of the new machine. Using Payback period, suggest the most profitable investment. Ignore taxation.

Year (at end)		Machine A	Machine B
Original Investment	₹	9,000	18,000
Estimated life of the machine	(Years)	4	5
Estimated savings in cost	₹	5,000	8,000
Estimated savings in wages	₹	60,000	80,000
Additional cost of maintenance	₹	8,000	10,000
Additional cost of supervision	₹	12,000	18,000

v) One Plant of a company is doing poorly and is being considered for replacement. Three mutually exclusive Plants A, B, and C, have been proposed. The Plants are expected to cost ₹ 2,00,000 each, and have an estimated life of 5 years, 4 years and 3 years, respectively, and have no salvage value. The company's required rate of return is 10%. The anticipated cash inflows after taxes for the three Plants are as follows :

Year	Plant A ₹	Plant B ₹	Plant C ₹
1	50,000	80,000	1,00,000
2	50,000	80,000	1,00,000
3	50,000	80,000	10,000
4	50,000	30,000	–
5	1,90,000	–	–

Find out the Payback, Average Rate of Return, Net Present Value and Profitability Index.

vi) A firm whose cost of capital is 10% is considering two mutually exclusive projects X and Y, the details of which are :

Year	Year	Plant X ₹	Plant Y ₹
Cost	0	70,000	70,000
Cash Inflows	1	10,000	50,000
	2	20,000	40,000
	3	30,000	20,000
	4	45,000	10,000
	5	60,000	10,000

Compute the Net Present Value at 10%, Profitability Index, and Internal Rate of Return for the two projects.

vii) The following (financially) mutually exclusive projects are considered :

	Project A ₹	Project B ₹
PV of cash inflows	20,000	8,000
Initial cash outlay	15,000	5,000
Net Present Value	5,000	3,000
Profitability Index	1.33	1.6
Which Project should be preferred and why ?		

viii) Management of Texmo Ltd., Tatanagar Ltd. has the option to buy either Machine A or Machine B. Machine A has a cost of ₹ 75,000. Its expected life is 6 years with no salvage value at the end. It would generate net cash flows of ₹ 20,000 per year. Machine B on the other hand, would cost ₹ 50,000. Its expected life is 6 years with no salvage value at the end. It would generate net cash flow of ₹ 15,000 per year. Assuming that the cost of capital of both the machines is 10 per cent, you are required to calculate :

a) Net Present Value for each Machine.

b) Internal Rate of Return for each machine.

c) Which machine should be recommend and why ?

ix) The management of Nirma Ltd., Nashik, is considering undertaking of a capital project. There are two mutually exclusive projects, Project A and Project B. The investment required for each project is ₹ 75,000. The net cash inflow estimated from these projects are as shown in table.

Year	Project A ₹	Project B ₹
1	15,000	20,000
2	20,000	25,000
3	30,000	30,000
4	40,000	40,000
5	25,000	30,000

The management wants return on investment at 18% p,a.

The present value of Re. 1 at 18% discount factor is as under:

1st year : ₹ 0.8475

2nd year : ₹ 0.7182

3rd year : ₹ 0.6086

4th year : ₹ 0.5158

5th year : ₹ 0.4371

Calculate the Net Present Value of Project A and Project B and advise the management with respect to the selection of the project.

■ ■ ■

Chapter **2**...

Cost of Capital

Synopsis...

2.1 MEANING

The **Cost of Capital** to a company is the rate of return it must earn on its investments in order to satisfy the expectation of investors who provide long-term funds to them. **Cost of Capital** means cost paid by the company for the use of capital, e.g. dividend is the cost paid by the company to use share capital, 'Interest' is the cost paid by a company to make use of borrowed capital. The **Cost of Capital** is a central concept in financial management, linking the investment and financial decisions.

The concept of **Cost of Capital** is very important in the realm of financial management. At the same time, it is also one of the most difficult and disputed topic in financial management, since conflicting opinions have been expressed by the financial experts and wizardry as regards the way in which the cost of capital can be computed.

The **Cost of Capital** is the minimum rate of return expected by the investors, which will maintain the market value of the shares constant at a particular level. Moreover, to achieve the predetermined objective of the financial management, viz. wealth maximisation, a firm has to necessarily earn a rate of return more than its cost of capital. The cost of capital in turns depends on the risk involved in the firm. Generally, higher the risk involved in a firm, the higher will be the Cost of Capital.

2.2 DEFINITIONS

Some of the important definitions given by certain eminent authors in the subject concerned are as follows :

i)   **Solomon Ezra:**

"Cost of Capital is the minimum required rate of earning or the cut-off rate for capital expenditures."

ii)   **Milton H. Spencer:**

"Cost of Capital is the minimum rate of return which a firm requires as a condition for undertaking an investment."

Thus Cost of Capital may be defined as cost to the company for procuring funds. This is equivalent to the average rate of return that an investor in a firm would expect for supplying capital. This is a minimum rate of return that a project must yield to keep the value of the firm in tact. The minimum rate of return tantamount to cost of capital.

It may be noted that Cost of Capital is always expressed in terms of percentage. Appropriate allowance is made for tax factor so that cost of capital may be compared with rates of return on capital expenditure projects that are based on cash benefits after taxes.

Importance of Cost of Capital:

The Cost of Capital can be used as a tool to evaluate the financial performance of top management. The actual profitability of any project is compared to the actual cost of capital funds raised to finance the project. If the actual profitability of the project is on the high side when compared to the actual cost of capital raised, the performance can be evaluated as satisfactory.

Cost of Capital plays a crucial role in capital budgeting decision. Any capital budgeting decision involves the consideration of the Cost of Capital. According to the net present value method of capital budgeting, if the present value of expected returns from the investment throughout its life period is greater than or equal to the cost of investment, the project may be accepted; otherwise the project may be rejected. The present value of expected returns is calculated by discounting the expected cash inflows at the cut-off rate, which is the Cost of Capital. It is clear from the above that the Cost of Capital serves as a very useful tool in the process of making capital budgeting decisions. The Cost of Capital acts as a determinant of capital mix in the designing of a balanced and appropriate capital structure. As a rule there should be a proper mix of debt and equity capital in financing a firm's assets. While designing an optimal capital structure of a firm, the management has to consider the objective of maximising the value of the firm and minimising the Cost of Capital. Computation of the weighted average cost of various sources of finance is very essential in planning and designing the capital structure of a firm. Thus, Cost of Capital provides useful guidelines in determining optimum capital structure of a company. The cost of capital can be conveniently employed as a tool in making other important financial decisions such as dividend policy, capitalisation of profit, rights issue and working capital, bonus issue and total capital structure. Investors feeling about expected income of a company and amount of risk inherent in it are reflected in the company's Cost of Capital. Cost of Capital is major standard of comparison used in modem financial decisions. Acceptance or rejection of an investment project depends on the cost of the company is required to pay for financing it.

2.3 ASSUMPTIONS

Following are the **assumptions** underlying the analysis of cost of capital.

i) Each new investment is deemed to be financed from a pool of funds in which the various sources of long-term financing are represented in the proportions in which they are found in the capital structure. For example, suppose the proportions of equity and debts in the capital structure of a firm are equal. The firm is planning to undertake two investments, in projects I_1 and I_2 each requiring an outlay of ₹ 200 lakhs. The total financing required for is ₹ 400 lakhs and this will be raised by issuing equity stock and debentures to the extent of ₹ 200 lakhs each. However, because of some 'lumpiness' in the process of financing, the firm would first raise ₹ 200 lakhs of equity financing at the time when project I_1 is undertaken and then it would raise ₹ 200 lakhs of debt financing when project I_2 is undertaken. According to the pool financing assumption, each project is deemed to be financed by a mixture of equity and debt in equal proportion, though the specific financing sought at the time of undertaking I_1 is only equity and at the time of undertaking I_2 is only debt.

ii) The risk characterising new investment proposals being considered is the same as the risk characterising the existing investment of the firm. In other words, the adoption of new investment proposals will not change the risk complexion of the firm.

iii) The capital structure of the firm will not be affected by the new investments. This means that the firm will continue to pursue the same financing policies.

iv) In general, if the firm uses n different sources of finance, the cost of capital is :

where, k_a = $\Sigma\ p_i k_i$

        k_a = Average Cost of capital

        p_i = Proportion of ith source of finance, and

        k_i = Cost of the ith source of finance.

Classification:

Cost of Capital can be classified in different ways which are shown below in Figure 2.1:

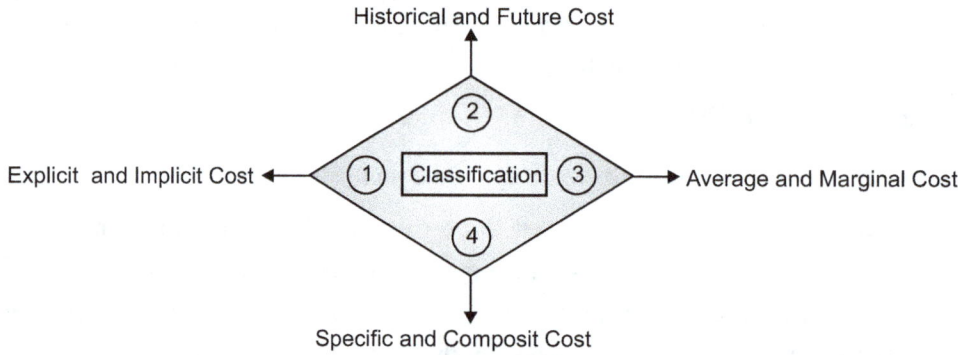

Fig. 2.1: Classification of Cost of Capital

2.4 EXPLICIT AND IMPLICIT COST

Explicit Cost refers the discount rate which equates the present value of cash inflows with the present value of cash outflows. Thus, the explicit cost is the internal rate of return which a company pays for procuring the required finances. The explicit cost of a specific source of finance may be determined with the help of the following formula :

$$I_0 = \frac{O_1}{(1+k)} + \frac{O_2}{(1+k)^2} + \dots + \frac{O_{P1}}{(1+k)^n} = \Sigma^n \frac{O_t}{(1+k)^t} \quad t = 1$$

where, I_0 = is the net cash inflow at zero point of time,

      O_t = is the outflow of cash in periods 1 to n,

      k = is the explicit cost of capital.

Implicit Cost represents the rate of return, which can be earned by investing the capital in alternative investments. The concept of opportunity cost gives rise to the implicit cost. For, the implicit cost represents the cost of the opportunity foregone in order to take up a particular project. For example, the implicit cost of retained earnings is the rate of return available to the shareholders by investing the funds elsewhere.

There are certain costs, besides the actual interest entailed by the debt but the company does not take note of it since it is not incurred directly. With induction of additional dose of debt beyond certain level the company may run the risk of bankruptcy. The shareholders may react to it strongly and in consequence, the share prices may tend to nose-dive. There may be further setback to share values caused by increased instability of earnings consequent upon unfavourable leverage. The loss in shares values owing to increased risk and greater instability of earnings is termed as **implicit cost** or invisible cost of debt capital.

Thus, with increase in doses of debt investors will demand higher interest rate because of the increased risk. Alongside in explicit cost, the implicit cost will also tend to rise as the company will be able to sell the bond at lower price.

To arrive at the actual cost of debt, capital hidden or implicit cost should be added in the explicit cost. But the problem lies in computation of the implicit cost of capital. The following formula may be used to adjust hidden cost of debt capital in the total cost of debt.

$$K_d = \frac{R + \frac{1}{n}(FV + SP) + LS/MP}{(FV + SP)/2}$$

where,

$$
\begin{aligned}
K_d &= (1 - T) = \text{Cost of debts,} \\
FV &= \text{Face value of security,} \\
SP &= \text{Sale proceeds from issue of security,} \\
1/n\,(FV + SP) &= \text{The amortisation of premium or discount,} \\
R &= \text{Annual interest payment,} \\
LS &= \text{Stand for possible losing share value and} \\
MP &= \text{Maturity period.}
\end{aligned}
$$

Historical and Future Cost:

It is defined as the costs which are ascertained after these have been incurred. **Historical Cost** represents the cost which has already been incurred for financing project. It is computed on the basis of past data collected. **Future Cost** represents the expected cost of funds to be raised for financing a project. Historical Cost is significant since it helps in projecting the future cost and in providing an appraisal of the past financial performance by comparison with the standard or predetermined costs. In financial decisions, future costs are more relevant than the historical costs. Historical Costs are only of historical value and not useful for cost control purposes.

Average and Marginal Cost:

Average Cost of capital refers to the weighted average cost calculated on the basis of cost of each source of capital and weights assigned to them in the ratio of their share to capital funds. **Marginal Cost** of capital refers to the average cost of capital, which has to be incurred to obtain additional funds required by a firm. Marginal cost of capital is considered as more important in capital budgeting and financing decisions. Actually, marginal cost is the total of variable cost.

Specific and Composit Cost:

Specific Cost refers to the cost of a specific source of capital, while composite cost of capital refers to the combined cost of various sources of capital. It is weighted average cost of capital. It is also termed as overall cost of capital. When more than one type of capital is employed in the business, it is the composit cost which should be considered for decision-making and not the specific cost. But where only one type of capital is employed in the business, the specific cost of that capital alone must be considered.

2.5 MEASUREMENT OF SPECIFIC COST

For ascertaining the overall cost of capital of a firm, the specific costs of different sources of finance raised by it have to be calculated, these sources are as shown in Figure 2.2.

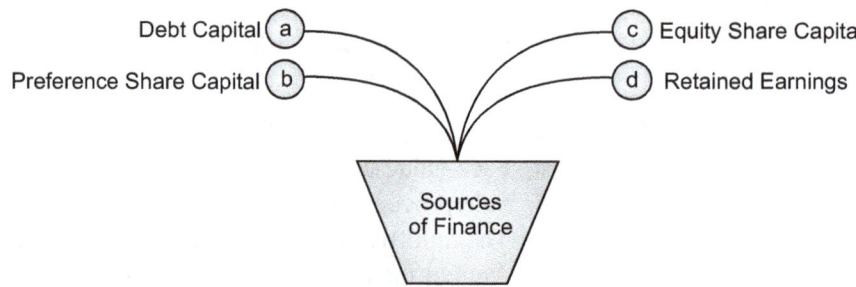

Fig. 2.2: Sources of Finance

The accurate measurement and understanding and interpretation of following specific cost related to difference sources of a finance becomes absolutely important.

2.5.1 COST OF DEBT

The cost of debt is the rate of interest payable on debt capital is obtained through the issue of debentures. The issue of debentures involves a number of floatation charges, such as printing of prospectus, advertisement, underwriting, brokerage etc. again, debentures can be issued at par or at times below par (at discount) or at times above par (at premium). These floatation charges and modes of issue have an important bearing on the cost of debt capital.

The formula adopted or calculating the cost of debt capital is given below :

i) $$K_p = \frac{I}{P}$$

where, K_d = Cost of debt (before tax),

I = Interest, and

P = Principal

In the case, the debt is raised by issue of debentures at premium or discount, one should consider P as the amount of net proceeds from the issue and not the face value of debentures. The formula may be modified as under :

ii) $K_d = \dfrac{I}{NP}$ (where, NP = Net proceeds)

When debt is used as a source of finance, the firm saves considerable amount in payment of tax since interest is allowed as a deductible expense in computation of tax. Hence, the effective cost of debt is reduced. In other words, the effective cost of debt, i.e. the after-tax cost of debt would be substantially less than the before-tax cost. The after-tax cost of debt may be calculated with help of following formula :

iii)   After-tax cost of debt = $K_d (1 - t)$ where, t is the tax-rate

ILLUSTRATION 1

i)   AB Ltd. issues ₹ 50,000, 8% debentures at par. The tax rate applicable to the company is 50%. Compute the cost of debt-capital.

ii)   CD Ltd. issues ₹ 50,000, 8% debentures at a premium of 10%. The tax rate applicable to the company is 60%. Compute the cost of debt-capital.

iii)   EF Ltd. issues ₹ 50,000, 8% debentures at a discount of 5%. The tax rate is 50%. Compute the cost of debt-capital.

iv)   GH Ltd. issues ₹ 50,000, 9% debentures at a premium of 10%. The costs of floatation are 2%. The tax rate applicable is 60%.

Compute cost of debt-capital.

SOLUTION

i) $K_d = \dfrac{I}{NP}(1-t) = \dfrac{₹\,4,000}{₹\,50,000}(1-0.5) = \dfrac{₹\,4,000}{₹\,50,000} \times 0.05 = 4\%$

ii) $K_d = \dfrac{I}{NP}(1-t) = \dfrac{₹\,4,000}{₹\,55,000}(1-0.6) = \dfrac{₹\,4,000}{₹\,55,000} \times 0.4 = 2.91\%$

iii) $K_d = \dfrac{I}{NP}(1-t) = \dfrac{₹\,4,000}{₹\,47,500}(1-0.5) = 4.21\%$

iv) $K_d = \dfrac{I}{NP}(1-t) = \dfrac{₹\,4,500}{₹\,53,900}(0.4) = 3.34\%$

Computation of Redeemable Debt Capital :

The **cost of redeemable debt capital** may be calculated as under :

i)   Before-tax cost of debt :

$$K_{db} = \dfrac{I + 1/n\,(P - NP)}{1/2\,(P + NP)}$$

where,

$$I = \text{Interest}$$

$$N = \text{Number of years in which debt is to be redeemed}$$

$$P = \text{Proceeds at par}$$

$$NP = \text{Net proceeds}$$

(b)   After-tax cost of debt,

$$K_{da} = K_{db} (1 - t) \frac{I + 1/n\,(P - NP)}{1/2\,(P + NP)} \times (1 - t)$$

ILLUSTRATION 2

Ashoka Ltd. Anand issues ₹ 5,00,000, 10% redeemable debentures at a discount of 5%. The cost of floatation amount to ₹ 15,000. The debentures are redeemable after 5 years. Calculate before-tax and after-tax cost of debt assuming a tax rate of 50%.

SOLUTION

Before-tax cost of debt,

$$K_{db} = \frac{I + 1/n\,(P - NP)}{1/2\,(P + NP)}$$

$$= \frac{₹\,50,000 + 1/5\,(₹\,5,00,000 - ₹\,4,60,000)}{1.2\,(₹\,5,00,000 + ₹\,4,60,000)}$$

$$= \frac{₹\,50,000 + ₹\,8,000}{₹\,4,80,000}$$

$$= \frac{₹\,58,000}{₹\,4,80,000} \times 100$$

$$= 12.09\%$$

After-tax cost of debt, $K_{db} = K_{db} (1 - t) = 12.09\,(1 - 0.5)$

$$= 12.09 \times 0.5 = 6.045\%$$

ILLUSTRATION 3

Barua Ltd. Bandra issues 5,000, 8% debentures of ₹ 100 each at a discount of 10% and redeemable after 10 years. The expenses of issues amounted to ₹ 10,000.

Calculate the cost of debt capital.

SOLUTION

$$K_{db} = \frac{I + 1/n\,(P - NP)}{1/2\,(P + NP)}$$

$$= \frac{₹\ 40,000 + 1/10\ (₹\ 5,00,000 - ₹\ 4,40,000)}{1/2\ (₹\ 5,00,000 + ₹\ 4,40,000)}$$

$$= \frac{₹\ 40,000 + ₹\ 6,000}{₹\ 4,70,000}$$

$$= \frac{₹\ 46,000}{₹\ 4,70,000} \times 100$$

$$= 9.79\%$$

Computation of Cost of using Debentures :

Interest is the cost paid by a company to use borrowed capital. Rate of cost of capital for using debentures is calculated as under :

ILLUSTRATION 4

i) Colgate Ltd. Chembur issued 1,000; 14% Debentures of ₹ 100 each; to be repaid (redeemed) after 10 years. Collection expenses are ₹ 2,000. Company's tax rate is 50%.

Calculate 'Rate of Cost of Capital for using debentures' per annum.

ii) Colgate Ltd. Chembur issued 1,000; 14% Debentures of ₹ 100 each to be repaid after 10 years at 5% premium. Collection Expenses are ₹ 2000. Company's tax rate is 50%.

Calculate Cost of Capital per annum.

iii) Colgate Ltd. Chembur issued 1000; 14% Debentures of ₹ 100 each, at 5% discount redeemable after 10 years. Collection expenses are ₹ 2000. Company's tax rate is 50%.

Calculate yearly Cost of Capital.

SOLUTION

Particulars		₹	₹
(a) Face value of Debentures (1,000 × ₹ 100)		1,00,000	
Less : Collection Expenses	(−)	2,000	
∴ Net Collection		**98,000**	
Interest p.a. (14% on ₹ 1,00,000)			14,000
Less : Tax Benefit			
• On Interest = ₹ 14,000 × 0.50		7,000	
• On Collection Expenses = $\frac{₹\ 2,000 \times 0.50}{10\ \text{years}}$	(+)	$\frac{100}{(-)}$	7,100
			6,900

$$\text{Hence, Average Cost of Capital} = \frac{\text{Net Cost of Capital}}{\text{Net Collection}} \times 100$$

$$= \frac{₹\,6,900}{₹\,98,000} \times 100$$

$$= 7.04\%$$

Particulars		₹	₹
ii) Face value of Debentures			1,00,000
Less : Collection Expenses	(−)		2,000
Net Collection			98,000
Interest p.a.			14,000
Add : Premium on Redemption (₹ 5,000/10 years)	(+)		500
			14,500
Less : • Tax Saving		7,000	
• On Interest		250	
• On Premium	(+)	100	7,350
On Collection Expense	(−)		
∴ Net Cost of Capital			7,150

$$\text{Hence, Cost of Capital per annum} = \frac{₹\,7,150}{₹\,98,000} \times 100 = 7.30\%$$

Particulars		₹	₹
iii) Face value of debentures			1,00,000
Less : Discount	(−)		5,000
			95,000
Less : Collection Expenses	(−)		2,000
Net Collection			**93,000**
Interest :			14,000
Less : Tax benefit on			
• Interest		7,000	
• Discount $\left(\frac{₹\,5,000}{10} \times 0.50\right)$		250	
Collection Expenses	(+)	100	(−) 7,350
∴ Net Cost of Capital			6,650

$$\text{Annual Cost of Capital} = \frac{\text{Net Cost of Capital}}{\text{Net Collection}} \times 100$$

$$= \frac{₹\,6,650}{93,000} \times 100 = 7.15\%$$

2.5.2 COST OF PREFERENCE SHARES

The **cost of preference share** capital is the dividend expected by its investors. Moreover, preference shareholders have a priority to dividend over the equity shareholders. In case dividends are not paid to preference shareholders, it will affect the fund raising capacity of the firm. Hence, dividends are usually paid regularly on preference shares except when there are no profits to pay dividends.

The cost of preference can be calculated as :

$$K_p = \frac{D}{P}$$

where,

K_p = Cost of preference capital

D = Annual preference dividend

P = Preference share capital (Proceeds)

Further, when preference shares are issued at premium or discount or when cost of floatation is incurred to issue preference shares, the nominal or par value of preference share capital has to be adjusted to find out the net proceeds from the issue of preference shares. In such a case, the cost of preference capital can be computed with the following formula :

$$K_p = \frac{D}{NP}$$

When redeemable preference shares are issued by a company, they can be redeemed or cancelled on maturity date. The cost of redeemable preference share capital can be calculated as :

$$K_{pr} = \frac{d + \dfrac{Mv - NP}{N}}{1/2\,(MV + NP)}$$

where,

K_{Pr} = Cost of redeemable preference shares

D = Annual preference dividend

MV = Maturity value of preference shares

NP = Net proceeds of preference shares

ILLUSTRATION 5

Dorabjee Ltd. Delhi issued 20,000, 10% preference shares of ₹ 100 each. Cost of issue is ₹ 2 per share. Calculate cost of preference capital if these shares are issued i) at par, ii) at premium of 10% and iii) at a discount of 5%.

SOLUTION

Cost of preference capital, $K_p = \dfrac{D}{NP}$

i)

$$K_p = \dfrac{₹\,2,00,000}{₹\,20,00,000 - ₹\,40,000} \times 100$$

$$= \dfrac{₹\,2,00,000}{₹\,19,60,000} \times 100$$

$$= 10.2\%$$

ii)

$$K_p = \dfrac{₹\,2,00,000}{₹\,20,00,000 + ₹\,2,00,000 - ₹\,40,000} \times 100$$

$$= \dfrac{₹\,2,00,000}{₹\,21,60,000} \times 100$$

$$= 9.26\%$$

iii)

$$K_p = \dfrac{₹\,2,00,000}{₹\,20,00,000 - ₹\,1,00,000 - ₹\,40,000} \times 100$$

$$= \dfrac{₹\,2,00,000}{₹\,18,60,000} \times 100$$

$$= 10.75\%$$

Cost of Irredeemable Preferred Stock :

The following formula can be used to determine the cost of the Irredeemable Stock :

$$K_p = \dfrac{DP}{MP}$$

where,

K_p = Cost of preferred stock

DP = Dividend per share

MP = Market price per share

ILLUSTRATION 6

Eros Ltd.. Elora issue 15% irredeemable preference shares of the face value of ₹ 100 each. Compute the cost of preferred stock, what will be cost of preferred stock if it is issued at 5% premium and 10% discount ?

SOLUTION

i) Issued at Par   …… $K_p = \dfrac{15}{₹\,100} = 15\%$ approximately

ii) Issued at Premium … $K_p = \dfrac{15}{₹\,105} = 14.29\%$ approximately

iii) Issued at Discount … $K_p = \dfrac{15}{₹\,90} = 16.67\%$ approximately

Cost of Redeemable Preferred Stock :

The explicit cost of redeemable preferred stock is the discount rate that equates the net proceeds from the sale of preference shares with the present value of the future dividends and principal repayments. The formula to determine the cost of redeemable preferred stock is the same used to calculate cost of redeemable debentures with a slight modification as set out below :

$$SP = \frac{Dp1}{(1 + Kp)^1} + \frac{Dp2}{(1 + Kp)^2} + \cdots \frac{Dpn}{(1 + Kp)^n} + \frac{Pn}{(1 + Kp)^n}$$

$$\sum_{E}^{n} = \frac{Dpt}{(1 + Kp)^1} + \frac{Pn}{(1 + Kp)^n}$$

Where,   SP = Expected sale proceed received per share from the issue of preferred stock,

dp = Dividend payment per share, and

Pn = Repayment of preference capital amount.

It should be noted here that the cost of preferred stock is always after taxes. Since dividend on preferred stock is not a tax deductible expense, no tax adjustment is called for in this case. Because dividend on preferred stock is usually fixed by contract, there is no problem to obtain the dividend figure, market price of the preferred stock is also easily available.

ILLUSTRATION 7

Finolex Ltd. Faizpur issued 1000, 9% preference shares of ₹ 100 each at a premium of 10% redeemable after 5 years at par.

Compute the cost of preference share capital.

SOLUTION

$$kpr = \frac{D + \frac{1}{N}(MV - NP)}{1/2\,(MV + NP)} \times 100$$

$$= \frac{₹\,9,000 + 1/5\,(₹\,1,00,000 - ₹\,1,10,000)}{1/2\,(₹\,1,00,000 + ₹\,1,10,000)}$$

$$= \frac{₹\,9,000 - ₹\,2,000}{₹\,1,05,000} \times 100$$

$$= \frac{₹\,7,000}{₹\,1,05,000} \times 100$$

$$= 6.7\%$$

ILLUSTRATION 8

Godrej Ltd. Gangapur issued 50,000, 10% preference shares of 100 each redeemable after 10 years at a premium of 5%. The cost of issue is ₹ 2 per share.

Calculate the cost of preference share capital.

SOLUTION

$$Kpr = \frac{D + \dfrac{MV - NP}{N}}{1/2 \ (MV + NP)} \times 100$$

$$= \frac{₹\ 5,00,000 + 1/10 \ (₹\ 52,50,000 - ₹\ 49,00,000)}{1/2 \ (₹\ 52,50,000 + ₹\ 49,00,000)} \times 100$$

$$= \frac{₹\ 5,00,000 + ₹\ 35,000}{₹\ 50,75,000} \times 100$$

$$= \frac{₹\ 5,35,000}{₹\ 50,75,000} \times 100$$

$$= 10.54\%$$

Cost of Preference Share Capital :

Calculation of Cost of Capital by Alternative Method :

The cost of preference capital which is redeemable is the value of K_p in the following expression :

$$P = \sum_{t=1}^{n} + \frac{D}{(1 + k_p)^T} + \frac{F}{(1 + k_p)^n}$$

where,

     P = Net amount realised per preference share

     D = Preference dividend per share payable annually

     F = Redemption price

     n = Maturity period

The cost of preference share capital may be obtained quickly by using the following approximation

$$k_p = \frac{D + (F - P)/n}{(P + F)/2}$$

ILLUSTRATION 9

Hindustan Ltd. Himmatpur issue ₹ 100 face value preference shares carrying 14% dividend which are repayable at par after 12 years. The net amount realised per share is ₹ 92.

What is the cost of preference capital ?

SOLUTION

The Cost of Preference Share Capital, K_p is approximately equal to :

$$= \frac{D + \frac{(F - P)}{n}}{(P + F)^2}$$

$$= \frac{14 + \frac{(100 - 92)}{12}}{(100 + 92/2)}$$

$$= 15.3\%$$

Perpetual Preference Capital :

The cost of preference capital which is perpetual is equal to Kp in the following equation; If the difference between F and P can be amortised equally over the life of the preference share, the cost of preference capital is the value of Kp in the equation :

$$P = \sum_{t=1}^{n} \frac{D - (F - P)T/n}{(1 + k_p)^t} + \frac{F}{(1 + k_p)^t} \qquad \ldots (1)$$

Here T stands for the tax rate; other symbols are the same as mentioned above . As per this equation :

$$k_p = \frac{D + (F - P)/n \, (1 - T)}{(P + F)/2}$$

$$P = \sum_{t=1}^{\infty} \frac{D}{(1 + k_p)^t}$$

where,   P = Net amount realised per share of preference capital

                D = Preference dividend per share payable annually

The value of KP in Equation (above) is simply : D/P.

2.5.3 COST OF EQUITY SHARES

The cost of equity share capital is by far the most difficult to compute. It is also inexact since it is based on forecast, which hardly turns out to be true. Unlike the preferred stock, dividend rate in the case of equity stock is not stipulated. The agreement with the equity stockholders provides that in return for a fixed capital contribution the investors would participate pro-rata according to their investment in the future fortunes of the company.

For the purpose of measuring the cost of equity, the capital will be divided into two parts viz. the external equity or the new issues (of shares) and the retained earnings.

The cost of external equity will normally be higher than the cost of retained earnings because of the floatation costs involved in the former. It is very difficult to measure the cost of equity in practice, since it is difficult to estimate the future dividends expected by the equity shareholders.

Methods used to calculate the Cost of Equity Capital :

There are different ways that can be employed to calculate the cost of equity capital. Moreover, the earning and dividends on equity share capital are generally expected to grow. The cost of equity capital can be computed by various methods as shown below in Figure 2.3.

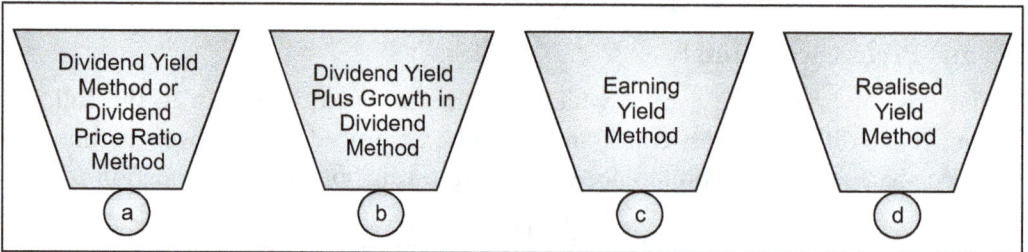

Fig. 2.3: Methods to calculate Cost of Equity Capital

a) Dividend Yield Method or Dividend Price Ratio Method :

Under this method, the cost of equity capital is the discount rate that equates the present value of expected future dividends per share with the net proceeds (or current market price) of a share symbolically,

$$K_e = \frac{D}{NP} \text{ or } \frac{D}{MP}$$

where, K_e = Cost of Equity Capital

       NP = Net proceeds per share

       D = Expected Dividend per share

       MP = Market Price per share

The basic assumptions underlying this method are that the investors give utmost importance to dividends and the risk in the firm remains constant.

The dividend price ratio method cannot be considered as a sound one for the following reasons :

i) It does not consider the growth in dividend.

ii) It does not consider future earnings on retained earnings and

iii) It does not take into account the capital is suitable only when the company has stable earnings and stable dividend policy over a period of time.

ILLUSTRATION 10

Indian Cable Ltd. Indore issued 5,000 equity shares of ₹ 100 each at premium of 10%. The company has been paying 20% dividend to equity shareholders for the past five years and expects to maintain the same in the future also.

Compute the cost of equity capital. Will it make any difference if the market price of equity share is ₹ 160 ?

SOLUTION

$$K_e = \frac{D}{NP}$$

$$= \frac{20}{110} \times 100$$

$$= 18.18\%$$

If the market price of a equity share is ₹ 160.

$$K_e = \frac{D}{MP}$$

$$= \frac{20}{160} \times 100$$

$$= 12.5\%$$

b) Dividend Yield Plus Growth in Dividend Method :

When the dividends of the firm are expected to grow at a constant rate and the dividend pay-out ratio is constant, this method may be the cost of equity capital is based on the dividends and the growth rate.

$$K_e = \frac{D}{NP} + G$$

Where,

K_e = Cost of equity of capital

D = Expected dividend per share

NP = Net proceeds per share

G = Rate of growth in dividends

Further, in case cost of existing equity share capital is to be calculated, the NP should be changed with MP (market price per share) in the above equation.

$$K_e = \frac{D}{MP} + G$$

ILLUSTRATION 11

i)   Jindal Ltd. Jalgoan issued 2,000 new equity shares of ₹ 100 each at par. The floatation costs are expected be 5% of the share price. The company pays a dividend of ₹ 10 per share initially and the growth in dividends is expected to be 5%.

Compute the cost of new issue of equity share.

ii) If the current market price of equity share is ₹ 200, calculate the cost of existing equity share capital.

SOLUTION

i)
$$K_e = \frac{D}{NP} + G$$

$$= \frac{10}{100 - 5} + 5\%$$

$$= 15.53\%$$

ii)
$$K_e = \frac{D}{MP} + G$$

$$= \frac{10}{200} + 5\%$$

$$= 10.0\%$$

c) **Earning Yield Method :**

Under this method, the cost of equity capital is the discount rate that equates the present value of expected future earnings per share with the net proceeds (or current marketing price) of a share. Symbolically,

$$K_e = \frac{\text{Earning per share}}{\text{Net proceeds}} = \frac{EPS}{NP}$$

where, the cost of existing capital is to be calculated,

$$K_e = \frac{\text{Earning per share}}{\text{Market price per share}} = \frac{EPS}{NP}$$

This method of computing cost of equity capital may be employed in the following cases :

i) When the earnings per share are expected to remain unchanged.

ii) When the dividend pay out ratio is 100 percent or when the retention ratio is zero, i.e. all the available profits are fully distributed as dividends

iii) When a firm is expected to earn an amount on new equity share capital, which is equal to the current rate of earnings

iv) The market price of the share is influenced by the earnings per share alone.

ILLUSTRATION 12

Kotak Ltd. Kochi is considering an expenditure of ₹ 80,00,000 for expanding its operations. Other particulars are as follows :

Number of existing equity shares = ₹ 10,00,000

Market value of existing share   = ₹ 60

Net earnings   = ₹ 90,00,000

Compute the cost of existing equity share capital and of new equity capital assuming that new shares will be issued at a price of ₹ 54 per share and the costs of new issue will be ₹ 2 per share.

SOLUTION

Cost of existing equity share capital

$$K_e = \frac{EPS}{MP}$$

$$\text{EPS, or Earnings per share} = ₹ \frac{90}{100} = ₹ 9$$

$$K_e = \frac{9}{60} \times 100 = 15\%$$

Cost of new equity capital, $K_e = \dfrac{EPS}{NP}$

$$= \frac{9}{54 - 2} \times 100 = \frac{9}{52} \times 100$$

$$= 17.30\%$$

d) Realised Yield Method :

The realised yield method which takes into consideration the actual average rate of return realised in the past, is employed to compute the cost of equity share capital while calculating the average cost of return realised, dividends received in the past along with the gain realised at the time of sale of shares, should be considered. The cost of capital is equal to the realised rate of return by the shareholders.

According to this approach the yield (rate of return) realised by equity shareholders historically is regarded as a proxy for the rate of return required by them. The yield on an equity stock for the year is given by the following equation :

$$Y_1 = \frac{D_1 + P_1}{P_{t-1}} - 1$$

where
Y_1 = Yield for year t

D_1 = Dividend per share for year t payable at the end of the year

P_1 = Price per share at the end of year t

P_{t-1} = Price per share at the end of year t − 1 that is at the beginning of year t

$\dfrac{D_1 + P_1}{P_{t-1}}$ is referred to as the wealth ratio, $W_n (W_1 \times W_2 \times x \ldots x\ W_n)^{1/n-1}$

The yield for an n-year period is,

where,

$$W_1 = \frac{D_1 + P_1}{P_0}$$

$$W_2 = \frac{D_2 + P_2}{P_1}$$

$$W_n = \frac{D_n + P_n}{P_{n-1}}$$

ILLUSTRATION 13

The dividend per share and price per share data of an equity stock relating to Liril Ltd. Lasalgoan are given below :

Year	1	2	3	4	5	6
	₹	₹	₹	₹	₹	₹
Dividend per share	1.00	1.00	1.20	1.25	1.15	1.30
Price per share at the beginning	9.00	9.75	11.50	11.00	10.60	12.50

The annual wealth ratios are as follows :					
Year	1	2	3	4	5	
Wealth Ratio	1.19	1.28	1.06	1.08	1.29	

Calculate the realized rate of return.

SOLUTION

The geometric rate of return (yield) over the five-year period is :

$$(1.19 \times 1.28 \times 1.06 \times 1.08 \times 1.29)^{1/5} - 1 = (2.25)^{1/5} - 1 = 2.25 \times 2.25 \div 5$$
$$= 0.0125 - 1 = 1.25\%$$

This method is based upon the following limitations :

i)   The firm will continue to remain and face the same risk, over the period.

ii) The investors expectations are based upon the past realised yield.

iii) The investors get the same rate of return as the realised yield even when invested elsewhere.

iv) The market price of shares remains unchanged.

2.5.4 COST OF RETAINED EARNINGS

Retained Earnings accrue to a firm only because of the sacrifice made by the shareholders is not getting the dividends declared out of the available profits fully. The cost of retained earnings is equal to the rate of return which is existing shareholders will obtain by investing the after-tax dividends in alternative investments. Thus it represents the opportunity cost of dividends foregone by the shareholders.

The opportunity cost here represents sacrifice of the dividend income, which the shareholders would have otherwise received it immediately. If the company had distributed its entire earnings; the stockholders would have invested it somewhere and earned a return thereon. They would however, not mind the company retaining the earnings if they are promised at least market rate of return (i.e. average dividend rate) on the income so retained. The management must earn the same return on retained earnings is the cost of equity capital (Ke).

Cost of retained earnings can be computed with the help of following formula :

$$K_r = \frac{D}{NP} + G$$

where,

K_r = Cost of retained earnings

D = Expected dividend

NP = Net proceeds of share issue

G = Rate of growth

Further, it is important to note that shareholders, usually, cannot obtain the entire amount of retained profits by way of dividends even if there is 100 percent payout ratio. It is so because the shareholders are required to pay tax on their dividend income. Hence, certain adjustment has to be made for tax. To make adjustment in the cost of retained earnings for tax and costs of purchasing new securities, the following formula may be adopted :

$$K_r = \left(\frac{D}{NP} + G\right) \times (1 - t) \times (1 - b)$$

or

$$K_r = K_e (1 - t) \times (1 - b)$$

where,

K_r = Cost of retained earnings

D = Expected dividend

G = Growth rate

NP = Net proceeds of equity issue

T = Tax rate

B = Cost of purchasing new securities, or brokerage costs

K_e = Rate of return available to shareholders

ILLUSTRATION 14

In Maxwell Ltd., Madurai return available to shareholders is 12%, the average, tax rate of shareholders is 50% and it is expected that 2% is brokerage cost that shareholders will have to pay while investing their dividends in alternative securities.

What is the cost of retained earnings ?

SOLUTION

Cost of retained Earnings, $K_r = K_r = (1 - t)(1 - b)$

where,

$K_e = $ Rate of return available to shareholders

$t = $ Tax rate

$b = $ Brokerage cost

So, $K_t = 12\% (1 - 0.5)(1 - 0.2)$

$= 12\% \times 0.5 \times 0.98 = 5.88\%$

Approaches for determining the Cost of Retained Earnings :

Two basic approaches have been suggested for determining the cost of retained earnings i) Tax-adjusted rate of return approach, and ii) external yield approach.

i) Tax-adjusted rate of return approach :

The cost of retained earnings is calculated as the post-tax rate of return available to the investors. This means that (K_s) has to be adjusted for ordinary and long-term capital gains tax as given below :

$$k_r = k_s \frac{1 - t_p}{1 - t_g}$$

where,

$k_r = $ Cost of retained earnings

$k_s = $ Rate of return required by equity investors

$t_p = $ Ordinary personal income tax rate

$t_g = $ Personal long-term capital gains tax rate

This approach is riddled with two problems viz. a) The ordinary personal income tax rate and the personal long term capital gains rate may vary widely across the shareholders of a company. Hence it may be impossible to establish a minimum rate of return that ensures that all the shareholders benefit if the company reinvests its cash flows instead of paying dividends, b) The alternative investment opportunities of the company are not considered.

ii) External Yield Approach :

The basic premise of this approach is that the company should evaluate the possibility of buying shares of other companies with similar risk characteristics by using retained earnings. Hence the opportunity cost of retained earnings is deemed equal to the rate of return that can be earned on such investment. Since that rate of return is equal to (K_s) the cost of retained earnings is simply equal to (K_s). This approach appears to be superior to the earlier approach.

2.5.5 WEIGHTED AVERAGE COST OF CAPITAL

Once the cost of individual capital components had been determined, they are combined to determine average or composit cost of capital so that the same may be compared with the discounted rate of return of the project. Such a cost of capital is termed as composit or weighted average cost of capital. The composit cost of capital can, therefore, be defined as the average of the costs of each source of funds employed by the company, properly weighted by the proportion they hold in the capital structure of the firm. Thus, the composit cost of capital is the weighted average cost of various sources of funds, weights being the proportion of each source of funds in the capital structure. It should also be remembered that it is the weighted average concept and not simple average, which is more relevant in calculating the overall cost of capital. As the firms do not use various sources of funds in equal proportion, the simple average cost of capital will not be appropriate to use, in the capital structure decisions making.

The following **steps are involved** in calculating the weighted average cost of capital.

i)   To calculate the cost of the specific sources of funds individually (i.e., cost of debt, cost of equity, cost of preference capital etc.)

ii) To multiply the cost of each source by its proportion in the capital structure and

iii) Add the weighted costs of all sources of funds to get the weighted cost of capital.

The cost of capital should always be calculated on the after-tax basis in financial decision-making. Hence, the component costs used for calculating the weighted average costs of capital should be after-tax costs. The following illustration shows the method of calculating the weighted average cost of capital.

ILLUSTRATION 15

The following is the capital structure of Nagarjun Ltd., Nashik.

Sources of Finance	Amount ₹	Proportion	After Text Cost
Equity Share Capital (40,000 shares of ₹ 10 each)	4,00,000	40 %	14.0 %
Retained Earnings (Reserves)	2,00,000	20 %	13.0 %
Preference Capital	1,00,000	10 %	12.0 %
Debt	3,00,000	30%	9.0 %

Calculate the weighted average cost of capital of the company.

SOLUTION

Sources (1)	Amount (2) ₹	Proportion (3)	After-tax (4)	Weighted Cost (5) = (3) × (4)
Equity capital (4,000 shares of ₹ 10 each)	4,00,000	40 %	14.0	5.60
Retained Earnings	2,00,000	20 %	13.0 %	2.60
Preference Capital	1,00,000	10 %	12.0 %	1.20
Debt	3,00,000	30 %	9.0 %	2.70
∴ Weighted Average Cost of Capital				12.1

The Weighted Average Cost of Capital of Nagarjun Ltd. can also be calculated as follows :

Sources (1)	Amount (2) ₹	After-tax Cost (Rate)	After-tax Cost (Amount) (4) = (2) × (3)
Equity Capital	4,00,000	14.0%	56,000
Retained Earnings	2,00,000	13.0%	26,000
Preference Capital	1,00,000	12.0%	12,000
Debt	3,00,000	9.0%	27,000
	10,00,000		1,21,000

$$\therefore \text{ Weighted Average Cost of Capital} = \frac{₹\ 1,21,000}{₹\ 10,00,000} \times 100 = 12.1\%$$

ILLUSTRATION 16

On January 1, 2013, the Total Assets of Omkar Ltd. Osmanabad were ₹ 100 crores. By the end of the year, total assets of the company are expected to be ₹ 150 crores. The company's capital structure shown below is considered to be optimum :

Debt (6 % bonds)   ₹ 40 crores

Preferred stock   ₹ 10 crores

Net worth   ₹ 50 crores

New bonds will have an 8 percent interest rate and will be sold at par preferred stock will have a 9 % rate and will be sold at 4% discount. Common stock currently selling at ₹ 50 a share can be sold to net the company ₹ 45 a share. Stockholders required rate of return is estimated to be 12 percent. Retained earnings are estimated to be ₹ 5 crores. The marginal tax rate of 25 percent.

Calculate the weighted average cost of capital.

| SOLUTION |

Sources of Funds (1)	Proportion of Total (2)	After-tax Cost (%) (3)	Weighted Cost (2 × 3/100) (4)
Debt	40.4	4.00	1.60%
Preferred Stock	10.1	9.47	0.95%
Common Stock	40.4	13.30	5.32%
Retained Earnings	10.1	9.37	1.00%
∴ Weighted Average Cost of Capital			8.87%

Working and Assumptions :

In this example, the overall cost of new capital of ₹ 50 crores has to be computed. The company's existing capital structure is considered optimal and hence weight to cost of each component of capital can be assigned in terms of their proportion to the capitalisation.

In the absence of break-up of net worth in the existing capital structure of the company, the relative proportion of common stock and retained earnings have been worked out in the following manner.

Since net worth represents 50% of the proposed company's capitalisation it will amount to ₹ 25 crores in the proposed expansion of funds. Out of this, retained earnings are expected to be ₹ 5 crores which means equity stock capital will figure ₹ 20 crores. Relative proportion of common stock capital and retained earnings in the capitalisation will then come to 40% and 10% respectively. Thus weighted average cost of capital of the Co. will be 8.87 %.

Book Value Vs. Market Weights :

The weighted cost of capital can be calculated by using either the book value or market value weights. If there is any difference between book value and market value weights, the weighted average cost of capital would also differ according to the weights used. When the market value of the share is higher than book value, the weighted average cost of capital calculated by using the book value weight will be much lower and vice versa. In the practice, the use of the book value weights is always preferred for the following reasons :

i)   The firm determines the capital structure targets in terms of book value only.

ii) The book value particulars can be easily obtained from the published statement of the company.

iii) Moreover the debt-equity ratio based on book values alone are analysed by the investors to evaluate the risk involved in their investment.

ILLUSTRATION 17

The capital structure of Pawan Ltd. Pune, consists of the following :

	₹
Equity Shares of ₹ 100 each	20 lakhs
Retained Earnings	10 lakhs
9% preference shares	12 lakhs
7% debentures	(+) 08 lakhs
∴ Total	50 lakhs

The company earns 12% on its capital. The income tax is 50%. The company requires sum of ₹ 25 lakhs to finance its expansion program for which following alternatives are available to it :

i)   Issue of 20,000 equity shares at a premium of ₹ 25 per share.

ii) Issue of 10 % preference shares.

iii) Issue of 8 % debentures.

It is estimated that the P/E ratios in the cases of equity; preference and debenture financing would be 21.4, 17 and 15.7 respectively. Which of the three financing alternatives would you recommend and why ?

SOLUTION

An alternative which would ensure the highest market price per share should be recommended. This analysis is carried out as follows.

Estimated Earnings per shares (EPS) and market price per share under the various financing plans :

Particulars	At Present (₹)	Equity Shares Plan (₹)	Preference Shares Plan (₹)	Debentures Plan (₹)
Earnings Before Interest and Tax (EBIT) @ 12%	6,00,000	9,00,000	9,00,000	9,00,000
Less : Interest Old :	56,000	56,000	56,000	56,000
New :	–	–	–	2,00,000
Profit Before Tax	5,44,000	8,44,000	8,44,000	6,44,000
Less : Tax @ 50%	2,72,000	4,22,000	4,22,000	3,22,000
Profit After Tax (PAT)	2,72,000	4,22,000	4,22,000	3,22,000
Less : Preference Dividend Old :	1,08,000	1,08,000	1,08,000	1,08,000
New :	–	–	2,50,000	–
Profit for Equity Shares	1,64,000	3,14,000	64,000	2,14,000
Number of Equity Shares	20,000	40,000	20,000	20,000
EPS (₹)	8.20	7.85	3.20	10.70
P.E. Ratio				
Market price per share (₹)	–	21.04	17	15.07
(EPS × P.E. Ratio)		1,67,99	54.40	167.99

The above analysis shows that the market price per share is the same in the case of equity financing and debenture financing. As such any of these two financing alternatives, viz. Equity financing or debenture financing can be adopted. However, EPS is higher in case of debenture financing without undue financial risk. Therefore, debenture financing alternative is recommended.

Cut-off Point :

Cut-off point is the optimal point of selecting viable projects. It is expressed in terms of percentage. After estimating the rates of return of different projects, they are compared with cut-off rate. Project promising rate of return higher or equal to cut-off rate are accepted for investment purposes. But those yielding below the cut-off rate are rejected.

ILLUSTRATION 18

Quick Ltd. Mumbai had decided to issue equity shares worth ₹ 10,00,000. The management expects to maintain the current dividend payment @ ₹ 10 per share. It is expected to grow at 5 % per year. The current market price of the shares is ₹ 50. Determine the cost of equity capital.

SOLUTION

$$K_e = \frac{₹\ 10}{₹\ 50} + 0.05 = 25\%$$

ILLUSTRATION 19

Rotex Ltd. Raipur, is planning to expand its business and accordingly the company desires to increase assets by 50 percent by the end of the year. The existing capital structure representing the optimal capital structure of the company is given as under :

	₹
8% Debentures (par value ₹ 1000 per debenture)	8,00,000
9% Preference shares (par value of ₹ 100 per share)	2,00,000
Equity shares (par value ₹ 100 per share)	(+) 10,00,000
∴ Total	20,00,000

New debentures can be sold at par at 10 % interest rate. Preference shares will have 12% dividend rate and can be sold at par. Equity shares can be sold to net ₹ 90 per share. The shareholders required rate of return is 18 percent, which is expected to grow at 4 percent. Retained earnings for the year are estimated to be ₹ 1,00,000.

You are required to calculate the cost of individual capital components and overall cost of capital.

SOLUTION

Cost of Individual Capital Components :

- Cost of Debentures = $10 (1 - 0.50) = 5\%$

- Cost of Preference Shares = $\frac{12}{100} \times 100 = 12\%$

- Cost of Equity Shares = $\frac{8}{90} + 0.04 = 12.9\ \%$ approx.

- Cost of Retained Earnings = $12.9 (1 - 0.50) = 6.45\ \%$ approx.

Overall Cost of Capital (K_0) :

Sources of Capital	Percentage Share	Specific Cost	Total Cost
Debt	36.0	5 %	180.00
Preferable Shares	9.0	12 %	108.00
Equity Shares	45.0	12.9 %	580.50
Retained Earnings	10.0	6.45 %	64.50
∴ Total	100.00		933.00

$$K_0 = \frac{933.00}{100} = 9.33\%$$

ILLUSTRATION 20

Sudarshan Ltd. Surat has a capital structure of 40% debt and 60% equity. The company is presently considering several alternative investment proposals costing less than ₹ 20 lakhs. The company always raises the required funds without disturbing its present debt equity ratio. The cost of raising the debt and equity are as under :

Project Cost	Cost of Debts	Cost of Equity
Up to ₹ 2 lakhs	10%	12%
Above ₹ 2 lakhs & up to ₹ 5 lakhs	11%	13%
Above ₹ 5 lakhs & up to ₹ 10 lakhs	12%	14%
Above ₹ 10 lakhs & up to ₹ 20 lakhs	13%	14.5%

Assuming the tax rate at 50%, calculate,

A) Cost of capital of two projects X and Y whose fund requirements are ₹ 6.5 lakhs and ₹ 14 lakhs respectively.

B) If a project is expected to give after tax return of 10% determine under what conditions it would be acceptable ?

SOLUTION

Calculation of weighted average cost of capital under different investment proposals with a Debt-Equity ratio of 4 : 6.

Project Cost	Financial Pattern	Debt Equity Ratio	Cost Before Tax %	Cost After Tax %	WACC (3) × (5) %	
• Upto ₹ 2 lakhs	Debt	0.4	10.0	5.0	2.0	
	Equity	0.6	12.0	12.0	7.2	9.2%
• Above ₹ 2 lakhs and upto 5 lakhs	Debt	0.4	11.0	5.5	2.2	
	Equity	0.6	13.0	13.0	7.8	10.0%
• Above ₹ 2 lakhs and upto 10 lakhs	Debt	0.4	12.0	6.0	2.4	
	Equity	0.6	14.0	14.0	8.4	10.8%
• Above ₹ 2 lakhs and upto 20 lakhs	Debt	0.4	13.0	6.5	2.6	
	Equity	0.6	14.5	14.5	8.7	11.3%

A) i)   Project X will require the funds of ₹ 6.5 lakhs and this project will come under the catetgory'Above ₹ 5 lakhs and upto ₹ 10 lakhs' and the concerned WACC is 10.8%.

ii)   Project Y need a capital investment of ₹ 14 lakhs whose WACC is 11.3% since it is coming under the classification of 'Above ₹ 10 lakhs' and up to ₹ 20 lakhs' Project cost.

B)   If the expected return of the project is 10% then the project must fall within the project cost of 'Above ₹ 20 lakhs and upto ₹ 5 lakhs investment.

In project appraisal, a project which gives above the return over the weighted cost of capital is preferred to implement.

ILLUSTRATION 21

Toshniwal Ltd., Tatanagar is considering raising of about ₹ 100 lakhs by one of two alternative methods, viz., 14% institutional term loan and 13% non-convertible debentures. The term loan option would attract no major incidental cost. The debentures would have to be issued at a discount of 2.5% and would involve cost of issue of ₹ 1 lakhs. Advise the company as to the better option based on the effective cost of capital in each. Assume a tax rate of 50%.

SOLUTION

Evaluation of raising ₹ 100 lakhs based on effective cost of capital (₹ lakhs)

Particulars	Option 1 (14% Term Loan)	Option 2 (13% NCD)
Face value of amount	100.00	100.00
Less : Discount	–	2.50
	100.00	97.50
Less : Cost of issue	–	1.00
Net effective amount raised	100.00	96.50
Interest charges p.a. on face value	14.00	13.00
Less : Savings in tax @ 50%	7.00	6.50
Net Interest Cost	7.00	6.50
Effective Cost of Capital : $\left[\dfrac{\text{Net Interest Cost}}{\text{Net effective amount raised}}\right] \times 100$	$\left[\dfrac{7}{100} \times 100\right]$ $= 7\%$	$\left[\dfrac{6.50}{96.50} \times 100\right]$ $= 6.74\%$

The cost of capital to the company is lower i.e., 6.74% if the company raises 13% non-convertible debentures (NCDs) and hence it is suggested to raise funds by issue of NCDs.

QUESTIONS FOR SELF-STUDY

I. **Theory Questions :**

i) How is the cost of debt computed ?

ii) State reasons for the importance of cost of capital.

iii) How is cost of preferred stock computed ?

iv) How is the weighted average cost of capital calculated ?

v) Explain the term Weighted Average Cost of Capital.

vi) How is the over-all cost of capital determined? What is its importance ?

vii) Define the term 'Cost of Capital'.

viii) 'The equity cost is free' do you agree? Give reasons.

ix) "Debt is the cheapest source of funds". Comment.

x) Explain the calculations for cost of debt under present value method.

II. Practical Problems :

i) Ashoka Ltd., Anantpur intends to issue 1,000, 10% debentures each of ₹ 1,000. In order to attract full subscription the firm proposes to sell the debentures at 5% discount. The income-tax rate applicable to the profit of the company is 50%. What is the cost of capital ?

    a) if the company sells without discount and

    b) if the company sells with discount

ii) Vijay Electronics Ltd. Vijapur issues 15 % debentures, face value ₹ 500. The cost of issue works out to 3 percent. The debentures are repayable after 7 years. The firm has a tax rate of 60 %. If the difference between the par value and the net amount realised can be amortised evenly over the life of the debentures, what is the cost of debentures to the firm ?

iii) Vaneeta Enterprises Vapi issues ₹ 100 face value preference stock which carries 12 percent dividend and is redeemable after 12 years at par. The net amount realised per preference share is ₹ 95. What is the cost of preference capital ?

iv) Superior Cement Ltd. Sholapur issues ₹ 100 face value preference stock which carries 12 percent dividend. The preference capital is repayable in two equal installments at the end of the tenth year and eleventh year respectively. The net amount realised per preference share is ₹ 95. What is the cost of preference of capital ?

v) Mysore Ltd., Mysore issues ₹ 100 face values debentures carrying interest of 15 %. The debentures are payable in three annual installments of ₹ 30, ₹ 30, ₹ 40 at the end of the seventh, eighth, and ninth year, respectively. The interest of course is payable only on the outstanding amount. The issue cost is 3 percent. The tax rate of the company is 60 percent. What is the cost of debenture capital to the company ?

vi) Your client has decided to float a transport company. He furnishes below a low down of the estimated cost of different capital structure options.

Long-term Debt to Equity	Cost of Debt		Dividend Expectation
	Source A	Source B	
1 : 6	20	15	12
1 : 4	20	16	12
3 : 7	22	16	15
2 : 3	22	16	16
1 : 1	22	18	18
3 : 2	24	18	20

He says that if the total debt as a percentage of equity is less than 45% loan from source A would be 30% of total loan, otherwise it would be 50% of total loan.

The tax rate applicable to the company is 50%. Decide for him the most appropriate capital mix and list your comment, if any.

vii) Sharda Ltd. Sangali is planning to issue 20 year, 10 percent debenture whose face value is ₹ 1,000 at 10 percent discount. What would be the cost of debenture, assuming corporate tax as 50 percent ?

viii) Caltex Ltd. Chennai decides to issues equity shares worth ₹ 10,00,000. The management expects to maintain the current dividend payment @ ₹ 10 per share. It is expected to grow at 5% per year. The current market price of the share is ₹ 50. Determine the cost of equity capital

ix) Dora Ltd. Daund is paying currently a dividend of ₹ 15 per share on its equity capital. The management is contemplating to float 1,000 equity shares of ₹ 100 each. They expect to net ₹ 90 per share from the market. Dividend payment at the current rate will be maintained in future.

Determine the cost of equity capital.

x) Kalwan Ltd. Karjat issued 1,000, 14% debentures of ₹ 100 each at 25% premium to be converted into equity shares after 5 years at 25% premium. Collection expenses are ₹ 2,000. Company's rate is 50%. Compute annual CoC, taking 10 years of use. Company pays 20% dividend on share capital.

xi) Following sources have been invested in the business of Delhi Ltd. New Delhi as on 31st March, 2013.

SOURCE	₹
Equity Share Capital	3,00,000
Reserves	10,00,000
14 % Debentures	6,00,000
18 % Bank Loan	(+) 8,00,000
Total	27,00,000

Company pays dividend at an average rate of 20%. Average post-tax earning rate in the industry is 15% company's tax liability is at 50%.

Calculate Cost of Capital for Delhi Ltd., New Delhi.

■■■

Chapter **3**...

Marginal Costing

Synopsis...

In the modern competitive era of global market, every manufacturing company has an ultimate objective i.e. to obtain maximum quality production from the available limited resources. They would like to increase their profits by increasing volume of production which will automatically involve additional cost. Such a decision would require a detailed analysis of additional costs and its behaviour as it has a direct bearing on the profitability of the concern. Any increase in the level of operation will decrease the firm's marginal profit, if it is already at its optimum level of existing operation. However, such a decision would definitely prove financially worth taking, if there exists any unutilised operational capacity. Thus, to reach at an accurate decision, management must know how costs will react to changes in activity. The analysis of cost behaviour reveals that the cost of a product can be divided as per their variability aspect into two major categories viz. the **fixed cost and variable cost**. In classifying a particular cost into fixed and variable, the volume or activity level is more important.

It is very clear that, **fixed cost** remains constant to a particular level of output whereas variable cost has a tendency to change proportionally with a change in the level of output. The following example will further clarify the concept.

Atlas Co., Ahmedabad made sales of 20,000 units at ₹ 1,000 per unit during the year 2012-2013 with the following details of expenditure on production.

- Raw material required to produce one unit of finished product 2 kg @ ₹ 2 per kg.,
- Wages ₹ 200 per unit,
- Rent of Factory ₹ 50,000 p.a.
- Salary of Executive ₹ 5,00,000 p.a.

Here, the costs of raw-material and wages change proportionately with the change in the level of output and, therefore they are known as **Variable Costs**. Whereas the rent of factory and salary of executive are such costs that are not subject to change with the change in output, they remain constant at every level of output and as such are known as **Fixed Costs**. On account of this reason, it is illogical to apportion fixed costs to production.

3.1 MEANING

Marginal Costing is the most important traditional technique which deals with the concept of variable cost, which is marginal in nature, very carefully and cautiously. **Marginal Costing** which is otherwise known as **"Variable Costing"** is used as a tool for decision-making by the management. It is also known as **"Direct Costing"** and this new concept is gaining wide popularity in the field of accounting. Marginal Costing is a technique through which variable costs are taken into account for the purposes of product costing, inventory valuation and other important management decisions. The term "Marginal Costing" is commonly used in U.K. and other European countries while the same is denoted as **"Direct Costing"** or **"Variable Costing"** in U.S.A. Marginal Costing is also known as variable or direct or differential costing.

The term "Marginal Costing" seems to be inappropriate since it has an exclusive meaning in Economics. Under the above circumstances, the term **'Variable Costing'** seems to be more appropriate and acceptable.

Marginal Costing is the technique of costing used by most of the manufacturing undertakings preferably for profit planning, cost control and managerial decision making. Marginal Costs reveal the lowest price at which a product can be sold during the period of trade depression, but they also indicate to management the most profitable lines during the period of intense trade activity. Hence, there is a basic need to understand **marginal costing concepts** which plays a vital role in controlling the costs, effectively and more efficiently.

3.1.1 MARGINAL COST

The term "**Marginal Cost**" is derived from the word "margin" which is a well known terminology in economics. As is used in economic parlance, the term "**Marginal Cost**" connotes the cost which arises from the production of additional increment of output.

Definitions :

The term 'Marginal Cost' has been defined by different experts and professional institutions in the manner stated below.

i) The **Institute of Cost and Works Accounts, London**, in its publication *"A Report of Marginal Costing" defines Marginal Cost as,*
"the amount at any given volume of output by which aggregate costs are changed if the volume of output is increased or decreased by one unit".

ii) "Marginal Cost", according to **the Institute of Chartered Accountants, England**,
"is the very expense (whether of production, selling or distribution) incurred by taking of a particular decision".

iii) **Blocker** and **Weltmore** defines Marginal Cost as,
"the increase or decrease in total cost which results from producing or selling additional or fewer units of a product or from a change in the method of production or distribution such as the use of improved machinery, addition or exclusion of a product or territory, or selection of an additional sales channel".

Thus, from the definitions quoted above, **Marginal Costs** in the short run will be synonymous with variable costs, i.e., prime costs and variable overheads; but in the long run the marginal costs will include fixed costs in planning production activities involving an increase in the production capacity. It is clear that the Marginal Costs are related to change in output under certain conditions. Thus, Marginal Cost is the cost incurred by a company for the additional output.

Marginal Costs reveal the lowest price at which a product can be sold during a trade depression, but they also reveal to management the most profitable times during a period of intense trade activity.

3.1.2 MARGINAL COSTING

Marginal Costing is an accounting technique which ascertains marginal cost by differentiating between fixed or period, and variable or product costs. This technique aims to charge only those costs of the product that vary directly with sales volumes. Those costs would be direct material, direct labour, and factory overhead expenses such as supplies, some indirect labour, and power. The cost of the product would not include fixed or non-variable expenses such as depreciation, factory insurance, taxes and supervisory salaries etc.

Definitions :

The term **'Marginal Costing'** has been defined by different experts and professional institutions as stated below :

i) Marginal costing is defined by the **National Association of Accountants**, as,
"This method proposes that fixed factory expenses be classified as period expenses and be written off currently as is generally done with selling and administration expenses, and that only the variable costs become the basis of inventory value and profit determination".

ii) According to the **Institute of Cost and Management Accounts, London,**

"Marginal Costing is the ascertainment of marginal costs and of the effect on profit of changes in volume or type of output by differentiating between fixed costs and variable costs. In this technique of costing only variable costs are charged to operations, processes or products, leaving all indirect costs to be written off against profits in the period in which they arise".

iii) The **Terminology of Management Accounting** has described Marginal Costing as,

"a costing principle whereby variable costs are charged to cost units and the fixed costs are attributable to the relevant period is written off in full against the contribution for that period".

Thus, **Marginal Costing** is a costing technique that considers only the costs that vary directly with volume i.e. direct materials, direct labour, and variable factory overheads and ignores fixed cost in additional output decisions. The technique of Marginal Costing lies in: i) differentiation between fixed and variable costs, ii) ascertainment of marginal costs, and iii) finding out effect on profit due to change in volume or type or output. It can very well be applied together with other techniques of costing such as standard costing, budgetary control and uniform costing.

The concept of marginal costing is evolved on the main distinction between product cost and period cost. While product cost relates to the volume of output, the period cost is mainly concerned with the period of time. Marginal Costing considers all those manufacturing costs which vary directly with the volume of output as product costs. This is in contradiction to the traditional system of costing under which all manufacturing costs - fixed as well as variable - are treated as product costs. It should also be remembered that variability with the volume of production is the basis for the classification of costs into product and period costs. Thus, marginal costing necessitates classification of costs into fixed and variable. Even the semi-variable costs have to be closely examined so as to separate fixed and variable components thereof depending upon the increase or decrease in the volume of output. Thus, marginal costs focus on the effect of costs on the varying level of output. In short, Marginal Costing has the following four important features :

i) Under marginal costing, all types of **operating costs** i.e. factory, selling and administrative, are separated into fixed and variable components and are recorded separately.

ii) **Variable cost** elements are handled as **product costs** i.e. they are charged to the product at the appropriate movements and follow the product through the inventory accounts, and thus become treated as expenses when the product is sold. Variable distribution costs normally are chargeable to product at or near the moment of sale, and thus do not become inclined in inventory values.

iii) **Fixed costs** including fixed factory overheads, are handled as **period costs**; i.e., they are written off as expenses in the period in which they are incurred. They do not follow the inventories through the accounts but rather are treated in the way which is traditional for selling and general administrative expenses.

iv) Marginal Costing is a method of **recording** as well as **reporting costs**. Unlike differential cost analysis and Break-Even analysis which utilise traditional records, variable costing requires a unique method of recording cost transactions as they originally take place.

Therefore, **marginal costing is a technique which deals with the effect on profits of changes in volume or type of output.**

3.2 ADVANTAGES

The following are the **Advantages of Marginal Costing** :

i) **Consistency :**

The marginal cost per unit of output remains the same irrespective of the volume of output.

ii) **Realistic Valuation of Stock :**

In Marginal Costing stocks of finished goods and work-in-progress are valued at their variable cost only. Therefore, it is more realistic and uniform. No fictitious profit arises.

iii) **No under/over Absorption of Overheads :**

In Marginal Costing there is no question of allocation, apportionment or absorption of fixed overheads. Hence, the tedious method of their accounting is eliminated.

iv) **Facilitates Cost Control :**

By separating the fixed and variable costs, marginal costing provides better means of controlling costs.

v) **Valuable Aid to Management :**

It helps the management with more appropriate information in taking vital business decisions like make or buy, sub-contracting, export order pricing, pricing under recession to continue or discontinue a product/division/ sales territory, selection of suitable product mix etc.

vi) **Aid to Profit Planning :**

The technique of Marginal Costing helps the management in profit planning. The management can plan the volume of sales for earning a required profit.

vii) **Relative Profitability :**

In case of multi-product and multi line of business activities, Marginal Costing facilitates the study of relative profitability of different products. It will show where the sales efforts should be concentrated.

viii) **Basis for Pricing :**

Marginal Costing furnishes a better and more logical basis for fixation of selling prices and tendering for contract particularly when business is dull.

ix) Valuable Adjunct to Other Techniques :

Marginal Costing is a valuable adjunct to budgeting and standard costing techniques.

x) Simple to Understand and in Application :

Marginal Costing method is simple in application and is easy for exercise of cost control. It is more informative and simple to understand.

xi) Cost Analysis Possible :

Profit-volume analysis is facilitated by the use of break-even charts and profit-volume graphs, and so on.

xii) Responsibility Accounting Becomes More Effective :

Responsibility accounting is more effective when based on marginal costing because managers can identify their responsibilities more clearly when fixed overhead is not charged arbitrarily to their departments or divisions.

> **Marginal Costing is more useful technique for cost control, profit planning and decision-making.**

3.3 LIMITATIONS

The following are the **Limitations of Marginal Costing**.

i) Difficulty in Analysing Overheads :

In Marginal Costing, costs are to be classified into fixed and variable costs. But it is not easy to classify all expenses into fixed and variable. It is very difficult to segregate semi-variable expenses into fixed and variable. Some expenses like bonus to workers, amenities to staff are caused by management decision and have no relation to the level of activity or with the time factor.

ii) Difficulty in Application :

The technique of Marginal Costing is difficult to apply in industries like ship building, contracts, etc. where the value of work-in-progress is large in proportion to turnover. Thus, if fixed overheads are not included in the closing value of work-in-progress, losses on contract may result every year, whereas on completion of contract, there may be huge profits.

iii) Improper Basis for Pricing :

In Marginal Costing prices are based on contribution which does not cover fixed costs. This may prove dangerous in the long-run.

iv) Ignores Time Factor :

In Marginal Costing time factor is ignored. For instance, the Marginal Cost of two jobs may be identical, but if one job takes twice as long to complete as the other the true cost of job taking longer time is higher than that of the other. This is not disclosed by Marginal Costing.

v) **Lack of Standard for Control :**
    Marginal Costing does not provide any standard for control purpose. In fact, Budgetary Control and Standard Costing are more effective tools in controlling costs. Hence, the technique of Marginal Costing need to be considered as unique from the cost control point of view.

> **The job of separation of overhead costs into fixed and variable costs is purely of academic nature, and practically very difficult hence the application of the technique of Marginal Costing is of limited use in marginal decision-making.**

vi) **Unrealistic Statements :**
    The exclusion of fixed overhead from stock valuation affects the Profit and Loss Account and also produces an unrealistic Balance Sheet.

vii) **Limited Scope :**
    With the increased use of automatic machinery the proportion of fixed costs (maintenance, depreciation etc.) increases. As Marginal Costing ignores fixed costs, this system becomes **less** effective in capital intensive industries.

viii) **Unacceptable by Taxation Authorities :**
    The income-tax authorities do not recognise the Marginal Cost for inventory valuation.

ix) **Faulty Conclusion :**
    Exclusion of fixed overheads from costs may lead to erroneous conclusions. It may create problems in interfirm comparison, higher demand for salaries and other benefits by employees, higher demand for tax by the Government authorities etc.

x) **Accepted Accounting Practices Deviate :**
    The exclusion of fixed overhead from inventory cost does not constitute an accepted accounting procedure, and therefore, adherence to Marginal Costing will involve deviation from accepted accounting practices.

xi) **Useful in short-run :**
    The distinction between fixed and variable costs holds good only in the short-run. In the long-run however, all costs become variable. As in Marginal Costing only variable costs are considered, it is useful for short-term assessment of profitability. However, long-term assessment of profit can be correctly determined on full costs basis only.

> **Marginal Costing technique is best suited for internal use by the management as an effective tool for managerial decision-making.**

3.4 FIXED AND VARIABLE COST

A) Fixed Cost :

Meaning :

The cost which remains fixed irrespective of level of output are known as fixed or rigid or constant costs. These costs remain fixed in total amount and do not increase or decrease with volume of production, but the fixed cost per unit increases when volume of **production decreases**, and **decreases when the volume of production increases**. Thus, fixed costs are constant in total amount but fluctuates per unit as production changes.

Examples :

Examples of Fixed Costs are Rent, Rates, Taxes, Insurance, Salaries, Depreciation etc.

For Example,

- If the fixed costs for producing 5,000 units at 40% capacity level is ₹ 10,000 then for producing 10,000 units at 80% capacity level also, the fixed cost will be the same i.e. ₹ 10,000, however the fixed cost per unit will reduce i.e.

- At 40% capacity $= \dfrac{₹\ 10,000}{5,000\ units} = ₹\ 2$ per unit

- At 80% capacity $= \dfrac{₹\ 10,000}{10,000\ units} = ₹\ 1$ per unit

Definition :

According to **ICMA, London Fixed Cost** is defined as,

"a cost which accrues in relation to the passage of time and which within certain output or turnover limits tends to be unaffected by fluctuations in volume of output or turnover".

Features :

The important **features of Fixed Costs** are as follows :

i)   Total fixed cost remains the same irrespective of changes in the volume of output.

ii) Increase or decrease in per fixed cost when volume of production changes.

iii) Fixed costs are apportioned to various departments on some equitable basis.

iv) Fixed costs are uncontrollable in nature in shorter run.

v)   In the longer run fixed costs can be controlled mostly by the top level management.

vi) Fixed costs are mostly concerned with the period hence are known as period costs also.

vii) Fixed costs are also termed as rigid costs or constant costs.

viii) Municipal taxes, office staff salaries, depreciation on factory premises are certain examples of fixed costs.

ix) Fixed costs are written off to Profit and Loss Account during the period in which they are incurred.

x)   Fixed costs can be calculated by using following formulae :

Fixed Costs   =   Total Costs (–) Variable Costs

xi) Fixed Costs are classified into cash fixed costs and non-cash fixed costs.

Graphical Presentation :

The **Graphical Presentation** indicating the Behaviour of Fixed Cost is shown below in Figure 3.1.

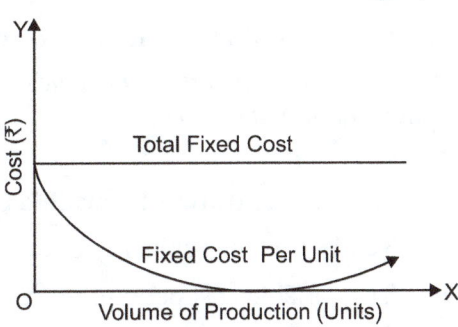

Fig. 3.1 : Behaviour of Fixed Cost

B) Variable Costs :

Meaning :

The cost which vary on the basis of volume of output are known as variable or marginal or direct costs. These costs are variable in total amount and increase or decrease with volume of production but the per unit variable cost remains fixed. Thus, variable costs are variable in total amount but remains fixed per unit even though the production changes.

Examples :

Examples of variable costs are direct material cost, direct labour cost, direct expenses, repairs and maintenance etc.

For Example,

If the total production is 10,000 units at 40% capacity and the variable costs is ₹ 20,000, then if the production is increased to 15,000 units at 60% capacity, the variable costs will be ₹ 30,000, but if the production is decreased to 5,000 units at 20% capacity the variable costs will be ₹ 10,000, however the variable cost units remains the same irrespective of the level of output i.e.

- At 40% capacity $= \dfrac{₹\ 20,000}{10,000\ \text{units}} = ₹\ 2$ per unit.

- At 60% capacity $= \dfrac{₹\ 30,000}{15,000\ \text{units}} = ₹\ 2$ per unit

- At 20% capacity $= \dfrac{₹\ 10,000}{5,000\ \text{units}} = ₹\ 2$ per unit

Definition :

According to **ICMA, London, Variable Cost** is defined as,

"a cost which in aggregate tends to vary in direct proportion to changes in the volume of output or turnover".

Features :

The important **features of Variable Costs** are as follows :

i)   Total variable cost increases or decreases when volume of production changes.

ii) The variable cost per unit remains the same irrespective of changes in the volume of output.

iii) Allocation and apportionment of variable costs to departments is a very simple task.

iv) Variable costs are controllable in nature hence treated with utmost importance for the purpose of cost control and decision-making.

v)   Variable costs can be controlled mostly by the departmental heads.

vi) Variable costs vary on the basis of production hence are known as product costs also.

vii) Variable costs are also termed as marginal costs or direct costs.

viii) Salesmen's commission, wages of machine operators, repairs of machine are certain examples of variable costs.

ix) Variable costs are charged to products directly.

x)   Variable costs can be calculated by using the following formulae,

Variable Costs   =   Total Costs (−) Fixed Costs

xi) Variable costs are classified into direct variable costs and indirect variable costs.

Graphical Presentation :

The graphical presentation indicating the **Behaviour of Variable Cost** is shown below in Figure 3.2.

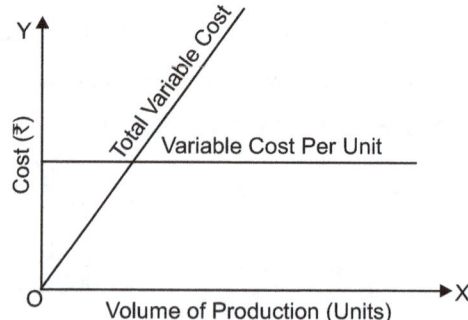

Fig. 3.2 : Behaviour of Variable Cost

The difference between **Fixed Costs and Variable Costs** is as follows :

	Fixed Costs		Variable Costs
i)	These are the costs which remain fixed in total irrespective of changes in the volume of output.	i)	These are the costs which vary in total due to changes in the volume of output.
ii)	Per unit fixed cost fluctuates when volume of production changes.	ii)	Per unit variable cost remains constant irrespective of changes in the volume output.
iii)	These costs are uncontrollable in nature.	iii)	These costs are controllable in nature.
iv)	In the longer run these costs can be controlled by the top level management.	iv)	These costs can be controlled by the departmental heads.
v)	These are period costs as they are concerned with period.	v)	These are product costs as they vary with production.
vi)	These costs are written off to Profit and Loss Account.	vi)	These costs are directly charged to production.
vii)	Rent, rates, taxes, insurance, depreciation etc. are the examples of fixed costs.	vii)	Direct material cost, direct labour cost, direct expenses etc. are the examples of variable costs.
viii)	These are also termed as Rigid or Constant Costs.	viii)	These are also termed as marginal or direct costs.
ix)	It can be calculated by using the following formula : Fixed Costs = Total Costs (−) Variable Costs	ix)	It can be calculated by using the following formula : Variable Costs = Total Costs (−) Fixed Costs
x)	They are classified into cash fixed costs and non-cash fixed costs.	x)	They are classified into direct variable costs and indirect variable costs.
xi)	Changes in fixed costs are much more significant to a company.	xi)	Changes in variable costs are not so much significant to a company, as they have the tendency to change as per the output changes.

In addition to these costs, **Semi-variable Costs** are also separated into fixed and variable elements and are added to their respective categories. Under the technique of marginal costing fixed and variable costs are kept separate for all purpose. Fixed costs do not find any place in the costs of products or in inventory valuation, which are written off to profit and loss account during the period in which they are incurred. Variable Costs are taken into account while calculating the cost of production and are charged to products directly.

EXAMPLE

Barua Ltd., Baroda submits the following information in respect of Semi-Variable Costs for 2013.

2013 Months	Production Units	Semi-Variable Costs ₹
January	25,000	1,50,000
February	15,000	1,32,000
March	40,000	2,00,000
April	30,000	1,70,000
May	50,000	2,30,000
June	35,000	1,90,000

During the month of July, 2013 the production was 20,000 units only.

Calculate the amount of fixed, variable and total semi-variable costs for the month of July, 2013.

ANSWER

Taking the level of activity of any two months, say March and May, the Variable Costs may be calculated as follows :

2013 Months	Production Units	Semi-variable Costs ₹	Fixed Costs ₹	Variable Costs ₹
March	40,000	2,00,000	80,000*	1,20,000*
May	50,000	2,30,000	80,000**	1,50,000**
Difference	10,000	30,000		

where,

$$\text{Variable Element} = \frac{\text{Change in Amount}}{\text{Change in Quantity}}$$

$$= \frac{₹\,30,000}{10,000\ \text{Units}}$$

$$= ₹\,3.00\ \text{per unit}$$

Hence,

*Variable Overheads for March   = Units 40,000 × ₹ 3.00

                         = ₹ 1,20,000

    Fixed Overheads for March   = ₹ 2,00,000 – ₹ 1,20,000

                         = ₹ 80,000

Overheads for May have been computed accordingly in the same manner.

Calculation of fixed, variable and Total Semi-variable Costs of ₹ 20,000 units for the month of July, 2013.

	₹
Variable Overheads (20,000 units × ₹ 3.00)	60,000
Fixed Overhead	(+) 80,000
∴ Total Semi-Variable Overheads	1,40,000

3.5 CONTRIBUTION

Meaning :

Contribution is considered as a special concept in the technique of marginal costing as it provides a scientific base for analytical search in the process of planning and decision making. It represents the difference between sales and variable cost of sales and is often referred to as gross margin, contribution margin, marginal income, marginal balance, marginal revenue, marginal contribution, variable profit or profit-pick up. It represents a sort of fund or pool of resources out of which all fixed costs, irrespective of their nature are to be met. It is termed as **'Contribution'** as it contributes to the recovery of fixed costs and assessment of the ultimate profit. The difference between contribution and fixed costs is either profit or loss. After the appropriate computation of contribution, it is absolutely necessary to analyse the same into changes in the contribution between budgeted results and actual results, so that steps may be taken to maximise it.

Definitions :

The term **'Contribution'** has been defined by different experts and professional institutes in the manner stated below :

i) According to **W. W. Bigg,** "**Contribution'** may be defined as,
    "the difference between sales value and the marginal cost of sales and no net profit arises until the contribution equal to the fixed overheads".

ii) **The Terminology of CIMA, London** defines **Contribution** as,
    *   *"Contribution per unit is the difference between the selling price of a unit of product or service and its marginal cost".*
    *   *"Contribution in total is the difference between the sales value and the marginal cost of such sales".*

Thus, **contribution** is the excess of sales revenue over marginal cost of sales and it shows the amount each unit contributes towards absorbing fixed costs and generating profits.

Accounting Formulaes :

*   **At break even point** total contribution is exactly sufficient to recover fixed cost hence,
    Total Contribution = Total Fixed Cost
∴ Total Contribution (–) Total Fixed Cost = No Profit No Loss
*   **At above break even point** total contribution is higher than total fixed cost hence,
    Total Contribution > Total Fixed Cost
∴ Total Contribution (–) Total Fixed Cost = Profit
*   **At below break even point** total contribution is lower than total fixed cost hence,
    Total Contribution < Total Fixed Cost
∴ Total Contribution (–) Total Fixed Cost = Loss

'**Contribution**' can be computed by using any of the following accounting formulaes considered appropriate in a given situation :

- Total Contribution = Total Sales (−) Total Variable Cost
- Contribution per unit = Selling price per unit (−) Variable Cost per unit
- Total Contribution = Contribution Per Unit (×) Number of units sold
- Contribution = Fixed Costs (+) Profit
- Contribution = Fixed Costs (−) Loss
- Selling Price (−) Variable Costs = Fixed Costs (+ or −) Profit/Loss
- Contribution = Sales (×) P/V Ratio
- Contribution = Fixed Costs/Break Even Units

Importance :

In short term period, as the fixed costs remain constant, more the contribution, higher will be the ultimate profit. **Contribution is of vital importance** for the technique of marginal costing because :

i)   it helps to ascertain the break-even point.

ii) it shows the potential of the existence of profit.

iii) it shows the profitability of products, processes, departments etc.

iv) it helps to select exact product mix or sales mix for profit maximisation.

v)   it helps to fix-up the selling prices under various conditions.

vi) it guides in deciding whether a production line should be continued or discontinued.

Improvement :

In the short run, as the fixed costs have a tendency to remain constant, maximum efforts should be made to increase the contribution substantially which ultimately helps to increase the profits of the company. The following are some of the important **steps which can be taken to improve the contribution** in the given situation.

i)   Increasing selling price without affecting sales.

ii) Reducing variable costs or

iii) Increasing the sales volume within the limited capacity.

iv) Making the product-mix more favourable.

Application :

Contribution can very well be used to find out :

i)   Break-even point,

ii) Profitability of products,

iii) An appropriate product mix and,

iv) To fix up the competitive selling price in the given situation.

Contribution and Profit

Contribution differs from profit which can be elaborated with the help of following example.

EXAMPLE

A product that sells at ₹ 50 has a variable cost of ₹ 30 and during the period ended 30th June 2013, 2,000 units were sold. Fixed costs for that period amounted to ₹ 25,000. The contribution and profit would be calculated, as shown below.

ANSWER

Statement showing Contribution and Profit

Particulars	Cost Per Unit ₹	Cost for 2,000 units ₹	% of Sales %
Selling Price	50	1,00,000	100
Less : Variable Costs (−)	30	(−) 60,000	(−) 60
∴ Contribution	20	40,000	40
Less : Fixed Costs		(−) 25,000	(−) 25
∴ Profit		15,000	15

From the above example, it can be observed that the contribution goes towards the recovery of the fixed overheads and profit. Marginal costing is a technique which can be used as part of the decision making process to show the effect of possible changes in demand and or selling prices and or variable costs. For example, it can be used to identify the most profitable projects; in make or buy decisions or in deciding whether or not to accept a special contract. Variable costs include only those costs which can be identified with and traced to products, e.g. direct labour, direct materials, direct expenses and variable overheads. The fixed costs are those which cannot be identified with and traced to the products. They tend to vary more with time than output, and are treated as period costs. This means that the fixed costs are not included in product costs. They are simply written off, in total, against the total contribution generated from the sale, of all the firm's products, for the period in which they were incurred.

Read the following statement to understand the concept of contribution and profit.

(Products) Particulars	A ₹	B ₹	C ₹	D ₹	Total ₹
Contribution	20	34	36	20	110
Less : Fixed Costs					(−) 78
∴ Profit					32

A Multi-product Environment

This treatment of fixed costs also means that because they are not included in product costs they are carried forward into the future as part of the valuation of the stocks of work in progress and finished goods.

EXAMPLE

From the following cost data relating to Charminar Ltd., Chennai, compute the amount of fixed cost from the information as per marginal cost equation.

		₹
Sales	:	2,40,000
Variable cost	:	1,20,000
Profit	:	60,000

ANSWER

As per Marginal Cost Equation

$$\text{Contribution} = \text{Sales} (-) \text{Variable Cost and}$$
$$\text{Contribution} = \text{Fixed Cost} \pm \text{Profit/Loss}$$
$$\text{Sales} - \text{Variable Costs} = \text{Fixed Cost} \pm \text{Profit/Loss}$$

$\therefore$ ₹ 2,40,000 − ₹ 1,20,000 = Fixed Cost + ₹ 60,000

$\therefore$ ₹ 1,20,000 = Fixed Cost + ₹ 60,000

$\therefore$ Fixed Cost = ₹ 1,20,000 − ₹ 60,000

$\therefore$ Fixed Cost = ₹ 60,000

Difference between Contribution and Profit :

The difference between Contribution and Profit is as follows :

Contribution	Profit
i) It is the difference between sales revenue and the variable cost of such sales.	i) It is the difference between total contribution and fixed cost.
ii) It is also termed as 'Gross Margin'.	ii) It is also termed as 'Net Margin'.
iii) This cost accounting concept is used in the traditional technique of marginal costing.	iii) This residual concept is used in accounting while preparing income statement as a part of final accounts.
iv) It is used for making vital managerial decisions.	iv) It is used for determining the individual operational results.
v) Changes in contribution reflect on efficiency of a company in a better way.	v) Changes in profit reflect on utilisation of available resources of a company in a better way.

EXAMPLE

Dorabjee Ltd.; Dombivali produces a single product and sells in the competitive market at ₹ 50 each. The variable cost of production is ₹ 30 each and the fixed cost is ₹ 1,500 per annum. You are required to calculate the contribution and profits for sales of 100 units, 400 units and 800 units separately.

ANSWER

In the books of Dorabjee Ltd.; Dombivali
Statement showing Contribution and Profits

Production Particulars	Units	100 ₹	400 ₹	800 ₹
Sales @ ₹ 50 per unit		5,000	20,000	40,000
Less : Variable Cost @ ₹ 30 per unit	(−)	3,000	12,000	24,000
$\therefore$ Contribution		2,000	8,000	16,000
Less : Fixed Cost	(−)	1,500	1,500	1,500
$\therefore$ Profits		**500**	**6,500**	**14,500**

3.6 BREAK-EVEN ANALYSIS

Break-Even Analysis establishes the relationship between costs and profit with sales volume. It represents a specific method of presenting and studying the inter-relationship between costs, volume and profits. It also helps in the determination of that volume of sales at which costs and revenues are in equilibrium. The equilibrium point is often referred to as the 'break-even point'. The break-even point may be defined as that point of sales volume at which the total revenue is equal to the total cost. Briefly, it is a no-profit, no-loss point. It should be remembered that the break-even point is purely incidental to the Cost Volume-Profit analysis. If all costs are assumed to be variable with sales volume, the break-even point would be at zero sales. On the other hand, if all costs remain fixed, profits would vary disproportionately with sales and the break-even point would be at a point where total sales revenue and fixed cost are in equilibrium.

Break-even analysis is a costing technique that helps executives in profit planning. The narrow interpretation of break-even analysis limits is to the study of break-even point. The break-even point is defined as the volume of activity at which total sales revenue exactly equals total costs of the output produced or sold. Since, at this level of operation sales revenue is adequate to cover all costs to manufacture and sell the product leaving no amount as profit, and therefore, this level is also known as no profit no loss level. Thus, in a situation where total costs of the output consist of only variable costs, the break-even point would be at zero of operation.

Break-even analysis need not be limited merely to seeking the break-even point. In broader sense, break-even analysts refers to the study of relationship between cost, volume and profit at different levels of sales or production which in technical terminology is known as cost-volume profit analysis. Cost-Volume Profit Analysis as a planning tool analysis the inherent relationship between prices, cost structure, volume and profit. **Ahmad Belkooni** defines **cost-volume-profit analysis** as "*an examination of cost and revenue behavioural patterns and their relationships with profit. The analysis separates costs into fixed and variable components and determines the levels of activity where costs and revenues are in equilibrium*".

According to **Schmiedicke and Nagy**, "*cost-volume profit analysis is an analytical technique which uses the degrees of cost variability for measuring the effect of changes in volume or resulting profits. Such analysis assumes that the plant assets of the firm will remain the same in the short-run, therefore, the established level of fixed cost will also remain unchanged during the period being studied*".

We define cost-volume-profit analysis as a mature model to study the inter-related relationship between cost, price and profit structure of a company. It is a formal profit planning approach based on established relationship between different factors affecting profit. The usual starting point in such an analysis is the determination of the company's break-even point. Thus, break-even analysis forms just one component of the total system of cost-volume profit analysis.

One of the important steps in cost-volume profit and break-even analysis is that of segregation of costs into fixed and variable costs. If the break-even point is to occur, it becomes essential that the business enterprise has some variable costs and some fixed costs.

Determination of Break-Even Point :

The Break-Even Point can be determined by the two following methods :

1. Algebraic Methods. (Mathematical)
   a) Contribution Margin Technique and
   b) Equation Technique.
2. Graphic Presentation
   a) Break-Even Chart and
   b) Profit Volume Graph.

The break-even point can be computed for a firm manufacturing single product only, in terms of units of product. The BEP is reached when the total proceeds of units sold are equivalent to the total cost incurred-fixed and variable. Each unit of the product sold will cover its variable cost and leave the remainder which is known as the contribution, to cover the fixed costs. The break-even point will occur when adequate units are sold so that total contribution would become equivalent to the total fixed costs. More precisely, contribution per unit while total contribution is equal to unit contribution multiplied by the total units sold. The profit of the unit is obtained by subtracting the fixed cost from the total contribution. The following equation can easily be remembered.

$$\text{Unit Contribution} = \text{Selling Price per unit} - \text{Variable Cost per unit}$$
$$\text{Total Contribution} = \text{Unit Contribution} \times \text{Number of units sold}$$
$$\text{Profit} = \text{Total Contribution} - \text{Fixed Costs}$$

1) Algebraic Methods (Mathematical) :

a) Contribution Margin Technique :

As has been stated earlier, contribution per unit represents the difference between selling price per unit and variable cost thereof and the profit represents the difference between the total contribution and the fixed costs. The BEP is reached when the total proceeds of units sold are equivalent to the total costs incurred - fixed and variable.

On an analysis of the above two statements, it would be clear that the Break-Even Point is reached when the profit is zero or more precisely when the total contribution is exactly equivalent to the fixed costs. The same thing can be represented in the form of equations as given below :

i) $\text{BEP (Units)} = \dfrac{\text{Fixed Cost}}{\text{Contribution per unit}}$

ii) $\text{BEP (₹)} = \text{BEP (Units)} \times \text{Selling Price per unit}$

iii) $\text{BEP (₹)} = \dfrac{\text{Fixed Cost}}{\text{Profit Volume Ratio}}$

iv) $\text{P/V Ratio} = \dfrac{\text{Marginal Contribution per unit}}{\text{Selling Price per unit}}$

From the above it is clear that Equation (3) is only the derivative of Equation (1) Multiplying both the numerator and the denominator with the common factor of sales, the following equation is obtained :

v) $\quad$ BEP (₹) $= \dfrac{\text{Fixed Cost} \times \text{Sales}}{\text{Sales} - \text{Variable Cost}}$

Again by dividing both the numerator and the denominator of the equation (5) by the common factor of sales, the following equation is obtained.

vi) $\quad$ BEP (₹) $= 1 - \dfrac{\text{Fixed Cost}}{\dfrac{\text{Variable Cost}}{\text{Sales}}}$

Despite the existence of the numerous formulae, it should be remembered that the following three formulae are always adopted for calculating the break-even point of the business rather than drawing a chart for ascertaining the same.

$$\text{BEP} = \frac{\text{FC} \times \text{S}}{\text{S} - \text{VC}} \text{ (or) } \frac{\text{FC}}{\text{P/V Ratio}}$$

b) Equation Technique :

Under mathematical approach, break-even can easily by computed by engaging the technique of unit contribution which is developed on the basis of marginal cost equation.

The equation can be stated as follows :

$$\text{Sales} = \text{Variable cost} + \text{Fixed Cost} + \text{Profit}$$

At the break-even point, profit is absent, therefore, the same equation for this purpose can be re-written as follows :

$$\text{Sales} = \text{Variable Cost} + \text{Fixed Cost} \quad \text{or}$$
$$\text{Sales} - \text{Variable Cost} = \text{Fixed Cost} \quad \text{or}$$
$$\text{Contribution} = \text{Fixed Cost}$$

The study of the above equation reveals that sales revenue of each unit leaves a certain amount in the shape of contribution margin to meet fixed costs. Thus, in order to work out the required number of units to break-even (where the amount of contribution will be sufficient to cover total fixed cost) the total fixed cost must be divided by the unit contribution. Accordingly, the break-even point can be calculated in terms of units by using the following equation :

$$\text{Break-Even Point (in terms of units)} = \frac{\text{Fixed Cost}}{\text{Unit Contribution Margin}} = \frac{\text{FC}}{\text{SP} - \text{VC}}$$

where,

$$\begin{aligned}
\text{BEP} &= \text{Break-Even Point} \\
\text{FC} &= \text{Total Fixed Cost} \\
\text{SP} &= \text{Selling Price per unit} \\
\text{VC} &= \text{Variable Cost per unit}
\end{aligned}$$

On the same basis, the break-even point in terms of rupees can be computed with the help of the equation as given under :

$$\text{BEP (in terms of rupees)} = \frac{FC}{CMR}$$

where,

$$FC = \text{Total Fixed Cost}$$
$$CMR = \text{Contribution Margin Ratio}$$

Where the selling price and variable cost per unit is not readily available, the following equation is applied to compute break-even point.

$$\text{BEP (in terms of rupees)} = \frac{FC}{\text{P/V Ratio}}$$

where,

$$FC = \text{Total Fixed Cost}$$
$$\text{P/V Ratio} = \text{Profit Volume Ratio}$$

EXAMPLE

Calculate the Break-Even Point from the following information :

Fixed Cost	:	₹ 1,200
Variable Cost	:	₹ 5,000
Sales in rupees	:	₹ 7,000
Sales in units	:	1,000 Units

ANSWER

$$\text{BEP (in units)} = \frac{FC}{SP - VC} = \frac{₹\,1,200}{₹\,7 - ₹\,5} = 600 \text{ units}$$

$$\text{BEP (in rupees)} = \frac{FC}{CMR^*} = \frac{₹\,1,200}{₹\,0.285} = ₹\,4,200$$

$$^*CMR = \frac{SP - VC}{SP} = \frac{₹\,7 - ₹\,5}{₹\,7} = ₹\,0.285$$

Working Notes :

i)   Calculation of Variable Cost $= \dfrac{₹\,5,000}{1,000 \text{ units}} = ₹\,5.00$

ii) Calculation of Selling Price (per unit) $= \dfrac{₹\,7,000}{1,000 \text{ units}} = ₹\,7.00$

EXAMPLE

Compute Break-Even Point from below given information :

Fixed Cost	:	₹ 3,600
Variable Cost	:	₹ 15,000
Sales	:	₹ 21,000

ANSWER

The Break-Even Point will be calculated with the help of P/V Ratio.

$$\text{BEP (in rupees)} = \frac{FC}{\text{P/V Ratio}} = \frac{₹\,3,600}{28.57/100} = \frac{₹\,3,600}{28.57} \times 100$$
$$= ₹\,12,600$$

Working Note :

- **Calculation of Profit/Volume Ratio :**

$$\text{P/V Ratio} = \frac{\text{Contribution}}{\text{Sales}} \times 100 = \frac{₹\,6,000}{₹\,21,000} \times 100 = 28.57\%$$

2) Graphic presentation :

a) Break-Even Chart :

The break-even analysis can also be demonstrated graphically, which is commonly known as Break-Even Chart. A Break-Even Chart is a graphical approach to the study of the relationship of cost, revenue and profit. The graphic instead of algebraic approach is often used because it tends to be more easily understood by persons whose acquaintance with mathematics is minimal and as it provides an immediate view of variable costs, fixed costs and profit at any level of activity.

Information for constructing a Break-Even Chart can be obtained from the income statement of the concern. However, the total cost i.e., fixed cost, variable cost, and semi variable cost must be separated only into two categories of costs : Fixed-Cost and Variable-Cost. A brief description of these costs is as follows :

i) Fixed Cost :

Fixed Costs are the costs which remain fixed for all practical purposes to a certain level of activity. Once that level of activity is increased, the fixed cost will also increase to a specific degree e.g. Cost of plant and machinery, salaries, rent etc. These costs are shown on the graph by means of a straight line.

ii) Variable Cost :

These cost vary in proportion to output. This means that they increase directly with the volume of production. Cost of material, wages, carriage etc. are some examples of variable cost. For graphic application, these costs will be aggregated with the fixed cost.

iii) Semi-Variable Cost :

Semi-variable costs posses the characteristics of both fixed and variable costs. These costs demand special attention from the management in splitting them into fixed and variable costs.

Constructing a Break-Even Chart :

1) The Traditional Break-Even Chart

EXAMPLE

Construct a Break-Even Chart, using the following information:

Output	:	1,25,000 units
Sales	:	₹ 5,00,000
Variable Cost	:	₹ 2,50,000
Fixed Cost	:	₹ 1,00,000

ANSWER

First we will have to draw-up the chart and then insert the sales line as shown below in Figure 3.3.

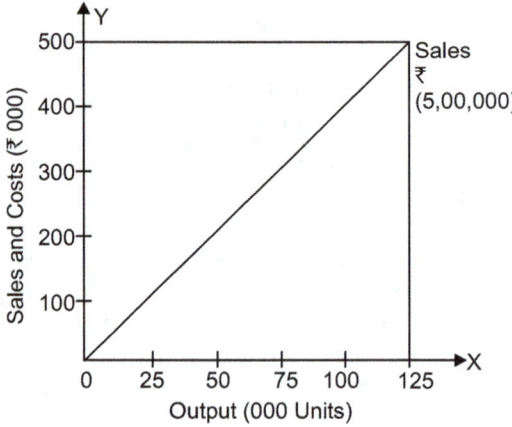

Fig. 3.3 : Sales Line

Next we will draw the fixed cost line which runs parallel to base of the chart i.e. the output as shown below in Figure 3.4.

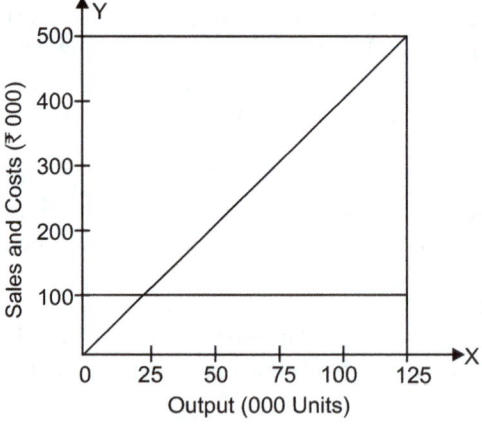

Fig. 3.4 : Sales and Fixed Cost Line

Then, we include the variable costs by adding them on to the fixed costs. This line is drawn from ₹ 1,00,000 at 0 output to ₹ 3,50,000 at 1,25,000 units of output. This line is the total cost line, i.e. fixed cost ₹ 1,00,000 plus variable cost ₹ 2.50,000 = ₹ 3,50,000 total cost as shown below in Figure 3.5.

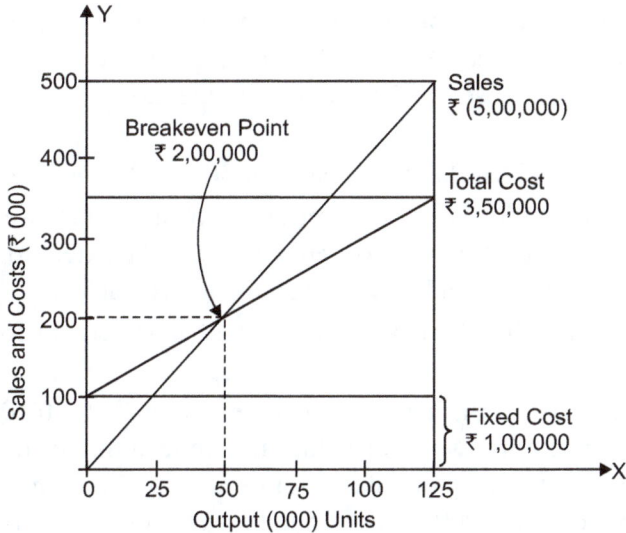

Fig. 3.5 : Break-Even Chart

Having completed our break-even chart Figure 3.5 we can read the break-even point at ₹ 200,000 Sales and Costs and 50,000 units of output, the point at which costs and revenue (sales / income) are equal, i.e. where the sales line intersects the total cost line.

After taking a closer look at the chart which we will complete finally showing the following information as shown below in Figure 3.6.

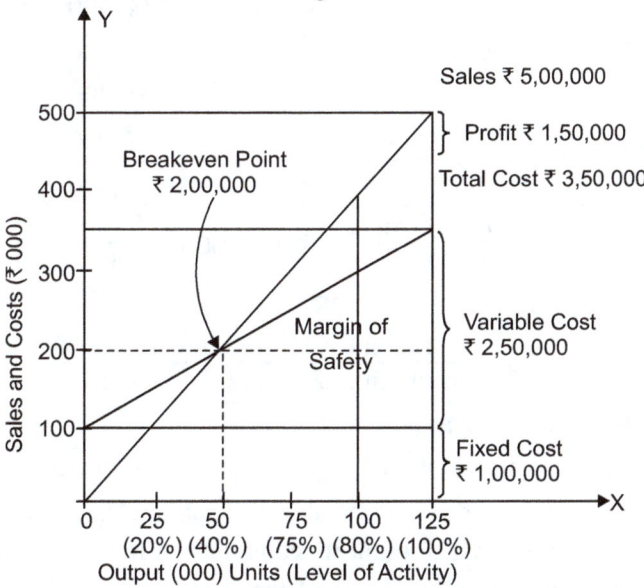

Fig. 3.6 : Conventional Break-Even Chart

i)   The logic of the calculations involved can be followed as per the righthand side of the chart, i.e. Sales ₹ 5,00,000 (Less) Total Cost ₹ 3,50,000 = Profit ₹ 1,50,000, Total Cost ₹ 3,50,000 = Variable Cost ₹ 2,50,000 + Fixed Cost ₹ 1,00,000.

ii) Above the Break-Even Point we make a profit and below it we make a loss.

iii) The margin of safety is the difference between the break-even point and the selected output / level of activity. This indicates the extent to which the level of activity must fall before a loss making situation is reached.

iv) The base of the chart can be expressed either in terms of output or level of activity.

v)   By projecting a vertical line from the base line, e.g. at 1,00,000 units of output (80% level of activity) we can use the chart to read the fixed cost, total cost and sales applicable to this particular level of activity. We can see that the vertical line drawn from 1,00,000 units of output (80% level of activity) cuts the fixed cost line at ₹ 1,00,000 the total cost line at ₹ 3,00,000 and the sales line at 4,00,000. The gap between sales and total cost of ₹ 1,00,000 represents the profit which should be achieved at the 80% level of activity.

Calculating the Break-Even Point

	Particulars		Unit Cost ₹	1,25,000 units ₹
	Sales		4	5,00,000
Less :	Variable Cost	(–)	2	2,50,000
	Contribution		2	2,50,000 (50% P/V Ratio)
Less :	Fixed Cost	(–)		1,00,000
	Profit			1,50,000

$$\text{Break-Even Point} = \frac{\text{Fixed Cost}}{\text{P/V Ratio}} = ₹\,1,00,000 \times \frac{₹\,100}{50} = ₹\,2,00,000$$

OR

$$= \frac{\text{Fixed Cost}}{\text{Contribution per unit}} = \frac{₹\,1,00,000}{₹\,2} = 50,000 \text{ Units}$$

The Contribution Break-Even Chart :

The Contribution Break-Even Chart is an alternative way of showing the information which used to construct our traditional break-even chart. Using the same information relating to earlier example, we will look at its construction in two phases. First, we draw up the chart and then insert the sales line and the variable cost line, both of which are drawn from the base line point as shown below in Figure 3.7.

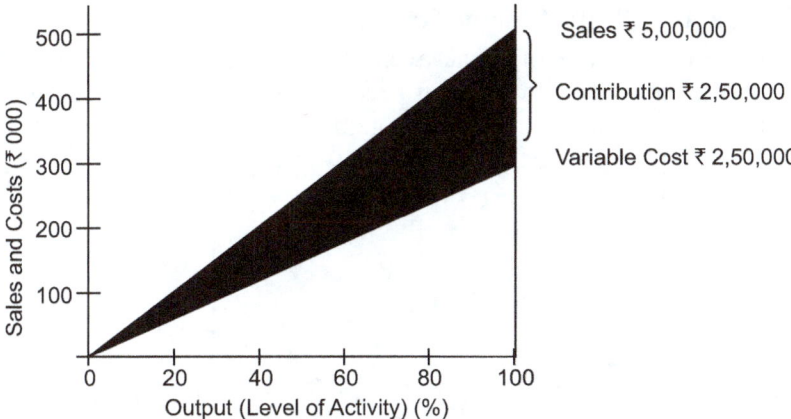

Fig. 3.7 : Income Break-Even Cost

This income break-even chart Figure 3.7 specifies that Sales ₹ 5,00,000 less variable cost ₹ 2,50,000 = contribution ₹ 2,50,000. The principal advantage of this chart is that it shows, very clearly, the contribution which is being generated at different levels of activity. The Fixed Costs of ₹ 1,00,000 are then added to the Variable Costs and the Total Cost line drawn from 1,00,000 at 0% level of activity to 3,50,000 at 100% level of activity, the Fixed Costs are plotted parallel to the Variable Costs as shown below in Figure 3.8.

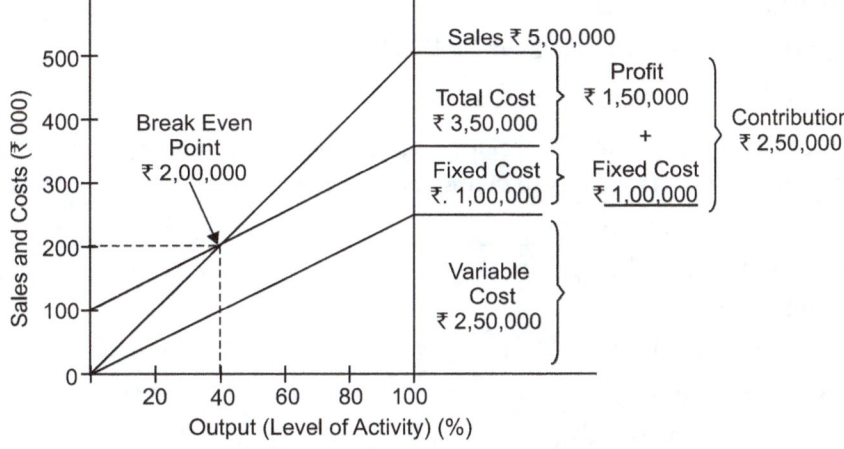

Fig. 3.8 : Contribution Break-Even Chart

Observations :

i)   This chart shows that below the break-even point the fixed costs are not being covered. When the contribution generated has covered fixed costs, the remainder is profit.

ii) The final contribution break-even chart i.e. Figure 3.9, illustrates that the contribution ₹ 2,50,000 (Less) Fixed Cost ₹ 1,00,000 = Profit ₹ 1,50,000.

b) The Profit Graph or Profit Volume Graph :

This is an alternative type of break-even chart and helps to understand the profit volume ratio more clearly. To draw it you need to know any two of the three figures : Fixed Cost, Profit and Break-Even Point. Again using the same figures as related to earlier example the graph would be as shown below in Figure 3.9.

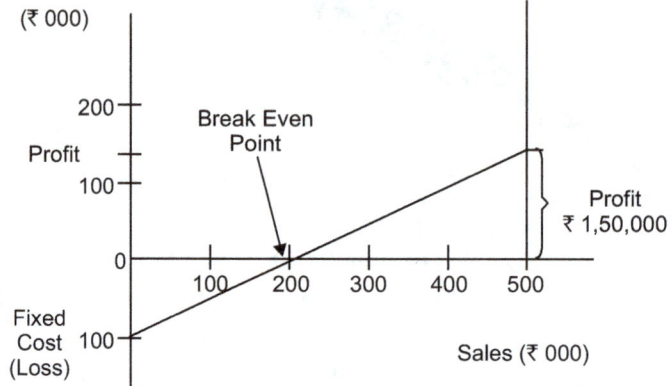

Fig. 3.9 : Profit Graph or Profit Volume Graph

Observations :

   i)   The line which joins the Fixed Costs to the Profit is, in fact, the Contribution Line, i.e. it represents Fixed Cost ₹ 1,00,000 + Profit ₹ 1,50,000 = ₹ 2,50,000 Contribution.

   ii) The Break-Even Point is again ₹ 2,00,000.

EXAMPLE

From the following particulars relating to the Ahmednagar Engineer Construction Ltd., Ahmednagar draw a Break-Even chart, and indicate the Break-Even Point.

Particulars	₹	₹
Sales (10,000 units at ₹ 20 per unit)		2,00,000
Less : Variable Costs :		
i) Direct Material	30,000	
ii) Direct Labour	50,000	
iii) Factory Overheads	20,000	
iv) Administrative and Selling Overheads (+)	20,000	(–) 1,20,000
∴ Contribution		80,000
Less : Fixed Costs :		
i) Factory Overheads	20,000	
ii) Administrative and Selling Overheads (+)	20,000	(–) 40,000
∴ Net Profit		40,000

ANSWER

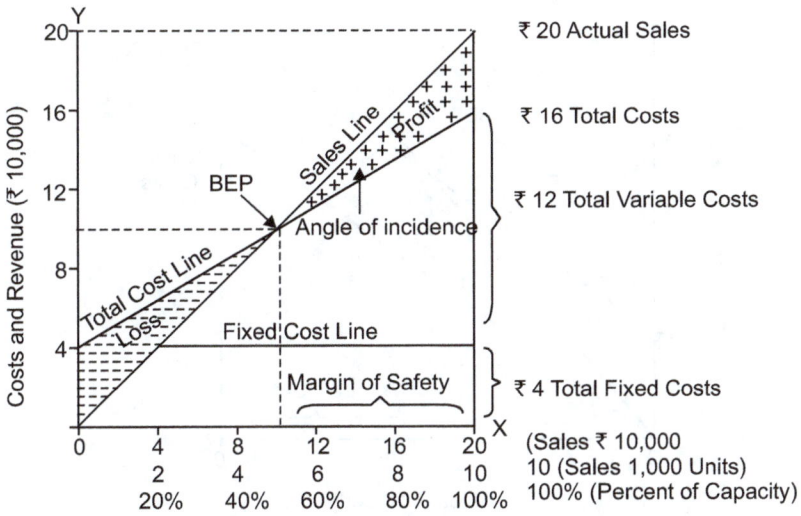

Fig. 3.10 : Break-Even Chart

In Figure 3.10, the fixed cost line is represented as the horizontal line parallel to the X-axis, whereas the Variable Cost line is represented by the area covered between the Total Cost and the Fixed Cost. The point of intersection between the Sales and the Total Cost lines represents the break-even point indicated as Break Even Point. It acquires at a Sales Volume of 5,000 units and Total Sales worth ₹ 1,00,000 (5,000 units × ₹ 20). The angle formed by the intersection of sales line and the Total Cost line is called the angle of incidence. The greater the angle of incidence, the lower will be the break-even point and vice-versa. While the area to the right of the break-even point represents the profit area, that to left of it represents the loss area which only reveals the uncovered fixed costs. The excess of actual sales over the break-even sales is known as the margin of safety.

Alternative Form :

In Figure 3.10, the Fixed Costs line is drawn first starting from the fixed cost point. It focuses the attention on the fact that Fixed Cost remains constant for different levels of sales. An alternative method of constructing the break-even chart is to draw the variable cost line followed by the total cost line from the fixed cost point. This total cost line will be parallel to the variable cost line.

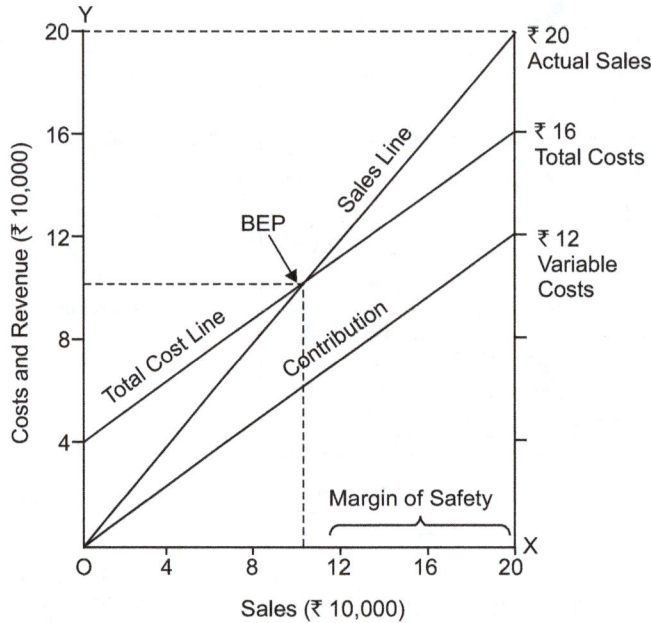

Fig. 3.11 : Alternative Form of Break-Even Chart

The alternative form of break-even chart discloses certain additional information not given by the first form. The fixed costs are indicated by the intercept of the total cost line on the vertical axis. There are three distinctive benefits of the alternative form. i) the variable costs are shown for different sales levels. ii) the marginal contribution at different sales levels is clearly represented by the difference between sales line and variable line. iii) the break-even chart clearly discloses the recovered as well as unrecovered amount of fixed costs at different levels of activity.

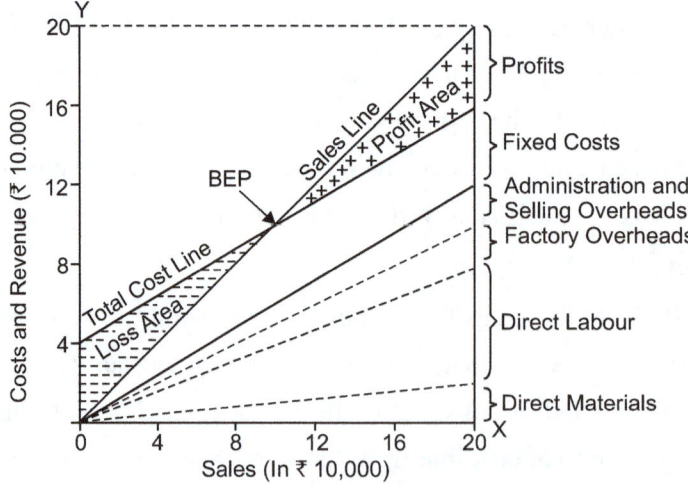

Fig. 3.12 : Alternative Break-Even Chart

It can be seen from the Figure 3.11 that when the sales are ₹ 80,000 (i.e. 40% of the capacity) the amount of contribution available to cover the fixed cost of ₹ 40,000 is only ₹ 32,000. Thus, the amount of fixed cost left unrecovered which represents loss to the business unit at this level of Sales is ₹ 8,000 (₹ 40,000 – ₹ 32,000). The third alternative is to construct a break-even chart portraying all the details of the components of fixed as well as Variable Costs as shown in Figure 3.12.

Margin of Safety (MOS)

The margin of safety represents the difference between actual and break-even sales. In Fig. 3.14 the margin of safety is indicated as ₹ 1,00,000 the difference between actual sales of ₹ 2,00,000 and the break-even sales of ₹ 1,00,000. It can also be calculated by the following formulae :

$$\text{Margin of Safety} \ = \ \text{Profit} \div \frac{\text{Sales} - \text{Variable Cost}}{\text{Sales}} \ \ (\text{or}) \ \ \frac{\text{Profit}}{\text{P/V Ratio}}$$

The margin of safety represents the extent to which sales can decline before the business unit sustains a loss. Larger the margin of safety, safer it will be for the business unit. A lower margin of safety will result for the business unit which has a low Profit-Volume Ratio. When both the margin of safety and the Profit-Volume Ratio are low, the management should either increase the selling price without adversely affecting the sales volume or reduce the variable cost by affecting improvements in the manufacturing process.

EXAMPLE

Nebula Ltd., Nashik manufactures 5,000 units with the existing plant and premises. An analysis of cost accounts indicates that :

i)   The expenditure on fixed overheads is ₹ 1,000.

ii)   The varibale costs are ₹ 0.60 per unit.

iii) Selling price per unit is ₹ 1.

The management is anxious to increase production and ascertain that the following increase in fixed expenses will occur if production is increased.

- Exceeding 5,000 units and not exceeding 10,000 units – ₹ 2,000 per annum.
- Exceeding 10,000 units - ₹ 2,000 per annum.

Incorporate the above information in a Break-Even Chart.

ANSWER

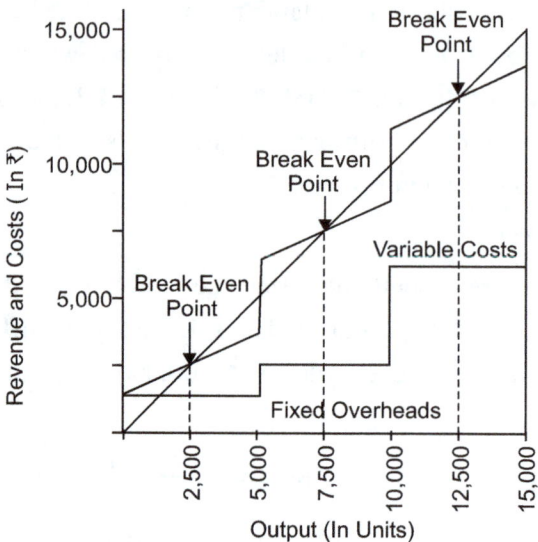

Fig. 3.13 : Break-Even Chart

Mathematical Verification :

Break Even Point at Sales of 5,000 units Variable Costs remain at ₹ 0.60 per unit, Fixed Overheads at ₹ 1,000 and Selling Price at ₹ 1 per unit.

i)   Break Even Point $= \dfrac{FC \times S}{S - VC}$

$$S = 5,000 \text{ units} \times ₹ 1 = ₹ 5,000$$

$$FC = ₹ 1,000 \text{ and } VC = 5,000 \text{ units} \times ₹ 0.60$$

$$= ₹ 3,000$$

$$= \dfrac{₹ 1,000 \times ₹ 5,000}{₹ 5,000 - ₹ 3,000} = \dfrac{₹ 50,00,000}{₹ 2,000}$$

$$= ₹ 2,500$$

ii)   Break Even Point at Sales of ₹ 10,000 units, cost remain at ₹ 0.60 per unit, Fixed Overheads at ₹ 3,000 and Selling Price at ₹ 1 per unit.

Break Even Point $= \dfrac{FC \times S}{S - VC}$

$$S = 10,000 \text{ units} \times ₹ 1 = ₹ 10,000$$

$$FC = ₹ 3,000 \text{ and } VC = 10,000 \text{ units} \times ₹ 0.60$$

$$= ₹ 6,000$$

$$= \dfrac{₹ 3,000 \times ₹ 10,000}{₹ 10,000 - ₹ 6,000} = \dfrac{₹ 3,00,00,000}{₹ 4,000}$$

$$= ₹ 7,500$$

iii) Break Even Point at Sales of 15,000 units, costs remain at ₹ 0.60 per unit, Fixed Overheads at ₹ 5,000 and Selling Price at ₹ 1 per unit.

$$\text{Break Even Point} = \frac{FC \times S}{S - VC}$$

$$S = 15{,}000 \text{ units} \times ₹\ 1 = ₹\ 15{,}000$$

$$FC = ₹\ 5{,}000 \text{ and } VC = 15{,}000 \text{ units} \times ₹\ 0.60$$

$$= ₹\ 9{,}000$$

$$= \frac{₹\ 5{,}000 \times ₹\ 15{,}000}{₹\ 15{,}000 - ₹\ 9{,}000} = \frac{₹\ 7{,}50{,}00{,}000}{₹\ 6{,}000}$$

$$= ₹\ 12{,}500$$

Assumptions of Break-Even Analysis :

Break-Even Analysis data are based upon certain assumed conditions which are rarely found in practice.

Some of these basic assumptions are given below :

i)   Costs can be classified into their fixed and variable components.

ii)   The principle of cost variability is valid.

iii)   Variable costs vary proportionately with the volume changes.

iv)   Fixed costs remain constant irrespective of the level of activity.

v)   Selling price does not change with the volume changes.

vi)   There is no change in the general price level.

vii)   There is only one product or in the case or multiple products sales mix remains constant.

viii) There is synchronisation between production and sales.

ix)   Productivity per worker remains constant.

x)   Revenue and costs are being compared with a common activity base, e.g., units produced or sales value of production.

xi)   Plant capacity and efficiency remain unaffected.

It is clear that a change in any one of the above factors will alter the break-even point such that profits are effected by changes in factors other than volume.

Usefulness of Break-Even Analysis :

Break-even analysis is considered to be the most useful technique of profit planning and control. It is an important device to explain the relationship between cost, volume and profit. The usefulness of the break-even analysis is as follows :

i)   It is simple tool employed to graphically represent complicated accounting data.

ii)   It is a more useful diagnostic tool.

iii)   It provides basic information facilitating further studies on improving the profit.

iv)   It is also used for analysing the risk implication of alternative actions.

v)   It is useful in marketing strategies also.

The break-even analysis serves as a useful tool for considering the risk implications of alternative actions. The problem of risk evaluation can be solved by considering the effects of the alternative actions on break-even point. While taking a decision, the business unit should not only consider the profits arising from the alternatives but also the probability of reaching the break-even point.

Limitations of Break-Even Analysis :

i)   The application of break-even analysis to a multi-product firm becomes very difficult.

ii) Since the break-even analysis is a short-run concept, it has a limited application in the long-range planning.

iii) The break-even tool is a static tool with very limited practical application.

iv) It is very difficult if not impossible to separate costs into fixed and variable components.

v)   The assumption that the total fixed cost remains constant over the entire volume range does not stand to reason.

3.7 PROFIT VOLUME RATIO

Meaning :

A Profit-Volume Ratio is the ratio of contribution to sales which is also termed as contribution to Sales Ratio, Marginal Ratio etc. It expresses the relationship between contribution and sales. It is the contribution per rupee of sales and since the fixed cost remains constant in the short-term period, Profit-Volume ratio also measures the rate of change of profit due to change in volume of sales. Hence, it is considered to be an important method of expressing the relationships between costs, revenues and volumes. It indicates the proportion of sales value available to recover the fixed costs and finally the earnings of profits. It is a particular rate at which profit increases with a corresponding increase in the volume. This ratio for any given product is assumed to remain constant for all levels of sales volume.

Definition :

According to **Chartered Institute of Management Accountants, London Profit-Volume Ratio** is defined as,

"the ratio that expresses the relationship of contribution to sales volume".

Thus, Profit-Volume ratio is regarded as an important test of the profitability of the business.

Accounting Formulaes :

P/V Ratio can be computed by using any of the following accounting formulaes considered appropriate in a given situation.

$$\bullet \qquad \text{P/V Ratio} = \frac{\text{Contribution}}{\text{Sales}} \times 100$$

$$\bullet \qquad \text{P/V Ratio} = \frac{\text{Change in Profit}}{\text{Change in Sales}} \times 100$$

$$\bullet \qquad \text{P/V Ratio} = \frac{\text{Change in Contribution}}{\text{Change in Sales}} \times 100$$

Importance :

P/V ratio states very clearly the actual rate of profitability growth with reference to the growth of sales value. P/V ratio is of vital importance for the technique of marginal costing because :

i)   Analysis of P/V ratio is an important tool in managerial decision-making.

ii) It helps in determining the profit which would be earned by any given volume of sales.

iii) The comparative analysis of P/V ratio helps in indicating the profitability of business units.

iv) It denotes specifically the profit making features of a firm.

v)   It is used for appraising profitability of alternative products.

vi) It can be used more effectively for scientific product analysis.

vii) It is an important indicator of the profit earning capacity of the business.

vii) It helps in inter-firm comparison.

viii) It helps to ascertain the break even point.

ix) It helps to determine the most profitable-product mix.

> **The profit is the product of P/V Ratio and the Margin of Safety.**

Implications :

i)   **A high P/V ratio** always indicates that with increase in sales above the break even point, profits will increase at a higher rate, assuming that there is no corresponding increase in the fixed costs. Under these situations, it is always beneficial to spend more and more on sales promotion, advertisement and publicity, to increase sales turnover and to generate higher profits, with lower risks.

ii) **A low P/V ratio** always indicates that with decrease in sales below the break even point, profits will decrease substantially. Under these situations, efforts should be made to improve P/V ratio by increasing the selling price and decreasing the direct cost. The overall profitability may also be increased by concentrating more on those products which have high P/V ratio.

Impact on P/V Ratio :

The **impact of fixed cost, variable cost and selling price on P/V ratio** can be summarised as follows :

i)   A change in fixed cost does not affect the P/V ratio.

   •   The increase in fixed cost will increase the BEP, but there will be no effect on P/V Ratio.

   •   The decrease in fixed cost will decrease the BEP, but there will be no effect on P/V ratio.

ii) A change in variable cost affect the P/V Ratio.

- The increase in variable cost per unit will decrease the contribution, this would decrease P/V Ratio.

- The decrease in variable cost per unit will increase the contribution, this would increase the P/V Ratio.

iii) A change in selling price affect the P/V Ratio.

- The increase in selling price will increase the contribution, this would increase the P/V Ratio.

- The decrease in selling price will decrease the contribution, this would decrease the P/V ratio.

Improvement :

The P/V Ratio can be improved if contribution is increased and contribution can be increased only by reducing variable costs or by increasing the selling price. The following can be some of the important measures undertaken to improve the P/V Ratio in a given situation :

i) increasing the selling price through product improvement,

ii) decreasing the variable costs by efficiency improvement,

iii) increasing the actual sales of more profitable products.

Application :

The P/V ratio can very well be used to find out,

i) the break even point,

ii) the profit at any volume of sales.

iii) the sales volume required to earn a desired amount of profit,

iv) profitability of products, processes or departments,

v) the variable cost for any volume of sales,

vi) various kinds of product analysis,

vii) the margin of safety.

Limitations :

However, the P/V Ratio is not very useful because it :

i) ignores the number of units sold or which can be sold and,

ii) does not consider the capital outlays required by the additional productive capacity.

EXAMPLE

From the following information compute, i) P/V Ratio, ii) Fixed Cost, and iii) Sales Volume to earn a profit of ₹ 1,20,000.

$$\text{Sales} \ : \ ₹\ 1,50,000$$
$$\text{Profit} \ : \ ₹\ 15,000$$
$$\text{Variable Cost} \ : \ 80\% \text{ of Sales Turnover}$$

ANSWER

- Computation of Variable Cost which are 80% of Sales Turnover.

$$= \frac{80}{100} \times ₹\ 1,50,000$$

$$= ₹\ 1,20,000$$

- Computation of P/V Ratio : $= \dfrac{\text{Contribution}}{\text{Sales}} \times 100$

$$= \frac{\text{Sales} - \text{Variable Cost}}{\text{Sales}} \times 100$$

$$= \frac{₹\ 1,50,000 - ₹\ 1,20,000}{₹\ 1,50,000} \times 100$$

$$= 20\%$$

- Computation of Fixed Cost

$$\text{Contribution} = \text{Fixed Cost} + \text{Profit}$$
$$₹\ 30,000 = \text{Fixed Cost} + ₹\ 15,000$$
$$\therefore \qquad \text{Fixed Cost} = ₹\ 30,000 - ₹\ 15,000$$
$$\text{Fixed Cost} = ₹\ 15,000$$

- Computation of Sales Volume to earn a profit of ₹ 1,20,000.

$$\text{Sales} = \frac{\text{Fixed Cost} + \text{Profit}}{\text{P/V Ratio}}$$

$$= \frac{₹\ 15,000 + ₹\ 15,000}{20\%}$$

$$= ₹\ 1,50,000$$

Therefore,		₹
Sales	:	1,50,000
Less : Variable Cost (80% of Sales)	:	(−) 1,20,000
∴ Contribution	:	30,000
Less : Fixed Cost	:	(−) 15,000
∴ Profit	:	15,000

EXAMPLE

Assuming that the cost structure and selling price remains the same in Ist and IInd quarter, find out the P/V Ratio.

Periods Quarters	Sales ₹	Total Cost ₹
I	2,80,000	2,50,000
II	3,20,000	2,80,000

ANSWER

- **Calculation of Profit :**

  (Where Profit = Sales – Total Cost)

Periods (Quarters)	Sales ₹	Total Cost ₹	Profit ₹
I	2,80,000	2,50,000	30,000
II	3,20,000	2,80,000	40,000

$$\text{P/V Ratio} = \frac{\text{Change in Profit}}{\text{Change in Sales}} \times 100$$

$$= \frac{₹\,10,000}{₹\,40,000} \times 100$$

$$= 25\%$$

3.8 LIMITING FACTOR

Every business organisation tries to achieve maximum profit but there are always certain factors which do not allow the organisation to earn more profits. These are the constraints of the business. For example, a company have very good sales network and can sell all the items produced. But there may be shortage of raw materials, which will limit the production to a certain extent. Sometimes, all other factors may be favourable, while sales becomes the problem. In this case, sales becomes the limiting or key factor.

A key factor can, therefore, be defined as that factor which limits the desired volume of production. When there is a key factor, the contribution per unit of that key factor is maximised so that we get the maximum advantage. To do this, ascertainment of the key factor is essential. If there is any mistake in finding out the key factor the decision based on it will go wrong. In dealing with a limiting factor problem the steps to be taken are as follows :

i) Identify the possibility that-there may be a limiting factor other than sales demand. There may be the maximum availability of one or more resources, so that sales demand cannot be met. This is done simply as follows

- Calculate the volume of resources required to produce enough units to satisfy sales demand. .

- Calculate the volume of resources available.

- Compare the two totals. If (a) exceeds (b) there is a limiting factor.

ii) If there is only one such limiting factor, the next step is to calculate the contribution earned by each product per unit of the scarce resource. The product(s) with the highest contribution per unit of scarce resource should receive priority in the allocation of the resource in the production budget.

If we know both the key factors as well as the contribution, we can find out the relative profitability of different products with the help of the following formula :

$$\text{Profitability} = \frac{\text{Contribution}}{\text{Key Factor}}$$

For example, if labour hour is the key factor, the profitability is found out as follows :

$$\text{Profitability} = \frac{\text{Contribution}}{\text{Labour hour per unit}}$$

Thus, when a limiting factor is in operation, the contribution per unit of such a factor should be criterion to judge the profitability of a line of activity. When two or more limiting factors are in operation simultaneously, it is necessary to take all of them into consideration to determine the profitability if it is the question of selecting a suitable product mix when a number of limiting factor operate, the technique of linear programming should be used.

EXAMPLE

You are given the following information when direct labour hour is the key factor, which is 800 hours.

Particulars		Product	
		X	Y
		₹	₹
Contribution per unit	(₹)	40	30
Direct Labour Hours Per unit	(Hrs.)	10	06

X and Y can be produced each 100 units, the fixed overhead are ₹ 800. Find out the total profit earned.

ANSWER

Particulars	Product	
	X	Y
	₹	₹
Contribution per unit (₹)	40	30
Direct Labour Hours Per unit (Hrs.)	10	06
$\therefore\ \text{Profitability} = \dfrac{\text{Contribution per unit}}{\text{Direct Labour Hours per unit}}$	$\dfrac{₹\,40}{\text{Hrs. }10}$ = ₹ 4 per hour	$\dfrac{\text{Rs. }30}{\text{Hrs. }06}$ = ₹ 5 per hour

Now, if direct labour hours are not the limiting factor, then product X is more profitable because it gives more contribution (₹ 40), than Y (₹ 30). But since only 800 hours are available, which is the limiting factor, we have to consider profitability of each product.

Now, Product Y is more profitable when direct labour is the key factor.

Hence, 100 units × 6 hours = 600 hours should be utilised to produce Y, while the balance (800 Hrs. − 600 Hrs.) = 200 Hrs. should be utilised to produced X (i.e. only 20 units of X can be produced).

Profitability Statement

Particulars		₹
Total Contribution from B = 100 units × ₹ 30		3,000
Total Contribution from A = 20 units × ₹ 40	(+)	800
Total Contribution		3,800
Less : Fixed Overheads	(−)	800
Profit		3,000

MARGINAL COST EQUATIONS

i) **Sales or Selling Price or Market Price or Value of Turnover or Invoice Price or Inflated Price Loaded Price :**

$$= \text{Total Cost} + \text{Profit}$$

$$= \text{Variable Cost} + \text{Fixed Cost} + \text{Profit}$$

$$= \text{Contribution} / \text{P/V Ratio}$$

$$= \text{Contribution} + \text{Variable Cost}$$

$$= \text{Marginal Cost} / \text{Marginal Cost Ratio}$$

ii) **Profit or Net Margin or Net Income :**

$$= \text{Sales} - \text{Total Cost}$$

$$= \text{Sales} - (\text{Variable Cost} + \text{Fixed Cost})$$

$$= \text{Contribution} - \text{Fixed Cost}$$

$$= \text{Margin of Safety} \times \text{P/V Ratio}$$

iii) **Loss :**

$$= \text{Total Cost} - \text{Sales}$$

$$= \text{Fixed Cost} - \text{Contribution}$$

iv) **Contribution or Gross Margin or Marginal Contribution :**

$$= \text{Sales} - \text{Variable Cost}$$

$$= \text{Fixed Cost} + \text{Profit}$$

$$= \text{Sales} \times \text{P/V Ratio}$$

$$= \text{Fixed Cost} - \text{Loss}$$

$$= \text{Fixed Cost} / \text{Break-Even units}$$

v) Fixed Cost, Rigid Cost or Constant Cost :

$$= \text{Total Cost} - \text{Variable Cost}$$

$$= \text{Contribution} - \text{Profit}$$

$$= \text{Contribution} + \text{Loss}$$

$$= \text{Sales} - (\text{Variable Cost} + \text{Profit})$$

vi) Variable Cost or Marginal Cost or Differential Cost :

$$= \text{Total Cost} - \text{Fixed Cost}$$

$$= \text{Sales} - \text{Contribution}$$

$$= \text{Sales} - (\text{Fixed Cost} + \text{Profit})$$

$$= \text{Direct Material} + \text{Direct Labour} + \text{Direct Expenses} + \text{Variable Overheads}$$

vii) Break-Even Point i.e. BEP (in units) or (in output) :

$$= \frac{\text{Total Fixed Cost}}{\text{Contribution per unit}}$$

$$= \frac{\text{Break-Even Sales in } ₹}{\text{Selling Price per unit}}$$

viii) Break-Even Point i.e. BEP (Sales in Rupees) :

$$= \frac{\text{Total Fixed Cost}}{\text{Contribution per unit}} \times \text{Selling Price per unit}$$

$$= \frac{\text{Total Fixed Cost}}{\text{Total Contribution}} \times \text{Total Sales}$$

$$= \frac{\text{Total Fixed Cost}}{\text{Profit/Volume Ratio}}$$

$$= \frac{\text{Total Fixed Cost}}{1 - \left(\dfrac{\text{Variable Cost}}{\text{Sales}} \right)}$$

$$= \text{Break-Even Point (Units)} \times \text{Selling Price per unit}$$

ix) Profit/Volume Ratio or Contribution to Sales Ratio or Contribution Ratio i.e. P/V Ratio :

$$= \frac{\text{Contribution}}{\text{Sales}} \times 100$$

$$= \frac{\text{Change in Profits}}{\text{Change in Sales}} \times 100$$

$$= \frac{\text{Change in Contribution}}{\text{Change in Sales}} \times 100$$

x) Margin of Safety :

$$\text{MS} = \text{Actual Sales} - \text{Break-Even Sales}$$

$$\text{MS} = \frac{\text{Profit}}{\text{P/V Ratio}}$$

$$\text{MS} = \frac{\text{Profit} \times \text{Selling Price per unit}}{\text{Selling Price per unit} - \text{Variable Cost per unit}}$$

xi) Margin of Safety Ratio :

$$\text{MS Ratio} = \frac{\text{Profit}}{\text{P/V Ratio}} \times 100$$

$$\text{MS Ratio} = \frac{\text{Margin of Safety}}{\text{Actual Sales}} \times 100$$

xii) Sales volume to earn required profit (in units) or Sales for desired profit (in units) :

$$= \frac{\text{Total Fixed Cost} + \text{Required Profit}}{\text{Contribution per unit}}$$

xiii) Sales volume to earn required profit (in value) or Sales for desired profit (in ₹) :

$$= \frac{(\text{Total Fixed Cost} + \text{Required Profit}) \times \text{ Sales}}{\text{Total Contribution}}$$

$$= \frac{\text{Total Fixed Cost} + \text{Required Profit}}{\text{P/V Ratio}}$$

xiv)   Profitability $= \dfrac{\text{Contribution}}{\text{Key Factor}}$

ILLUSTRATIONS

ILLUSTRATION 1

Rotex India Ltd., Raipur produces 1,00,000 units and sells them @ ₹ 10 each. The Variable Cost per unit is ₹ 6 and Total Fixed Cost amounted to ₹ 2,00,000.

Calculate Break-Even Point in units and sales by following formulae method and graphical presentation method. Also calculate margin of safety showing angle of incidence.

SOLUTION

A) Formulae Method :

i) Break-Even Point (Units) $= \dfrac{\text{Total Fixed Cost}}{\text{Contribution per unit}}$

But,

Contribution per unit = Selling Price per unit – Variable Cost per unit

∴ Break-Even Point (Units) $= \dfrac{\text{Total Fixed Cost}}{\text{Selling Price per unit} - \text{Variable Cost}}$

$= \dfrac{₹\,2,00,000}{₹\,10 - ₹\,6}$

$= \dfrac{₹\,2,00,000}{₹\,4}$

= 50,000 units

ii) Break-Even Point (Sales) $= \dfrac{\text{Break-Even Point}}{\text{(Units)}} \times \dfrac{\text{Selling price}}{\text{per unit}}$

= 50,000 units × ₹ 10

= ₹ 5,00,000

iii) Margin of Safety = Actual Sales – Break-Even Sales

= ₹ 10,00,000 – ₹ 5,00,000

= ₹ 5,00,000

B) Graphical Presentation Method :

Break-Even Chart is a graphical representation of marginal costing. It indicates the graphical relationship between cost, volume and profits. On the basis of cost data, the Break-Even Chart can be drawn as shown below in Figure 3.14.

		₹
i)	Total Actual Sales	10,00,000
	(1,00,000 units × ₹ 10)	
ii)	Total Fixed Cost	2,00,000
iii)	Total Variable Cost	6,00,000
	(1,00,000 units × ₹ 6)	
iv)	Total Profit	2,00,000

Scale,

OX axis ... 1 cm = 10, 000 units ... Output in units

OY axis ... 1 cm = ₹ 1,00,000 ... Costs and Sales Revenue

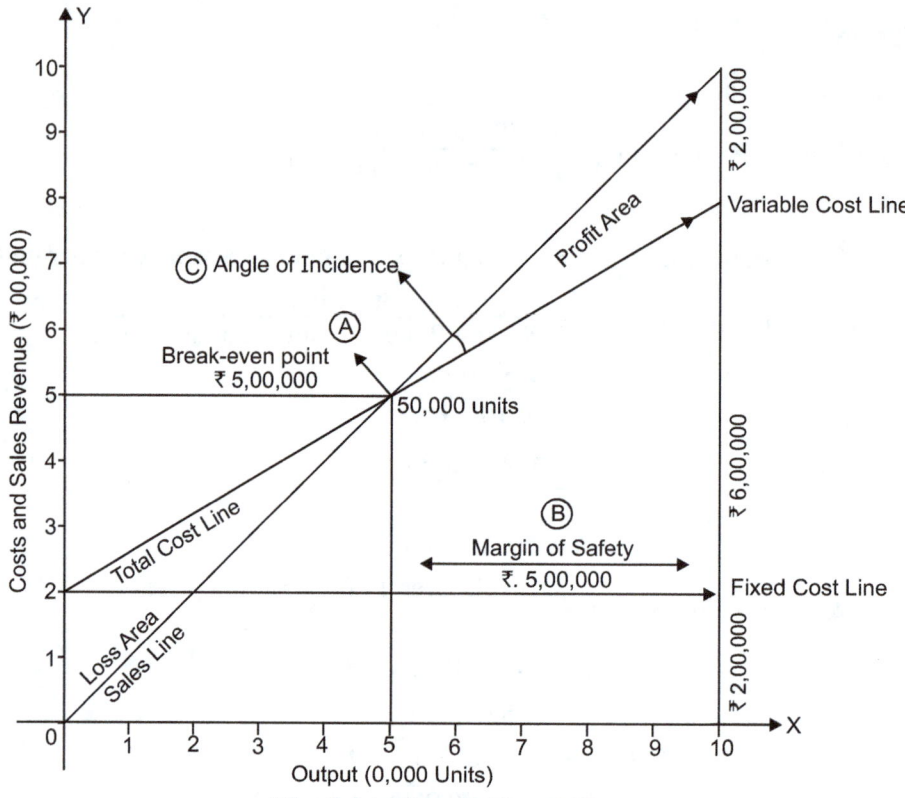

Fig. 3.14 : Break-Even Chart

ILLUSTRATION 2

From the following particulars calculate :

i)   Contribution per unit

ii) P/V Ratio

iii) BEP (units and in rupees)

iv) What will be the selling price per unit if BEP is brought down to 25,000 units ?

Fixed expenses ₹ 1,50,000,

Selling price per unit ₹ 15,

Variable Cost per unit ₹ 10.

SOLUTION

i)   **Contribution per unit :**

= Selling Price per unit – Variable Cost per unit

= ₹ 15 – ₹ 10

= ₹ 5

ii) **P/V Ratio :**

$$= \frac{\text{Contribution per unit}}{\text{Selling Price per unit}} \times 100$$

$$= \frac{₹\,5}{₹\,15} \times 100$$

$$= \frac{1}{3} \times 100$$

$$= 33\,{}^1/_3\%$$

iii) **BEP (in rupees) :**

$$= \frac{\text{Fixed Cost}}{\text{P/V Ratio}}$$

$$= \frac{₹\,1,50,000}{33\,{}^1/_3\%}$$

$$= \frac{₹\,1,50,000}{{}^1/_3}$$

$$= ₹\,1,50,000 \times \frac{3}{1}$$

$$= ₹\,4,50,000$$

BEP (units) :

$$= \frac{\text{Fixed Cost}}{\text{Contribution per unit}}$$

$$= \frac{₹\,1,50,000}{₹\,5} = 30,000 \text{ units}$$

iv) **Selling Price per unit :**

where,

$$\text{BEP (units)} = \frac{\text{Fixed Cost}}{\text{Contribution per unit}}$$

$$\therefore \quad \text{Contribution per unit} = \frac{\text{Fixed Cost}}{\text{BEP (Units)}}$$

$$= \frac{₹\,1,50,000}{\text{Units } 25,000}$$

$$= ₹\,6 \text{ per unit}$$

$$\text{Selling Price per unit} = \text{Variable Cost per unit} + \text{Contribution per unit}$$

$$= ₹\,10 + ₹\,6$$

$$= ₹\,16$$

ILLUSTRATION 3

Gasco Ltd., Gurgaon provides you with the following additional cost data regarding its operations for 2012-13.

- Invoice price   ₹ 20 per unit
- Works on Cost – Fixed   ₹ 61,000 p.a.
- Production Cost – Marginal   ₹ 11 per unit
- Selling Overheads – Rigid   ₹ 29,000 p.a.
- Distribution Overheads – Differential   ₹ 3 per unit

Calculate –

i)   Break-Even Point in amount of sales in rupees.

ii) Number of units to be sold to earn a profit of ₹ 30,000 per year.

SOLUTION

- **Calculation of Contribution per unit :**

			Unit Cost ₹
	Invoice Price		20
Less :	Variable Cost		
	i) Production Cost – Marginal	11	
	ii) Distribution Overheads – Differential	(+) 3	
			(−) 14
∴	**Contribution**		**06**

- **Calculation of P/V Ratio :**

where,

$$\text{P/V Ratio} = \frac{\text{Contribution}}{\text{Sales}} \times 100$$

$$= \frac{₹\,6}{₹\,20} \times 100$$

$$= 30\%$$

i)   Break-Even Point in amount of Sales in rupees :

$$= \frac{\text{Fixed Cost}}{\text{P/V Ratio}}$$

$$= \frac{\overset{\text{Works on Cost}}{₹\,61,000} + \overset{\text{Selling Overheads}}{₹\,29,000}}{30\%}$$

$$= ₹\,90,000 \times \frac{100}{30}$$

$$= ₹\,3,00,000$$

ii) Number of units to be sold to earn a profit of ₹ 30,000 per year :

$$= \frac{\text{Fixed Cost + Desired Profit}}{\text{Contribution per unit}}$$

$$= \frac{₹\ 90,000}{₹\ 6}$$

= 15,000 units

ILLUSTRATION 4

From the following cost data calculate :

a)   BEP (units)

b)   BEP (units) if selling price is reduced by 10%.

c)   Selling price per unit if BEP is 8,000 units.

Fixed Cost-₹ 1,00,000, Variable cost per unit-₹ 10, Selling price per unit- ₹ 20.

SOLUTION

i)   BEP (units) :

$$= \frac{\text{Fixed Cost}}{\text{Contribution per unit}}$$

But, Contribution per unit = Selling Price per unit – Variable Cost per unit

∴   BEP (units) $= \dfrac{\text{Fixed Cost}}{\text{Selling Price per unit – Variable Cost per unit}}$

$$= \frac{₹\ 1,00,000}{₹\ 20 - ₹\ 10}$$

$$= \frac{₹\ 1,00,000}{₹\ 10}$$

= 10,000 units.

ii)   BEP (units) if selling price is reduced by 10% :

Original Selling Price per unit – Reduction by 10% = New Selling Price per unit.

₹ 20   –   ₹ 2   =   ₹ 18

BEP (units) :

$$= \frac{\text{Fixed Cost}}{\text{Contribution per unit}}$$

But, Contribution per unit = Selling Price per unit – Variable Cost per unit

∴   BEP (units) $= \dfrac{\text{Fixed Cost}}{\text{Selling Price per unit – Variable Cost per unit}}$

$$= \frac{₹\ 1,00,000}{₹\ 18 - ₹\ 10}$$

$$= \frac{₹\ 1,00,000}{₹\ 8}$$

= 12,500 units

iii) **Selling Price per unit if BEP is 8,000 units :**

Let X' be the Selling Price per unit.

where, $\quad$ BEP (units) $= \dfrac{\text{Fixed Cost}}{\text{Contribution per unit}}$

But,

$\qquad$ Contribution per unit $=$ Selling Price per unit – Variable Cost per unit

$\therefore \qquad$ BEP (units) $= \dfrac{\text{Fixed Cost}}{\text{Selling Price per unit – Variable Cost per unit}}$

$\therefore \qquad$ 8,000 units $= \dfrac{₹\ 1,00,000}{X - ₹\ 10}$

$\therefore \quad$ 8,000 units $\times$ (X – ₹ 10) $= \qquad\qquad$ ₹ 1,00,000

$\therefore \qquad$ 8,000 X – ₹ 80,000 $=$ ₹ 1,00,000

$\therefore \qquad\qquad$ 8,000 X $=$ ₹ 1,00,000 + ₹ 80,000

$\therefore \qquad\qquad\quad$ X $= \dfrac{₹\ 1,80,000}{8,000\ \text{units}}$

$\therefore \quad$ Selling Price per unit $=$ ₹ 22.50

ILLUSTRATION 5

From the following cost data of Onida Co. Ltd., Otur calculate BEP (units) and also new BEP (units) if selling price is reduced by 10%.

	₹
Direct Materials per unit	3
Depreciation on Plant and Machinery	1,00,000
Basic Labour per unit	1.50
Salaries to Staff – Middle Level	80,000
Prime Cost Expenses per unit	0.50
Workshop Rent	20,000
Value of Turnover per unit	10

SOLUTION

i) **Calculation of Variable Cost per unit :** $\qquad$ ₹

Direct Materials per unit	3.00
Add : Basic Labour per unit	1.50
Add : Prime Cost expenses per unit	(+) 0.50
$\therefore$ **Total Variable Cost per unit**	**5.00**

ii) **Calculation of Total Fixed Cost :** $\qquad$ ₹

Depreciation of Plant and Machinery	1,00,000
Add : Salaries to Staff – Middle Level	80,000
Add : Workshop Rent	(+) 20,000
$\therefore$ **Total Fixed Cost**	**2,00,000**

BEP (units) : $= \dfrac{\text{Fixed Cost}}{\text{Contribution per unit}}$

But, Contribution per unit = Selling Price per unit – Variable Cost per unit

$\therefore$ BEP (units) $= \dfrac{\text{Fixed Cost}}{\text{Selling Price per unit – Variable Cost per unit}}$

$= \dfrac{₹\,2,00,000}{₹\,10 - ₹\,5}$

$= \dfrac{₹\,2,00,000}{₹\,5}$

$= 40,000$ units

Calculation of new BEP (units) if Selling Price is reduced by 10% :

Original Selling Price per unit – Reduction by 10% = New Selling Price per unit

$₹\,10 - ₹\,1$ $= ₹\,9$

BEP (units) $= \dfrac{\text{Fixed Cost}}{\text{Contribution per unit}}$

But, Contribution per unit = Selling Price per unit – Variable Cost per unit

$\therefore$ BEP (units) $= \dfrac{\text{Fixed Cost}}{\text{Selling Price per unit – Variable Cost per unit}}$

$= \dfrac{₹\,2,00,000}{₹\,9 - ₹\,5}$

$= \dfrac{₹\,2,00,000}{₹\,4}$

$= 50,000$ units

ILLUSTRATION 6

The following cost details are made available by Indian Plastics Ltd., Indapur for the month July, 2013.

Prime Cost Labour per unit	₹ 3.50
Fixed Overheads	₹ 20,000
Value of Turnover per unit	₹ 20
Productive Wages – Outstanding per unit	₹ 0.50
Basic Material Cost per unit	₹ 6
Variable Overheads – 100% of Direct Labour Cost	10%

You are required to calculate :

i) Break-Even Point (Sales Value)

ii) Net Profit, if Sales are 10% and 15% above the Break-Even Volume.

SOLUTION

- **Calculation of Contribution per unit :**

			Unit Cost ₹
where,

Selling Price — — — 18.00

$\left(\begin{array}{cc} \text{Value of Turnover} & \text{Trade Discount @ 10\%} \\ ₹ 20 & ₹ 2 \end{array}\right)$

Less : Variable Cost

i) Basic Material Cost — 6.00

ii) Direct Labour Cost — 4.00
- Prime Cost Labour — 3.50

Add : Productive Outstanding Wages (+) 0.50

iii) Variable Overheads — 4.00
(100% of Direct Labour Cost i.e. ₹ 4) (+)_____

(−) 14.00

∴ **Contribution** **4.00**

i) - **Break-Even Point (Units) :**

$$= \frac{\text{Total Fixed Cost}}{\text{Contribution per unit}}$$

$$= \frac{₹ 20,000}{₹ 4}$$

= ₹ 5,000 Units

- **Break-Even Point (Sales Value) :**

	₹
Gross Sales at Break-Even	1,00,000
(5,000 Units × ₹ 20)	
Less : Trade Discount	10,000
(10% of ₹ 1,00,000) (−)	
∴ **Net Sales at Break-Even**	**90,000**

ii) a) Net Profit, if Sales are 10% above break-even volume :
Revised Sales are 10% above Break-Even Volume i.e.

= 5,000 units + (10% of above i.e.) 500 units
= 5,500 units

- Calculation of Net Profit :
where,

Contribution = Fixed Cost + Profit

∴ Profit = Contribution − Fixed Cost
= (5,500 units × ₹ 4) − ₹ 20,000
= ₹ 22,000 − ₹ 20,000
= ₹ 2,000

b) Net Profit, if Sales are 15% above break-even volume :
Revised Sales are 15% above Break-Even Volume i.e.

$$= 5,000 \text{ units} + (15\% \text{ above i.e.}) \ 750 \text{ units}$$
$$= 5,750 \text{ units}$$

• Calculation of Net Profit :
where,

$$\text{Contribution} = \text{Fixed Cost} + \text{Profit}$$

∴ $\text{Profit} = \text{Contribution} - \text{Fixed Cost}$
$$= (5,750 \text{ units} \times ₹ 4) - ₹ 20,000$$
$$= ₹ 23,000 - ₹ 20,000$$
$$= ₹ 3,000$$

ILLUSTRATION 7

Bokaro India Ltd., Badalpur provides the following cost data relating to one unit of output.

Productive Materials	₹ 50
Variable Works Overheads : 75% of Prime Cost Labour	
Direct Labour	₹ 80
Yearly Fixed Establishment Overheads	₹ 2,40,000
Market Price	₹ 230

You are required to calculate,

i)   the number of units to be produced and sold in a year to break-even.

ii)   the number of units to be manufactured and sold in a year to make a profit of ₹ 80,000.

iii) the number of units to be produced and sold to break-even if the selling price is reduced by ₹ 16 each.

SOLUTION

• Calculation of Contribution per unit :
where,

	Unit Cost ₹
Market Price	230
Less : Variable Cost	
i) Productive Materials	50
ii) Direct Labour	80
iii) Variable Works Overheads	60
(75% of Prime Cost labour i.e. ₹ 80)	(+)____
	(−) 190
∴ **Contribution**	**40**

i) Number of units to be produced and sold in a year to break-even :

where, Break-Even Points (units) =

$$= \frac{\text{Fixed Cost}}{\text{Contribution per unit}}$$

$$= \frac{₹\,2,40,000}{₹\,40}$$

= 6,000 units.

ii) Number of units to be manufactured and sold in a year to make a profit of ₹ 80,000 :

$$= \frac{\text{Fixed Cost + Desired Profit}}{\text{Contribution per unit}}$$

$$= \frac{₹\,2,40,000 + ₹\,80,000}{₹\,40}$$

$$= \frac{₹\,3,20,000}{₹\,40}$$

= 8,000 units.

iii) Number of units to be produced and sold to break-even if the selling price is reduced by ₹ 16 each :

• Calculation of Revised Selling Price :

$$\underset{₹\,230}{\text{Old Selling Price}} - \underset{₹\,16}{\text{Reduction by}} = \underset{₹\,214}{\text{Revised Selling Price}}$$

• Calculation of Revised Contribution per unit :

where,

	Unit Cost ₹
Market Price	214
Less : Variable Cost	(–) 190
∴ Contribution	24

Break Even Point (units) :

$$= \frac{\text{Fixed Cost}}{\text{Contribution per unit}}$$

$$= \frac{₹\,2,40,000}{₹\,24}$$

= 10,000 units

ILLUSTRATION 8

The Burma-Shell Ltd., Bandra has submitted the following data :	₹
Selling price per unit	20
Variable cost per unit	16
Total Fixed Cost	20,000

Calculate BEP (units). Also calculate the effect on BEP (units) if

i)   Selling price is increased by ₹ 1
ii) Selling price is decreased by ₹ 1
iii) Variable cost is increased by ₹ 1
iv) Variable cost is decreased by ₹ 1
v)   Fixed cost is increased by ₹ 5,000
vi) Fixed cost is decreased by ₹ 5,000

SOLUTION

BEP (units) :

$$= \frac{\text{Fixed Cost}}{\text{Contribution per unit}}$$

But,

Contribution per unit = Selling Price per unit – Variable Cost per unit

∴ $$\text{BEP (units)} = \frac{\text{Fixed Cost}}{\text{Selling price per unit} - \text{Variable cost per unit}}$$

$$= \frac{₹\,20,000}{₹\,20 - ₹\,16} = \frac{₹\,20,000}{₹\,4}$$

$$= 5,000 \text{ units}$$

Calculation of effect on BEP (units) if,

i) Selling Price is increased by ₹ 1 :

Original Selling Price per unit + Increase by ₹ 1 = New Selling Price per unit

₹ 20 + ₹ 1   = ₹ 21

$$\text{BEP (units)} = \frac{\text{Fixed Cost}}{\text{Selling Price per unit} - \text{Variable Cost per unit}}$$

$$= \frac{₹\,20,000}{₹\,21 - ₹\,16} = \frac{₹\,20,000}{₹\,5}$$

$$= 4,000 \text{ units}$$

ii) Selling Price is decreased by ₹ 1 :

Original Selling Price per unit – Decrease by ₹ 1 = New Selling Price per unit

₹ 20 – ₹ 1   = ₹ 19

$$\text{BEP (units)} = \frac{\text{Fixed Cost}}{\text{Selling Price per unit} - \text{Variable Cost per unit}}$$

$$= \frac{₹\,20,000}{₹\,19 - ₹\,16}$$

$$= \frac{₹\,20,000}{₹\,3}$$

$$= 6,667 \text{ units}$$

iii) Variable Cost is increased by ₹ 1 :

Original Variable Cost per unit + Increase by ₹ 1 = New Variable Cost per unit

₹ 16 + ₹ 1   = ₹ 17

$$\text{BEP (units)} = \frac{\text{Fixed Cost}}{\text{Selling Price per unit} - \text{Variable Cost per unit}}$$

$$= \frac{₹\,20,000}{₹\,20 - ₹\,17}$$

$$= \frac{₹\,20,000}{₹\,3}$$

$$= 6,667 \text{ units}$$

iv) Variable Cost is decreased by ₹ 1 :

Original Variable Cost per unit – Decrease by ₹ 1 = New Variable Cost per unit

₹ 16 – ₹ 1   = ₹ 15

$$\text{BEP (units)} = \frac{\text{Fixed Cost}}{\text{Selling Price per unit} - \text{Variable Cost per unit}}$$

$$= \frac{₹\,20,000}{₹\,20 - ₹\,15}$$

$$= \frac{₹\,20,000}{₹\,5}$$

$$= 4,000 \text{ units}$$

v) Fixed Cost is increased by ₹ 5,000 :

Original Fixed Cost + Increase by = New Fixed Cost

₹ 20,000   ₹ 5,000   ₹ 25,000

$$\text{BEP (units)} = \frac{\text{Fixed Cost}}{\text{Selling Price per unit} - \text{Variable Cost per unit}}$$

$$= \frac{₹\,25,000}{₹\,20 - ₹\,16}$$

$$= \frac{₹\,25,000}{₹\,4}$$

$$= 6,250 \text{ units}$$

vi) Fixed Cost is decreased by ₹ 5,000 :

Original Fixed Cost – Decrease by = New Fixed Cost

₹ 20,000   ₹ 5,000   ₹ 15,000

$$\text{BEP (units)} = \frac{\text{Fixed Cost}}{\text{Selling Price per unit} - \text{Variable Cost per unit}}$$

$$= \frac{₹\,15,000}{₹\,20 - ₹\,16}$$

$$= \frac{₹\,15,000}{₹\,4}$$

$$= 3,750 \text{ units}$$

ILLUSTRATION 9

Birla Ltd., Baroda has prepared the following budget estimated for the year 2012-13.

Sales	Units 15,000
Fixed Cost	₹ 34,000
Sales Value	₹ 1,50,000
Variable Cost per unit	₹ 6

You are required to calculate,

A)   P/V Ratio, BEP (Sales) and Margin of Safety

B)   Also calculate the effect of the following.

     i)   decrease of 10% in selling price

     ii) increase of 10% in variable cost.

SOLUTION

$$\text{Selling Price per unit} = \frac{\text{Sales value}}{\text{Sales units}}$$

$$= \frac{₹\ 1,50,000}{15,000\ \text{units}} = ₹\ 10$$

A)   1)   P/V Ratio :

$$= \frac{\text{Contribution per unit}}{\text{Selling Price per unit}} \times 100$$

But,   Contribution per unit = Selling price per unit – Variable Cost per unit

∴   P/V Ratio $= \dfrac{\text{Selling Price per unit} - \text{Variable Cost per unit}}{\text{Selling Price per unit}} \times 100$

$$= \frac{₹\ 10 - ₹\ 6}{₹\ 10} \times 100$$

$$= \frac{₹\ 4}{₹\ 10} \times 100 = 40\%$$

2)   BEP (Sales) :

$$= \frac{\text{Fixed Cost}}{\text{P/V Ratio}}$$

$$= \frac{₹\ 34,000}{40\%}$$

$$= ₹\ 34,000 \times \frac{100}{40} = ₹\ 85,000$$

3)   Margin of Safety :

= Actual Sales – Break-Even Sales

$$= \begin{array}{l} ₹\ 1,50,000 - ₹\ 85,000 \\ (15,000\ \text{units} ₹\ 10) \end{array}$$

= ₹ 65,000

B) i) Decrease of 10% in Selling Price :

Original Selling Price per unit – Decrease of 10% = New Selling Price per unit

$$₹ 10 - ₹ 1 \qquad\qquad = ₹ 9$$

1) P/V Ratio :

$$= \frac{\text{Contribution per unit}}{\text{Selling Price per unit}} \times 100$$

But, Contribution per unit = Selling Price per unit – Variable Cost per unit

∴ P/V Ratio $= \dfrac{\text{Selling Price per unit – Variable Cost per unit}}{\text{Selling Price per unit}} \times 100$

$$= \frac{₹ 9 - ₹ 6}{₹ 9} \times 100$$

$$= \frac{₹ 3}{₹ 9} \times 100 = 33\tfrac{1}{3}\%$$

2) BEP (Sales) :

$$= \frac{\text{Fixed Cost}}{\text{P/V Ratio}}$$

$$= \frac{₹ 34,000}{33\tfrac{1}{3}\%}$$

$$= \frac{₹ 34,000}{1/3}$$

$$= ₹ 34,000 \times \frac{3}{1}$$

$$= ₹ 1,02,000$$

3) Margin of Safety :

$$= \text{Actual Sales – Break-Even Sales}$$

$$= \frac{₹ 1,35,000 \qquad - \quad ₹ 1,02,000}{(15,000 \text{ units} \times ₹ 9)}$$

$$= ₹ 33,000$$

B) ii) Increase of 10% in Variable Cost :

Original Variable Cost per unit + Increase of 10% = New Variable Cost per unit

$$₹ 6 + ₹ 0.60 \qquad = ₹ 6.60$$

1) P/V Ratio :

$$= \frac{\text{Contribution per unit}}{\text{Selling Price per unit}} \times 100$$

But, Contribution per unit = Selling Price per unit – Variable Cost per unit

∴ P/V Ratio $= \dfrac{\text{Selling Price per unit – Variable Cost per unit}}{\text{Selling Price per unit}} \times 100$

$$= \frac{₹ 10 - ₹ 6.60}{₹ 10} \times 100$$

$$= \frac{₹ 3.40}{₹ 10} \times 100 = 34\%$$

2) BEP (Sales) :

$$= \frac{\text{Fixed Cost}}{\text{P/V Ratio}}$$

$$= \frac{₹\,34,000}{34\%}$$

$$= ₹\,34,000 \times \frac{100}{34}$$

$$= ₹\,1,00,000$$

3) Margin of Safety :

$$= \text{Actual Sales} - \text{Break-Even Sales}$$

$$= ₹\,1,50,000 - ₹\,1,00,000$$

$$= ₹\,50,000$$

ILLUSTRATION 10

Activa Engineering Co. Ltd., Ahmednagar provides you with the following cost details :

Non-variable Cost	₹ 2,000
Variable Cost of Sales	60%
Total Turnover	₹ 10,000
Net Margin	₹ 2,000

Calculate the following :

i) Break-Even Sales

ii) Sales Volume to earn a profit of ₹ 6,000 and

iii) Margin of Safety when Sales are ₹ 25,000.

SOLUTION

As Variable Cost of Sales are 60%, the P/V Ratio will be (i.e. 100% – 60%) 40%.

i) Break-Even Sales :

$$= \frac{\text{Fixed Cost (i.e. Non-variable Cost)}}{\text{P/V Ratio}}$$

$$= \frac{₹\,2,000}{40\%}$$

$$= ₹\,2,000 \times \frac{100}{40}$$

$$= ₹\,5,000$$

ii) Sales Volume to earn a profit of ₹ 6,000 :

where, $\text{P/V Ratio} = \dfrac{\text{Contribution}}{\text{Sales}}$

But, $\text{Contribution} = \text{Fixed Cost} + \text{Profit}$

∴ $\text{P/V Ratio} = \dfrac{\text{Fixed Cost} + \text{Profit}}{\boxed{\text{Sales}}}$

$$\therefore \quad \text{Sales} = \frac{\text{Fixed Cost} + \text{Profit}}{\text{P/V Ratio}}$$

$$= \frac{₹\,2,000 + ₹\,6,000}{40\%}$$

$$= ₹\,8,000 \times \frac{100}{40}$$

$$= ₹\,20,000$$

iii) **Margin of Safety when Sales are ₹ 25,000 :**

where,

Margin of Safety = Actual Sales – Break-Even Sales

= ₹ 25,000 – ₹ 5,000 = ₹ 20,000

ILLUSTRATION 11

Bajaj Auto Ltd., Bilaspur has submitted the following cost data.

	₹
Invoice Price per unit	40
Fixed Production Overheads	1,50,000
Variable Manufacturing Cost per unit	5
Selling on Cost – Fixed	20,000
Prime Cost Materials per unit (Variable Cost)	18
Fixed - Distribution Expenses	10,000
Variable Selling Overheads per unit	2

Calculate :

i) BEP (Sales)

ii) Number of units to be sold to earn a profit of ₹ 1,20,000.

iii) Number of units to be sold to earn an income of 25% of Sales.

SOLUTION

Calculation of Total Fixed Cost : ₹

Fixed Production Overheads	1,50,000
Add : Selling on Cost – Fixed	20,000
Add : Fixed Distribution Expenses	(+) 10,000
$\therefore$ **Total Fixed Cost**	**1,80,000**

Calculation of Total Variable Cost per unit ₹

Variable Manufacturing cost per unit	5
Add : Prime Cost materials per unit	18
Add : Variable Selling Overheads per unit	(+) 2
$\therefore$ **Variable Cost per unit**	**25**

Calculation of P/V Ratio :

$$= \frac{\text{Contribution per unit}}{\text{Selling Price per unit}} \times 100$$

But,   Contribution per unit = Selling Price per unit – Variable Cost per unit

$\therefore$ P/V Ratio $= \dfrac{\text{Selling Price per unit – Variable Cost per unit}}{\text{Selling Price per unit}} \times 100$

$$= \frac{₹\,40 - ₹\,25}{₹\,40} \times 100$$

$$= \frac{₹\,15}{₹\,40} \times 100$$

$$= 37.50\%$$

i)   BEP (Sales) :

$$= \frac{\text{Fixed Cost}}{\text{Contribution per unit}} \times \text{ Selling Price per unit}$$

But,   Contribution per unit = Selling Price per unit – Variable Cost per unit

$\therefore$ BEP (Sales) $= \dfrac{\text{Fixed Cost}}{\text{Selling Price per unit – Variable Cost per unit}} \times \begin{array}{c}\text{Selling}\\\text{Price}\\\text{per unit}\end{array}$

$$= \frac{₹\,1,80,000}{₹\,40 - ₹\,25} \times 40$$

$$= \frac{₹\,1,80,000}{₹\,15} \times ₹\,40$$

$$= ₹\,12,000 \text{ units} \times ₹\,40$$

$$= ₹\,4,80,000$$

ii)   Number of units to be sold to earn a profit of ₹ 1,20,000 :

where,   P/V Ratio $= \dfrac{\text{Contribution}}{\boxed{\text{Sales}}}$

But,   Contribution = Fixed Cost + Profit

$\therefore$ P/V Ratio $= \dfrac{\text{Fixed Cost + Profit}}{\boxed{\text{Sales}}}$

$\therefore$ Sales $= \dfrac{\text{Fixed Cost + Profit}}{37.5\%}$

$$= \frac{₹\,1,80,000 + ₹\,1,20,000}{37.5\%}$$

$$= ₹\,3,00,000 \times \frac{100}{37.5}$$

$$= ₹\,8,00,000$$

But,

$$\text{Number of units to be sold} = \frac{\text{Total Sales}}{\text{Selling Price per unit}}$$

$$= \frac{₹\,8,00,000}{₹\,40}$$

$$= 20,000 \text{ units}$$

iii) Number of units to be sold to earn an income of 25% on Sales :

Let x be the number of units to be sold.

$$\therefore \qquad x = \frac{\text{Fixed Cost + Required Profit}}{\text{Contribution per unit}}$$

But, Contribution per unit = Selling Price per unit – Variable Cost per unit

$$\therefore \qquad x = \frac{\text{Fixed Cost + Required Profit}}{\text{Selling Price per unit – Variable Cost per unit}}$$

$$\therefore \qquad x = \frac{₹\,1,80,000 + 25\%\,(x \times 40)}{₹\,40 - Rs.\,25}$$

$$x = \frac{₹\,1,80,000 + 10x}{₹\,15}$$

$$\therefore \qquad 15x = ₹\,1,80,000 + 10x$$

$$\therefore \qquad 15x - 10x = ₹\,1,80,000$$

$$\therefore \qquad 5x = ₹\,1,80,000$$

$$\therefore \qquad x = \frac{₹\,1,80,000}{₹\,5}$$

$$= 36,000 \text{ units}$$

∴ Number of units to be sold to earn an income of 25% of Sales = 36,000 units.

ILLUSTRATION 12

The following information is obtained from Godrej Ltd., Gulbarga for the year ended 31st March, 2013.

	₹
Sales (1,00,000 Units)	1,00,000
Marginal Cost	60,000
Fixed Cost	30,000

Calculate :

i) P/V Ratio,

ii) BEP (Sales-value)

iii) Sales to earn a profit of ₹ 15,000

iv) Profit when sales amounted to ₹ 1,40,000

SOLUTION

i) **P/V Ratio :**

$$= \frac{\text{Contribution}}{\text{Sales}} \times 100$$

But,

$$\text{Contribution} = \text{Sales} - \text{Variable Cost}$$

$$\therefore \quad \text{P/V Ratio} = \frac{\text{Sales} - \text{Variable Cost}}{\text{Sales}} \times 100$$

$$= \frac{₹\,1,00,000 - ₹\,60,000}{₹\,1,00,000} \times 100$$

$$= \frac{₹\,40,000}{₹\,1,00,000} \times 100$$

$$= 40\%$$

ii) **BEP (Sales-value) :**

$$= \frac{\text{Fixed Cost}}{\text{P/V Ratio}}$$

$$= \frac{₹\,30,000}{40\%}$$

$$= ₹\,30,000 \times \frac{100}{40}$$

$$= ₹\,75,000$$

iii) **Sales to earn a profit of ₹ 15,000 :**

where,

$$\text{P/V Ratio} = \frac{\text{Contribution}}{\boxed{\text{Sales}}}$$

But, $\quad \text{Contribution} = \text{Fixed Cost} + \text{Profit}$

$$\therefore \quad \text{P/V Ratio} = \frac{\text{Fixed Cost} + \text{Profit}}{\boxed{\text{Sales}}}$$

$$\therefore \quad \text{Sales} = \frac{\text{Fixed Cost} + \text{Profit}}{\text{P/V Ratio}}$$

$$= \frac{₹\,30,000 + ₹\,15,000}{40\%}$$

$$= ₹\,45,000 \times \frac{100}{40}$$

$$= ₹\,1,12,500$$

iv) Profit when Sales amounted to ₹ 1,40,000 :

where,

$$\text{P/V Ratio} = \frac{\text{Contribution}}{\text{Sales}}$$

But, Contribution = Fixed Cost + Profit

$$\therefore \quad \text{P/V Ratio} = \frac{\text{Fixed Cost} + \boxed{\text{Profit}}}{\text{Sales}}$$

$$\therefore \quad \text{P/V Ratio} \times \text{Sales} = \text{Fixed Cost} + \boxed{\text{Profit}}$$

$$\therefore \quad \text{Profit} = (\text{P/V Ratio} \times \text{Sales}) - \text{Fixed Cost}$$

$$= (40\% \times ₹ 1,40,000) - ₹ 30,000$$

$$= ₹ 56,000 - ₹ 30,000$$

$$= ₹ 26,000$$

ILLUSTRATION 13

From the following cost data relating to Force India Ltd., Faizpur for the year 2012-13 you are required to calculate,

i)   Sales at Break-Even,

ii) Profit at budgeted sales,

iii) Profit, if actual sales be at 80% capacity.

Budgeted Sales for the year 2012-13	₹ 12,00,000
(At 100% Capacity)	
Rigid cost in total	₹ 1,00,000
Chargeable Expenses	2% of Sales
Variable Manufacturing Overheads	10% of Sales
Administrative and Selling Cost – Variable	8% of Sales
Direct Materials	35% of Sales
Prime Cost Labour	20% of Sales

SOLUTION

In the books of Force India Ltd., Faizpur
Profitability Statement for the year 2012-13 (Normal Capacity – 100%)

Particulars		₹
	Budgeted Sales	12,00,000
Less : Variable Cost :		
• Chargeable Expenses 24,000		
(02% of Sales i.e. 2% of ₹ 12,00,000)		
• Variable Manufacturing Overheads 1,20,000		
(10% of Sales i.e. 10% of ₹ 12,00,000)		
• Administrative and Selling on Cost – Variable 96,000		
(08% of Sales i.e. 8% of ₹ 12,00,000)		
• Direct Materials 4,20,000		
(35% of Sales i.e. 35% of ₹ 12,00,000)		
• Prime Cost Labour 2,40,000		
(20% of Sales i.e. 20% of ₹ 12,00,000) (+)_____		
(−)		9,00,000
∴ Contribution		3,00,000
Less : Fixed Cost		
i) Rigid Cost (−)		1,00,000
∴ Profit at Budgeted Sales		**2,00,000**

Calculation of P/V Ratio :
    where,

$$\text{P/V Ratio} = \frac{\text{Contribution}}{\text{Sales}} \times 100$$

$$= \frac{₹\,3,00,000}{₹\,12,00,000} \times 100$$

$$= 25\%$$

i) Sales at Break-Even :
    where,

$$\text{Break-Even Point (Sales)} = \frac{\text{Fixed Cost}}{\text{P/V Ratio}}$$

$$= \frac{₹\,1,00,000}{25\%}$$

$$= ₹\,1,00,000 \times \frac{100}{25}$$

$$= ₹\,4,00,000$$

ii) **Profit at Budgeted Sales :**

where,

$$\text{Contribution} = \text{Fixed Cost} + \text{Profit}$$

∴ $$\text{Profit} = \text{Contribution} - \text{Fixed Cost}$$

$$= ₹\, 3,00,000 - ₹\, 1,00,000$$

$$= ₹\, 2,00,000$$

iii) **Profit, if actual sales be at 80% capacity :**

- Calculation of actual sales at 80% capacity

If 100% Capacity = ₹ 12,00,000 Actual Sales

∴ 80% Capacity = ?

$$= \frac{80 \times ₹\, 12,00,000}{100}$$

$$= ₹\, 9,60,000$$

- Calculation of profit if actual sales are ₹ 9,60,000

where,

$$\text{P/V Ratio} = \frac{\text{Contribution}}{\text{Sales}}$$

But,

$$\text{Contribution} = \text{Fixed Cost} + \text{Profit}$$

∴ $$\text{P/V Ratio} = \frac{\text{Fixed Cost} + \boxed{\text{Profit}}}{\text{Sales}}$$

∴ $$\text{P/V Ratio} \times \text{Sales} = \text{Fixed Cost} + \boxed{\text{Profit}}$$

∴ $$\text{Profit} = (\text{P/V Ratio} \times \text{Sales}) - \text{Fixed Cost}$$

$$= (25\% \times ₹\, 9,60,000) - ₹\, 1,00,000$$

$$= ₹\, 2,40,000 - ₹\, 1,00,000$$

$$= ₹\, 1,40,000$$

ILLUSTRATION 14

From the following data calculate,

i) Total Profits, ii) BEP (Sales) and iii) Margin of Safety

Number of units sold	Units – 20,000
Fixed Overheads	₹ 50,000
Selling Price per unit	₹ 10
Variable Overheads per unit	₹ 6

SOLUTION

i)   Total Profits :

$$
\begin{aligned}
\text{Sales} &= \text{Total Cost} + \text{Profit} \\
\text{But,} \quad \text{Total Cost} &= \text{Fixed Overheads} + \text{Variable Cost} \\
\therefore \quad \text{Sales} &= \text{Fixed Overheads} + \text{Variable Cost} + \text{Profit} \\
\therefore \quad \text{Profits} &= \text{Sales} - (\text{Fixed Overheads} + \text{Variable Cost}) \\
&= (20{,}000 \text{ units} \times ₹\ 10) - (₹\ 50{,}000) + (20{,}000 \text{ units} \times ₹\ 6) \\
&= ₹\ 2{,}00{,}000 - ₹\ 50{,}000 + ₹\ 1{,}20{,}000 \\
&= ₹\ 2{,}00{,}000 - ₹\ 1{,}70{,}000 \\
&= ₹\ 30{,}000
\end{aligned}
$$

ii)   BEP (Sales) :

$$
= \frac{\text{Fixed Cost}}{\text{Contribution per unit}} \times \text{Selling Price per unit}
$$

But,

$$
\text{Contribution per unit} = \text{Selling Price per unit} - \text{Variable Cost per unit}
$$

$$
\begin{aligned}
\therefore \quad \text{BEP (Sales)} &= \frac{\text{Fixed Cost}}{\text{Selling Price per unit} - \text{Variable Cost per unit}} \times \text{Selling Price per unit} \\[2mm]
&= \frac{₹\ 50{,}000}{₹\ 10 - ₹\ 6} \times ₹\ 10 \\[2mm]
&= \frac{₹\ 50{,}000}{₹\ 4} \times ₹\ 10 \\[2mm]
&= ₹\ 12{,}500 \times ₹\ 10 \\
&= ₹\ 1{,}25{,}000
\end{aligned}
$$

iii) Margin of Safety :

$$
\begin{aligned}
&= \text{Actual Sales} - \text{Break-Even Sales} \\
&= (20{,}000 \text{ units} \times ₹\ 10) - ₹\ 1{,}25{,}000 \\
&= ₹\ 2{,}00{,}000 - ₹\ 1{,}25{,}000 \\
&= ₹\ 75{,}000
\end{aligned}
$$

ILLUSTRATION 15

You are given with the following cost data :

Total Sales	₹ 4,00,000
Total Variable Cost	₹ 2,00,000
Total Fixed Cost	₹ 1,00,000
Total Units sold	Units 1,00,000

Calculate,

i)   Contribution per unit
ii)   BEP - units and sales
iii) Margin of Safety
iv)   Profit
v)   Units to be sold to earn a profit of ₹ 1,40,000.

SOLUTION

i) **Contribution per unit :**

where,

$$\text{Contribution} = \text{Sales} - \text{Variable Cost}$$
$$= ₹\,4,00,000 - ₹\,2,00,000$$
$$= ₹\,2,00,000$$

But,

Contribution per unit :

$$= \frac{\text{Total Contribution}}{\text{Total units sold}}$$

$$= \frac{₹\,2,00,000}{1,00,000 \text{ units}}$$

$$= ₹\,2 \text{ per unit}$$

ii) **BEP (units) :**

$$= \frac{\text{Total Fixed Cost}}{\text{Contribution per unit}}$$

$$= \frac{₹\,1,00,000}{₹\,2}$$

$$= 50,000 \text{ units}$$

Calculation of Selling price per unit :

$$\frac{\text{Total Sales}}{\text{Total units sold}} = \frac{₹\,4,00,000}{1,00,000 \text{ units}}$$

$$= ₹\,4 \text{ per unit}$$

BEP (Sales) :

$$= \frac{\text{Total Fixed Cost}}{\text{Contribution per unit}} \times \text{Selling Price per unit}$$

$$= \frac{₹\,1,00,000}{₹\,2} \times ₹\,4$$

$$= 50,000 \text{ units} \times ₹\,4$$

$$= ₹\,2,00,000.$$

iii) Margin of Safety :

$$= \text{Actual Sales} - \text{Break-Even Sales}$$
$$= ₹\,4,00,000 - ₹\,2,00,000$$
$$= ₹\,2,00,000$$

iv) **Profit :**

where,

$$\text{Contribution} = \text{Fixed Cost} + \text{Profit}$$

$$\therefore \qquad \text{Profit} = \text{Contribution} - \text{Fixed Cost}$$

$$= ₹\,2,00,000 - ₹\,1,00,000$$

$$= ₹\,1,00,000$$

v) **Units to be sold to earn a profit of ₹ 1,40,000 :**

Sales volume to earn required profit (units) :

$$= \frac{\text{Total Fixed Cost} + \text{Required Profit}}{\text{Contribution per unit}}$$

$$= \frac{₹\,1,00,000 + ₹\,1,40,000}{₹\,2}$$

$$= \frac{₹\,2,40,000}{₹\,2}$$

$$= 1,20,000 \text{ units}$$

ILLUSTRATION 16

Kiddy Toy's Co. Kalyan provides the following costing data :

		% of Sales	₹
•	Marginal Cost	80%	8,00,000
•	Fixed Cost	10%	1,00,000
•	Profit	10%	1,00,000
•	Sales	100%	10,00,000

You are required to calculate :

i) P/V Ratio ii) BEP (Sales) iii) Margin of Safety and iv) Margin of Safety Ratio

SOLUTION

i) **P/V Ratio :**

$$= \frac{\text{Contribution}}{\text{Sales}} \times 100$$

But, Contribution = Sales – Variable Cost

$$\therefore \qquad \text{P/V Ratio} = \frac{\text{Sales} - \text{Variable Cost}}{\text{Sales}} \times 100$$

$$= \frac{₹\,10,00,000 - ₹\,8,00,000}{₹\,10,00,000} \times 100$$

$$= \frac{₹\,2,00,000}{₹\,10,00,000} \times 100$$

$$= 20\%$$

ii) BEP (Sales) :

$$= \frac{\text{Fixed Cost}}{\text{P/V Ratio}}$$

$$= \frac{₹\,1,00,000}{20\%}$$

$$= ₹\,1,00,000 \times \frac{100}{20}$$

$$= ₹\,5,00,000$$

iii) Margin of Safety :

$$= \frac{\text{Profit}}{\text{P/V Ratio}}$$

$$= \frac{₹\,1,00,000}{20\%}$$

$$= ₹\,1,00,000 \times \frac{100}{20}$$

$$= ₹\,5,00,000$$

iv) Margin of Safety Ratio :

$$= \frac{\text{Actual Sales} - \text{Break-Even Sales}}{\text{Actual Sales}} \times 100$$

$$= \frac{₹\,10,00,000 - ₹\,5,00,000}{₹\,10,00,000} \times 100$$

$$= \frac{₹\,5,00,000}{₹\,10,00,000} \times 100$$

$$= 50\%$$

ILLUSTRATION 17

The following is the cost structure of a product Gemini for 2012-13.

Particulars		Unit Cost ₹
Direct Material		100
Add : Productive Wages		80
Add : Variable Overheads	(+)	20
∴ Total Variable Cost		200
Add : Fixed Cost	(+)	40
∴ Total Cost		240
Add : Profit	(+)	60
Sales		300

Company produced and sold 5,000 units.

You are required to calculate :

i)   P/V Ratio
ii)   BEP (Sales)
iii) Margin of Safety
iv)   Profit when Sales are ₹ 30,00,000
v)   Sales when Profits are ₹ 1,00,000

SOLUTION

i)   P/V Ratio :

$$= \frac{\text{Contribution per unit}}{\text{Selling Price per unit}} \times 100$$

But,

Contribution per unit = Selling Price per unit – Variable Cost per unit

∴   P/V Ratio $= \dfrac{\text{Selling Price per unit – Variable Cost per unit}}{\text{Selling Price per unit}} \times 100$

$$= \frac{₹\,300 - ₹\,200}{₹\,300} \times 100$$

$$= \frac{₹\,100}{₹\,300} \times 100$$

$$= 33\,^1/_3\%$$

ii)   BEP (Sales) :

$$= \frac{\text{Total Fixed Cost}}{\text{P/V Ratio}}$$

$$= \frac{₹\,40 \times 5,000\ \text{units}}{33\,^1/_3\%}$$

$$= \frac{₹\,2,00,000}{1/3}$$

$$= ₹\,2,00,000 \times \frac{3}{1}$$

$$= ₹\,6,00,000$$

iii) Margin of Safety :

= Actual Sales – Break-Even Sales

= (₹ 300 × 5,000 units) – ₹ 6,00,000

= ₹ 15,00,000 – ₹ 6,00,000

= ₹ 9,00,000

iv) **Profit when Sales are ₹ 3,00,000 :**

where,

$$\text{P/V Ratio} = \frac{\text{Contribution}}{\text{Sales}}$$

But, Contribution = Fixed Cost + Profit

$$\therefore \quad \text{P/V Ratio} = \frac{\text{Fixed Cost} + \boxed{\text{Profit}}}{\text{Sales}}$$

$$\therefore \text{P/V Ratio} \times \text{Sales} = \text{Fixed Cost} + \boxed{\text{Profit}}$$

$$\therefore \quad \text{Profit} = (\text{P/V Ratio} \times \text{Sales}) - \text{Fixed Cost}$$
$$= (33\tfrac{1}{3}\% \times ₹\,30,00,000) - (₹\,40 \times 5,000 \text{ units})$$
$$= ₹\,10,00,000 - ₹\,2,00,000$$
$$= ₹\,8,00,000$$

v) **Sales when Profit are ₹ 1,00,000 :**

where,

$$\text{P/V Ratio} = \frac{\text{Contribution}}{\boxed{\text{Sales}}}$$

But,

$$\text{Contribution} = \text{Fixed Cost} + \text{Profit}$$

$$\therefore \quad \text{P/V Ratio} = \frac{\text{Fixed Cost} + \text{Profit}}{\boxed{\text{Sales}}}$$

$$\therefore \quad \text{Sales} = \frac{\text{Fixed Cost} + \text{Profit}}{\text{P/V Ratio}}$$
$$= \frac{(₹\,40 \times 5,000 \text{ units}) + ₹\,1,00,000}{33\tfrac{1}{3}\%}$$
$$= \frac{₹\,2,00,000 + ₹\,1,00,000}{1/3}$$
$$= ₹\,3,00,000 \times \frac{3}{1}$$
$$= ₹\,9,00,000$$

ILLUSTRATION 18

Bajaj Industries, Bandra provides the following cost data :

	₹
Sales	1,50,000
Marginal Cost	1,20,000
Gross Profit	60,000
Fixed Overheads	20,000
Net Profit	40,000

You are required to calculate :

i)   P/V Ratio,

ii)   BEP (Sales),

iii)   Margin of Safety when Sales are ₹ 4,00,000,

iv)   Net Profit when Sales are ₹ 4,00,000 and

v)   Sales required to earn a profit of ₹ 80,000.

SOLUTION

i)   **P/ V Ratio :**

$$= \frac{\text{Contribution}}{\text{Sales}} \times 100$$

But,   Contribution = Sales – Variable Cost

$\therefore$ P/V Ratio $= \dfrac{\text{Sales – Variable Cost}}{\text{Sales}} \times 100$

$$= \frac{₹\,1,50,000 - ₹\,1,20,000}{₹\,1,50,000} \times 100$$

$$= \frac{₹\,30,000}{₹\,1,50,000} \times 100$$

$$= 20\%$$

ii)   **BEP (Sales) :**

$$= \frac{\text{Fixed Cost}}{\text{P/V Ratio}}$$

$$= \frac{₹\,20,000}{20\%}$$

$$= ₹\,20,000 \times \frac{100}{20}$$

$$= ₹\,1,00,000$$

iii)   **Margin of Safety when Sales are ₹ 4,00,000 :**

Margin of Safety = Actual Sales – Break-Even Sales

$$= ₹\,4,00,000 - ₹\,1,00,000$$

$$= ₹\,3,00,000$$

iv)   **Net Profit when Sales are ₹ 4,00,000 :**

where,

$$\text{P/V Ratio} = \frac{\text{Contribution}}{\text{Sales}}$$

But,

     Contribution = Fixed Cost + Profit

$\therefore$ P/V Ratio $= \dfrac{\text{Fixed Cost} + \boxed{\text{Profit}}}{\text{Sales}}$

$\therefore$ P/V Ratio $\times$ Sales = Fixed Cost + $\boxed{\text{Profit}}$

$$\therefore \quad \text{Profit} = (\text{P/V Ratio} \times \text{Sales}) - \text{Fixed Cost}$$

$$= (20\% \times ₹\,4,00,000) - ₹\,20,000$$

$$= ₹\,80,000 - ₹\,20,000$$

$$= ₹\,60,000$$

v) Sales required to earn a Profit of ₹ 80,000 :

$$\text{where,} \quad \text{P/V Ratio} = \frac{\text{Contribution}}{\boxed{\text{Sales}}}$$

$$\text{But,} \quad \text{Contribution} = \text{Fixed Cost} + \text{Profit}$$

$$\therefore \quad \text{P/V Ratio} = \frac{\text{Fixed Cost} + \text{Profit}}{\boxed{\text{Sales}}}$$

$$\therefore \quad \text{Sales} = \frac{\text{Fixed Cost} + \text{Profit}}{\text{P/V Ratio}}$$

$$= \frac{₹\,20,000 + ₹\,80,000}{20\%}$$

$$= ₹\,1,00,000 \times \frac{100}{20}$$

$$= ₹\,5,00,000$$

ILLUSTRATION 19

Calculate,

i)   P/V Ratio, if a company has fixed expenses of ₹ 90,000 with Sales at ₹ 3,00,000 and a profit of ₹ 60,000.

ii)   BEP (Sales), if budgeted output is 80,000 units, fixed cost is ₹ 4,00,000, Selling price per unit is ₹ 20 and Variable cost per unit is ₹ 10.

iii)   Sales, if Marginal Cost is ₹ 2,400 and P/V Ratio is 20%.

iv)   Margin of Safety if profit is ₹ 20,000 and P/V Ratio is 40%.

SOLUTION

i)   P/V Ratio :

$$= \frac{\text{Contribution}}{\text{Sales}} \times 100$$

$$\text{But,} \quad \text{Contribution} = \text{Fixed Cost} + \text{Profit}$$

$$\therefore \quad \text{P/V Ratio} = \frac{\text{Fixed Cost} + \text{Profit}}{\text{Sales}} \times 100$$

$$= \frac{₹\,90,000 + Rs.\,60,000}{₹\,3,00,000} \times 100$$

$$= \frac{₹\,1,50,000}{₹\,3,00,000} \times 100$$

$$= 50\%$$

ii) BEP (Sales) :

$$= \frac{\text{Fixed Cost}}{\text{Contribution per unit}} \times \text{Selling Price per unit}$$

But,

Contribution per unit = Selling Price per unit – Variable Cost per unit

$\therefore$ BEP (Sales) $= \dfrac{\text{Fixed Cost}}{\text{Selling Price per unit} - \text{Variable Cost per unit}} \times \begin{array}{c}\text{Selling Price}\\ \text{per unit}\end{array}$

$$= \frac{₹\,4,00,000}{₹\,20 - ₹\,10} \times ₹\,20$$

$$= \frac{₹\,4,00,000}{₹\,10} \times ₹\,20$$

$$= ₹\,40,000 \text{ units} \times ₹\,20$$

$$= ₹\,8,00,000$$

iii) Sales :

$$= \frac{\text{Marginal Cost}}{\text{Marginal Cost Ratio}}$$

But,

Marginal Cost Ratio = 100 – (P/V Ratio)

$\therefore$ Sales $= \dfrac{\text{Marginal Cost}}{100 - \text{P/V Ratio}}$

$$= \frac{₹\,2,400}{100\% - 20\%} = \frac{₹\,2,400}{80\%}$$

$$= ₹\,2,400 \times \frac{100}{80}$$

$$= ₹\,3,000$$

iv) Margin of Safety :

$$= \frac{\text{Profit}}{\text{P/V Ratio}}$$

$$= \frac{₹\,20,000}{40\%}$$

$$= ₹\,20,000 \times \frac{100}{40}$$

$$= ₹\,50,000$$

ILLUSTRATION 20

Mobilink Co., Malad has fixed overheads of ₹ 90,000 with a turnover of ₹ 3,00,000 and a profit of ₹ 60,000 during the first half year. If in the next half year they suffered a loss of ₹ 30,000, calculate :

a) P/V Ratio, BEP (Sales) and Margin of Safety for the first half year.

b) Expected sales volume for the next half year assuming that selling price and fixed cost remain unchanged.

c) BEP (sales) and Margin of Safety for the whole year.

SOLUTION

a) i) P/V Ratio :

$$= \frac{\text{Contribution}}{\text{Sales}} \times 100$$

But,

$$\text{Contribution} = \text{Fixed Cost} + \text{Profit}$$

$$\therefore \quad \text{P/V Ratio} = \frac{\text{Fixed Cost} + \text{Profit}}{\text{Sales}} \times 100$$

$$= \frac{₹\,90,000 + ₹\,60,000}{₹\,3,00,000}$$

$$= \frac{₹\,1,50,000}{₹\,3,00,000} \times 100$$

$$= 50\%$$

ii) BEP (Sales) :

$$= \frac{\text{Fixed Cost}}{\text{P/V Ratio}}$$

$$= \frac{₹\,90,000}{50\%}$$

$$= ₹\,90,000 \times \frac{100}{50}$$

$$= ₹\,1,80,000$$

iii) Margin of Safety :

$$= \text{Actual Sales} - \text{Break-Even Sales}$$

$$= ₹\,3,00,000 - ₹\,1,80,000$$

$$= ₹\,1,20,000$$

b) Expected sales volume for the next half year :

where,

$$\text{P/V Ratio} = \frac{\text{Contribution}}{\boxed{\text{Sales}}}$$

But,   Contribution = Fixed Cost – Loss

∴   P/V Ratio $= \dfrac{\text{Fixed Cost} - \text{Loss}}{\boxed{\text{Sales}}}$

∴   Sales $= \dfrac{\text{Fixed Cost} - \text{Loss}}{\text{P/V Ratio}}$

$$= \dfrac{₹\,90,000 - ₹\,30,000}{50\%}$$

$$= ₹\,60,000 \times \dfrac{100}{50}$$

$$= ₹\,1,20,000$$

c) **i)** **BEP (Sales)** for the whole year :

$$= \dfrac{\text{Fixed cost for the whole year}}{\text{P/V Ratio}}$$

$$= \dfrac{₹\,90,000 + ₹\,90,000}{50\%}$$

$$= ₹\,1,80,000 \times \dfrac{100}{50}$$

$$= ₹\,3,60,000$$

  ii) **Margin of Safety :**

= Actual Sales – Break-Even Sales

= (₹ 3,00,000 + ₹ 1,20,000) – ₹ 3,60,000

= ₹ 4,20,000 – ₹ 3,60,000

= ₹ 60,000

ILLUSTRATION 21

Roadstar Co. Ltd., Raipur furnished you the following information relating to half year ended 31st March, 2013.   ₹

Fixed Cost	45,000
Sales Value	1,50,000
Profit	30,000

During the second half of the year the company has projected a loss of ₹ 10,000.

Calculate :

i)   Variable Cost for the 1st half year.

ii)   P/V Ratio for the 1st half year.

iii)   BEP (Sales) for the 1st half year.

iv)   Margin of Safety for the 1st half year.

v)   Expected sales volume for the 2nd half year assuming that the P/V Ratio and Fixed Cost remains constant in the 2nd half year also.

SOLUTION

i) **Variable Cost, for the 1st half year :**

where,

$$\text{Sales} = \text{Total Cost} + \text{Profit}$$

But,

$$\text{Total Cost} = \text{Fixed Costs} + \text{Variable Cost}$$

$$\therefore \quad \text{Sales} = \text{Fixed Cost} + \text{Variable Cost} + \text{Profit}$$

$$\therefore \quad \text{Variable Cost} = \text{Sales} - (\text{Fixed Cost} + \text{Profit})$$

$$= ₹\,1,50,000 - (₹\,45,000 + ₹\,30,000)$$

$$= ₹\,1,50,000 - ₹\,75,000 = ₹\,75,000$$

ii) **P/V Ratio, for the 1st half year :**

$$\text{P/V Ratio} = \frac{\text{Contribution}}{\text{Sales}} \times 100$$

But,   Contribution = Fixed Cost + Profit

$$\therefore \quad \text{P/V Ratio} = \frac{\text{Fixed Cost} + \text{Profit}}{\text{Sales}} \times 100$$

$$= \frac{₹\,45,000 + ₹\,30,000}{₹\,1,50,000} \times 100$$

$$= \frac{₹\,75,000}{₹\,1,50,000} \times 100$$

$$= 50\%$$

iii) **BEP (Sales), for the 1st half year :**

$$\text{BEP (Sales)} = \frac{\text{Fixed Cost}}{\text{P/V Ratio}}$$

$$= \frac{₹\,45,000}{50\%}$$

$$= ₹\,45,000 \times \frac{100}{50}$$

$$= ₹\,90,000$$

iv) **Margin of Safety, for the 1st half year :**

$$\text{Margin of Safety} = \text{Actual Sales} - \text{Break-Even Sales}$$

$$= ₹\,1,50,000 - ₹\,90,000$$

$$= ₹\,60,000$$

v) **Expected sales volume for the 2nd half year assuming that the P/V Ratio and Fixed Cost remains constant in the 2nd half year also :**

where,   P/V Ratio $= \dfrac{\text{Contribution}}{\boxed{\text{Sales}}}$

But,   Contribution $=$ Fixed Cost $-$ Loss

$\therefore$ P/V Ratio $= \dfrac{\text{Fixed Cost} - \text{Loss}}{\boxed{\text{Sales}}}$

$\therefore$ Sales $= \dfrac{\text{Fixed Cost} - \text{Loss}}{\text{P/V Ratio}}$

$= \dfrac{₹\,45,000 - ₹\,10,000}{50\%}$

$= ₹\,35,000 \times \dfrac{100}{50}$

$= ₹\,70,000$

ILLUSTRATION 22

The sales and profits during the last two years of Ashoka Ltd. were as follows :

Year	Sales ₹	Profits ₹
2011-12	15,00,000	2,00,000
2012-13	17,00,000	2,50,000

Annual fixed cost is ₹ 1,75,000.

You are required to calculate,

i)   P/V Ratio

ii)   BEP (Sales)

iii)   The profits made when Sales are ₹ 25,00,000

iv)   The sales required to earn a profit of ₹ 4,00,000.

SOLUTION

i) **P/V Ratio :**

$= \dfrac{\text{Change in Profits}}{\text{Change in Sales}} \times 100$

$= \dfrac{₹\,2,50,000 - ₹\,2,00,000}{₹\,17,00,000 - ₹\,15,00,000} \times 100$

$= \dfrac{₹\,50,000}{₹\,2,00,000} \times 100$

$= 25\%$

ii) BEP (Sales) :

$$= \frac{\text{Fixed Cost}}{\text{P/V Ratio}}$$

$$= \frac{₹\,1,75,000}{25\%}$$

$$= ₹\,1,75,000 \times \frac{100}{25}$$

$$= ₹\,7,00,000$$

iii) The profits made when sales are ₹ 25,00,000

where,   P/V Ratio $= \dfrac{\text{Contribution}}{\text{Sales}}$

But,   Contribution = Fixed Cost + Profit

$\therefore$ P/V Ratio $= \dfrac{\text{Fixed Cost} + \boxed{\text{Profit}}}{\text{Sales}}$

$\therefore$ P/V Ratio $\times$ Sales = Fixed Cost + $\boxed{\text{Profit}}$

$\therefore$ Profit = (P/V Ratio $\times$ Sales) – Fixed Cost

$$= (25\% \times ₹\,25,00,000) - ₹\,1,75,000$$

$$= ₹\,6,25,000 - ₹\,1,75,000$$

$$= ₹\,4,50,000$$

iv) The sales required to earn a profit of ₹ 4,00,000 :

where,   P/V Ratio $= \dfrac{\text{Contribution}}{\boxed{\text{Sales}}}$

But,

Contribution = Fixed Cost + Profit

$\therefore$ P/V Ratio $= \dfrac{\text{Fixed Cost} + \text{Profit}}{\boxed{\text{Sales}}}$

$\therefore$ Sales $= \dfrac{\text{Fixed Cost} + \text{Profit}}{\text{P/V Ratio}}$

$$= \frac{₹\,1,75,000 + ₹\,4,00,000}{25\%}$$

$$= ₹\,5,75,000 \times \frac{100}{25}$$

$$= ₹\,23,00,000$$

ILLUSTRATION 23

From the following comparative cost data of Joel India Ltd., Jabalpur for 2012 and 2013 you are required to find out : i) P/V Ratio, ii) Break-Even Point, Sales Value and iii) Margin of Safety, separately.

Particulars	2012 ₹	2013 ₹
Rigid Expenses	4,000	4,000
Direct Materials	22,000	30,000
Cash Sales	10,000	15,000
Productive Wages	10,000	12,000
Credit Sales	50,000	75,000
Prime Cost Expenses	4,000	3,000
Indirect Costs – Fixed	11,000	14,000

SOLUTION

In the books of Joel India Ltd., Jabalpur

Profitability Statement for the period ended ……

Particulars		2012 ₹	2013 ₹
Sales : Cash + Credit		60,000	90,000
2012 : ₹ 10,000 + ₹ 50,000			
2013 : ₹ 15,000 + ₹ 75,000			
Less : Variable Cost			
• Direct Materials		22,000	30,000
• Productive Wages		10,000	12,000
• Prime Cost Expenses	(–)	4,000	3,000
∴ Contribution		24,000	45,000
Less : Fixed Cost			
• Rigid Expenses		4,000	4,000
• Indirect Costs – Fixed	(–)	11,000	14,000
∴ Net Profit		**9,000**	**27,000**

i) **Profit Volume Ratio :**

$$= \frac{\text{Contribution}}{\text{Sales}} \times 100$$

$$2012 \ = \frac{₹\,24,000}{₹\,60,000} \times 100$$

$$= 40\%$$

$$2013 \ = \frac{₹\,45,000}{₹\,90,000} \times 100$$

$$= 50\%$$

ii) **Break-Even Point, Sales Value :**

$$= \frac{\text{Fixed Cost}}{\text{P/V Ratio}}$$

$$2012 = \frac{₹ 15,000}{40\%}$$

$$= ₹ 37,500$$

$$2013 = \frac{₹ 18,000}{50\%}$$

$$= ₹ 36,000$$

(iii)   **Margin of Safety :**

$$= \frac{\text{Profit}}{\text{P/V Ratio}}$$

$$2012 = \frac{₹ 9,000}{40\%}$$

$$= ₹ 22,500$$

$$2013 = \frac{₹ 27,000}{50\%}$$

$$= ₹ 54,000$$

ILLUSTRATION 24

The sales (units) and profit or loss during the last two periods were as follows :

Period	Sales Units	Profit/Loss ₹
I	7,000	10,000 (Loss)
II	9,000	10,000 (Profit)

The selling price per unit was ₹ 100.

Calculate,

i)   Fixed Cost

ii)   BEP (Sales)

iii)   The number of units to be sold to earn a profit of ₹ 40,000

iv)   The amount of profits when sales are ₹ 20,000 units.

SOLUTION

The additional Sales of ₹ 2,00,000 in Period II (2,000 units × ₹ 100) has given an additional contribution of ₹ 20,000 (i.e. change in profits ₹ 20,000), which has wiped off the loss of ₹ 10,000 of Period I and gave a profit of ₹ 10,000 for Period II.

i) **Fixed Cost :**
   - **Calculation of P/V Ratio**

$$= \frac{\text{Change in Profits}}{\text{Change in Sales}} \times 100$$

$$= \frac{₹\ 10,000\ (P) - ₹\ 10,000\ (L)}{₹\ 9,00,000 - ₹\ 7,00,000} \times 100$$

$$= \frac{₹\ 20,000}{₹\ 2,00,000} \times 100$$

$$= 10\%$$

   - **Calculation of Contribution of Period I**

$$\text{Contribution} = \text{Sales} \times \text{P/V Ratio}$$

$$= ₹\ 7,00,000 \times 10\%$$

$$= ₹\ 70,000$$

   - **Calculation of Fixed Cost of Period I**

where,

$$\text{Contribution} = \text{Fixed Cost} - \text{Loss}$$

$$\therefore \quad \text{Fixed Cost} = \text{Contribution} + \text{Loss}$$

$$= ₹\ 70,000 + ₹\ 10,000$$

$$= ₹\ 80,000$$

ii) **BEP (Sales) :**

$$= \frac{\text{Fixed Cost}}{\text{P/V Ratio}}$$

$$= \frac{₹\ 80,000}{10\%}$$

$$= ₹\ 80,000 \times \frac{100}{10}$$

$$= ₹\ 8,00,000$$

iii) **The number of units to be sold to earn a profit of ₹ 40,000 :**

where,

$$\text{P/V Ratio} = \frac{\text{Contribution}}{\boxed{\text{Sales}}}$$

But,

$$\text{Contribution} = \text{Fixed Cost} + \text{Profit}$$

$$\therefore \quad \text{P/V Ratio} = \frac{\text{Fixed Cost} + \text{Profit}}{\boxed{\text{Sales}}}$$

$$\therefore \quad \text{Sales} = \frac{\text{Fixed Cost + Profit}}{\text{P/V Ratio}}$$

$$= \frac{₹\,80,000 + ₹\,40,000}{10\%}$$

$$= \frac{₹\,1,20,000}{10\%}$$

$$= ₹\,1,20,000 \times \frac{100}{10}$$

$$= ₹\,12,00,000$$

$$\text{Sales Units} = \frac{\text{Total Sales}}{\text{Selling price per unit}}$$

$$= \frac{₹\,12,00,000}{₹\,100}$$

$$= 12,000 \text{ units}$$

iv) **The amount of profits when Sales are 20,000 units (i.e. 20,000 units × ₹ 100 = ₹ 20,00,000)**

where,

$$\text{P/V Ratio} = \frac{\text{Contribution}}{\text{Sales}}$$

But,

$$\text{Contribution} = \text{Fixed Cost + Profit}$$

$$\therefore \quad \text{P/V Ratio} = \frac{\text{Fixed Cost} + \boxed{\text{Profit}}}{\text{Sales}}$$

$$\therefore \text{ P/V Ratio} \times \text{ Sales} = \text{Fixed Cost} + \boxed{\text{Profit}}$$

$$\therefore \quad \text{Profit} = (\text{P/V Ratio} \times \text{ Sales}) - \text{Fixed Cost}$$

$$= (10\% \times ₹\,20,00,000) - ₹\,80,000$$

$$\therefore \quad = ₹\,2,00,000 - ₹\,80,000$$

$$= ₹\,1,20,000$$

ILLUSTRATION 25

In Ness Co., Navapur, the sales and profits for the two periods are as given below :

Period	Sales ₹	Profit ₹
I	1,00,000	9,000
II	1,20,000	13,000

You are required to calculate,
i)   P/V Ratio,
ii) BEP (Sales),
iii) Profits when Sales are ₹ 1,50,000,
iv) Sales required to earn a profit of ₹ 50,000,
v)   Margin of Safety in Period – II and
vi) Variable Cost for both the periods.

SOLUTION

i)   **P/V Ratio :**

$$= \frac{\text{Change in Profits}}{\text{Change in Sales}} \times 100$$

$$= \frac{₹\,13,000 - ₹\,9,000}{₹\,1,20,000 - ₹\,1,00,000} \times 100$$

$$= \frac{₹\,4,000}{₹\,20,000} \times 100$$

$$= 20\%$$

ii)   **BEP (Sales) :**

$$= \frac{\text{Fixed Cost}}{\text{P/V Ratio}}$$

$$= \frac{₹\,11,000}{20\%}$$

$$= ₹\,11,000 \times \frac{100}{20}$$

$$= ₹\,55,000$$

iii)   **Profits when Sales are ₹ 1,50,000 :**

where,

$$\text{P/V Ratio} = \frac{\text{Contribution}}{\text{Sales}}$$

But,

$$\text{Contribution} = \text{Fixed Cost} + \text{Profit}$$

$$\therefore \quad \text{P/V Ratio} = \frac{\text{Fixed Cost} + \boxed{\text{Profit}}}{\text{Sales}}$$

$$\text{P/V Ratio} \times \text{Sales} = \text{Fixed Cost} + \boxed{\text{Profit}}$$

$$\therefore \quad \text{Profit} = (\text{P/V Ratio} \times \text{Sales}) - \text{Fixed Cost}$$

$$= (20\% \times ₹\,1,50,000) - ₹\,11,000$$

$$= ₹\,30,000 - ₹\,11,000$$

$$= ₹\,19,000$$

iv)   **Sales required to earn a profit of ₹ 50,000 :**

where,

$$\text{P/V Ratio} = \frac{\text{Contribution}}{\boxed{\text{Sales}}}$$

But, $\text{Contribution} = \text{Fixed Cost} + \text{Profit}$

$$\therefore \quad \text{P/V Ratio} = \frac{\text{Fixed Cost} + \text{Profit}}{\boxed{\text{Sales}}}$$

$$\therefore \quad \text{Sales} = \frac{\text{Fixed Cost} + \text{Profit}}{\text{P/V Ratio}}$$

$$= \frac{₹\,11,000 + ₹\,50,000}{20\%}$$

$$= ₹\,61,000 \times \frac{100}{20}$$

$$= ₹\,3,05,000$$

v) **Margin of Safety in Period II :**

Margin of Safety = Actual Sales – Break Even Sales

$$= ₹\,1,20,000 - ₹\,55,000$$

$$= ₹\,65,000$$

vi) **Variable Cost for both the periods :**

Here, P/V Ratio i.e. Contribution Margin is 20% which means Variable Cost will be 80% of Sales.

Hence,

Variable Cost = 80% of Sales

Period I : 80% of ₹ 1,00,000 = ₹ 80,000

Period II : 80% of ₹ 1,20,000 = ₹ 96,000

ILLUSTRATION 26

Philips Radio Co., Pune produced and sold 10,000 radios during the year 2012-2013 at a price of ₹ 5,000 each, the cost structure per radio is as follows :

Particulars		₹
Add : Direct Materials		1,000
Add : Prime Cost Labour		500
Add : Variable Overheads	(+)	250
Marginal Cost		**1,750**
Add : Fixed Overheads	(+)	2,000
Total Cost		**3,750**
Add : Profits for the year	(+)	1,250
Selling Price		**5,000**

Due to heavy competition the selling price has to be reduced to ₹ 4,250 for the coming year. Assuming that there will be no change in costs, find out how many radios shall be sold to ensure the same amount of profits as last year.

SOLUTION

i) **Calculation of Contribution per unit for the coming year :**

where,

Contribution per unit = Selling price per unit – Variable cost per unit

$$= ₹\,4{,}250 - ₹\,1{,}750$$

$$= ₹\,2{,}500$$

ii) **Calculation of Sales volume to earn the required profits, in units :**

$$= \frac{\text{Total Fixed Cost + Total Required Profits}}{\text{Contribution per unit}}$$

$$= \frac{(₹\,2{,}000 \times 10{,}000 \text{ Radios}) + (₹\,1{,}250 \times 10{,}000 \text{ Radios})}{₹\,2{,}500}$$

$$= \frac{₹\,2{,}00{,}00{,}000 + ₹\,1{,}25{,}00{,}000}{₹\,2{,}500}$$

$$= \frac{₹\,3{,}25{,}00{,}000}{₹\,2{,}500}$$

$$= 13{,}000 \text{ Radios}$$

ILLUSTRATION 27

Rally Industries, Rajgad produces two different products X and Y. The standard time taken to produce them is 4 hours and 5 hours respectively. Recommend which product you would suggest when,

a)   Labour is the key factor and

b)   Sales is the key factor

The data of X and Y is as follows :

Particulars	Product	
	X ₹	Y ₹
• Direct Materials	40	80
• Operating Labour (₹ 5 per hour)	20	25
• Variable Overheads (₹ 6 per hour)	24	30
• Selling Price	200	300

| SOLUTION |

i) **Calculation of Contribution per product :**

Contribution per product　=　Selling price per unit – Variable cost per unit

Product X　:　₹ 200 – ₹ 84 = ₹ 116

Product Y　:　₹ 300 – ₹ 135 = ₹ 165

ii) **Calculation of Contribution per labour hour :**

$$= \frac{\text{Contribution per product}}{\text{Labour hours per product}}$$

Product X　　　　　**Product Y**

$$= \frac{₹ 116}{\text{Hrs. 4}} \qquad = \frac{₹ 165}{\text{Hrs. 5}}$$

$$= ₹ 29 \text{ per hour} \qquad = ₹ 33 \text{ per hour}$$

iii) **Calculation of Contribution per Rupee of Sales :**

$$= \frac{\text{Contribution per product}}{\text{Selling Price per product}}$$

Product X　　　　　**Product Y**

$$= \frac{\text{Rs. } 116}{₹ 200} \qquad = \frac{₹ 165}{₹ 300}$$

$$= ₹ 0.58 \text{ per rupee} \qquad = ₹ 0.55 \text{ per rupee}$$

Recommendation :

- When labour is the key factor, Product Y is recommended because contribution per labour hour of Y is more than X.
- When Sales is the key factor, Product X is recommended because contribution per rupee of Sales of X is more than Y.

| ILLUSTRATION 28 |

From the following data, which product would you recommend to be manufactured in the factory, time being the key factor.

Particulars		Product A Per Unit	Product B Per Unit
• Direct Material	₹	24	14
• Basic Labour (₹ 1 per hour)	₹	2	3
• Variable Overheads (₹ 2 per hour)	₹	4	6
• Selling Price	₹	100	110
• Standard time to produce	Hrs.	2	3

SOLUTION

i) Calculation of P/V Ratio :

$$= \frac{\text{Contribution per unit}}{\text{Selling Price per unit}} \times 100$$

But,

Contribution per unit = Selling Price per unit – Variable Cost per unit

$\therefore$ P/V Ratio $= \dfrac{\text{Selling Price per unit} - \text{Variable Cost per unit}}{\text{Selling Price per unit}} \times 100$

$$A = \frac{₹\,100 - ₹\,30}{₹\,100} \times 100 = \frac{₹\,70}{₹\,100} \times 100$$

$$= 70\%$$

$$B = \frac{₹\,110 - ₹\,23}{₹\,110} \times 100 = \frac{₹\,87}{₹\,110} \times 100$$

$$= 79.09\%$$

ii) Calculation of Profitability per hour :

$$= \frac{\text{Contribution per unit}}{\text{Standard Time per unit}}$$

$$A = \frac{₹\,70}{\text{Hrs. 2}}$$

$$= ₹\,35 \text{ per hour}$$

$$B = \frac{₹\,87}{\text{Hrs. 3}}$$

$$= ₹\,29 \text{ per hour}$$

Recommendation :

It is true that, Product B has higher P/V Ratio than Product A and hence the production of B should be increased, but as time is the key factor, contribution per hour need to looked at to consider the profitability. Hence, Product A is more profitable and should be produced more as it gives more contribution per hour than product B.

ILLUSTRATION 29

The following cost data is available from the records of Atlas Tyre Co. Akola, manufacturing products Cee and Dee.

Particulars	Products	
	Cee **Unit Cost** ₹	**Dee** **Unit Cost** ₹
Selling Price	100	200
Material @ ₹ 10 per kg.	20	50
Wages @ ₹ 3 per hour	30	60
Marginal Overheads	10	20
Fixed Cost : ₹ 5,000	–	–

State which product is better to be produced and why, in the following cases :

i)   if the total sales in units is key factor.

ii)   if total sales in value is key factor.

iii)   if raw material is in short supply.

iv)   if labour hours is the limiting factor.

v)   if raw materials available is 2,000 kgs. and maximum sale of each product is 500 units.

SOLUTION

- **Calculation of Contribution per unit :**

  where,   Contribution = Selling Price per unit – Variable Cost per unit

  $$\text{Cee} = ₹\,100 - ₹\,60 \left(\text{i.e.} \underset{₹\,20}{\text{Materials}} + \underset{₹\,30}{\text{Wages}} + \underset{₹\,10}{\text{Marginal Overheads}} \right)$$

  $$= ₹\,40 \text{ per unit}$$

  $$\text{Dee} = ₹\,200 - ₹\,130 \left(\text{i.e.} \underset{₹\,50}{\text{Materials}} + \underset{₹\,60}{\text{Wages}} + \underset{₹\,20}{\text{Marginal Overheads}} \right)$$

  $$= ₹\,70 \text{ per unit}$$

- **Calculation of P/V Ratio :**

  where, $\text{P/V Ratio} = \dfrac{\text{Contribution per unit}}{\text{Selling Price per unit}} \times 100$

  $$\text{Cee} = \dfrac{₹\,40}{₹\,100} \times 100$$

  $$= 40\%$$

  $$\text{Dee} = \dfrac{₹\,70}{₹\,200} \times 100$$

  $$= 35\%$$

- **Calculation of Contribution per kg of raw material :**

  $$= \dfrac{\text{Contribution per unit}}{\text{Raw material consumption per unit}}$$

  $$\text{Cee} = \dfrac{₹\,40}{2 \text{ kg}}$$
  (i.e. ₹ 20/₹ 10)

  $$= ₹\,20 \text{ per kg.}$$

  $$\text{Dee} = \dfrac{₹\,70}{5 \text{ kg.}}$$
  (i.e. ₹ 50/₹ 10)

  $$= ₹\,14 \text{ per kg.}$$

- **Calculation of Contribution per Labour Hour :**

$$= \frac{\text{Contribution per unit}}{\text{Labour Hours per unit}}$$

$$\text{Cee} = \frac{₹\,40}{\text{Hrs. 10}}$$
(i.e. ₹ 30/₹ 3)

$$= ₹\,4 \text{ per hour}$$

$$\text{Dee} = \frac{₹\,70}{\text{Hrs. 20}}$$
(i.e. ₹ 60/₹ 3)

$$= ₹\,3.50 \text{ per hour}$$

Comment :

i) If total sales in units is key factor, product Dee is better because it gives higher contribution per unit (i.e. Dee ₹ 70 > Cee ₹ 40).

ii) If total sales in value is key factor, product Cee is better because of its higher P/V Ratio (i.e. Cee - 40% > Dee - 35%).

iii) If Raw Material is in short supply, product Cee is better because it gives higher contribution per kg of raw material (i.e. Cee ₹ 20 > Dee ₹ 14).

iv) If labour hours is the limiting factor, product Cee is preferred as it gives higher contribution per labour hour (i.e. Cee ₹ 4 > Dee ₹ 3.50).

v) If raw material available is 2,000 kgs. and maximum sale of each product is 500 units, product Cee is to be produced first to the maximum limit of 500 units because its contribution per kg of raw material is higher (i.e. Cee ₹ 20 > Dee ₹ 14) and remaining material will be used to produce product Dee.

ILLUSTRATION 30

Fill in the blanks for each of the following independent situations.

Particulars		A	B	C	D	E
• Selling Price per unit	₹	?	50	20	?	30
• Variable Cost as a percentage of Selling Price	%	60	?	75	75	?
• Number of Units sold	units	10,000	4,000	?	6,000	5,000
• Marginal Contribution	₹	20,000	80,000	?	25,000	50,000
• Fixed Costs	₹	12,000	?	1,20,000	10,000	?
• Profit/Loss	₹	?	20,000	30,000	?	15,000

SOLUTION

1) Situation A :

i) Calculation of Contribution per unit :

$$= \frac{\text{Marginal Contribution}}{\text{Number of units sold}}$$

$$= \frac{₹\ 20,000}{\text{Units } 10,000}$$

$$= ₹\ 2 \text{ per unit.}$$

ii) Calculation of Selling Price per unit :

But,

       Variable Cost is 60% of Selling Price

       Selling Price − Variable Cost = Contribution

          100   −   60   = 40

           ?   = ₹ 2

∴   If 40 Contribution = 100 Selling Price

∴   ₹ 2 = ?

$$= \frac{₹\ 2 \times 100}{40}$$

$$= ₹\ 5 \text{ per unit}$$

iii) Calculation of Profit/Loss :

where,

        Profit = Contribution − Fixed Cost

             = ₹ 20,000 × ₹ 12,000

              (₹ 2 × 10,000 units)

             = ₹ 8,000

2) Situation B :

i) Calculation of Contribution per unit :

$$= \frac{\text{Marginal Contribution}}{\text{Number of units sold}}$$

$$= \frac{₹\ 80,000}{\text{Units } 4,000}$$

$$= ₹\ 20 \text{ per unit}$$

ii) Calculation of Fixed Cost :

where,

        Fixed Cost = Contribution − Profit

              = ₹ 80,00 − ₹ 20,000

              = ₹ 60,000

iii) Calculation of Variable Cost as a % of Selling Price :

where,

$$\text{Variable Cost per unit} = \text{Selling Price per unit} - \text{Contribution per unit}$$
$$= ₹\,50 - ₹\,20$$
$$= ₹\,30 \text{ per unit}$$
$$\text{If } ₹\,50 = ₹\,30 \text{ Variable Cost}$$
$$\therefore \quad 100 = ?$$
$$= \frac{100 \times ₹\,30}{₹\,50}$$
$$= 60\%$$

3) Situation C :

i) Calculation of Marginal Contribution :

where,

$$\text{Marginal Contribution} = \text{Fixed Costs} + \text{Profit}$$
$$= ₹\,1,20,000 + ₹\,30,000$$
$$= ₹\,1,50,000$$

ii) Calculation of Contribution per unit :

where,

$$\text{Contribution per unit} = \text{Selling Price per unit} - \text{Variable Cost per unit}$$
$$= ₹\,20 - ₹\,15 \ (75\% \text{ of } ₹\,20)$$
$$= ₹\,5$$

iii) Calculation of number of units sold :

$$= \frac{\text{Marginal Contribution}}{\text{Contribution per unit}}$$
$$= \frac{₹\,1,50,000}{₹\,5}$$
$$= 30,000 \text{ units}$$

4) Situation D :

i) Calculation of Profit :

where,

$$\text{Profit} = \text{Marginal Contribution} - \text{Fixed Costs}$$
$$= ₹\,25,000 - ₹\,10,000$$
$$= ₹\,15,000$$

ii) Calculation of Contribution per unit

$$= \frac{\text{Marginal Contribution}}{\text{Number of units sold}}$$
$$= \frac{₹\,25,000}{\text{Units } 6,000}$$
$$= ₹\,4.167 \text{ per unit}$$

iii) Calculation of Selling Price per unit :

But,

Variable Cost is 75% of Selling Price.

Selling Price – Variable Cost	=	Contribution
100 75	=	25
?		₹ 4.167

If 25 Contribution = 100 Selling Price

$$\therefore ₹ 4.167 = ?$$

$$= \frac{₹ 4.167 \times 100}{25}$$

$$= ₹ 16.67 \text{ per unit}$$

5) Situation E :

i) Calculation of Contribution per unit :

$$= \frac{\text{Marginal Contribution}}{\text{Number of units sold}}$$

$$= \frac{₹ 50,000}{\text{units } 5,000}$$

$$= ₹ 10 \text{ per unit}$$

ii) Calculation of Fixed Cost :

where,

Fixed Cost = Contribution – Profit

$$= ₹ 50,000 – ₹ 15,000$$

$$= ₹ 35,000$$

iii) Calculation of Variable Cost as a % of Selling Price :

where,

Variable Cost per unit = Selling Price per unit – Contribution per unit

$$= ₹ 30 – ₹ 10$$

$$= ₹ 20$$

If ₹ 30 SP = ₹ 20 VC

$$\therefore \qquad 100 = ?$$

$$= \frac{100 \times ₹ 20}{₹ 30}$$

$$= 66.67\%$$

QUESTIONS FOR SELF-STUDY

I. Theory Questions

i) Define the concept of 'Marginal Cost' and 'Marginal Costing'. State the important characteristics of Marginal Costing.

ii) What is 'Marginal Costing' ? Explain the objectives of Marginal Costing.

iii) State the advantages and limitations of Marginal Costing.

iv) Explain Marginal Costing as a technique of costing.

v)   Explain the following concepts :

a) Fixed Cost, b) Variable Cost, c) Marginal Cost, d) Contribution, e) Profit Volume Ratio.

vi)   Explain the technique of Marginal Costing and state its importance in decision-making.

vii)   How are variable costs and fixed costs treated in Marginal Costing ?

viii)   Define the term 'Marginal Costing'. Explain the practical uses of Marginal Costing.

ix)   State the utility of Marginal Costing in price fixation during trade depression and for export promotion.

x)   In what circumstances would you recommend the management to make use of Marginal Costing ?

xi)   What is 'Contribution' ? How it differs from 'Profit' ?

xii)   What do you understand by P/V Ratio ? Discuss the importance of P/V Ratio. How P/V Ratio can be improved ?

xiii)   What is Break-Even Analysis ? State the assumptions of Break-Even Analysis.

xiv)   State the advantages and limitations of Break-Even Analysis.

xv)   What is Break-Even Point ? Explain the importance of Break-Even Point.

xvi)   Explain the concept of 'Break-Even-Point'. What factors influences Break-Even Point.

xvii)   "Limitations of Break-Even Charts arise from the assumptions involved in preparing such charts". Discuss.

xviii) What is Break-Even Chart. State the important purposes of constructing Break-Even Chart ?

xix)   What is Margin of Safety ? How it can be improved ?

xx)   Discuss the importance of the following in relation to Marginal Costing

(a) Break-Even Point, (b) Margin of Safety, (c) Contribution, (d) Angle of Incidence.

xxi)   Explain the concept 'Margin of Safety'. State various ways of improving Margin of Safety.

xxii)   Draw a Break-Even Chart taking suitable data and show the (i) Break-Even Point, (ii) Angle of Incidence, (iii) Margin of Safety, clearly on the chart itself.

xxiii) What is Cost-Volume-Profit Analysis ? State the advantages and limitations of Cost-Volume-Profit Analysis.

xxiv)   What do you mean by 'Cost-Volume-Profit Analysis' ? State the assumptions underlying Cost-Volume-Profit Analysis.

xxv)　What is Differential Cost Analysis ? Explain the usefulness of Differential Cost Analysis.

xxvi)　Explain the concept of Differential Cost Analysis. Explain the important features of Differential Cost Analysis.

xxvii)　Explain the concept of 'Key Factor' in Marginal Costing.

xxviii)　Explain the various managerial problems which are simplified by the use of Marginal Costing technique.

xxix)　"Marginal Costing technique helps in decision-making as also in controlling costs". Discuss.

xxx)　"Marginal Costing is a useful technique for cost control, profit planning and decision-making". Comment.

xxxi)　"The technique of Marginal Costing is more useful to provide a reasonable and sound basis for managerial decisions than to arrive at product cost". Discuss.

xxxii)　"Profit planning is very important tool in management decision-making". Comment.

xxxiii)　In what way Marginal Costing contributes to cost control, performance evaluation and profit planning ?

xxxiv)　Explain the importance of Marginal Costing in decision-making.

xxxv)　Explain the consideration influencing (i) Discontinuance of a product line and (ii) Make or by decisions.

xxxvi)　State the applications of Marginal Costing technique in solving problems of management in decision-making.

xxxvii)　"The effect of price reduction is always to reduce the P/V Ratio, to raise Break-Even Point and to short-term the margin of safety". Explain

xxxviii)　How the following affect the Break-Even Point and P/V Ratio ?

(a) Increase in Fixed Cost, (b) Increase in Sales, (c) Decrease in Variable Cost.

xxxix)　What are the various applications of Marginal Costing ?

xxxx)　Why is the contribution that a product makes towards the recovery of non-escapable costs a better measure of its profitability than the profit or loss reported on its sale after it has been charged with its fair share of all costs ?

xxxxi)　How is Marginal Costing useful in the decision-making of a firm ?

xxxxii) Explain the circumstances under which selling price below the Marginal Cost may be justified ?

xxxxiii) Write short notes on :

a) Marginal Cost, b) Fixed Cost, c) Marginal Costing, d) Variable Cost, e) Contribution, f) Margin of Safety, g) Angle of Incidence, h) Profit Volume Ratio, i) Break-Even Analysis, j) Break-Even Point, i) Cost-Volume-Profit Analysis, l) Differential Cost Analysis, m) Key Factor, n) Application of Marginal Costing Technique, o) Shut Down Point, p) Characteristics of Marginal Costing, q) Objectives of Marginal Costing, r) Limitations of Marginal Costing, s) Advantages of Marginal Costing, t) Importance of Profit Volume Ratio, u) Limitations of Break-Even Analysis, v) Importance of Break-Even Point, w) Buy or Make Decision

xxxxiv) **Differentiate between :**

a) Fixed Cost and Variable Cost, b) Contribution and Profit, c) Marginal Costing and Differential Costing, d) Break-Even-Point and Shut-Down Point.

II. Practical Problems :

i) The following are the budgeted cost data of Atlas Co. Ltd., Ahmedabad.

	₹
Total Turnover	6,00,000
Marginal Costs	3,00,000
Fixed Costs	1,50,000

Find out the Break-Even Point at i) The budgeted data and ii) 20% increase in variable cost.

ii) The turnover and profits during the two periods were as follows :

Period	Sales ₹	Profit ₹
One	40,00,000	4,00,000
Two	60,00,000	8,00,000

Assuming that the cost structure and selling price remains the same in the two periods. Calculate – a) Profit-Volume Ratio, b) Break-Even Point Sales Value), c) The sales required to earn a profit of ₹ 10,00,000, d) Margin of Safety in period two, e) Profit when Sales are ₹ 50,00,000.

iii) From the following cost data calculate – a) Fixed Cost, b) Break-Even Point, c) The number of units to be sold to earn a profit of ₹ 40,000.

The selling price is ₹ 100 per unit.

Period	Sales (Units)	Profit/Loss ₹
One	7,000	Loss – 10,000
Two	9,000	Profit – 10,000

iv) From the following find out, a) P/V Ratio, b) Break-Even Point, c) Net Profit if the sales were ₹ 2,50,000, d) Sales to earn a profit of ₹ 70,000.

In the books of Atlas Ltd., Akurde Cost Statement for year ended 31-03-2013

Particulars		₹
Value of Turnover		2,00,000
Less : Variable Cost	(–)	1,20,000
∴ Contribution		80,000
Less : Fixed Cost	(–)	20,000
∴ Profit		60,000

v) Morgan Ltd., Mahim has prepared the following budget estimates for the year 2012-13.

Sales   – 20,000 units

Sales value   – ₹ 2,00,000

Variable Cost per unit   – ₹ 5

Fixed Cost   – ₹ 20,000.

You are required to calculate :

a) P/V Ratio, Break-Even Point and Margin of Safety in each of the following cases.

- Decrease of 10% in selling price.
- Increase of 10% in variable cost.

vi) Calculate the Break-Even point in the following cases :

Sales (estimated)   – ₹ 5,00,000

Fixed costs   – ₹ 2,00,000

Variable cost per unit   – ₹ 10

Selling price per unit   – ₹ 50

vii) Amol Industries Agra supply you with the following information :

Sales   – ₹ 2,00,000

Fixed cost   – ₹ 1,00,000

Variable cost   – ₹ 1,30,000

Find out the increase in sales required to break-even.

viii) Chaby Ltd. Chembur furnishes you the following information. Calculate the break-even point and show the same by drawing a graph.

Sales (value)   – ₹ 1,50,000

Sales (units)   – 15,000

Fixed cost   – ₹ 50,000

Variable costs   –

Direct Material   – ₹ 40,000

Direct Labour   – ₹ 45,000

Variable overheads   – ₹ 35,000

ix) From the following particulars draw a break-even chart and find out the break-even point.

Variable cost per unit   – ₹ 15

Fixed cost   – ₹ 54,000

Selling price per unit   – ₹ 20

x) From the following particulars find out the a) P/V Ratio, b) BEP (Sales) and c) Margin of Safety.

	₹	% of Sales
Variable cost –	10,000	80%
Fixed cost –	5,000	5%
Profit –	15,000	15%
	30,000	**100%**

xi) The sales and profit during two years are given below :

	Sales	Profit
2007 –	₹ 20 lakhs	₹ 2 lakhs
2008 –	₹ 30 lakhs	₹ 4 lakhs

Calculate (a) P/V Ratio, (b) Sales required to earn a profit of ₹ 5 lakhs.

xii) Ashim Ltd. Anand gives you the following information :

Sales   – ₹ 50,000

Variable cost   – ₹ 25,000

Fixed cost   – ₹ 10,000

Calculate P/V Ratio, BEP and Margin of Safety. Also calculate the effect of 20% increase in sales price and 20% decrease in sales price.

xiii) The following are the figures obtained from the cost records of Neel Industries Nagpur :

		₹	₹
Sales – 5,000 units @ ₹ 4 per unit			20,000
Direct material –		4,000	
Direct labour –		5,000	
Variable overheads –	+	3,000	
		12,000	
Fixed overheads –	+	4,000	+ 16,000
Net profit		4,000	

The company has decided to reduce the selling price by 10%. What extra units should be sold to obtain the same amount of profit ?

xiv) The P/V Ratio and Margin of Safety of Bardhan Industries Baroda are 50% and 40% respectively. The Company has a sales volume of ₹ 8,00,000. Calculate the net profit.

xv) The following are the details of Manoj Ltd. Mysore for the two products A and B :

	A Per unit ₹	B Per unit ₹
Sales price –	100	120
Material (₹ 10 per kg) –	20	40
Wages –	30	20
Variable overheads –	8	12
Total fixed costs – ₹ 10,000		

When material is the limiting factor, suggest which product should be produced more.

xvi) The following two proposals are under consideration –

a) 10% reduction in price to give an increase in sales volume from 5,000 units to 6,500 units.

b) 10% increase in price with decrease in sales volume from 5,000 units to 4,000 units.

Following cost data is also being made available :

Variable Cost per unit – ₹ 50
Selling Price per unit – ₹ 100
Fixed Cost – ₹ 1,00,000.

State which of the two proposals should be recommended to the management so as to get more profits.

xvii) Godrej Ltd., Goregaon are currently operating at full capacity, manufactures and sells a product at ₹ 6 each. The existing production is 1,00,000 units per year for which the cost structure is as follows :

	₹
Direct Materials	2,00,000
Prime Cost Labour	50,000
Variable on Cost	2,00,000
Fixed Overheads	50,000
Sales	6,00,000

There is an offer from a reputed buyer for 20,000 units at ₹ 5.50 per unit. Acceptance of this order would result in additional fixed cost of ₹ 20,000 per year for hire of special machinery and payment of overtime premium of 20% for the extra direct labour required. Should the order be accepted ?

xviii) Domino Plastics Co., Dombivali make plastic trays. An analysis of their cost accounting record reveals the following :

Selling price per tray	₹ 80
Variable cost per tray	₹ 20
Fixed cost for the year	₹ 50,000
Production capacity per year	Trays - 2,000

You are required to find out :

(a) Break-Even Point (in units)

(b) The number of trays to be sold to get a profit of ₹ 30,000.

(c) If the company can produce 600 trays more per year with an additional fixed cost of ₹ 2,000, what should be the new selling price of a tray to maintain ₹ 30,000, as at the original data ?

xix) Two competing companies Honda Ltd. Hazaribaug and Kinetic Ltd. Kanpur produce and sell the same type of product in the same market. For the year ended 31st March, 2013 their forecasted Profit and Loss Account are as follows :

Particulars	Honda Ltd. ₹		Kinetic Ltd. ₹	
Sales		4,50,000		4,50,000
Less : Variable Cost	2,70,000		3,60,000	
Less : Fixed Cost (+)	1,35,000		45,000	
	(−)	4,05,000	(−)	4,05,000
Forecasted Net Profit		45,000		45,000

You are required to calculate,

    a)   Profit/Volume Ratio,

    b)   Break-Even Point (Sales Value),

    c)   State which company is likely to keep greater profit in conditions of :

        • Low demand and

        • High demand.

xx) From the following data, which products would you recommend to produce in a factory, time being the key factor.

Particulars		Product X Unit Cost	Product Y Unit Cost
Prime Cost Materials	₹	24	14
Direct Labour @ ₹ 1 per hour	₹	2	3
Variable Overheads @ ₹ 2 per hour	₹	4	6
Selling Price	₹	100	110
Standard time to produce	Hrs.	2	3

■■■

Chapter 4...

Short Run Managerial Decision Analysis

Synopsis...

4.1 INTRODUCTION

Decision Making is a regular phenomenon of the business. Managers have to analyse the relevant costs and other related factors to take right decisions. The decision criterion most often used are **cost minimisation**, **profit maximisation** and **contribution maximisation**. The accounting world slowly accepted the idea that the accounting information for decision is different from the accounting information recorded in the books of cost and financial account. For **short-term decision making**, absorption costing may give totally misleading decision information. For example, the total cost of a cosmetic article is ₹ 40, made up of ₹ 28 as variable cost and ₹ 12 as fixed cost. The sales manager is having difficulty in selling the article and a customer has offered ₹ 32 each. The following positions may be observed :

i)   If there is no other customer for the article, ₹ 32 may be better than nothing and the product may be sold on short-term basis to improve his income.

ii)   If the company has spare capacity, it may be possible to manufacture and sell more of the cosmetic articles, if customers are willing to pay ₹ 32 for each extra article. As the contribution per unit will increase by ₹ 4 for each article, the profit will increase marginally by ₹ 4 for each unit manufactured and sold.

iii) In absorption costing terms, the product makes a loss of ₹ 8 per article but if the sales demand is less or market share is lost, the loss would be substantial and the total fixed cost of the concern will remain the same.

Thus, **short-term decisions** or decision affecting the use of spare capacity, absorption costing fails to guide management in proper decision-making. In marginal costing, when cost are analysed into variable and fixed a suitable decision for short-term is made possible.

Hence, the most useful contribution of marginal costing is the assistance that it render to the management in vital **decision making**. Therefore, marginal costing is an invaluable aid to managerial decision-making.

4.2 ANALYTICAL FRAMEWORK

Short-run decisions concentrate on the maximum utilisation of existing resources while **long-term decisions** are usually concerned with acquiring large capital investments. In the short-run, fixed costs remain unchanged so that the marginal cost, revenue and contribution of each alternative is relevant. In making business decisions, managers bring together all the relevant information, identify alternative courses of action and then decide on the course of action to be taken.

Short-term and Long-term Decisions :

The short-term decision refers to a decision-horizon usually not exceeding one year over which the capacity of the organisation would remain unchanged. The main distinction between short-term and long-term decisions arises from the need to incorporate time value of money in the latter, while in the short-run analysis the amount of costs and profits is important but their timing is assumed to be unimportant.

Relevant Data/Information :

The type of **information required for decision-making** depends on the decision situation under consideration. The information required for such decisions is called 'relevant data'. The relevant data refers to decision-making elements required to meet the needs of specific situations. The conventional accounting data would not serve the purpose. They have to be altered or modified in terms of addition or deletion to tailor the historical costs to the requirements of decision-making.

In making business decisions, managers must identify the financial information relevant to a particular decision, i.e., information related to costs and revenue. Managers making business decisions always have to choose among alternative courses of action. In a choice among alternative courses of action, the only information that is relevant is the information which varies among the various actions being considered. Factors and information which remain the same among alternatives courses are not taken into account in making the business decisions.

Decision-making essentially involves choosing one or more of several available alternatives. The main task is to determine how costs and profits would be affected if a particular alternative is chosen. The process is called **differential or incremental analysis. Differential Analysis** is the process of estimating the consequences of alternative actions that a decision-maker may take. It is used both for short-term and long-term decisions.

i) The first element of the relevant data is that it is future-oriented, that is, it relates to a future period. The underlying consideration is that these decisions imply some future activity. In other words, while historical cost represents what has happened under existing conditions, the future costs refer to what is expected to happen under an assumed set of conditions. They are special purpose costs that are applicable only to the situations for which they are constructed.

ii) The second component of the analytical framework of short-term decision-making is that it is primarily quantitative (tangible). Factors having a bearing on decision-making can be either qualitative (intangible) defined as, factors which are not amenable to precise and direct measurement, or quantitative which can be expressed in numerical terms

Very frequently, managers have to make decisions and choose from among various alternatives. This could involve dropping a particular product or adding a new line of product or making parts that earlier had been purchased or raising the price of the product and so on. Both qualitative and quantitative data are important in deciding among various alternative courses of action. Usually, quantitative data is utilised is making-decisions. However, many times a decision might be taken based on certain overriding qualitative factors that are economically not very sound.

Thus, **short-term decision-making** is based on quantifiable, future accounting information. This is derived from the alteration of the historical cost data. The modification is based on the following cost concepts :

A)   Relevant Costs.

B)   Incremental or Differential Costs.

C)   Opportunity Costs.

D)   Sunk or Committed Costs.

E)   Avoidable or Escapable or Discretionary Costs.

A. Relevant Costs

Relevant Costs are pertinent costs, related solely to a particular decision. These are specific costs which get changed in the short-run as a result of some management decision. Costs and benefits which are independent of a decision are not relevant and will not be considered when making that decision. Drury defines them as, "future cash flows which will differ between the various alternatives being considered". In essence, these are "future differential costs". Thus, the two characteristic features of relevant costs are :

i) Expected Future Costs :

Relevant Costs are prospective in nature. These are projected costs over the future life of assets. These are forward-looking based on expected factor for the planning period. Selection of one alternative over another does not affect the past cash flows. Current fixed costs, which will not change irrespective of the decision are hardly significant. These are sunk or historical costs. Since, decisions are made unto the future circumstances, they must also include anticipated costs. Relevant costing no doubt, is the modification and extention of marginal costing it is not exactly the same. There are material points of difference.

Relevant Costs are future costs and arise as a direct consequence of a decision. Relevant costs are cash flows and non-cash item such as depreciation, notional charges, absorbed fixed overheads which do not reflect additional cash flows should be ignored. A distinction between relevant and irrelevant costs is as follows.

Relevant Costs	Irrelevant Costs
i) Marginal or Variable Costs.	i) General or Absorbed Fixed Cost.
ii) Additional or Specific or Unavoidable Fixed Cost, Differential or Incremental Costs.	ii) Committed Costs.
iii) Opportunity Costs (where alternative choices exist).	iii) Sunk or Past Costs. (having no relevancy in the future)

ILLUSTRATION 1

Aspi Enterprises, Anand finds at the beginning of an accounting year that there is a stock of ₹ 10,000 at cost of maxi skirts which are outdated and have to be sold as scrap (Alternative I) for ₹ 2,000 or remake them incurring a cost of ₹ 5,000 and sell at ₹ 8,000 (Alternative II).

You are required to prepare a statement:

a)   Showing net profit or loss of each alternative, for decision making,

b)   Under relevant cost approach to make a decision by the management.

SOLUTION

a) Statement showing Net Profit or Loss of each alternative.

Particulars		Alternative I		Alternative II	
		₹	₹	₹	₹
	Sales		2,000		8,000
Less :	Opening Stock	10,000		10,000	
	Remaking Costs	–	(–) 10,000	5,000	(–) 15,000
∴ **Loss**			8,000		7,000

Thus, alternative II is preferable as the loss could be reduced by ₹ 1,000 from ₹ 8,000 in Alternative I to ₹ 7,000 in Alternative II.

b) In this case, the value of opening stock is a sunk cost and is irrelevant for making a decision so it can be omitted considering opportunity cost the position can be shown in Alternative I as follows :

Alternative I

Particulars		₹
Sales (as scrap)		2,000
Less : i) Opportunity Cost		
(benefit foregone in not availing Alternative II)	(−)	3,000
∴ Net Disadvantage		1,000

Alternatively, the position can be shown with Alternative II as follows :

Alternative II

Particulars			₹
Sales (after remaking)			8,000
Less : i) Remaking Cost	5,000		
ii) Opportunity Cost	(+) 2,000		7,000
(benefit foregone in not availing Alternative I)	(−)		
∴ Net Advantage over Alternative I			1,000

Thus, in relevant cost approach, the opening stock becomes sunk cost i.e. irrelevant, whereas opportunity cost is taken into consideration for decision-making.

ii) Different in Different Alternatives :

Only costs that differ among various alternatives are relevant to a decision. These are different between each of the alternative courses of action. **Differential Costs** are defined as, "the amount of difference (increase or decrease) in cost expected from one alternative compared to the amount expected from another". Thus, it is obtained by subtracting the cost of one alternative from the cost of other alternative. For example, when management is considering a change in the level of production, differential cost will be calculated by subtracting the cost at lower level of production from that of a higher level.

ILLUSTRATION 2

The cost data relating to various alternatives relating to Bosco Traders, Baramati are as follows :

Output in Units	Alternative I	Alternative II	Differential Cost
	10,000	15,000	5,000
	₹	₹	₹
Material	80,000	1,00,000	20,000
Labour	24,000	30,000	6,000
Variable Overheads	16,000	20,000	4,000
Fixed Overheads (+)	20,000	22,000	2,000
∴ **Total**	**1,40,000**	**1,72,000**	**32,000**

Comment on the situation.

SOLUTION

Thus, in order to produce additional 5,000 units, additional cost is ₹ 32,000 (i.e. ₹ 1,72,000 – ₹ 1,40,000). In other words, differential cost for 5,000 units is ₹ 32,000. It should be noted that in this example, if additional output does not involve any additional fixed cost to be incurred, the differential cost will be equal to marginal variable cost. Thus, when fixed costs remain constant, the differential cost is synonymous with the variable costs of producing the n-units. It is for this reason that differential cost is sometimes referred to as marginal cost. Sometimes the term incremental cost is also interchangeably used with differential cost. Incremental cost means only an increase in cost from one alternative to another, generally costs are differential costs.

The two elements, or criteria of costs that differ among alternatives are, Incremental Costs, and Opportunity Costs.

Both are added with a view to choose between the competing schemes. These are being taken up for a detail discussion as follows.

B. Incremental Costs

In effect, differential cost are **incremental costs**. These are the additional costs of manufacturing and marketing new products. These would not be incurred if the firm does not proceed with the project. These represent a change in aggregate costs that accompany the addition or deletion of a batch or block of output. If total costs do not change as a result of a decision, the incremental cost would be zero. They are thus avoidable or out-of-pocket costs and need be compared with differential revenue. Unless incremental revenue exceeds the incremental costs, the proposed decision is not good enough.

C. Opportunity Costs

The **opportunity cost** of a decision is the net benefit of the best alternative that is foregone. It is represented by the potential revenue that might be earned if the contemplated actions were not implemented. It is cost of one course of action in terms of the opportunities, which are relinquished given up to carry on that action. In fact, these are shadow prices, not collected within the accounting system. These are not paid out in cash of a third party. They are imputed in terms of a measurable advantage of a lost opportunity. It is important to note opportunity costs only apply to the use of scarce resource. Where resources are not scarce, no sacrifice exists from using these resources.

Applications and Uses of Relevant Costing :

The relevant costing principles give a fresh and refreshing insight. It clearly indicates the minimum price which must be charged to cover variable costs. It reveals the most profitable lines in all conditions of trade. It does this by showing the contribution each product makes towards fixed costs and profit.

The typical situations in which relevant costing is useful are the following short-run, special ad hoc, or non-routine decision. The term short-run is applied to decision horizons over which capacity will be unchanged. This is generally taken as one year. Short-term decision effect cash flow for such a short period that the time value of money is immaterial, for example:

i) Capacity utilisation, ii) Selection of a plant, replacement of existing machine with a newer model, iii) Introduction of a new product, iv) Accepting tender, exploring possibilities of foreign market, v) Alternative course of action, vi) Sell a partially completed product or process the product further, vii) Make or buy decisions, viii) Pricing decisions, ix) Maintaining a desired level of profit, x) Selection of suitable product mix, xi) Dropping a product line.

For decision-making, as choice between alternative mix, replacement etc. orthodox system cannot be used with advantage, as fixed or irrelevant cost distorts the analysis. This is the special domain of Marginal Costing. In planning Marginal Costing is thus more helpful. In preparation of Budget too, Marginal Analysis is more helpful, as it is not vitiated by allocation of different types of fixed overheads. For control purpose too, the Marginal Analysis is more dependable, as a person is responsible for direct expenses under him and not for expenses occurring elsewhere and allocated on different bases on which he has no control whatsoever. Of course, from control point of view Standard Costing is superior to Marginal Costing form.

In the short-run the time horizon is conventionally limited to one year. The plant capacity, therefore, remains unchanged. The objective function is of **"maximising contribution margin"**. For such non-routine, adhoc problem-solving, relevant costing principles are utilised. These examine both revenue and cost effects. But in some cases, only costs may be looked into as revenues remain unaffected by the decision choice.

D. Sunk Costs

Such Costs are historical costs that are irrevocable in a given situation. They are the costs that have been incurred by a decision that was made in the past and cannot be changed by any decision that would be made in the future. They are, therefore, irrelevant in decision-making and have to be deleted from the historical costs.

E. Avoidable Costs

These costs can be avoided in the future as a result of managerial choices because management can choose not to incur them. **Avoidable Costs** are relevant costs when particulars decision-alternatives are compared.

4.3 DECISION SITUATIONS

Incremental Analysis is an important tool for evaluating the effects of short-term changes in revenues and costs. We will now consider some of the typical short-term decisions. Here, we can discuss the application of incremental or differential costs and revenue data for decision-making in the various situations viz. Sales volume related, Sell or further process, Make or buy, Addition/dropping of product lines/divisions/departments, Short-term use of scarce resources, Joint outputs of common processing operations, and Operate or shut-down.

These decision situations are summarised in Figure 4.1 as shown below:

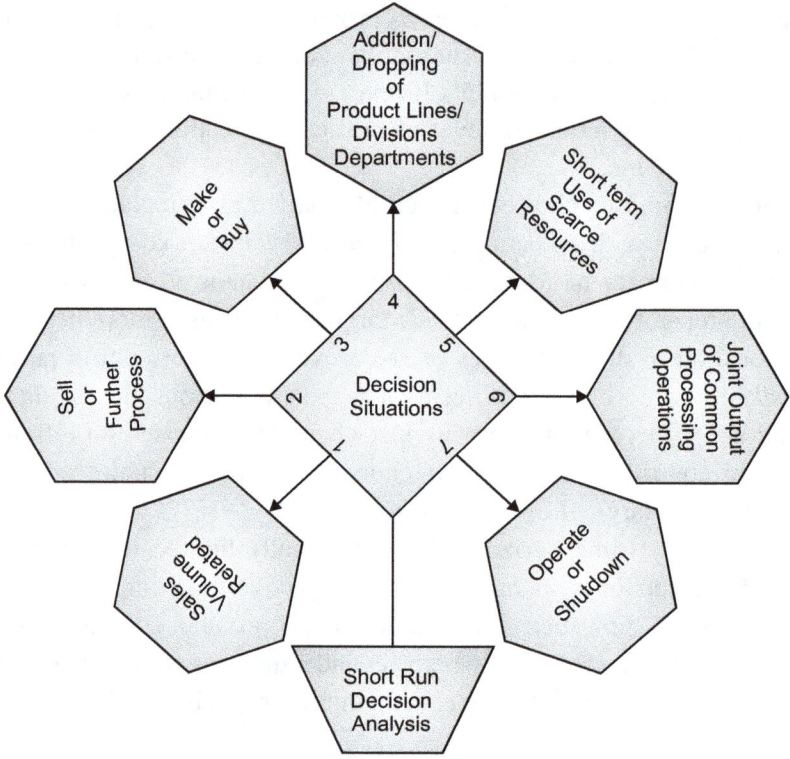

Fig. 4.1: Decision Situations

4.3.1 SALES VOLUME RELATED DECISIONS

Such type of decisions cover, a) Accepting a special order or extra sales orders, b) Disposing of inventories and c) Loss leaders, as shown below in Figure 4.2.

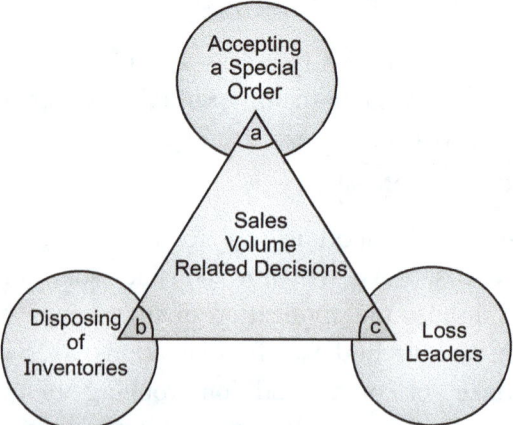

Fig. 4.2: Sales Volume Related Decisions

a) Accepting a Special Order or Extra Sales Orders :

In evaluating the merits of a special order decision, managers must consider not only their cost structures but also the potential effect of the special order on sales at regular prices. Special orders, either short-term or long-term require careful study.

Several factors should be considered appropriately in deciding whether to accept a special order or extra sales order or not. One of the important factor is to verify the effect of accepting the special order upon the concerns having regular sales volume and affordable prices. No business can continue indefinitely without covering all its costs which they have incurred.

If such special sales do not affect the normal sales, the accept-reject decision would be based on the incremental contribution. In case, the special sale would affect the future sales volume and/or selling price, the opportunity cost in terms of lost revenue will also be relevant to the decision-making.

ILLUSTRATION 3

Charvi and Co. Chembur produces a product X that it sells for ₹ 50. The current production is at 5,000 units per month which represents 80% of capacity. Currently, the fixed costs are ₹ 1,00,000 per month. The firm has an opportunity to utilise its spare capacity if it accepts an offer from a departmental store. The departmental store is willing to purchase 1250 units of product X at a price of ₹ 40 per unit. Acceptance of the special order will increase fixed costs by ₹10,000. The variable costs of product X are ₹ 20 per unit. Should the firm accept the special offer ?

SOLUTION

The present position is as follows :

Particulars		₹
	Sales (Units 5,000 × ₹ 50)	2,50,000
Less :	Variable Cost (Units 5,000 × ₹ 20) (−)	1,00,000
	∴ Contribution	1,50,000
Less :	Fixed Cost (−)	1,00,000
	∴ Net Profit	50,000

The cost-structure for the special order is as under :

Particulars		₹
	Sales (Units 1,250 × ₹ 40)	50,000
Less :	Variable Costs (Units 1,250 × ₹ 20) (−)	25,000
	∴ Contribution	25,000
Less :	Fixed Cost (−)	10,000
	∴ Net Profit	**15,000**

In this example, accepting the special order increases net income by ₹ 15,000. Hence, the firm should accept the special offer as it improves the profit earnings.

Thus, based on purely quantitative data, the offer should be accepted. However, in some situations, certain qualitative factors also need to be considered, before a final decision is taken. Operating at capacity may help the firm avoid lay offs and other related problems. Also the firm must find out if accepting the special order is the most profitable way of using spare capacity.

ILLUSTRATION 4

Domino Corporation, Delhi has normal production capacity 3,00,000 units per annum and current production is 2,00,000 units per annum. At present there is 'no' alternative use for the idle facilities. The company receives an offer from a foreign customer to buy 1,00,000 units at ₹ 10 per unit. The current market price is ₹ 14 per unit. The current manufacturing and selling costs are as under :

Particulars		Unit Cost ₹	Total Cost ₹
Total Variable Cost :			
• Direct Labour		2	4,00,000
• Direct Material		3	6,00,000
• Variable Overheads		2	4,00,000
• Variable Selling Cost	(+)	1	2,00,000
		8	16,00,000
Fixed Overheads :			
• Manufacturing Overheads		2.50	5,00,000
• Selling Overheads	(+)	0.50	1,00,000
∴ **Total Cost:**		11.00	22,00,000

    i)   Should the offer be accepted assuming that shipment charges of ₹ 50,000 are to be borne by the seller ? There will be a special packing of the products which will involve packing cost of ₹ 0.25 per unit. Being an export order, the management is convinced of the fact that the regular market price of ₹ 14 a unit will not be affected.

    ii)   Assume that the order is from a local supplier and, therefore, should the order be accepted, all products in future are to be offered at the special order price.

SOLUTION

The decision analysis in situations i) and ii) is given below :

Situation. i)   **DECISION ANALYSIS STATEMENT**

Particulars	Without Special Order (Units × ₹)	Amount ₹	With Special Order (Units × ₹)	Amount ₹
Sales	(2,00,000 × 14)	28,00,000	(2,00,000 × 14)	28,00,000
	(+)		(1,00,000 × 10)	10,00,000
		28,00,000		38,00,000
Less : Incremental Costs				
i) Direct Labour	(2,00,000 × 2)	4,00,000	(3,00,000 × 2)	6,00,000
ii) Direct Material	(2,00,000 × 3)	6,00,000	(3,00,000 × 3)	9,00,000
iii) Direct Overheads	(2,00,000 × 2)	4,00,000	(3,00,000 × 2)	6,00,000
iv) Packing Costs	–	–	(1,00,000 × 0.25)	25,000
v) Selling Costs	(2,00,000 × 1)	2,00,000	(2,00,000 × 1)	2,00,000
vi) Shipment Costs	– (–)	–		50,000
∴ Contribution		12,00,000		14,25,000

The incremental contribution is ₹ 2,25,000 and therefore the order should be accepted.

Situation ii)   **DECISION ANALYSIS STATEMENT**

Particulars	Amount ₹	Amount ₹
Sales (3,00,000 × ₹ 10)		30,00,000
Less : Relevant Costs :		
i) Manufacturing Variable Costs (Units 3,00,000 × ₹ 7)	21,00,000	
ii) Packing Costs (Units 1,00,000 × ₹ 0.25)	25,000	
iii) Variable Selling Costs (2,00,000 × ₹ 1)	2,00,000	
iv) Shipment Costs (+)	50,000	23,75,000
∴ Contribution (–)		6,25,000

Since, the contribution has declined, the order from the local supplier should not be accepted.

b) Disposing of Inventories :

When due to damage or lack of demand, inventory may not be saleable through normal distribution channels in such cases incremental analysis is appropriate for decision-making. In such a situation all priority costs of producing/acquiring inventory are sunk costs and therefore, they are irrelevant to the decisions. The following example illustrates the decision.

ILLUSTRATION 5

Elite Bros. Elora has on hand 10,000 units of a product that cannot be sold through regular sales. These were produced at a total cost of ₹ 3,00,000 and would normally have been sold for ₹ 40 per unit. Three alternatives are being considered which are as follows :

i)   Sell the items as scrap for ₹ 2 per unit.
ii) Repackage at a cost of ₹ 40,000 and sell them at ₹ 8 per unit.
iii) Dispose them off at the city dump at removal cost of ₹ 1,000.
Which alternative should be accepted ?

SOLUTION

DECISION ANALYSIS STATEMENT

Particulars	Alternatives		
	i) Sell as scrap ₹	**ii) Repackage and sell** ₹	**iii) Disposal** ₹
Sales Revenue	20,000 (10,000 units × ₹ 2)	80,000 (10,000 units × ₹ 8)	–
Less :			
i) Repackage Cost	–	40,000	–
ii) Removal Cost	–	–	1,000
Contribution Loss	20,000	40,000	(1,000)

Alternative ii) should be accepted without any hesitation.

c) Loss Leaders :

'Loss Leader' means an article offered by a retail store at cost or less than at cost to attract customers. It means sometime an item or article may be deliberately priced so low that the business house has to suffer loss in the expectation that additional sales will be generated which will offset the loss. Such sales are referred to as **"loss leaders"**.

ILLUSTRATION 6

Femina Trading Corporation, Faizpur has regular monthly gross sales average ₹ 4,00,000. It's contribution margin is 50%. Monthly fixed costs are ₹ 1,00,000. To increase the sales, the company plans to sell a special product at ₹ 8 each. If 10,000 units of this item can be purchased for ₹ 12 per unit, determine the increase in the sales revenue of the normally priced items to make the promotion in a worthy manner.

SOLUTION

DECISION ANALYSIS STATEMENT

Particulars		Amount ₹
	Incremental Revenue (10,000 units × ₹ 8)	80,000
Less :	Incremental Costs (10,000 units × ₹ 12) (–)	1,20,000
	∴ Incremental Loss	(40,000)
	Desired increase in Sales Revenue = Loss ₹ 40,000	
	CV Ratio (0.50)	(40,000)
	∴ Desired increase in Sales Revenue	80,000

The interpretation of ₹ 80,000 is that the increase in the Sales Revenue exceeding this amount will justify the promotional efforts.

4.3.2 SELL OR FURTHER PROCESS

When an item of manufacturing passes through various processes, it is saleable at different stages or points deciding at what stage to sell the product, the two variables are to be considered. viz. Identification of Sunk Costs and Ascertainment of Incremental Return at various sales alternatives.

i) Identification of Sunk Costs :

All costs either fixed or variable, incurred before the sell or process to further point, should be treated as sunk costs and therefore, irrelevant costs.

ii) Ascertainment of Incremental Return Relevant to the Decisions :

It is the difference between the costs that are incurred beyond the decision points and the revenues.

Role of Opportunity Cost in Decision-making :

If the fixed resources would remain idle as a result of not processing the product further and if they could be diverted to some other use, opportunity cost would also become relevant to the decision-making process.

ILLUSTRATION 7

(Additional Processing - Single Product)

Galaxy Ltd., Goregaon manufacturers a single product, which it sells to firms which process it further before sale. The normal monthly operating volume for the company is 50,000 units produced and sold. The necessary relevant cost information is as follows :

Particulars	₹	₹
Selling Price		10.00
Less : Standard Costs :		
i) Direct Materials	3.00	
ii) Direct Labour	1.50	
iii) Variable Manufacturing Overheads	1.00	
iv) Fixed Manufacturing Overheads (₹ 25,000 per month)	0.50	
v) Variable Selling Overheads	1.00	
vi) Fixed Selling Expenses (₹ 12,500 per month) (+)	0.25	(–) 7.25
∴ Standard Profit per unit		2.75

The company management is considering the possibility of further processing it itself, necessary for the operation to sell directly to the customers. The management estimates that the product can be sold at ₹ 14 per unit after further processing. The following are the estimates of the additional costs of processing 50,000 units.

Particulars	₹
Direct Labour ……………………..……………………... per unit	1.00
Variable Manufacturing Overheads ………....…………… per unit	0.50
Variable Selling Costs …………………………………… per unit	0.20
Additional Fixed Manufacturing Overheads …………..……… per month	10,000
Additional Sales Expenses ……………………………… per month	2,500

You are required to decide whether further processing should be done or not.

SOLUTION

DECISION ANALYSIS STATEMENT

Particulars	Without further processing		With further processing		Incremental revenues and costs	
	Per Unit	Total	Per Unit	Total	Per Unit	Total
	₹	₹	₹	₹	₹	₹
Sales	10.00	5,00,000	14.00	7,00,000	4.00	2,00,000
Less : Incremental Costs :						
i) Direct Material	3.00	1,50,000	3.00	1,50,000	–	–
ii) Direct Labour	1.50	75,000	2.50	1,25,000	1.00	50,000
iii) Manufacturing Overheads	1.00	50,000	1.70*	85,000	0.70*	35,000
iv) Selling Overheads (–)	1.00	50,000	1.30*	65,000	0.30*	15,000
∴ Contribution	3.50	1,75,000	5.50	2,75,000	2.00	1,00,000

*   Including additional Fixed Overheads.

Manufacturing Overheads (Additional) ₹ 10,000 ÷ 50,000 units = ₹ 0.20

(0.50 + 0.20 = 0.70).

Additional Sales Expenses : ₹ 2,500 ÷ 50,000 units = 0.05 (0.25 + 0.05 = 0.30)

The new proposal should be accepted, because further processing would result in a greater contribution and more profitable.

ILLUSTRATION 8

(Sell or Process Further – Multiple Products)

Himali Traders, Himmatpur produces three products, viz. X, Y and Z. Company uses one type of raw material for all three products. Initially, the raw material enters the process in Department 'P' of the factory. Department 'P' separates material for products X, Y and Z. During the month, material worth ₹ 4,00,000 was issued to Department 'P'. Other direct costs of operating Department 'P' were ₹ 2,00,000. The output of products from Department 'P' was : X – 10,000 units; Y – 5,000 units and Z – 2,000 units.

Product X, Y and Z can be sold after being processed from Department 'P' (split-off point) at prices of ₹ 60, ₹ 30 and ₹ 20, respectively. After the split-off, product X could be processed further in Department 'Q'. With additional processing cost of ₹ 50,000, this product can be sold for ₹ 70 per unit. After the split-off, product Y could be processed further in Department 'R' for ₹ 30,000 additional cost and will then fetch ₹ 35 per unit. Product 'Z' is not suitable for further processing and has to be sold at the point of split-off. Suggest what action should the company take.

SOLUTION

DECISION ANALYSIS STATEMENT

Particulars			Sell Now ₹	Process Further ₹	Incremental Revenues and Costs ₹
			Product X		
	Sales		6,00,000	7,00,000	1,00,000
Less :	Separable Costs	(–)		50,000	50,000
	∴ Contribution		6,00,000	6,50,000	50,000
			Product Y		
	Sales		1,50,000	1,75,000	25,000
Less :	Separable Costs	(–)		30,000	30,000
	Contribution		1,50,000	1,45,000	(5,000)

Comments :

Assumed that there is no other opportunity cost for using the facilities of Department 'Q' and Department 'R', above information indicate that it is profitable to process product. 'X' further because it yields an incremental contribution of ₹ 50,000. The company is advised to process product X further and sell product Y as it is.

4.3.3 MAKE OR BUY

Marginal Cost Analysis renders useful assistance when a decision has to be taken by the management of whether a component part should be manufactured internally or purchased from an outside firm. This is particularly so when a component part is available in the market at a price below firm's own total cost. Such a decision can be arrived at by comparing the outside price with firm's own marginal cost. On the face of it, since the only extra cost to manufacture the component is the marginal cost, then the amount by which this falls below supplier's price is the saving that arises in making. Therefore, it will be profitable to buy from outside only when supplier's price is below firm's own marginal cost. This decision from economic point of view, requires accurate calculations involving the concepts of differential costing and opportunity cost.

ILLUSTRATION 9

In its manufacturing operations, Infra Ltd., Indore uses a component 'WWS' that can be purchased from a supplier for ₹ 40 per unit. The same component 'WWS' is manufactured by the company at the following unit cost.

Particulars		Unit Cost ₹
Direct Material		10
Direct Labour		12
Variable Overheads (125% of Direct Labour)		15
Fixed Overheads (75% Direct Labour)	(+)	9
∴ Total Cost		46

Give your suggestion whether to make or buy this component.

SOLUTION

It the component 'WWS' is purchased it will cost ₹ 40 per unit. However that purchasing cost should not always be compared with the full cost of internal manufacture, which amounts to ₹ 46. For short run decision-making purpose, fixed overheads will remain constant regardless of the alternative chosen. Therefore, the outside purchase price should be compared only with internal manufacturing costs that can be avoided if the outside purchase is made. These avoidable cost include,

Particulars		Unit Cost ₹
Direct Material		10
Direct Labour		12
Variable Overheads	(+)	15
∴ Total Avoidable Costs		37

Thus, Total Avoidable Costs of ₹ 37 per unit is less than the ₹ 40 outside purchase price, hence, it is suggested that the company, should continue to manufacture the components 'WWS'.

ILLUSTRATION 10

In Jolly Co., Jaipur manufacture of product A takes 20 hours of machine No. 101. It has a selling price of ₹ 150 and marginal cost of ₹ 110. A component part Y could be made on machine No. 101 in 4 hours. The marginal cost of component part is ₹ 9 of which supplier's price is ₹ 15.

Should one make or buy component ? Assume machine time as the key factor.

SOLUTION

Contribution per unit A = ₹ 150 – ₹ 110 = ₹ 40.

Contribution per unit of key factor i.e. machine hour $= \dfrac{₹\ 40}{20\ \text{Hrs.}} = ₹\ 2$ per hour.

If component Y takes. 4 hours, the loss of contribution is ₹ 8 (i.e. 4 hrs. × ₹ 2). The total cost to make will be ₹ 9 + ₹ 8 = ₹ 17.

This is more than supplier's price of ₹ 15 and so it is better to buy than to make component Y.

If, however, there was some unutilised machine capacity, then there would be no loss of contribution and so the making cost would only be its marginal cost i.e. ₹ 9. In such a case, it would be economical to make the product than to buy it.

ILLUSTRATION 11

(Dropping of Product Line)

Kanishka Enterprises, Kanpur is currently operating at 70% capacity and producing 10,000 units a year. The manager of the enterprise is considering various possibilities to increase its sales. At present the enterprises purchases its product from a supplier at a unit price of ₹ 30. Estimates show that the enterprises can manufacture the product at ₹ 11 per unit direct material cost and ₹ 8 Direct Labour Cost, Variable Factory Overheads are ₹ 64,000 and Fixed Factory Overheads are ₹ 90,000.

    a)   Should the company Make or Buy?
    b)   If the company could rent out the currently unused part of the factory for ₹ 1,500 a month, would this affect your decision in part (a) ?

SOLUTION

a)   Statement showing Differential Cost (for Product of 10,000 units)

Particulars	Make ₹	Buy @ ₹ 30 per unit	Difference ₹
Raw Materials @ ₹ 11 per unit	1,10,000	–	–
Direct Labour @ ₹ 8 per unit	80,000	–	–
Variable Overheads (+)	64,000	–	–
∴ Total Variable Cost	2,54,000	3,00,000	46,000

Thus the company can save ₹ 46,000 by making its own component.

b)   The Opportunity cost of utilising the factory space will be ₹ 18,000 per year. This will not alter the decision in (a) above but the net benefits will be reduced to ₹ 28,000.

4.3.4 PRODUCT LINES / DIVISIONS / DEPARTMENTS

Frequently managers have to decide whether to discontinue or replace an unprofitable product line, so that the overall profitability of the company can be improved. This is specially applicable in case of a company which has a range of products, one of which is supposed to be unprofitable.

When a firm is divided into multiple sales outlets, product lines, divisions, departments, segments, it may have to evaluate their individual performances to decide whether or not to continue operations of each of these segments or add a new segment. The decision criterion would be the segment margin. The segment margin equals to segment's contribution margin less fixed costs that are directly traceable to that segment.

ILLUSTRATION 12

Lijjat Ltd., Lonavala manufactures three products, the income statement for which are given below. Management is considering whether or not to discontinue product Y as it is showing a loss.

a)   Based on the above data should product Y be dropped ?

b)   What other factors would you take into account before making a final decision ?

Income Statement

Particulars	Product X ₹	Product Y ₹	Product Z ₹	Total ₹
Sales	60,000	50,000	80,000	1,90,000
Less : Variable Cost (−)	25,000	30,000	35,000	90,000
∴ Contribution Margin	35,000	20,000	45,000	1,00,000
Less : Fixed Costs				
i) Joint	8,000	9,000	10,000	27,000
ii) Separate (+)	15,000	15,000	18,000	48,000
Total (−)	23,000	24,000	28,000	75,000
∴ Net Income / (Loss)	12,000	(4,000)	17,000	25,000

SOLUTION

a) If product Y is dropped, the joint costs remain the same and have to be absorbed by the remaining products. i.e. ₹ 3,000 by product X and ₹ 6,000 by product Y. The revised Income Statement will appear as shown below :

Revised Income Statement

Particulars		Product X ₹	Product Z ₹	Total ₹
Sales		60,000	80,000	1,40,000
Less : Variable Cost	(−)	25,000	35,000	60,000
∴ Contribution margin		35,000	45,000	80,000
Less : Fixed Costs :				
i) Joint		11,000	16,000	27,000
ii) Separate	(+)	15,000	18,000	33,000
Total	(−)	26,000	34,000	60,000
∴ Net Income		9,000	11,000	20,000

Thus, dropping product Y with a loss of ₹ 4,000 reduces total profits by ₹ 5,000. The company would loose ₹ 20,000 contribution margin while saving only ₹ 15,000 in separate fixed costs. The common costs allocated to the other products will not change. Hence, dropping product Y reduces total profit by ₹ 5,000 (₹ 20,000 lost contribution margin - ₹ 15,000 in fixed cost savings).

b) Other factors taken into account before making a final decision :

Various other factors should also be considered in a decision of whether to discontinue a product line.

i)   The company may want to avoid laying-off employees or want to maintain a reputation for offering its customers a "full-line of products".

ii)   Will dropping product Y result in the complete elimination of joint costs to product Y ? If this is so, eliminating product Y may be a worthwhile decision.

iii) Will dropping product Y cause sales to increase for the company's other two products ? If yes, then discontinuing product Y may be the correct decision. Thus, the effects of expected changes in the sales of other products should also be examined.

iv)   What alternative use can the company make of the production and the other facilities now used in manufacturing product Y ?

ILLUSTRATION 13

(Addition of Second Shift)

Metro Ltd., Mysore produces a single product in its plant. This product sells for ₹ 100 per unit. The standard production cost per unit is as follows :

Particulars		Unit Cost ₹
Raw Materials (5 kgs. @ ₹ 8)		40
Direct Labour (2 hours @ ₹ 5)		10
Variable Manufacturing Overheads		10
Fixed Manufacturing Overheads	(+)	20
∴ Total		80

The plant is currently operating at full capacity of 1,00,000 units per year on a single shift. This output is inadequate to meet the projected sales demand and the sales manager has estimated that the firm will lose sales of 40,000 units next year if the capacity is not expanded.

Plant capacity could be doubled by adding a second shift. This would require additional out-of-pocket fixed manufacturing overhead costs of ₹ 10,00,000 annually. Also, a night work wage premium equal to 25% of the standard wage would have to be paid during the second shift. However, if annual production volume were 1,30,000 units or more, the company could take advantage of 2% quantity discount on its raw material purchases.

You are required to advise whether it would be profitable to add the second shift in order to obtain the sales volume of 40,000 units per year ?

SOLUTION

DECISION ANALYSIS STATEMENT

Particulars		Profit without Expansion ₹	Profits with Expansion ₹
Sales Revenue		1,00,00,000	1,40,00,000
Less : Variable Costs			
i) Raw Materials			
(₹ 40 × Units 1,00,000)		40,00,000	
(₹ 39.20 × Units 1,40,000)			54,88,000
ii) Direct Labour		10,00,000	15,00,000
iii) Variable Manufacturing Overhead	(−)	10,00,000	14,00,000
∴ Contribution		40,00,000	56,12,000
Less : Fixed Costs (Units 1,00,000 × ₹ 20)	(−)	20,00,000	30,00,000
∴ Net Income		20,00,000	26,12,000

It would be profitable to add the second shift as it would increase profits by ₹ 6,12,000.

ILLUSTRATION 14

(Elimination of Division)

The management of Netco Ltd. Nanded wants to determine if Division X should be eliminated. Given below provides the Income Statement for the company.

Divisional Profit Statement

Particulars		Division Netco Ltd. ₹	Division X ₹	Total Company ₹
Sales		1,25,000	10,000	1,35,000
Less : Variable Cost	(−)	42,500	6,500	49,000
∴ Contribution Margin		82,500	3,500	86,000
Less : Traceable Fixed Cost	(−)	45,500	10,500	56,000
Divisional Income		37,000	(7,000)	30,000
Less : Unallocated Fixed Cost	(−)	–	–	15,000
∴ Income Before Tax				15,000

SOLUTION

Profitability Statement

Particulars		Keep Division 'X' ₹	If it decides to Eliminate Division 'X' ₹	Cost to Eliminate Division 'X' ₹	Ultimate Effect
Sales		1,35,000	1,25,000	(10,000)	Sales Decrease
Less : Variable Cost	(−)	49,000	42,500	6,500	Cost Reduction
∴ Contribution Margin		86,000	82,500	(3,500)	C.M. Decrease
Less : Total Fixed Costs	(−)	71,000	60,500	10,500	Cost Reduction
∴ Income Before Tax		15,000	22,000	7,000	Profit Increase

Above statement shows that the profits Netco Ltd. increase by ₹ 7,000 if Division X is eliminated.

Incremental Revenue and Cost Analysis

Advantage of eliminating division X	Amount ₹
Increase in Sales	–
Decrease in Costs (₹ 6,500 + ₹ 10,500)	17,000
∴ Total Advantage	17,000
Disadvantage of eliminating Division X	**Amount ₹**
Decrease in Sales	10,000
Increase in Costs	–
Total Disadvantage	10,000

Incremental profit from eliminating division X is greater than the disadvantage of eliminating division X. Hence, it is observed that whether to discontinue a segment or not, contribution margin format helps in identifying traceable and avoidable fixed costs relevant to the decision whereas incremental revenue and cost analysis helps in comparing the operating results with and without the segment.

ILLUSTRATION 15

(Elimination of a Product Line)

Olyster Ltd. Osmanabad manufactures readymade garments and uses its cut-pieces of cloth to manufacture hanky. The following statement of cost has been prepared :

Particulars		Readymade Garments ₹	Hanky ₹	Total ₹
Direct Material		80,000	6,000	86,000
Direct Labour		13,000	1,200	14,200
Variable Overheads		17,000	2,800	19,800
Fixed Overheads	(+)	24,000	3,000	27,000
∴ Total Cost		1,34,000	13,000	1,47,000
Sales	(−)	1,70,000	12,000	1,82,000
∴ Profit/Loss		36,000	(1,000)	35,000

The cut-pieces used in hanky have a scrap value of ₹ 1,000 if sold in the market. As there is a loss of ₹ 1,000 in the manufacturing of hanky, it is suggested to discontinue their manufacture. Advise the management.

SOLUTION

DECISION ANALYSIS STATEMENT

Particulars	Production of Hanky ₹	Non-production of Hanky ₹
Sales Revenue	12,000	–
Scrap Value of Cut-pieces	–	1,000
Less : Avoidable Costs		
i) Direct Material	6,000	
ii) Direct Labour	1,200	
iii) Variable Overheads (–)	2,800	
Differential Revenue	2,000	1,000

The management is advised that the differential revenue favours continuation of production of Hanky.

4.3.5 SHORT-RUN USE OF SCARCE RESOURCES

Short-term incremental analysis can be applied to allocate the resources that are limited in quantity i.e. key-factor. In this process, alternative courses of action be compared in a way that takes resource availability into account. While calculating result, the decision criterion in such a situation is the contribution margin per unit of the key-factor. This will maximise the total contribution of the firm.

ILLUSTRATION 16

Prestige Ltd., Pune are producing to specific orders. Their manufacturing capacity is limited by one major machine forming a critical cost centre through which all orders pass. The factory normally works for 250 days in a year on 24 hours, 3 shifts a day and 5 days a week basis. Their maximum achievable capacity is 80% corresponding to the average level of activity in the critical cost centre. The operating results of previous year are summarised in the following statement.

(₹ in lakhs)

Particulars	Amount ₹	Amount ₹
Sales		48
Less :		43
i) Materials	18.00	
ii) Labour Variable Costs	5.75	
iii) Factory Variable Costs	6.25	
iv) Factory Fixed Costs	3.00	
v) Selling and Administration Costs (+)	10.00	
∴. Profit	(–)	5

The average profitability experienced during the previous years is being maintained during the current year also. The company has an opportunity of taking any one of two large contracts either of which will substitute for a large amount of current production without affecting the hourly variable production costs. Details of the contracts are as follows :

Particulars		Contract X	Contract Y
Material Cost per unit	₹	375	1,750
Machine Hours (critical cost centre) per unit	Hrs.	2	3
Contract Price per unit	₹	1,500	3,750
Extra Selling Expenses per unit	₹	25	50

Advise the managing director making your recommendations as to which of the two contracts should be preferred.

SOLUTION

Working Notes :

i)   Machine Hours available =
     (Working days × 24 hours) = 250 Days × 25 Hrs. = 6,000 Hrs.
     Operating Capacity available 80% × 6,000 Hrs. = 6,800 Hrs.

ii) Variable Production Costs (other than materials) per hour :
     (₹ 5,75,000 + ₹ 6,25,000) ÷ 4,800 Hrs. = ₹ 250 per hour.

iii) It is assumed that the company, at present, is operating at its maximum achievable capacity, i.e. 4,800 hours. In operational terms, the variable production costs (labour and other variable costs) are at the level of 4,800 hours.

iv) The company would be in a position to sell all the units of Y contract.

v)   Selling and Administration Overheads are assumed to be fixed.

DECISION ANALYSIS STATEMENT

Particulars	Contract X 2,400 units (4,800 Hrs. ÷ 2 Hrs.)		Contract Y 1,600 units (4,800 Hrs. ÷ 3 Hrs.)	
	Per Unit ₹	Total ₹	Per Unit ₹	Total ₹
Contract Price	1,500	36,00,000	3,750	60,00,000
Less : Incremental Costs				
i) Material Costs	375	9,00,000	1,750	28,00,000
ii) Other Variable Production Cost	500	12,00,000	750	12,00,000
iii) Additional Selling Expenses (−)	25	60,000	50	80,000
∴ Contribution	600	14,40,000	1,200	19,20,000
Contribution per machine-hour i.e. key factor	300		400	
Less : Fixed Costs				
i) Factory Overheads		3,00,000		3,00,000
ii) Selling and Administration (assumed) (−)		10,00,000	(−)	10,00,000
∴ Profit		1,40,000		6,20,000
Present Profit ... ₹ 5,00,000				

*   Contribution per machine-hour (Contract X) = ₹ 600 ÷ 2 Hrs. = ₹ 300.

**   Contribution per machine-hour (Contract Y) = ₹ 1,200 ÷ 3 Hrs. = ₹ 400.

The Managing Director is advised to accept Contract Y as its contribution margin per machine-hour as well as profit is higher.

Joint Outputs of Common Processing Operations :

A related short-term decision involves selecting an alternative processing plan for joint products when the proportions of the output (sale-mix) from common processing cost can be varied.

Sales mix denotes the proportion in which various products are sold or produced. The problem of selecting a profitable mix of sales thus arises only when a business enterprise has a variety of product lines and each making a contribution of its own. Any change in sales mix also results in the change in profit position. The technique of marginal costing informs the management regarding the most profitable sales mix. The most profitable sales mix is one which yields the largest overall contribution.

ILLUSTRATION 17

Quality Ltd. Patna gives you the following information :

Particulars	Product A ₹	Product B ₹
Fixed Overheads : ₹ 10,000 p.a.	–	–
Direct Materials	20	25
Direct Labour @ ₹ 1 per hour	10	15
Variable Overheads (100% of Direct Labour)	–	–
Selling Price	60	100

You are required to present a statement showing the marginal cost of each product and recommend which of the following sales mix should be adopted :

1) 900 units of A and 600 units of B.
2) 1,800 units of A only.
3) 1,200 units of B only.
4) 1,200 units of A and 400 units of B.

SOLUTION

Marginal Cost Statement

Particulars		A	B
i) Direct Materials		20	25
ii) Direct Labour		10	15
iii) Variable Overheads	(+)	10	15
∴ Marginal Cost		40	55
Add : Contribution	(+)	20	45
∴ Selling Price		60	100

Statement of Contributions and Profits of Different Sales Mixture

Sales Mix	Contribution per unit ₹		Contribution ₹	Total Contribution ₹	Fixed Cost ₹	Profit ₹
1) A : 900 units	20		18,000			
B : 600 units	45	(+)	27,000	45,000	10,000	35,000
2) A : 1,800 units	20		36,000			
B : Nil	–	(+)	Nil	36,000	10,000	26,000
3) A : Nil	–		Nil			
B : 1,200 units	45	(+)	54,000	54,000	10,000	44,000
4) A : 1,200 units	20		24,000			
B : 400 units	45	(+)	18,000	42,000	10,000	32,000

Thus, sales mix (3) is recommended as it yield the highest profit of ₹ 44,000. This is because contribution per unit of B is more than that of A and therefore, any sales mixture that takes into account the maximum number of units of B would be more profitable.

ILLUSTRATION 18

Rotex Enterprises, Raipur submit the following information of costs in respect of its two products :

	Product X (per unit) ₹	Product Y (per unit) ₹
Direct Material	25	30
Direct Wages	15	20
Variable Overheads	15	20
Fixed Overheads - ₹ 15,000 p.a.	–	–
Selling Price	75	125

You are required to recommend the management the profitable sales mix from following alternatives :

1) 300 units of X and 200 units of Y.   2) 600 units of X only.
3) 800 units of Y only.   4) 100 units of X and 300 units of Y.

SOLUTION

Marginal Cost Statement

Particulars		X ₹	Y ₹
Selling Price		75	125
Less : Variable Cost			
i) Direct Material		25	30
ii) Direct Wages		15	20
iii) Variable Overheads	(+)	15	20
∴ Total Marginal Cost		55	70
∴ Contribution		20	55

Statement of Sales Mixture

Particulars	X ₹	Y ₹	Total ₹
1) 300 Units of X and 200 Units of Y			
Contribution :	6,000	11,000	17,000
X (Units 300 × ₹ 20) and Y (Units 200 × ₹ 55)			
Less : Fixed Overheads		(−)	15,000
∴ Profit			2,000
2) 600 Units of X only			
Contribution (Units 600 × ₹ 20)	12,000		12,000
Less : Fixed Overheads		(−)	15,000
∴ Loss			(3,000)
3) 800 Units of Y only			
Contribution (Units 800 × ₹ 55)		44,000	44,000
Less : Fixed Overheads		(−)	15,000
∴ Profit			29,000
4) 100 Units of X and 300 Units of Y			
Contribution			
X (Units 100 × ₹ 20) and Y (Units 300 × ₹ 55)	2,000	16,500	18,500
Less : Fixed Overheads		(−)	15,000
∴ Profit			3,500

Comments :

As the sales mixture (3) i.e., 800 units of Y only gives maximum profit, it is recommended.

4.3.6 OPERATE OR SHUT DOWN

The management under certain circumstances, might feel that plant should be shut down i.e. closing down the business is better than operating at a loss, but a marginal costing analysis may prove that this is not so. This type of situation usually arises when sufficient business cannot be secured. This type of decision may be either temporary suspension of production activities, or permanent closing down of production. Temporary suspension of activities is a short term concept. The object is usually to stop operations until trade depression has passed. The problem before management is when should operations be suspended, or in other words, how long should operations be continued. The answer to this problem is that if products are making a contribution towards fixed cost, then generally speaking, production should not be suspended. This is so because continuing production will help minimising loss which would be incurred if plant is shut down. Thus, the information needed to solve this type of problem involves a comparison between probable loss at a given level of output and the loss that would be suffered in production is suspended temporarily.

ILLUSTRATION 19

Swastic Ltd. Surat supplies you the following information :

Normal Capacity of plant	: 10,000 Units
Fixed Costs	: ₹ 2,00,000
Marginal Cost	: ₹ 150
Estimated Selling Price	: ₹ 160
Estimated Sales Volume at the selling price	: 5,000 Units

Advise the company whether plant is to be operated or not ?

SOLUTION

Marginal Cost Statement

	Particulars		Amount ₹
	Sales (5,000 Units × ₹ 160)		8,00,000
Less :	Marginal Costs (5,000 Units × ₹ 150)	(–)	7,50,000
∴	Contribution		50,000
Less :	Fixed Cost	(–)	2,00,000
	Loss		(1,50,000)

If plant is shut down the loss due to fixed charges would be ₹ 2,00,000, whereas if plant is operated, the loss would only be ₹ 1,50,000. This is because selling price is above the marginal cost and is making a contribution towards fixed cost.

ILLUSTRATION 20

Toya Ltd., Tatanagar produces 24,000 Units. The cost sheet gives the following information :

	₹
Direct Material	1,20,000
Direct Wages	84,000
Variable Overheads	48,000
Semi-Variable Overheads	28,000
Fixed Overheads	(+) 80,000
∴ Total Cost	3,60,000

The product is sold at ₹ 20 per unit. The management proposes to increase the production by 3,000 units for sales in the foreign market. It is estimated that the semi-variable overheads will increase by ₹ 1,000. But the product will be sold at ₹ 14 per unit in the foreign market. However, no additional capital expenditure will be incurred. The management seeks your advice as a cost accountant.

What will you advise them ?

SOLUTION

Marginal Cost Statement for 24,000 units

Particulars		Total Cost ₹	Unit Cost ₹
	Sales	4,80,000	20.00
Less :	Variable Cost		
	i) Direct Materials	1,20,000	5.00
	ii) Direct Wages	84,000	3.50
	iii) Variable Overheads (−)	48,000	2.00
∴	Contribution	2,28,000	9.50

If production of additional 3,000 units is undertaken for sale in the foreign market, the position of cost and profit will be as follows :

Particulars		Total Cost ₹	Unit Cost ₹
	Additional Sales	42,000	14.00
Less :	Marginal Cost (−)	31,500	10.50
∴	Additional Contribution	10,500	3.50
Less :	Increase in Semi-Variable Overheads (−)	1,000	–
∴	Net addition to Profit	9,500	–

Acceptance of this offer for sale in the foreign market at ₹ 14 per unit will yield an additional profit of ₹ 9,500. Therefore, the offer should be accepted.

ILLUSTRATION 21

The following production or sales mix are capable of achievement in United Ltd, Ujjain.

1) 2,000 Units of product A and 2,000 Units of product C.
2) 4,000 Units of product B only.
3) 1,000 Units of product A, 2,000 Units of product B and 1,600 Units of product C.

The unit cost is as follows :

Particulars	A ₹	B ₹	C ₹
Direct Materials	20	16	40
Direct Wages	8	10	20

Fixed Cost is ₹ 20,000 and Variable Overheads per unit of A, B and C are ₹ 2, ₹ 4 and ₹ 8 respectively. Selling Prices of A, B and C are ₹ 36, ₹ 40 and ₹ 100 per unit respectively. Determine the marginal contribution per unit of A, B and C and the profit resulting from product mixes 1), 2) and 3).

SOLUTION

Marginal Cost Statement

Particulars	Unit Cost of Products		
	A ₹	B ₹	C ₹
Selling Price	36	40	100
Less Marginal Cost			
i) Direct Material	20	16	40
ii) Direct Wages (+)	8	10	20
iii) Variable Overheads	2	4	8
Total (−)	30	30	68
∴ Contribution	06	10	32

Statement showing Comparative Profitability

Sales Mix	Contribution ₹	Total Contribution ₹	Fixed Cost ₹	Profit ₹
1) A : 2,000 Units	12,000			
C : 2,000 Units	64,000	76,000	20,000	56,000
2) B : 4,000 Units	40,000	40,000	20,000	20,000
3) A : 1,000 Units	6,000			
B : 2,000 Units	20,000			
C : 1,600 Units	51,200	77,200	20,000	57,200

Comments :

The sales mix (3) is the most profitable as it yields the highest amount of profit i.e. ₹ 57,200.

ILLUSTRATION 22

Vedant Ld. Vijapur produces part No. 201 of an article. The cost of making part No. 201 is given below :

Particulars	Cost of making part No. 201	
	Per Unit ₹	10,000 Units ₹
Direct Materials	1	10,000
Direct Labour	8	80,000
Variable Overheads	4	40,000
Fixed Overhead Charges (+)	5	50,000
∴ Total Cost	18	1,80,000

Another manufacturer offers to sell Vedant Ld. the same part for ₹ 16 per unit. The analysis of Fixed Overhead charged showed that ₹ 30,000 represents (such costs like depreciation, insurance, allocated executive salaries etc.) those costs that will continue regardless of the decision.

Should Vedant Ltd. make or buy the part ?

SOLUTION

It is obvious that Vedant Ltd. should buy. But if the key factor, that is, how best to utilise the available facilities taken into account is then the decision will be different.

Suppose the capacity now used to make parts will become idle if the parts are purchased. The relevant computations are as follows :

Particulars	Per Unit Cost		Total Cost	
	Make ₹	Buy ₹	Make ₹	Buy ₹
Direct Materials	1		10,000	
Direct Labours	8		80,000	
Variable Overhead	4		40,000	
Fixed Overhead (that can be avoided by not making) (+)	2		20,000	
∴ Total	15	16	1,50,000	1,60,000
Difference in favour of making	1		10,000	

The above analysis of cost indicates that making the parts is a better choice in absence of the alternative use of released facilities.

QUESTIONS FOR SELF-STUDY

I. Theory Questions :

i) Briefly explain the meaning of short-term as it relates to short-term decisions.

ii) Briefly explain the meaning of the following concepts :
  a) Make-or-buy decision.
  b) Relevant Cost.
  c) Dropping a product line.

iii) How do you determine which data are relevant to a make-or-buy decision ?

iv) For 'pricing a special order' when should fixed overhead costs be included excluded from the analysis. Under what circumstances are fixed costs relevant to the pricing decision ?

v) What is meant by relevant decision information ? What are the important factors that should be taken into account in this decision ?

vi) What are the factors that must be considered in a decision to drop a product line ?

vii) What does the term 'short-term' mean as it relates to short-term decision ?

viii) Explain the meaning of the term 'segment analysis'. Can all business firms use this concept successfully in their organisations ? Elucidate with example.

ix) Write short notes on :

    a) Relevant Data   b) Incremental Costs

    c) Opportunity Costs   d) Use of Relevant Costing

    e) Decision Situations   f) Sales Volume related decisions

    g) Loss Leaders   h) Sell or Process further decisions

x) Distinguish between :

    a) Relevant Cost and Irrelevant Costs.

II. Practical Problems :

i) Asmita Ltd., Anand manufactures and sells three products. The income statement for the company is given below :

Particulars		Product A ₹	Product B ₹	Product C ₹	Total ₹
	Sales	10,000,000	6,00,000	4,00,000	20,00,000
Less :	Variable Cost (−)	4,00,000	2,70,000	2,40,000	9,10,000
	Contribution Margin	6,00,00	3,30,000	60,000	10,90,000
Less :	i) Fixed Cost	2,40,000	1,44,000	96,000	4,80,000
	ii) Joint Separable	1,00,000	80,000	70,000	2,50,000
		3,40,000	2,24,000	1,66,000	7,30,000
	Net Income (Loss)	2,60,000	1,06,000	(6,000)	3,60,000

You are required to,

a) Should the company drop product C ? Explain.

b) Prepare a revised income statement assuming that product C was dropped.

c) Suppose that the sales of the XYZ Electronics Co. increase by 25% if product C is dropped. Will this change your answer ? Explain.

ii) The following are the estimated costs to produce a unit of item M for the next budget period :

Particulars		Unit Cost ₹	Total Cost ₹
Direct Material		6.00	30,000
Direct Labour		18.00	90,000
Variable Overhead		8.00	40,000
Joint Fixed Overhead		6.00	30,000
Separable Fixed Overhead	(+)	4.00	(+) 20,000
		42.00	2,10,000

X Ltd. a competitor has offered to make item M for ₹ 40 per unit, with no sacrifice in quality.

Should the offer of X Ltd. be accepted ? Explain.

iii) Bipin Ltd., Bandra has three divisions, M.N.O. the divisional income summarised for 2013 revealed the following :

Income Statement for 2013

Particulars	M ₹	N ₹	O ₹	Total ₹
Sales	1,90,000	4,30,000	7,40,000	13,60,000
Less : Variable Cost (−)	50,000	3,20,000	4,80,000	8,50,000
∴ Contribution Margin	1,40,000	1,10,000	2,60,000	5,10,000
Less : Traceable Fixed Costs (−)	1,00,000	1,50,000	1,50,000	4,00,000
∴ Divisional Income	40,000	(40,000)	1,10,000	1,10,000
Less : Unallocated Fixed Cost (−)	5,000			35,000
∴ Net Income before Taxes	35,000			75,000

A detailed analysis of the traceable fixed costs revealed the following information :

Particulars	M ₹	N ₹	O ₹
Avoidable Fixed Cost	70,000	1,35,000	1,10,000
Unavoidable Fixed Cost	30,000	15,000	40,000
Total	1,00,000	1,50,000	1,50,000

Is it profitable for the Co. to eliminate one or more of its segments based on the 2013 income statement ? Prepare revised income statement if any divisions are eliminated.

iv) The income statement for Comex Ltd., Chinchwad producing three products is as shown below :

Particulars		Products		
		A ₹	B ₹	C ₹
	Sales	65,800	1,00,000	85,500
Less :	Variable Cost (−)	25,000	55,000	35,000
∴	Total Contribution Margin	40,800	45,000	50,500
Less :	Allocated Fixed Cost (−)	20,500	47,000	32,800
	Profit/Loss	20,300	(2,000)	17,700

Should the Co. drop product B ? Prepare a revised income statement if product B was dropped.

v) Sumadhur Co., Surat (SCS) manufactures cassette record players. It is operating at full capacity of 10,000 units annually with a sales price of ₹ 3,000 per unit. The cost data are : a) Raw Materials, ₹ 900 per unit, b) Direct Labour, ₹ 400 per unit, c) Variable Overheads, ₹ 300 per unit and d) Fixed Cost, ₹ 60,00,000.

While the SCS was planning to expand its operations, Audiocon Ltd. launched a new competitive product: HiFi CD player at ₹ 3,500 per unit. To meet the competition from this new product, the SCS has under consideration two alternatives: a) Reduce the price of the cassette player to ₹ 2,499 b) Add new features to the product by further processing and sell for ₹ 3,700.

The further processing of the product would involve the following.

i)   Raw Materials cost, ₹ 600 per unit;

ii) Labour Charges, ₹ 300 per unit;

iii) Additional Variable Overheads, ₹ 300 per unit and

iv) Additional Fixed Costs, ₹ 40,00,000.

As a consultant, what course of action would you recommend the SCS to follow ?

vi) Bata Shoes, Baroda which has a chain of shoe shops throughout the country has two shops in Madras of which Shop I makes a profit and Shop II makes a loss. The following is the summarised Profit and Loss Account of shop II for the current year ended March 31, 2013.

Particulars		₹	₹
	Sales		6,00,000
Less :	Cost of Sales		4,92,000
	∴ Gross Profit	(−)	1,08,000
Less :	Expenses		
	• Commission to Salesmen	6,000	
	• Manager's Salary	12,000	
	• Head Office Expenses	10,500	
	• Motor Van Expenses		
	• Fixed (Allocated)	6,900	
	• Variable (Allocated)	2,400	
	• Other Items (+)	1,09,950	1,47,750
	∴ Loss for the year	(−)	(39,750)

The commission to salesmen is a fixed percentage on turnover. There is a common manager for the two shops and his salary is equally shared by the two shops. The motor van is also common to the two shops. Its fixed expenses are shared equally by the two shops but the running expenses are apportioned on the basis of the turnover.

Prepare a report explaining the financial implication of the closing down Shop II, assuming that 20% of its turnover will be gained by Shop I without that shop needing any additional staff.

vii) Liberty Ltd., Lonavala is currently buying a component from a local supplier at ₹ 15 each. The supply is tending to be irregular. Two proposals are under consideration :

a) Buy and instal a semi-automatic machine for manufacturing this component, which would involve an annual fixed cost of ₹ 9,00,000 and a variable cost of ₹ 6 per manufactured component.

b) Buy and instal an automatic machine for manufacturing this component, incurring an annual fixed cost of ₹ 15,00,000 and a variable cost of ₹ 5 per manufactured component. Determine with necessary computation :

- The annual volume required in each case to justify the switchover from "outside purchase" to "own manufacture".

- The annual volume required to justify selection of the automatic machine instead of semi-automatic machine.

- If the annual requirement for the coming year is expected to be 5,00,000 units and the volume is expected to increase rapidly thereafter, would you recommended the automatic or semi-automatic machine ? Justify your recommendation.

viii) Henley Ltd., Himmatpur produces two products, X and Y. As per the existing operations, raw materials are processed in Department 1, and the two products are separated at the end of this processing. For every unit of product X, 3 units of Y are obtained. X is then finished in Department 2 and Y in Department 3. Budgeted operating data for year 1 are as follows :

Particulars	Departments		
	1	2	3
Units Produced and Sold :			
Product X - Units	1,00,000	1,00,000	–
Y - Units	3,00,000	–	3,00,000
Costs incurred :	₹	₹	₹
i) Direct Materials	6,00,000	1,20,000	1,60,000
ii) Direct Labour	3,20,000	40,000	80,000
iii) Variable Manufacturing Overheads	80,000	1,00,000	1,40,000
iv) Fixed Manufacturing Overheads	3,60,000	1,00,000	1,40,000

All costs are directly traceable to the individual departments. At present, X is sold for ₹ 10 per unit and Y for ₹ 5 per unit. Both products are also readily saleable at the completion of processing in Department 1 – Product X for ₹ 8 per unit and product Y for ₹ 3 per unit.

You are required to advise the company whether each product should be sold after final completion or at the split-off point.

ix) Mahima Ltd., Malegaon manufactures three products, A, B and C from common facilities. Production was standardised for some months at a mix of 27,000 units of product A and 18,000 units each of products B and C. The total fixed costs come to ₹ 3,15,000 per month. At the above production volume per month, the variable costs are of the order of ₹ 9,00,000 per month. The cost ratios among the products, excluding fixed costs are 2 : 3 : 4 for A, B and C respectively. With the unit selling prices being ₹ 12. ₹ 15 and ₹ 30 each, for products A, B and C respectively, losses are being suffered at present. Three proposals for change of product-mix have been put up, which are as follows.

Mix	A ₹	B ₹	C ₹	Total ₹
1	32,000	22,000	13,000	67,000
2	27,000	10,000	23,000	60,000
3	25,000	5,000	30,000	60,000

Which do you consider to be the most desirable mix ? Compile the statement showing profit or loss pertaining to current mix and proposed alternatives.

■■■

Chapter 5...

Budget and Budgetary Control

Synopsis...

5.1 MEANING AND DEFINITIONS

5.1.1 BUDGET

Managerial Control becomes essential in case of public limited companies and Government undertakings, which are run by hired managerial personnel with little interest in the results of such enterprises. The proprietors have, therefore, to think of a device which may encourage the management to work with greater care and caution to serve the interests of all by optimising the use of investments in the form of man, money and materials.

Budgeting is one such device which helps the management to understand the business programmes in their right perspective and take steps to achieve business objectives. Budgeting means planning for future. It involves the preparation of departmental budgets, budgetary control and related issues. The **Budgetary Control** is concerned with the management of business activities with the help of budgets. In this way, **Budgets** serve as a control device.

The term **'Budget'** is derived from the French word **'bougette'** which means a little bag, containing documents and accounts. A **Budget** is a plan which relates to a definite period of time and which is expressed in quantitative terms. It is thus, a predetermined statement which incorporates the policy of the management during a given period and serves as a standard for comparing the actual results.Thus, a **Budget** is a tool in the hands of the management which serves as a guide for all the employees in achieving their goals, objectives and targets. A **Budget** helps in planning and co-ordination with all the employees and departments, but the most important factor is that it is used for control purposes at all levels of management.

> **Budgets provide a discipline that brings planning to the forefront as a key managerial responsibility.**

There is a difference between budget and budgetory control. A **Budget** is a quantitative statement prepared in advance and keeping it as the base, the actuals are compared. **Budgetary Control** on the other hand means use of the budgets. Thus, **Budgetary Control** involves use of the budgeting techniques to help the management for carrying out various functions viz. Planning, Organising, Co-ordinating and Controlling the activities of a business.

The term **Budget** has been defined by different experts and professional institutes in the manner stated below :

i) **The Chartered Institute of Management Accountants (CIMA), London** :

"A financial and/or quantitative statement, prepared and approved prior to a defined period of time, of the policy to be pursued during the period for the purpose of attaining a given objective. It may include income, expenditure and employment of capital".

ii) **Kohler :**

"A financial plan serving as a pattern for and a control over future operations".

iii) **Brown and Howard**

"It is a pre-determined statement of management policy during a given period which provides a standard for comparison with the results actually achieved".

> **A Budget is a vital tool for carrying out effectively short term planning and control in business units.**

Thus, from the above definitions the **important features of budget** are outlined as follows :

   i)   it is a statement expressed in numbers.
   ii) it is a financial and/or quantitative statement.
   iii) it is prepared for a future specified period of timc.
   iv) it is prepared and approved prior to the budget period.
   v)   it is based on the policies to be pursued.
   vi) it is prepared for the purpose of attaining a given objective.
   vii) it may relate to incomes, expenses, capital receipts and expenditure.
   viii) it may be prepared for a short, medium or long period.
   ix) it may relate to whole of the organisation or for various divisions of the organisation.
   xi) it is an instrument of financial control.

5.1.2 BUDGETARY CONTROL

The term **Budgetary Control** has been defined by different experts and professional institutes in the manner stated below :

i) **The Chartered Institute of Management Accountants (CIMA), London :**
"the establishment of budgets relating to the responsibilities of executives to the requirements of a policy, and the continuous comparison of actual with the budgeted results, either to secure by individual action the objective of that policy or to provide a basis for its revision".

ii) **W. W. Bigg :**
"the term Budgetary control is applied to a system of management and accounting control by which all operations and output are forecast as far ahead as possible and actual results when known, are compared with the budget estimates".

iii) **J. A. Scott :**
"it is the system of management control and accounting in which all operations are forecasted and planned so far as possible ahead, and the actual results compared with the forecasted and planned ones".

iv) **Robert Anthony :**
"it is process by which the managers assure that efficiently in the accomplishment of the goals of the organisation".

v) **Brown and Howard :**
"it is a system of controlling costs which includes the preparation of budgets, co-ordinating the departments and establishing responsibilities, comparing actual performance with the budgeted and acting upon results to achieve maximum profitability".

vi) **J. Betty :**
"it is a system which uses budgets as a means of planning and controlling all aspects of producing and selling commodities or services".

Thus, from the above definitions the **important features of budgetary control** are outlined as follows :

    i)   establishment of budgets for each department or function of the organisation.

   ii)   co-ordination of various budgets as a total plan for the entire organisation.

  iii)   recording and reporting of actual results.

  iv)   comparing the actual result continuously with the budgeted performance.

   v)   finding out the variances.

  vi)   analysing the reasons for such variables.

 vii)   fixing the responsiblities for every controllable variances.

viii)   taking corrective action wherever possible.

  ix)   to see that the mistakes of the past are not repeated in the future.

  xi)   revising the budgets in the light of changes in plans and policies.

Thus, Budgetary control is an important tool very frequently used by the management for the purpose of planning, co-ordination and control.

Rowland and Harr, the professional authority on the subject of 'Budgeting for Management Control' has made a clearcut variation between the original concepts of budget, budgeting and bugetary control as follows :

'Budgets' are the individual objectives of a particular department in the organisation.

'Budgeting' is the ultimate process of building up the specific budget.

'Budgetary control' includes all this and additionally, it is the science of planning the budgets themselves and the utilisation of the same to effect an overall management tool for effective business planning and efficient control.

Hence, **Budgets** are the future estimates. **Budgeting** is based on incrementalism. Budgetary control is a broader term than budgeting. **Budgtary control** is a most useful technique of implementing the objectives of the company with minimum possible cost and maximum possible efficiency.

Generally, Budgetary Control is concerned with three basic aspects viz. planning, co-ordination and control.

i) Planning :

A Budget is nothing but a plan. Without planning no modern business can function. Planning is related to production sales, stocks, requirement of labour, etc. The advantage of planning is that we can anticipate the problems before hand. Planning through budgetary control is necessary at all levels of management. It is a process of thinking which enables the management to get newer ideas.

ii) Co-ordination :

It means co-operation by the different people in the organisation to achieve the common goal. To have effective co-ordination, proper communication is essential which can be achieved through implementation of budgets and planning helps in this process. A detailed budgetary control system is one where the plans are written down and these plans are circulated to all the levels of management.

iii) Control :

It ensures that the goals of the management as stated in the budgetary control system have been achieved. For this fixing of standards is necessary. Thus, through the budgets the standards are fixed which enables the management to control the activities so that the goals are achieved. Thus, through budgetary control, we can compare the standards with the actuals and the analysis of the variances becomes possible and corrective action can be taken wherever necessary.

It encourages research as budgetary control schedules are usually based on past experience.

> **Budget and Budgetary Control, both are used as important managerial tools for planning, co-ordination, motivation, communication and control so as to promote optimum utilisation of available scarce resources.**

Objectives of Budgetary Control :

The important basic objective of the technique of budgetary control is to exercise managerial control over the different activities of the organisation through effective planning, proper co-ordination and strict control. However, the other important **objectives of budgetary control** are as follows :

i) to identify the overall aims of the business enterprise.

ii) to determine specific targets of performance for each division of the business.

iii) to fix up the responsibilities of the top executives and other personnel.

iv) to provide a basis for comparison of actual performance with the predetermined targets.

v) to analyse the variances more carefully for maximisation of quality production.

vi) to ensure the best use of the available resources for maximisation of quality production.

vii) to co-ordinate the overall activities of the business for effecting centralised control and decentralised responsibilities.

viii) to delegate authority for increasing efficiency.

ix) to provide a suitable basis for necessary revision of current and future policies.

xi) to draw long-term plan with absolute accuracy.

(xi) to provide a suitable standard performance with which actuals can be compared.

(xii) to find out capital requirements for achieving planned targets.

Essentials of Budgetary Control :

The most effective and successful implementation of a budgetary control system depends on certain important features. The following are some of the **Essentials of Budgetary Control** :

i) Sound Organisation :

A good organisation is necessary to carry out the plans and policies of the management. It means that the organisational structure should be such that each one knows what the management expects from him and also his responsibilities.

ii) Cost Factor :

The cost benefit analysis should be made before the budget is introduced. It means that the cost of operation of the budget should be less than the benefits derived out of it.

iii) Interpersonal Relationship :

The management should develop interpersonal relationship, which means that the management should be able to know the personal difficulties of the executives and managers in implementing the budgets. This will ensure that the budget is not imposed on anyone without studying his ability to undertake the responsibility.

iv) Systematic Accounting Systems :

It is necessary so that the management can hold the concerned person responsible in the organisation in terms of monetary consideration.

v) High Profits :

The main aim or goal of the management should be to earn maximum profits and this factor should be kept in mind while preparing the budget.

vi) Goals should be Achievable :

The management should fix the goals in such a way that they should be attainable. Otherwise there will be confusion in the organisation.

vii) Constant Review :

Constant review of the performance should be made to evaluate the actual results as compared with the budgets so that corrective action can be taken at the right time.

viii) Fixing of Responsibilities and Preparation of Budget :

It should be noted that the person who will execute the budgets should be made responsible for the preparation of it.

ix) Budget Committee :

A Budget Committee is necessary to carry out the policies effectively so that the committee consisting of the directors and the executives of various departments are responsible for its implementation.

x) Involvement of Top Management :

Unless the top management co-operates in implementing the budget in true spirit, the budgetary control system cannot be successful. It means that the top management should carry out the plans and policies as laid down in the budget strictly.

Advantages of Budgetary Control :

> **Budgetary Control is the most effective tool available with the modern management for the purposes of efficient cost control and ultimately the maximisation of profits, only.**

The **important advantages of budgetary control system** are as follows :

   i) It locates the inefficient areas and persons in the business.

   ii) It helps to increase the efficiency, reduce wastages and control costs.

   iii) It helps to co-ordinate the activities of the various employees, departments and thus helps to achieve the goal of the management.

   iv) With the help of budgeting, the responsibilities of the managers can be fixed for planning, so that they can think ahead, anticipate and be prepared to meet the challenges ahead.

   v) Maximisation of profits is possible through budgeting.

vi) It helps to introduce the standard costing technique.

vii) It helps to ensure cash flow and hence bank credit can be obtained.

viii) It creates cost consciousness in the minds of all the employees in the organisation.

ix) Authority can be delegated and responsibilities fixed.

x) It rewards the efficient workers and the managers can show their efficiency by achieving the goals fixed by the management through the budgets.

xi) It ensures that the capital of the firm is utilized in a proper way and that there is no misutilisation of funds.

xii) Vital decisions can be taken by the management based on the budgets.

xiii) Actual results can be compared with the budgets so that corrective action can be taken in time.

xiv) It is like a barometer which enables us to study the changes in the business conditions.

Limitations of Budgetary Control :

> **The Limitations of Budgetary Control system arise mainly due to poor implementation of the entire budgetary process.**

Though there are many advantages of Budgetary Control System, it suffers from many defects also. Hence, the persons using the budgets should be very careful and should be fully aware of the limitations. The **important limitations of budgetary control system** are as follows :

i) Budgetary control does not replace management :

It cannot replace the management because in business all vital decisions have to be taken by the management.

ii) Too much reliance on budgets is harmful :

Budgetary control is only a technique and tool in the hands of the management. To execute the budget, all the employees must take active part and co-operate with each other so that the budgetary goal can be achieved. But the budgets should not be taken as the only means through which the business should run. Though sometimes, through budgetary control it is possible to have utmost success in business, it should not be depended upon totally.

iii) Less flexibility :

A Budgetary control system should be more flexible and should be changed according to the changing circumstances. The alternative systems should be added, deleted, improved, replaced or compared with the present system of budgetary control.

iv) Budgets are based on estimated figures :

Budgets are prepared in anticipation of various factors. These factors are estimated by knowing the past and forecasting for the future which may or may not happen in actual life. Thus, it is not an exact prediction of figures, but based on estimates.

v) Costly system :

The installation of the system and its execution is expensive affair. This is because specialised persons have to be appointed and extra costs have to be incurred for carrying out the operations. Hence, small scale units cannot go in for budgetary control system.

vi) Budgetary control deals with quantitative data only : In budgetary control system, only the figures are considered and hence the quantitative data i.e. the facts are not considered. e.g. if a worker is inefficient, he may be so because of the conditions or environment where he works are not suitable to his health. Here budgets are of no use because budgets will only measure his efficiency in terms of quantity produced and will not consider other factors.

5.2 SCOPE OF BUDGET AND BUDGETARY CONTROL

Normally, a budget statement is expressed in both the terms-currency and quantitative units. Currency refers to the cost or value and quantity refers to the activity level or volume of function. Certain budgets can be expressed only in currency as the function cannot be quantified. A budget is a statement of estimated performance for a specific period of time. The natural means of performance evaluation is the comparison between the ideas and the actual. Here, the ideas are the budgeted or standard specifications which are set before the budget period begins. So the actual performance is compared with the standard performance and such comparison gives an idea about the degree of success as a result of the actual performance.

The scope of budgetary control is very wide and broad based and it includes within its fold, a variety of aspects of business operations. The scope of budgetary control extend to cover the operations of a department of the whole organisation. e.g. budgets are prepared for production department, selling and distribution department, purchase department, research and development department etc. and also for the whole company. Therefore, budgetary control is more extensive in its scope. Budgetary control can be applied over to a part of the business. Budgetary control system can be operated without standard costing.

Generally Budgetary Control system involves the following steps :
1) Preparation of various types of budgets i.e. :
   i)   According to Time :
        Long-term, Short-term and Current Budget
   ii) On the Basis of Flexibility :
        Static or Fixed Budgets and Flexible or Variable Budgets
   iii) According to Functions :
        Purchase, Production, Production Cost, Sales, Cash, Labour, R & D, Overhead, Capital Expenditure Budget and Master Budget
   iv) Management Control Instruments :
        Programme Budgeting, Performance Budgeting, Revenue Budgets and Zero Base Budgeting.

2) Measurement of actual performance at the end of the budget period.

3) Comparison of actual performance with the budgetary performance to find out whether the company has achieved the target set in the budget.

4) Analysis of the reasons for not achieving the target so that remedial measures may be taken.

Budgetary Control is largely a matter of management action which is taken on the basis of information on variances. It could be described as **'forwarding costing'**, establishment of budgets and then their application with a view to monitoring and controlling the activities of a concern. In recent years, there have been some notable changes in the concept and techniques of budgets with the introduction of zero base budgeting and performance budgeting. These approaches are particularly useful in government and non-profit organisations where benefits cannot be traced to the costs.

5.3 TYPES OF BUDGET

The budgets are of different types which are classified according to the bases considered as shown in Figure 5.1 as under :

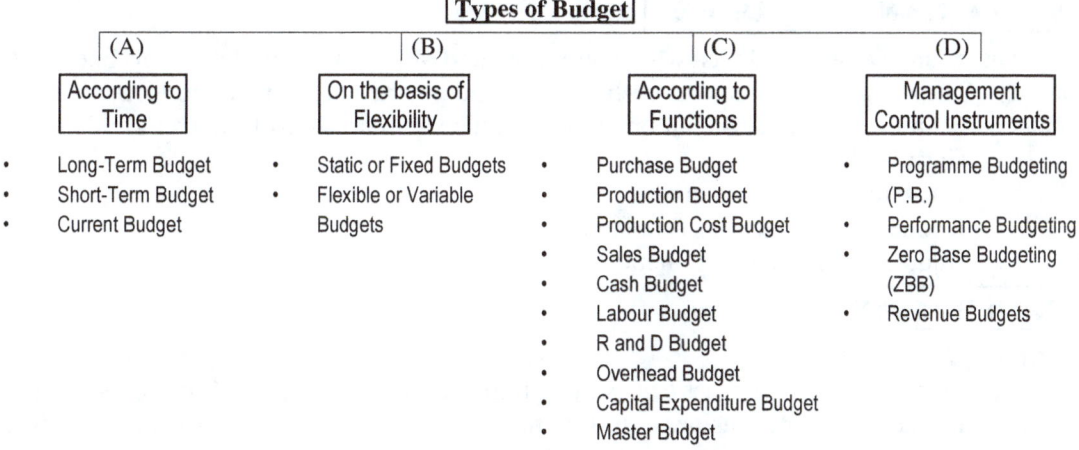

Fig. 5.1: Types of Budget

Budgeting in an undertaking may be done for a particular segment or it may cover all the activities depending upon the need and resources of the enterprise. The large scale business enterprises prepare different types of budgets covering almost all activities where control is desired. In order to understand the nature of budgets, it is desirable to know their classification which is usually done on time, flexibility, functions and management control instrument basis.

A) According to Time :

According to time, budgets can be of three types viz. Long-term Budgets, Short-term Budgets, and Current Budgets. Long-term budgets are concerned with planning activities for a long-period – a period of 5 to 10 or more years whereas short-period budgets cover a period of one to two years. Current budgets relate to the current period i.e. less than or one year. An yearly budget is generally broken on monthly, quarterly or half yearly basis for effective implementation of the same.

B)   On the Basis of Flexibility

On the basis of flexibility, budgets are grouped into two categories, viz. i) Fixed budget, and ii) Flexible or Variable budgets.

C)   According to Functions :

According to functions, a budget relates to a particular activity which can be selling, production, purchasing or any other activity. The budgets prepared according to functions are known as functional budgets. The popular functional budgets prepared in a large scale enterprise are : Sales Budget, Production Budget, Purchase Budget, Capital Expenditure Budget, Overhead Cost Budgets, Cash Budget, Research and Development Budget, Production Cost Budget, Labour Budget, Master Budget.

D)   Management Control Instruments :

Budget or Budgeting as a management control instrument can be classified as Programme Budgeting, Performance Budgeting, Zero Base Budgeting and Revenue Budgets.

5.3.1 FINANCIAL BUDGET

These are certain budgets which are prepared after the completion of operating budgets. They relate to estimate of cash receipts and payments, financial performance and financial position. Hence, financial budgets are to be summarised as follows :

- Cash Budget.
- Budgeted Income Statement.
- Budgeted Statement of Retained Earnings.
- Budgeted Position Statement.

Cash Budget

Meaning :

Cash Budget is the forecast of cash position for a particular period. It represents the cash requirements of the business during the budget period. It is a financial budget prepared after the preparation of all the functional budgets.

Definition :

A Cash Budget is usually defined as,

"an estimate of receipts and payments for each month or any other relevant period forming part of the entire budget period".

Thus, it is the future plan of receipts and payment of cash for the budget period, analysed to show the monthly flow of cash drawn up in such a way that the balance can be forecasted at regular intervals. It is a 'means budget' prepared by the chief accountant in terms of money value. It may be prepared for a short period or a long period depending on the requirements e.g. weekly, fortnightly, monthly, quarterly, half yearly, annually etc. A company may have divisional and departmental cash budgets in addition to a cash budget for the overall organisation.

Necessity :

Generally, a cash budget is prepared to achieve the following necessities :

i) To obtain necessary working capital easily from the banks and financial institutions for smooth running of the business.

ii) To enable the top management to make necessary arrangements of cash in case of emergency situations.

iii) To ensure that sufficient cash is made available throughout the financial period to meet the required payments.

iv) To ascertain any expected shortage of cash and to make it available through bank loan or sale of fixed assets.

Utility :

A cash budget **is more useful** to the organisation in the following manner.

i) It helps in co-ordinating activities of different divisions of a corporate sector.

ii) It helps the company to plan for dividend and interest payments.

iii) It helps in proper planning for long-term capital requirement.

iv) It helps the management to know the type of capital required to be raised.

v) It helps the management to raise the finance from economical sources.

vi) It is useful in knowing the flow of funds and their requirements.

vii) It helps in providing sufficient information on the probable profits to be realised during the budgeted period.

viii) It is useful in analysing the estimated changes in receipts and planned payments in the budget period.

ix) It highlights the fluctuations in cash due to various financial transactions.

x) It indicates the surplus or deficiency of cash at the end of every budgeted period.

Cash Budget is a most important tool for financial planning.

Methods of Preparation of Cash Budget :

Generally, a Cash Budget can be prepared by any one of the three methods viz. Receipts and Payments Method, Cash Flow Statement Method and the Balance Sheet Method. But a Receipts and Payments Method seems to be more popular because of its own advantages as well as, the Receipts and Payments Method is useful for short-term cash budget whereas the other two methods are used for long-term cash budgets.

A) Receipts and Payments Method :

According to this method, Cash Budget includes all the cash receipts whether they are on revenue account or capital account. Similarly, all expected capital and revenue expenditures are brought in a cash budget. The accruals i.e. income earned but not received and expenditure due but not paid are excluded from the cash budget. Thus, a cash budget is a sort of cash account which records cash receipts and cash payments and shows expected cash balance at the end of the budget period. The informations for cash budget are derived from other budgets. For example, the sales budget will provide the amount of sales and the receipts from sales and realisation from debtors can be estimated by taking into account the terms of sales. The raw materials purchase budget, labour budget and overheads budget will provide information relating to payments for raw materials, wages and overhead charges. The management can forecast payments on account of capital expenditure, tax, dividend etc. The difference of cash receipts and cash payments for a period is either positive or negative, which is carried to next period.

In this method, all the cash receipts which are expected and all the cash payments which are expected to be made are taken into account. Thus, the cash balance will represent the difference between the total cash receipts expected (including the opening cash balance) and the total cash payments to be made.

The following are the **sources and application of cash**.

a) **Sources of Cash :**
   - **Collection from debtors i.e. credit customers :** This can be ascertained from the Sales Budget. The terms and conditions of sale, lag in payments and other factors should be considered while estimating the cash receipts.
   - Cash receipts from other sources viz. dividends received interest on investments, rent received, sale of investments, sale of fixed assets etc.

b) **Applications of Cash :**
   - Cash payments for purchase of raw materials, payment of wages and other expenses are estimated from various budgets viz. purchase budgets, personnel budget and overhead/expenses budget. The suppliers credit period, terms and conditions of purchases, cash discount allowed, law about payment of wages etc. should be considered.
   - Cash payments for capital expenditure can be ascertained from the capital expenditure budget.
   - Cash payments for dividends, income tax etc.

EXAMPLE

From the following budgeted data relating to Atlas Industries Ltd., Amaravati, prepare Cash Budget as per Receipts and Payments Method for three months from February to April, 2013.

2013 Months	Sales ₹	Purchases ₹	Wages ₹	Overheads ₹
January	85,000	48,000	10,000	12,500
February	90,000	52,000	11,000	13,500
March	1,20,000	60,000	14,000	15,000
April	1,30,000	62,000	14,000	16,000

Other Information :
   i) 20% sales is for cash and the remaining amount is realised in the month following that of sales.
   ii) Suppliers supply raw materials at one month's credit.
   iii) Wage-bill is paid in the first week of next month.
   iv) Overheads are paid in cash in the same month.
   v) Payment of monthly rent amounts to ₹ 1,000.
   vi) Advance Income Tax of ₹ 15,000 is payable in April.
   vii) Bonus of ₹ 10,000 is payable to workers in February.

viii) Plant costing ₹ 80,000 is due to be installed in February. The part of the bill will be paid in March amounting to ₹ 18,500.

ix) Half year interest on 12% ₹ 50,000 Debentures is to be received in February and August every year.

x) Cash at Bank on 1st February, 2013 estimated at ₹ 5,000.

ANSWER

In the books of Atlas Industries Ltd., Amaravati
Cash Budget as per Receipts and Payments Method
for the three months ended 30th April, 2013

Particulars		February ₹	March ₹	April ₹
Cash at Bank Opening	**(A)**	(+) 5,000	(+) 11,500	(+) 10,000
Add : Receipts :				
i) Cash Sales i.e. 20% of Sales				
ii) Collection from Debtors i.e. 80% of Sales –		18,000	24,000	26,000
One month credit		68,000	72,000	96,000
iii) Interest on Debentures received				
@ 12% p.a. on ₹ 50,000 for six months	**(+)**	3,000	–	–
∴ **Actual Receipts**	**(B)**	89,000	96,000	1,22,000
	(+)			
∴ **Total Receipts (A + B)**	**(C)**	94,000	1,07,500	1,32,000
Less : Payments :				
i) to suppliers for purchase of raw materials –				
One month credit		48,000	52,000	60,000
ii) wage bill – One month credit		10,000	11,000	14,000
iii) overheads – Paid on same month		13,500	15,000	16,000
iv) Monthly Rent		1,000	1,000	1,000
v) Advance Income Tax Payable		–	–	15,000
vi) Plant installation and payment of bill		–	18,500	–
vii) Bonus to workers		10,000	–	–
	(+)			
∴ **Total Payments**	**(D)**	**82,500**	**97,500**	**1,06,000**
	(–)			
∴ **Cash at Bank Closing (C – D)**	**(E)**	(+) 11,500	(+) 10,000	(+) 26,000

B) Adjusted Profit and Loss Method :

Under this method, the profits as shown in the Profit and Loss Account prepared in the conventional manner forms the basis for cash forecast. The profit is adjusted by adding back to it the non-cash items such as depreciation, outstanding expenses, other provisions etc. The other items which increase the total cash inflows are the increase in share capital, debenture and loans, current liabilities (creditors) and decrease in fixed assets, debtors and stock etc. Out of the total cash-inflows calculated as above, the items which results in cash outflow are subtracted to arrive at the cash position at the end of the period. The items which reduce the cash position are accrued incomes, advance payments, dividend payment redemption of debentures and loans, decrease in creditors, payment for fixed assets, increase in debtors and stock etc. This method of cash forecast may also be called as the Cash Flow Statement method as the net income as per the conventional income statement is converted into a cash flow forecast. The main sources of information for cash forecast as per this method are the profit and loss account and balance sheet. This method is suitable to prepare cash budget for long period.

EXAMPLE

From the following Balance Sheet and Projected Profit and Loss Account of Aptech Ltd., Ahmedabad prepare the Cash Budget according to Adjusted Profit and Loss Account method for the year ended 31st December, 2013.

Balance Sheet as on 31st December, 2013

Liabilities	₹	Assets	₹
Share Capital	1,50,00,000	Land and Buildings	1,25,00,000
General Reserve	50,00,000	Plant and Machinery	80,00,000
Profit and Loss	25,00,000	Furniture and Fixtures	15,00,000
Debentures	80,00,000	Sundry Debtors	75,00,000
Creditors	1,00,00,000	Stock	50,00,000
Bills Payable	20,00,000	Bills Receivable	10,00,000
Outstanding Salaries	3,00,000	Prepaid Rent	3,00,000
		Cash at Bank and in Hand	70,00,000
	4,28,00,000		**4,28,00,000**

Dr.   Projected Profit and Loss Account for the year ended 31st December, 2013   Cr.

Particulars		₹	Particulars	₹
To Opening Stock		50,00,000	By Sales	3,00,00,000
To Purchases		2,25,00,000	By Closing Stock	45,00,000
To Gross Profit C/D		70,00,000		
		3,45,00,000		**3,45,00,000**
To Salaries	10,00,000		By Gross Profit B/D	70,00,000
Less : Last years				
Outstanding	(−) 3,00,000			
	7,00,000			
Add : Outstanding				
for current year	(+) 1,00,000	8,00,000		
To Commission		1,50,000		
To Rent	9,00,000			
Add : Last years prepaid				
	(+) 3,00,000	12,00,000		
To Interest		8,00,000		
To Establishment Charges		2,50,000		
To Advertising Expenses		2,00,000		
To Depreciation :				
i) Plant and Machinery				
	8,00,000			
ii) Land and Buildings	6,00,000			
iii) Furniture	(+) 1,50,000	15,50,000		
To Net Profit C/D		20,50,000		
		70,00,000		**70,00,000**
To Dividend		30,00,000	By Net Profit B/D	20,50,000
To General Reserve		10,00,000	By Profit and Loss	25,00,000
To Balance C/D		5,50,000		
		45,50,000		**45,50,000**

On 31st December, 2013, the position of some of the items was as under :

		₹
•	Share Capital	2,00,00,000
•	Debentures	1,00,00,000
•	Creditors	80,00,000
•	Debtors	90,00,000
•	Bills Payable	25,00,000
•	Bills Receivable	8,00,000

Purchase of Plant and Machinery during 2013 amounted to ₹ 28,00,000 and Purchase of Furniture and Fixtures ₹ 21,50,000.

ANSWER

In the books of Aptech Ltd., Ahmedabad
Cash Budget as per Adjusted Profit and Loss Method
for the year ended 31st December, 2013

		Particulars	₹	₹	₹
		Cash at Bank and in Hand - Opening			70,00,000
Add :					
	i)	Net Profit for 2013		20,50,000	
	ii)	Depreciation :			
		• Plant and Machinery	8,00,000		
		• Land and Buildings	6,00,000		
		• Furniture (+)	1,50,000	15,50,000	
	iii)	Decrease in Prepaid Rent		3,00,000	
	iv)	Decrease in Stock		5,00,000	
	v)	Decrease in Bills Receivable		2,00,000	
	vi)	Increase in Bills Payable		5,00,000	
	vii)	Issue of Share Capital		50,00,000	
	viii)	Issue of Debentures (+)		(+) 20,00,000	1,21,00,000
				(+)	1,91,00,000
Less :					
	i)	Purchase of Plant and Machinery		28,00,000	
	ii)	Purchase of Furniture and Fixtures		21,50,000	
	iii)	Dividend		30,00,000	
	iv)	Decrease in Outstanding Salaries		2,00,000	
	v)	Increase in Debtors		15,00,000	
	vi)	Decrease in Creditors		(+) 20,00,000	(−) 1,16,50,000
		Cast at Bank and in Hand – Closing			**74,50,000**

C) Balance Sheet Method :

As per this method, a projected Balance Sheet is prepared in which cash balance is not an estimated item but a difference between total projected assets and total estimated liabilities. In other words, the excess of projected assets over projected liabilities, represents cash balance. If the liabilities are more than the assets, the balance shows the overdraft.

EXAMPLE

Using the cost data of previous example of Aptech Ltd., Ahmedabad, prepare a projected Balance Sheet as on 31st December, 2013 to show the cash position as on that date :

ANSWER

In the books of Aptech Ltd., Ahmedabad
Cash Budget as per Projected Balance Sheet Method as on 31st December, 2013

Liabilities	₹	Assets	₹
Share Capital	2,00,00,000	Land and Buildings 1,25,00,000	
Debentures	1,00,00,000	**Less :** Depreciation (–) 6,00,000	1,19,00,000
General Reserve	60,00,000	Plant and Machinery 80,00,000	
Profit and Loss	5,50,000	**Less :** Depreciation(–) 8,00,000	
Creditors	80,00,000	72,00,000	
Bills Payable	25,00,000	**Add :** Purchases (+) 28,00,000	1,00,00,000
Outstanding Salaries	1,00,000	Furniture and Fixtures 15,00,000	
		Less : Depreciation (–) 1,50,000	
		13,50,000	
		Add : Purchases (+) 21,50,000	35,00,000
		Debtors	90,00,000
		Bills Receivable	8,00,000
		Stock	45,00,000
		Cast at Bank and in Hand (Balancing figure)	74,50,000
	4,71,50,000		**4,71,50,000**

Proforma of Cash Budget
The proforma of Cash Budget can be shown by two methods as follows :
i)   **Proforma of Cash Budget under Rolling Period Basis :**
In the books of a Company
Cash Budget (under Rolling Period Basis) for the period ended ......

Budget Actual Comparison Month – I		Particulars		Month 1	Month 2	Month 3
Budget	Actual					
		(A) **Sales Receipts :**				
		i) Cash Sales and Advances				
		ii) Sundry Debtors Collection				
		iii) Cash Subsidies, Rebate etc.	(+)			
		Total	**(A)**			
		(B) **Operations Distribution**				
		i) Cash Purchases and Advances				
		ii) Sundry Creditors Payment				
		iii) Wages, Salaries etc.				
		iv) Rent, Electricity etc.				
		v) Selling Expenses				
		vi) Administrative Expenses				
		vii) Income Tax paid				
		Total	**(B)**			

contd. ...

(C)	**Cash Flow Through**					
	Operations	(A – B)				
(D)	**Miscellaneous Receipts :**					
	(Interest, Rent, Royalties etc.)					
(E)	**Capital Receipts :**					
i)	Debenture Issues					
ii)	Term Loans					
iii)	Issue of Share Capital					
iv)	Sales of Assets					
	Total	(E)				
(F)	**Non-Operating Distributions**					
i)	Interest and Financial Cost					
ii)	Donations					
iii)	Dividends					
iv)	Capital Expenditures					
v)	Debt redemption					
	Total	(F)				
(G)	**Net Cash Flow (C + D + E – F)**					
Add :	Opening Balance Cash Position	(+)				
Less :	Minimum Cash Required					
	Bank Loan (Increase)/					
	decrease					
	Cumulative Bank Position					
	(Drawing Power)	(–)				

ii) **Proforma of Cash Budget under Receipts and Payments Basis :**

In the books of a Company

Cash Budget (under Receipts and Payments Basis) for the period ended ......

Particulars	January ₹	February ₹	March ₹	Total ₹
Opening Balance of Cash	....	....	....	....
Add : Receipts :				
• Cash Sales	....	....	....	....
• Receipts from Debtors	....	....	....	....
• Issue of Shares and Debentures	....	....	....	....
• Dividends etc. (+)				
Total **(A)**	....	....	....	....
Less : Payments :				
• Cash Purchases	....	....	....	....
• Creditors	....	....	....	....
• Wages	....	....	....	....
• Capital Expenditure	....	....	....	....
• Dividend Payable	....	....	....	....
• Interest Payable	....	....	....	....
• Income-Tax Payable	....	....	....	....
Total **(B)**	....	....	....	....
∴ Closing Cash Balance : (A – B)	....	....	....	....

Thus, a Cash Budget helps the business to plan their future cash requirements in such a way so that sufficient cash liquidity is always being made available to meet their urgent needs to make use of idle cash in the most profitable but secured manner.

ILLUSTRATIONS

ILLUSTRATION 1

Prepare a Cash Budget for three months ended 31st March, 2013 from the following particulars relating to Bharat Forge Co. Ltd., Bengaluru.

2012-2013 Months	Credit Sales ₹	Purchases ₹	Wages ₹
November, 2012	1,00,000	80,000	5,000
December, 2012	90,000	70,000	6,000
January, 2013	1,10,000	1,00,000	4,500
February, 2013	60,000	95,000	5,500
March, 2013	80,000	1,30,000	7,000

Additional Data :

40% of the credit sales will be realised in the month following the sales and the remaining 60% in the second month following it. The creditors will be paid in the month following the purchases. Interest of ₹ 5,000 will have to be paid in the month of February, 2013. Income-tax of ₹ 15,000 will have to be paid in the month of March, 2013. Wages are paid in the same month. The opening balance of cash as on 1st January, 2013 was ₹ 20,000.

SOLUTION

In the Books of Bharat Forge Ltd., Bengaluru
Cash Budget for the three months ending 31st March, 2013

Particulars		January ₹	February ₹	March ₹
Cash Balance Opening :	(A)	20,000	41,500	29,000
Add Receipts :				
i) Collection from Debtors				
• 40% of Credit Sales - one month credit		36,000	44,000	24,000
• 60% of Credit Sales - two months credit	(+)	60,000	54,000	66,000
∴ **Actual Receipts**	(B)	**96,000**	**98,000**	**90,000**
	(+)			
∴ **Total Receipts (A + B)**	(C)	**1,16,000**	**1,39,500**	**1,19,000**
Less Payments :				
i) Creditors for purchases one month credit		70,000	1,00,000	95,000
ii) Interest		–	5,000	–
iii) Income-tax		–	–	15,000
iv) Wages	(+)	4,500	5,500	7,000
∴ **Total Payments**	(D)	**74,500**	**1,10,500**	**1,17,000**
	(–)			
Cash Balance Closing (C – D)	(E)	**41,500**	**29,000**	**2,000**

ILLUSTRATION 2

Cadbury India Ltd., Cochin wants to avail overdraft facility with Bank of India for the period October - December 2013 for meeting the orders.

From the following particulars prepare a Cash Budget and find out the amount of overdraft facility required.

2013 Months	Credit Sales ₹	Purchases ₹	Wages ₹
July	1,30,000	1,60,000	14,000
August	2,10,000	1,55,000	15,000
September	2,20,000	1,80,000	18,000
October	3,00,000	3,20,000	15,000
November	1,50,000	2,20,000	17,000
December	1,50,000	3,50,000	16,000

The credit sales are realised as below :

- 50% of the amount in the second month following the sales two months or
- 50% of the amount in the third month following the sales three months

The creditors for purchases are paid in the month following the month of purchase.

The bank pass book showed a balance in the current account as on 30th September 2013 as ₹ 10,000.

SOLUTION

In the Books of Cadbury India Ltd., Cochin
Cash Budget for the three months ending 31st December, 2013

Particulars		October ₹	November ₹	December ₹
Cash at Bank Opening :	(A)	(+) 10,000	(–) 15,000	(–) 1,37,000
Add Receipts :				
i) Collection from Debtors				
• 50% of Credit Sales - two months credit		1,05,000	1,10,000	1,50,000
• 50% of Credit Sales - three months credit	(+)	65,000	1,05,000	1,10,000
∴ **Actual Receipts**	(B)	**1,70,000**	**2,15,000**	**2,60,000**
	(+)			
∴ **Total Receipts (A + B)**	(C)	**1,80,000**	**2,00,000**	**1,23,000**
Less Payments :				
i) Wages		15,000	17,000	16,000
ii) Creditors for purchases one month credit	(+)	1,80,000	3,20,000	2,20,000
∴ **Total Payments**	(D)	**1,95,000**	**3,37,000**	**2,36,000**
	(–)			
∴ Cash at Bank Closing (C – D)	(E)	**(–) 15,000**	**(–) 1,37,000**	**(–) 1,13,000**

ILLUSTRATION 3

Denso Ltd., Delhi wishes to arrange overdraft facility with its bankers during the period April to June, 2013 when it will be manufacturing mostly for stock. Prepare a Cash Budget for the above period from the following cost data indicating the extent of bank facilities the company will require at the end of each month.

Cost Data made available is as follows :

2013 Months	Sales ₹	Purchases ₹	Wages ₹
February	1,80,000	1,24,800	12,000
March	1,92,000	1,44,000	14,000
April	1,08,000	2,43,000	11,000
May	1,74,000	2,46,000	10,000
June	1,26,000	2,68,000	15,000

Additional Information :

a) 50% of Credit Sales are realised in the month following the sales and the remaining 50% in the second month following it.

b) Creditors are paid in the month following the month of purchases.

c) Wages are paid in the month following the month of wages.

d) Cash at Bank on 1st April, 2013 estimated at ₹ 25,000.

SOLUTION

In the Books of Denso Ltd., Delhi

Cash Budget for the three months ending 30th June, 2013

Particulars		April ₹	May ₹	June ₹
Cash at Bank Opening :	(A)	(+) 25,000	(+) 53,000	(–) 51,000
Add Receipts :				
i) Collection from Debtors				
• 50% of Credit Sales - one month credit		96,000	54,000	87,000
• 50% of Credit Sales - two months credit	(+)	90,000	96,000	54,000
∴ **Actual Receipts**	**(B)**	**1,86,000**	**1,50,000**	**1,41,000**
	(+)			
∴ **Total Receipts (A + B)**	**(C)**	**2,11,000**	**2,03,000**	**90,000**
Less Payments :				
i) Payment to Creditors for purchase of materials – one month credit		1,44,000	2,43,000	2,46,000
ii) Payment of wages in the month following the month of wages	(+)	14,000	11,000	10,000
∴ **Total Payments**	**(D)**	**1,58,000**	**2,54,000**	**2,56,000**
	(–)			
∴ **Cash at Bank Closing (C – D)**	**(E)**	**(+) 53,000**	**(–) 51,000**	**(–) 1,66,000**

ILLUSTRATION 4

Eskay Ltd. Ernakulam wishes to prepare Cash Budget from January. Prepare a Cash Budget for the first six months from the following estimated revenue and expenses of 2013.

2013 Months	Total Sales ₹	Materials ₹	Wages ₹	Overheads	
				Production ₹	Selling and Distribution ₹
January	20,000	20,000	4,000	3,200	800
February	22,000	14,000	4,400	3,300	900
March	24,000	14,000	4,600	3,300	800
April	26,000	12,000	4,600	3,400	900
May	28,000	12,000	4,800	3,500	900
June	30,000	16,000	4,800	3,600	1,000

Cash balance on 1st January, 2013 was ₹ 10,000. A new machine is to be installed at ₹ 30,000 on credit to be repaid by two equal instalments in March and April 2013. Sales commission @ 5% on total sales is to be paid within the month following actual sales. ₹ 10,000 being the amount of 2nd call may be received in March 2013. Share premium amounting to ₹ 2,000 is also receivable with 2nd call.

- Period of credit allowed by suppliers – 2 months.
- Period of credit allowed to customers – 1 month
- Delay in payment of overheads – 1 month
- Delay in payment of wages – 1/2 month.
Assume cash sales to be 50% of total sales.

SOLUTION

In the Books of Eskay Ltd., Ernakulam
Cash-Budget for six months ending 30th June, 2013

Particulars		Jan. ₹	Feb. ₹	March ₹	April ₹	May ₹	June ₹
Cash Balance Opening	(A)	10,000	18,000	29,800	20,000	6,100	8,800
Add Receipts :							
i) Share 2nd Call		–	–	10,000	–	–	–
ii) Share Premium		–	–	2,000	–	–	–
iii) Cash Sales : 50% of Total Sales		10,000	11,000	12,000	13,000	14,000	15,000
iv) Collection from Debtors 50% of Total Sales 1 month credit	(+)		10,000	11,000	12,000	13,000	14,000
∴ **Actual Receipts**	(B) (+)	10,000	21,000	35,000	25,000	27,000	29,000
∴ **Total Receipts (A + B)**	(C)	20,000	39,000	64,800	45,000	33,100	37,800
Less : Payments							
i) Purchase of Machine				15,000	15,000		
ii) Sales Commission @ 5% on Total Sales			1,000	1,100	1,200	1,300	1,400
iii) Payment to Suppliers for purchase of material (2 months credit)				20,000	14,000	14,000	12,000
iv) Payment of Production Overheads (1 month credit)			3,200	3,300	3,300	3,400	3,500
v) Payment of Selling and Distribution (1 month credit)			800	900	800	900	900
vi) Payment of Wages (1/2 month credit)	(+)	2,000	4,200	4,500	4,600	4,700	4,800
∴ **Total Payment**	(D) (−)	2,000	9,200	44,800	38,900	24,300	22,600
∴ **Cash Balance Closing (C – D)**	(E)	18,000	29,800	20,000	6,100	8,800	15,200

ILLUSTRATION 5

Summarised below are the income and expenditure forecasts for the month of March to August, 2013 of Flex Industries Ltd., Faridabad.

Month	Credit Sales ₹	Credit Purchases ₹	Wages ₹	Manufacturing Expenses ₹	Office Expenses ₹	Selling Expenses ₹
March	60,000	36,000	9,000	4,000	2,000	4,000
April	62,000	38,000	8,000	3,000	1,500	5,000
May	64,000	33,000	10,000	4,500	2,500	4,500
June	58,000	35,000	8,500	3,500	2,000	3,500
July	56,000	39,000	9,000	4,000	1,000	4,500
August	60,000	34,000	8,000	3,000	1,500	4,500

You are given the following further information :

i) Plant costing ₹ 16,000 is due for delivery in July 2013, payable 10% on delivery and balance after three months.

ii) Advance Tax of ₹ 8,000 each is payable in March and June, 2013.

iii) Period of credit allowed
- by suppliers 2 months and
- to customers one month

iv) Lag in payment of manufacturing expenses half month.

v) Lag in payment of all other expenses one month.

You are required to prepare a Cash Budget for three months starting on 1st May, 2013 when there was a cash balance of ₹ 8,000.

SOLUTION

In the Books of Flex Industries Ltd., Faridabad
Cash-Budget for three months ended on 31st July, 2013

Particulars		May ₹	June ₹	July ₹
Cash Balance Opening :	(A)	8,000	15,750	12,750
Add Receipts :				
i) Collection from customers for credit sales i.e. one month credit	(+)	62,000	64,000	58,000
∴ **Actual Receipts**	(B) (+)	**62,000**	**64,000**	**58,000**
∴ **Total Receipts (A + B)**	(C)	**70,000**	**79,750**	**70,750**
Less : Payments :				
i) Purchase of Plant		–	–	1,600
ii) Advance-Tax		–	8,000	–
iii) Payment to suppliers for credit purchase (2 months credit)		36,000	38,000	33,000
iv) Payment of Manufacturing Expenses - half month credit		3,750 (1,500 + 2,250)	4,000 (2,250 + 1,750)	3,750 (1,750 + 2,000)
v) Wages - one month credit		8,000	10,000	8,500
vi) Office expenses - one month credit		1,500	2,500	2,000
vii) Selling Expenses - one month credit	(+)	5,000	4,500	3,500
∴ **Total Payments**	(D) (–)	**54,250**	**67,000**	**52,350**
∴ **Cash Balance Closing (C – D)**	(E)	**15,750**	**12,750**	**18,400**

ILLUSTRATION 6

From the following information relating to Gesco Ltd., Gurgaon prepare a Cash Budget for half year ended 30th June, 2013.

2013 Months	Sales ₹	Materials ₹	Wages ₹	Selling Expenses ₹	Works Overheads ₹	Manufacturing Expenses ₹
January	72,000	25,000	10,040	4,000	6,000	1,500
February	97,000	31,000	12,190	5,000	6,300	1,700
March	86,000	25,500	10,620	5,500	6,000	2,000
April	88,600	30,600	25,042	6,700	6,500	2,200
May	1,02,500	37,000	22,075	8,500	8,000	2,500
June	1,08,700	38,800	23,039	9,000	8,200	2,500

Additional Information :

The Cash Balance on 1st January, 2013 is ₹ 2,500. Assume that 50% of the total sales are cash sales. Assets are to be acquired in the month of February and April 2013, hence, provision should be made for the payment of ₹ 8,000 and ₹ 25,000 respectively for the same. An application has been made to the bank for the grant of a loan of ₹ 30,000 and it is expected that it will be received in May, 2013. It is also anticipated that a dividend of ₹ 35,000 will be paid in June. Debtors are allowed one months credit whereas creditors, for goods or overheads, grant one months credit. Sales commission @ 3% on total sales is to be paid in the same month.

SOLUTION

In the Books of Gesco Ltd., Gurgaon
Cash-Budget for the six months ended on 30th June, 2013

Particulars		Jan. ₹	Feb. ₹	March ₹	April ₹	May ₹	June ₹
Cash Balance Opening	(A)	2,500	26,300	51,200	85,500	81,100	1,35,500
Add Receipts :							
i) Cash Sales – 50% of Total Sales		36,000	48,500	43,000	44,300	51,250	54,350
ii) Collection from Debtors – 50% of Total Sales one months credit		–	36,000	48,500	43,000	44,300	51,250
iii) Grant of Bank Loan	(+)					30,000	
∴ **Actual Receipts**	(B) (+)	36,000	84,500	91,500	87,300	1,25,550	1,05,600
∴ **Total Receipts (A + B)**	(C)	38,500	1,10,800	1,42,700	1,72,800	2,06,650	2,41,100
Less : Payments							
i) Credit for purchase of materials One months credit			25,000	31,000	25,500	30,600	37,000
ii) Wages		10,040	12,190	10,620	25,042	22,075	23,039
iii) Creditors for selling expenses One months credit		–	4,000	5,000	5,500	6,700	8,500
iv) Creditors for Works Overheads One months credit		–	6,000	6,300	6,000	6,500	8,000
v) Creditors for Office on Cost One months credit		–	1,500	1,700	2,000	2,200	2,500
vi) Purchase of Asset		–	8,000		25,000	–	–
vii) Dividend		–	–	–	–	–	35,000
viii) Sales Commission @ 3% on Total Sale (+)		2,160	2,910	2,580	2,658	3,075	3,261
∴ **Total Payments**	(D) (–)	12,200	59,600	57,200	91,700	71,150	1,17,300
∴ **Cash Balance Closing (C – D)**	(E)	26,300	51,200	85,500	81,100	1,35,500	1,23,800

ILLUSTRATION 7

Prepare a Cash Budget of India Nippon Ltd., Navapur for the three months ended 30th June, 2013 in a columner form using the following cost data.

2013 Months	Total Sales ₹	Total Purchases ₹	Wages ₹	Overheads ₹
January - Actual	80,000	45,000	20,000	5,000
February - Actual	80,000	40,000	18,000	6,000
March - Actual	75,000	42,000	22,000	6,000
April - Budgeted	90,000	50,000	24,000	7,000
May - Budgeted	85,000	45,000	20,000	6,000
June - Budgeted	80,000	35,000	18,000	5,000

Additional Information :

i)   10% of the Purchases and 20% of the Sales are for cash.

ii) The average collection period of the company is half a month and the credit purchases are paid-off regularly after one month.

iii) Wages are paid off half monthly and the taxes of ₹ 500 included in Overheads are paid off on monthly basis.

iv) Cash balance on 1st April, 2013 was ₹ 15,000 and the company has decided to maintain it at the end of every month at the same amount, the excess cash if any, is deposited into fixed deposit account.

SOLUTION

In the books of India Nippon Ltd., Navapur
Cash Budget for the three months ending 30th June, 2013

Particulars		April ₹	May ₹	June ₹
Cash Balance Opening :	**(A)**	15,000	15,000	15,000
Add : Receipts				
i) Cash Sales i.e. 20% of Total Sales		18,000	17,000	16,000
ii) Collection from Debtors from				
Credit Sales i.e. 80% of Total Sales –		66,000	70,000	66,000
Average collection period half a month		(30,000 +	(36,000 +	(34,000 +
		36,000)	34,000)	32,000)
	(+)			
∴ **Actual Receipts**	**(B)**	84,000	87,000	82,000
∴ **Total Recepts : (A + B)**	**(C)**	99,000	1,02,000	97,000
Less : Payments :				
i) Cash Purchases i.e. 10% of Total Purchases		5,000	4,500	3,500
ii) Payment to Creditors from Credit Purchases				
i.e. 90% of Total Purchases – One month credit		37,800	45,000	40,500
iii) Wages - Half a month credit		23,000	22,000	19,000
		(11,000 +	(12,000 +	(10,000 +
		12,000)	10,000)	9,000)
iv) Overheads - Monthly basis		6,500	5,500	4,500
v) Taxes - Monthly basis	(+)	500	500	500

contd. ...

Particulars		April ₹	May ₹	June ₹
∴ Total Payments :	(D)	72,800	77,500	68,000
	(–)			
∴ Actual Cash Balance Closing (C – D)	(E)	26,200	24,500	29,000
Less : Excess cash deposited into Fixed Deposit				
Account	(–)	11,200	9,500	14,000
∴ Required Cash Balance Closing		**15,000**	**15,000**	**15,000**

ILLUSTRATION 8

From the following forecast of income and expenditures of Forex Engineering Co. Ltd., Faizpur, prepare a Cash Budget for three months ended 31st August, 2013.

2013 Months	Total Turnover ₹	Purchases ₹	Prime Cost Labour ₹	Works Overhead ₹	Selling on Cost ₹
April	50,000	39,700	5,000	20% of Direct Wages	5% of Market Price
May	80,000	49,600	5,000	20% of Direct Wages	5% of Invoice Price
June	60,000	51,050	6,000	20% of Direct Wages	5% of Inflated Price
July	70,000	38,340	6,000	20% of Direct Wages	5% of Loaded Price
August	60,000	28,910	7,000	20% of Direct Wages	5% of Selling Price

The additional information made available is as follows :

i)   One-fifth of the Sales are on cash basis. Of the remaining credit sales, fifty percent are to be recovered in the next month whereas other fifty percent after two months. Cash Sales are made on five percent cash discount.

ii) All Purchases are credit and the payment to suppliers is made after two months.

iii) Wages are paid fifteen days in arrears.

iv) Overheads are paid in the same month.

v)   A Texmo machine costing ₹ 60,000 is to be purchased in July, 2013.
     Fifty percent of the total amount is to paid in the same month as down payment whereas the balance is to be paid in three equal instalments together with interest at eighteen percent per annum.

vi) On 31st May, 2013 cash balance is estimated at ₹ 36,000.

SOLUTION

In the books of Forex Engineering Co. Ltd., Faizpur
Cash Budget for the three months ending 31st August, 2013

Particulars		June ₹	July ₹	August ₹
Cash Balance Opening :	(A)	36,000	50,000	29,000
Add : Receipts				
i) Cash Sales i.e. 20% of Total Sales				
Less : 5% Cash Discounts		11,400	13,300	11,400
ii) Collection from Debtors - from Credit Sales				
i.e. 80% of Total Sales	(+)	52,000	56,000	52,000
∴ **Actual Receipts :**	(B)	63,400	69,300	63,400
	(+)			
∴ **Total Receipts : (A + B)**	(C)	99,400	1,91,300	92,400
Less : Payments :				
i) Payment to Creditors from Credit Purchases -				
Two months credit		39,700	49,600	51,050
ii) Prime Cost labour i.e. Wages -				
15 days in arrears		5,500	6,000	6,500
		(2,500 +	(3,000 +	(3,000 +
		3,000)	3,000)	3,500)
iii) Works Overhead - in the same month				
i.e. 20% of Direct Wages				
(i.e. actual Prime Cost Labour)		1,200	1,200	1,400
iv) Selling on Cost - in the same month				
i.e. 5% of market price (i.e. Total Turnover)		3,000	3,500	3,000
v) Purchase of Machine and payment of 'down		–	30,000	–
payment' and payment of equal instalment				
togetherwith interest of 18% p.a.		–	–	10,450
	(+)			
∴ **Total Payments**	(D)	49,400	90,300	72,400
	(–)			
∴ **Cash Balance Closing (C – D)**	(E)	50,000	29,000	20,000

Working Notes :

1) **Calculation of Net Cash Sales :**

Particulars		June ₹	July ₹	August ₹
Actual Cash Sales		12,000	14,000	12,000
(i.e. 20% of Total Sales)				
Less : Cash Discount)				
(i.e. 5% of Cash Sales	(–)	600	700	600
∴ **Net Cash Sales**		**11,400**	**13,300**	**11,400**

2) Calculation of Net Cash Collection from Debtors - from Credit Sales i.e. 80% of Total Sales :

Particulars	June ₹	July ₹	August ₹
i) 50% of Credit Sales - One month credit	32,000	24,000	28,000
ii) 50% of Credit Sales - Two months credit	20,000	32,000	24,000
(−)			
∴ **Net Cash Sales**	**52,000**	**56,000**	**52,000**

3) Calculation of instalment amount to be paid on purchase of machine :

	₹
• Cost price of 'Texmo' machine - July, 2013	60,000
• Down Payment i.e. 50% of total amount	30,000
• Total Amount due on 31st July, 2013	30,000
• To be paid in three equal instalments of	10,000
• Togetherwith interest @ 18% p.a. (i.e. 18% of ₹ 30,000 or mone month)	450
Hence, total instalment to be paid in August	10,450
will be (i.e. ₹ 10,000 + ₹ 450).	

ILLUSTRATION 9

Prepare a Cash Budget for the three months ending 30th September, 2013 based on the following cost data relating to Hikal Industries Ltd., Himmatpur.

i)   Cash Balance as on 1st July, 2013 was ₹ 25,000.

ii)   Monthly Salaries estimated to be ₹ 10,000.

iii)   Interest payable in August, 2013 amounted to ₹ 5,000.

Other estimated cost details are as follows :

Particulars	June ₹	July ₹	August ₹	September ₹
Cash Turnover	−	1,40,000	1,52,000	1,21,000
Purchases - Credit	1,60,000	1,70,000	2,40,000	1,80,000
General Expenses	−	20,750	22,500	21,250
Sales Credit	1,00,000	80,000	1,40,000	1,20,000

Additional Cost Data :

Credit Sales are collected 50% in the month sales are made and remaining 50% in the month following. Collection from Credit Sales are subject to 5% cash discount if payment is received during the month of Sales and $2^1/_2$% if payment is received in the following month of Sales. Creditors are paid either on a prompt or 30 days credit basis. It is estimated that 10% of the Total Creditors are in the prompt category.

SOLUTION

Working Notes :

1) Calculation of Total Collection from Debtors :

Particulars	July		August		September	
	₹	₹	₹	₹	₹	₹
i) 50% of Credit Sales in the same month	40,000	38,000	70,000	66,500	60,000	57,000
Less : Cash Discount	(–) 2,000		(–) 3,500		(–) 3,000	
ii) 50% of Credit Sales - One month credit	50,000	48,750	40,000	39,000	70,000	68,250
Less : 2½ Cash Discount	(–) 1,250	(+)	(–) 1,000	(+)	(–) 1,750	(+)
∴ **Total**		**86,750**		**1,05,500**		**1,25,250**

2) Calculation of Total Payment to Creditors :

Particulars	July ₹	August ₹	September ₹
i) 90% of Credit Purchases			
30 days credit basis (i.e. one month)	1,44,000	1,53,000	2,16,000
ii) 10% of Credit Purchases - Prompt basis	17,000	24,000	18,000
	(+)		
∴ **Total**	**1,61,000**	**1,77,000**	**2,34,000**

In the books of Hikal Industries, Ltd., Himmatpur
Cash Budget for the three months ending 30th September, 2013

Particulars		July ₹	August ₹	September ₹
Cash Balance Opening :	**(A)**	**25,000**	**60,000**	**1,03,000**
Add : Receipts				
i) Cash Turnover		1,40,000	1,52,000	1,21,000
ii) Total Collection from Debtors		86,750	1,05,500	1,25,250
	(+)			
∴ **Actual Receipts :**	**(B)**	**2,26,750**	**2,57,500**	**2,46,250**
	(+)			
∴ **Total Receipts (A + B)**	**(C)**	**2,51,750**	**3,17,500**	**3,49,250**
Less : Payments				
i) Monthly Salaries		10,000	10,000	10,000
ii) Interest Payable		–	5,000	–
iii) Total payment to Crediors		1,61,000	1,77,000	2,34,000
iv) General Expenses		20,750	22,500	21,250
	(+)			
∴ **Total Payments**	**(D)**	**1,91,750**	**2,14,500**	**2,65,250**
	(–)			
∴ **Cash Balance Closing (C – D)**	**(E)**	**60,000**	**1,03,000**	**84,000**

ILLUSTRATION 10

Prepare a Cash Budget for three months ending 30th June, 2013 from the following particulars related to Atlas Cycle Co., Ajmer.

2013 Months	Total Sales ₹	Material Purchases ₹	Salary ₹	Selling on Cost ₹
January	80,000	40,000	6,000	3,800
February	1,00,000	80,000	8,000	4,200
March	60,000	80,000	8,000	6,100
April	1,20,000	1,00,000	10,000	3,800
May	1,60,000	1,43,000	12,000	4,300
June	1,40,000	1,00,000	10,000	6,800

Additional Information :

i)   30% of Credit Sales will be realised in the second month whereas remaining 70% of Credit Sales will the realised in the month following the sales.

ii)   The Materials Purchases will be on credit and the Creditors to be paid in the month following the purchases.

iii) Delay in payment of salary is half a month.

iv)   Selling on costs are to be paid in the same month.

v)   The proportion of cash turnover to credit turnover is 1 : 3 in total turnover.

vi)   Advance income tax is to be paid in the month of April amounting to ₹ 4,000.

vii) The Cash at Bank on 1st April, 2013 is estimated at ₹ 40,000.

SOLUTION

In the books of Atlas Cycle Co., Ajmer
Cash Budget for the three months ended 30th June, 2013

Particulars		April ₹	May ₹	June ₹
Cash Balance Opening :	(A)	**(+) 40,000**	**(+) 26,000**	**(+) 26,000**
Add : Receipts				
i) Cash Sales i.e. 1/4th of Total Sales		30,000	40,000	35,000
ii) Collection from Debtors - from Credit Sales				
i.e. 3/4th of Total Sales				
• 70% of Credit Sales - One month credit		31,500	63,000	84,000
• 30% of Credit Sales - Two months credit		22,500	13,500	27,000
	(+)			
∴ **Actual Receipts**	(B)	**84,000**	**1,16,500**	**1,46,000**
	(+)			

contd. ...

Particulars		April ₹	May ₹	June ₹
∴ **Total Receipts (A + B)** (C)		1,24,000	1,42,500	1,72,000
Less : Payments				
i) Purchase of materials and payment to Creditors - One month credit		80,000	1,00,000	1,43,000
ii) Delay in payment of salary - half a month		9,000	11,000	11,000
		(4,000 + 5,000)	(5,000 + 6,000)	(6,000 + 5,000)
iii) Selling on Cost - Payment in same month)		3,800	4,300	6,800
iv) Advance Income Tax		4,000	–	–
v) Carriage on Sales		1,200	1,200	1,200
	(+)			
∴ **Total Payments** (D)		98,000	1,16,500	1,62,000
	(–)			
∴ **Cash Balance Closing (C – D)** (E)		(+) 26,000	(+) 26,000	(+) 10,000

ILLUSTRATION 11

Intel Co. Ltd., Indapur expects to have ₹ 37,500 Cash at Bank opening on 1st April, 2013 and requires you to prepare an estimate of cash position during the three months ended 30th June, 2013. The cost data made available to you is as follows :

2013 Months	Sales ₹	Purchases ₹	Wages ₹	Works Overhead ₹	Management on Cost ₹	Selling Expenses ₹
February	75,000	45,000	3,000	7,500	6,000	4,500
March	84,000	48,000	9,750	8,250	6,000	4,500
April	90,000	52,500	10,500	9,000	6,000	3,500
May	1,20,000	60,000	13,500	11,250	6,000	2,250
June		60,000	14,250	14,000	7,000	7,000

Additional information :

i) Period of credit allowed by suppliers is two months.

ii) 20% of Total Sales are for cash and period of credit allowed to customers for credit sales is one month.

iii) Delay in payment of all other expenses is one month.

iv) Preference share divided amounting to ₹ 57,500 is to be paid on 1st June, 2013.

v) The company is to pay bonus to workers of ₹ 22,500 in the month of April.

vi) Plant has been ordered to be received and paid in May, which will cost ₹ 1,20,000.

vii) Income-tax of ₹ 15,700 is due to be paid in April, 2013.

SOLUTION

In the books of Intel Co. Ltd., Indapur
Cash Budget for the three months ended 30th June, 2013

Particulars		April ₹	May ₹	June ₹
Cash at Bank Opening :	**(A)**	(+) 37,500	(+) 11,000	(–) 90,000
Add : Receipts				
i) Cash Sales i.e. 20% of Total Sales		18,000	24,000	27,000
ii) Collection from Debtors - from Credit Sales				
i.e. 80% of Total Sales - One month credit		67,200	72,000	96,000
	(+)			
∴ **Actual Receipts :**	**(B)**	**85,200**	**96,000**	**1,23,000**
	(+)			
∴ **Total Receipts (A + B)**	**(C)**	**1,22,700**	**1,07,000**	**33,000**
Less : Payments :				
i) Payment to suppliers on credit purchases -				
Two months' credit		45,000	48,000	52,500
ii) Wages - One month delay		9,750	10,500	13,500
iii) Works Overhead - One month delay		8,250	9,000	11,250
iv) Management on Cost - One month delay		6,000	6,000	6,000
v) Selling Expenses - One month delay		4,500	3,500	2,250
vi) Preference Share Dividend		–	–	57,500
vii) Bonus to Workers		22,500	–	–
viii) Purchase of Plant		–	1,20,000	–
ix) Income-tax		15,700	–	–
	(+)			
∴ **Total Payments**	**(D)**	**1,11,700**	**1,97,000**	**1,43,000**
	(–)			
∴ **Cash at Bank Closing (C – D)**	**(E)**	(+) 11,000	(–) 90,000	(–) 1,10,000

ILLUSTRATION 12

Sunil Shetty has recently set up a modern restaurant in a prominent shopping complex near Pune. His business is very good but because of heavy personal withdrawls, he is facing liquidity problems. To get a better handle over his cash flow, he requests you to prepare a Cash Budget for the next quarter, January to March, 2013 for him. He has provided you with the following information.

- Sales (i.e. cash turnover) are expected to be as follows :

    January - ₹ 50,000, February - ₹ 55,000 and March - ₹ 60,000.

- His establishment purchases are estimated to be as follows :

  January - ₹ 20,000, February - ₹ 22,000 and March - ₹ 25,000.

- Payments for purchases will be made after a lag of one month. Outstanding on account of purchases in December last are ₹ 22,000.

- The monthly rent is ₹ 5,000 and his personal withdrawls per month are amounting to   ₹ 5,000.

- Salaries and other expenses payable in cash are expected to be as follows :

  January - ₹ 15,000, February - ₹ 18,000 and March - ₹ 20,000.

- He plans to buy Furniture worth ₹ 25,000 and Cash payment in February.

- The cash at bank at present is ₹ 5,000. The target cash balance is however ₹ 8,000.

What will be the surplus or deficit of cash in relation to his target cash balance ?

SOLUTION

In the books of Sunil Shetty, Pune
Cash Budget for the quarter ended 31st March, 2013

Particulars		January ₹	February ₹	March ₹
Cash at Bank Opening	(A)	(+) 5,000	(+) 8,000	(–) 10,000
Add : Receipts :				
i) Cash Turnover		50,000	55,000	60,000
	(+)			
∴ **Actual Receipts :**	(B)	50,000	55,000	60,000
	(+)			
∴ **Total Receipts (A + B)**	(C)	55,000	63,000	50,000
Less : Payments				
i) Establishment Purchases - lag of one month		22,000	20,000	22,000
ii) Monthly Rent		5,000	5,000	5,000
iii) Personal withdrawals per month		5,000	5,000	5,000
iv) Salaries and Other Expenses		15,000	18,000	20,000
v) Purchase of Furniture		–	25,000	–
	(+)			
∴ **Total Payments**	(D)	47,000	73,000	52,000
	(–)			
∴ **Cash at Bank Closing (C – D)**	(E)	(+) 8,000	(–) 10,000	(–) 2,000
Target Cash Balance :		8,000	8,000	8,000
∴ **Surplus/Deficit of Cash :**		NIL	18,000	10,000
		–	Deficit	Deficit

5.3.2 MASTER BUDGET

Meaning:

The **master budget** is expressed in financial terms and sets out management's plans for the operations and resources of the firm for a given period of time. It is a summary of the budget schedule in capsule form made for the purpose of presenting in one report the highlights of the budget period.

Definitions:

    i)   The Institute of Cost and Management Accounts, London defines it as, *"The summary budget, incorporating its component functional budget which is finally approved, adopted and employed."*

    ii) Davidson : *"The master budget, sometimes called the comprehensive budget is complete blueprint of the planned operations of the firm for a period."*

Thus, **master budget** is an overall budget of the firm which includes all other small departmental budgets. It is a network consisting of many separate budgets that are interdependent. It co-ordinates various activities of the business and puts them on correct lines. In fact, the master budget contains consolidated summary of all the budgets prepared by the organisation. Few top executive of the business are supplies with the copies of the master budgets. Such budget is no use to department executives. It draws the attention of the management to those issues which must require immediate attention or which must be avoided without any delays in the interest of the business.

Preparation of the Master Budget :

Preparation of Master Budget is a complete process that requires much time and effort by management at all levels. It includes the preparation of a projected Profit and Loss Account i.e. income statement and projected Balance Sheet. However, preparation of a master budget involves the following step :

    i)   Preparation of a Sales Budget.

    ii)   Preparation of Production Cost Budget.

    iii)   Preparation of the Cost Budget.

    iv)   Preparation of the Cash Budget.

    v)   Preparation of projected Profit and Loss Account on the basis of information collected from above stated four steps

    vi)   Preparation of projected Balance Sheet from the information available in lasts year's Balance Sheet and with the help of five steps stated above.

A Master Budget is the summary of all the functional budgets taken together. The Master Budget is finally approved, adopted and implemented by the management. Thus when all the functional budgets are prepared and consolidated into a master budget we can get the :

    i)   Budgeted Profit and Loss Account

    ii)   Budgeted Profit and Loss Appropriation Account

    iii)   Budgeted Balance Sheet.

Thus a Master Budget shows an overall business plan and contains the financial statements which we prepare as usual. But the only difference between a Master Budget and the financial statement is that in case of a Master Budget, the budgeted figure i.e. estimated amounts are taken, while in case of the financial statements prepared by the account department, the past data is considered i.e. the accounts are prepared from the vouchers for which the expenses have already accrued.

The Master Budget is prepared by the Budget Committee on the basis of the consolidated functional budgets. When the Master Budget is approved by the management, it becomes the business plan of the company.

When the functional budget have been drawn up, a Master budget can be built up by summarising all the functional budgets and expressing and incorporating them under Budgeted Profit and Loss Account and a Budget Balance Sheet. Such Master Budget must contain the budgeted Profit and Loss Account for the current year as well as for previous year showing clearly why there has been a change.

Format of Master Budget:

Table A

.... Co. Ltd.

Master Budget for the year ended .....

Projected Profit and Loss Account for the year ending ......

Particulars	Previous period Amount (₹)	Budgeted period Amount (₹)	Particulars	Previous period Amount (₹)	Budgeted period Amount (₹)
To Cost of Product (as per Production Cost Budget) **To Direct Materials** (– Unit @ ₹) xxx **Add :** Direct Wages xxx **To Prime Cost** **Add :** Factory Overheads (a) Variable xxx (b) Fixed xxx **To Works Cost** **Add :** Administrative, Selling and Distribution Overheads To Net Profit C/D			By Sales (As per Sales Budget) i) X Product ... units @ ₹ ... ii) Y Product ... units @ ₹ ...		

Table B
Budgeted Balance Sheet

Liabilities	Previous period Amount	Budgeted period Amount	Assets	Previous period Amount	Budgeted period Amount
Shareholder's Equity • Pref. Share Capital • Equity Share Capital **Current Liabilities :** • Bills Payable • Sundry Creditors • Bank Loan			**Fixed Assets :** • Plant and Machinery • Buildings • Furniture **Current Assets :** • Bills Receivable • Sundry Debtors • Cash in Hand and at Bank • Inventories		
Total			**Total**		

The following specimen of Budget Profit and Loss Account and the Budgeted Balance Sheet, provides the summary of all revenue accounts and the summary of all capital items respectively, with imaginary figures.

Master Budget
Budgeted Profit and Loss Account for the year ending 31st March 2013

Particulars			Budget Period		Previous Period	
			Amount ₹	%	Amount ₹	%
	Sales		50,000	100	40,000	100
Less :	Cost of Production	(–)	30,000	60	24,800	62
	Gross Profit (A)		**20,000**	**40**	**15,200**	**38**
Less :	Operating Expenses :					
•	Administrative		2,500	5	2,200	5.5
•	Selling and Distribution		3,500	7	3,000	7.5
•	Advertisement	(–)	1,000	2	1,000	2.5
	Total (B)		**7,000**	**14**	**6,200**	**15.5**
∴	Operating Profit (A – B)		13,000	26	9,000	22.5
Add : Other Income (Investments)		(+)	600	1.2	600	1.5
	Net Profit Before Tax		**13,600**	**27.2**	**9,600**	**24.0**

Budgeted Balance-Sheet as on 31st March, 2013

Liabilities	Budget Period ₹	Previous Year ₹	Assets	Budget Period ₹	Previous Period ₹
Share Capital			**Fixed Assets (Net)**		
• Equity Shares	1,25,000	1,25,000	• Buildings	90,000	1,00,000
Reserves and Surplus			• Plant and Machinery	22,500	25,000
• General Reserves	25,000	25,000	• Furniture & Fixtures	22,500	25,000
• Profit and Loss	22,500	17,500	**Current Assets**		
Current Liabilities			• Stocks	19,000	20,000
• Creditors	11,500	25,000	• Debtors	10,000	12,500
			• Cash and Bank (+)	20,000	10,000
	1,84,000	**1,92,500**		**1,84,000**	**1,92,500**

5.3.3 FLEXIBLE BUDGET

Meaning:

A flexible budget is a concise statement of how costs are related to fluctuations in output. It is one which is designed to change according to the level of activity actually achieved. The budgeted figures can be changed according to the changing conditions. Hence a flexible budget is just the opposite of a fixed budget. Thus, it is more elastic, practical and useful in the real life. These budgets are prepared for the purpose of ultimate cost control.

Definition :

ICMA, London Terminology defines a **Flexible Budget** as,

"one which by recognising the difference between fixed, semi-fixed and variable costs, is designed to change in relation to the level of activity attained".

Generally, Flexible budgets are prepared under the following situations :

- Where the business depends upon some scarce material.
- Where the exact demand cannot be estimated e.g. in new business.
- Where the business depends upon nature e.g. rainfall.
- In some business where the sales cannot be predicted.
- Where sufficient labour force is necessary for running the business smoothly.

Distinction between Fixed Budget and Flexible Budget :

The difference between Fixed Budget and Flexible Budget is as follows :

Fixed Budget	Flexible Budget
i) It is prepared for a particular level of activity.	i) It is designed to change in accordance with the level of activity actually attained.
ii) It is prepared only for one level of activity.	ii) It is prepared for any level of activity.
iii) It is static and does not change with the changes in the level of activity attained.	iii) It is variable and can change on the basis of activity level to be achieved.
iv) Here costs are not classified according to behaviour.	iv) Here costs are classified according to the behaviour i.e. fixed, variable and semi-variable.
v) Formation of budget equation is not necessary.	v) Budget equation is formed for each and every cost.
vi) It is difficult to ascertain the cost under changing circumstances.	vi) It is possible to ascertain cost at different levels of activity.
vii) Fixation of price do not give a correct picture.	vii) It facilitates fixation of selling price.
viii) It has very limited use in controlling costs.	viii) It is more useful technique for cost control.
ix) Tendering quotations do not give correct picture.	xi) It helps a lot in tendering quotations.
x) It is not useful for performance evaluation.	x) It is useful for performance evaluation.

Methods of preparing Flexible Budgets :

Generally, a Flexible Budget can be prepared in the following manner :

At first a number of fixed budgets are prepared for each manufacturing budget centre. Within the limits of these budgets, the flexible budgets are prepared. In flexible budgets clear differences are drawn between fixed, semi-fixed and variable costs.

There are three methods of preparing Flexible Budgets which are as follows :

i) **Tabular Method :**

In this method, a table is prepared wherein different capacities are shown in horizontal columns and the budget. The budgeted figures are shown against different capacities in the vertical columns. The expenses are recorded as variable, semi-variable and fixed. Various capacity levels showing different volumes of production are shown in the flexible budgets.

ii) **Charting Method :**

In this method, the expenses are analysed according to their nature or behaviour i.e. variable, semi-variable and fixed. The budgeted expenses are prepared and these are plotted on a graph paper against different levels of activity. The budgeted expenses relating to the level of activity actually attained can be read from this chart.

iii) **Ratio Method :**

If the activities of a company are standardised and the expenses are of uniform nature, most of the expenses can be worked out as percentage level of activity. The method is that the common costs are estimated for the normal production, i.e. the normal level of activity. From this we can work out various ratios which show the relationships of each expenses with each increase in the level of activity. Then the budgeted cost for any level of activity can be ascertained by using these ratios.

Utility :

Flexible Budgets are more useful in actual practice because,

- It is more realistic and has great practical utility in the business.
- The efficiency of the managers can be measured.
- It helps to control the costs.
- It is more realistic than a fixed budget because a fixed budget deals with only one level of activity of condition.
- The figures in a flexible budget can be changed according to the change in the volume of activity.

> **Flexible Budgets are more useful for effective cost control, viable pricing decisions and appropriate performance evaluation.**

Proforma of Flexible Budget :

Usually, the following format of Flexible Budget is preferably used in actual practice.

In the books of a Company
Flexible Budget for the period ended ......

Normal Activity : Units
Capacity :   %

Production Units						
Capacity %						
Particulars	Unit Cost ₹	Total Cost ₹	Unit Cost ₹	Total Cost ₹	Unit Cost ₹	Total Cost ₹
A) Fixed Expenses : • Salaries • Depreciation • Insurance • Rent						
B) Variable Expenses : • Direct Material • Direct Labour • Direct Expenses • Indirect Material/Labour/Expenses • Variable Overheads						
C) Semi-Variable Expenses : • Electricity • Repairs and Maintenance • Administrative Expenses • Selling Expenses • Distribution Expenses (+)						
∴ **Total Cost**	–	–	–	–	–	–
Add : Profit						
Less : Loss (–)						
∴ **Sales**						

EXAMPLE

Prepare a Flexible Budget for overhead expenses on the basis of the following data relating to Aspro India Ltd., Ajmer and determine the overhead rates at 70%, 80% and 90% capacity level.

Overheads	At 70% Capacity ₹
A) Fixed Overheads :	
i) Plant Depreciation	52,000
ii) Buildings Insurance	23,000
iii) Premises Rent	1,65,000
B) Variable Overheads :	
i) Stores and Spares	91,000
ii) Unproductive Labour	35,000
iii) Indirect Expenses	14,000
C) Semi-variable Overheads :	
i) Power and Fuel (Variable – 70%)	1,00,000
ii) Repairs and Maintenance (Fixed – 30%) (+)	20,000
∴ **Total**	**5,00,000**

The estimated direct labour hours at different capacity levels are as under :

Capacity Level	Direct Labour Hours
70%	62,500 Hrs.
80%	76,000 Hrs.
90%	94,000 Hrs.

ANSWER

In the books of Aspro India Ltd., Ajmer
Flexible Budget

Normal Activity Units :
Capacity   %   :   70

Production	Units	70	80	90
Capacity	%	Total Cost ₹	Total Cost ₹	Total Cost ₹
Particulars				
A) **Fixed Overheads**				
i) Plant Depreciation		52,000	52,000	52,000
ii) Buildings Insurance		23,000	23,000	23,000
iii) Premises Rent (+)		1,65,000	1,65,000	1,65,000
∴ **Total** **A)**		**2,40,000**	**2,40,000**	**2,40,000**
B) **Variable Overheads**				
i) Stores and Spares		91,000	1,04,000	1,17,000
ii) Unproductive Labour		35,000	40,000	45,000
iii) Indirect Expenses (+)		14,000	16,000	18,000
∴ **Total** **(B)**		**1,40,000**	**1,60,00**	**1,80,000**
C) **Semi-variable Overheads :**				
i) Power and Fuel 1,00,000				
F) Fixed 30% 30,000		30,000	30,000	30,000
V) Variable 70% (+) 70,000		70,000	80,000	90,000
ii) Repairs and Maintenance 20,000				
F) Fixed 30% 6,000		6,000	6,000	6,000
V) Variable 70% (+) 14,000 (+)		14,000	16,000	18,000
∴ **Total** **(C)**		**1,20,000**	**1,32,000**	**1,44,000**
∴ **Total Overheads (A + B + C)** **(D)**		**5,00,000**	**5,32,000**	**5,64,000**
Calculation of Overhead Rates on the basis of Labour Hours : Overhead Rate = $\dfrac{\text{Total Overheads (D)}}{\text{Direct Labour Hours}}$		$=\dfrac{\text{Rs. } 5,00,000}{\text{Hrs. } 62,500}$ $= ₹\,8$	$=\dfrac{\text{Rs. } 5,32,000}{\text{Hrs. } 76,000}$ $= ₹\,7$	$=\dfrac{\text{Rs. } 5,64,000}{\text{Hrs. } 94,000}$ $= ₹\,6$

ILLUSTRATIONS

ILLUSTRATION 1

The budgeted expenses for production at 100% capacity of Infosys Ltd., Islampur are given below.

Particulars	At 100% Capacity ₹
Direct Materials	6,00,000
Variable Works Overheads	2,00,000
Basic Wages	2,00,000
Fixed Production Overheads	80,000
Productive Expenses – Marginal	40,000
Administrative Expenses – Rigid	40,000
Selling Overheads (10% Fixed)	1,20,000
Distribution on Cost (80% Variable)	60,000

Prepare a Flexible Budget for the production at 60% and 80% capacity showing separately,

i) Prime Cost, ii) Works Cost, iii) Cost of Production and iv) Cost of Turnover.

In the Books of Infosys Ltd., Islampur
Flexible Budget

Normal Activity : Units
Capacity :   100%

Production Capacity			Units %	60 Total Cost ₹	80 Total Cost ₹	100 Total Cost ₹
	Direct Materials			3,60,000	4,80,000	6,00,000
Add :	Basic Wages			1,20,000	1,60,000	2,00,000
Add :	Productive Expenses – Marginal		(+)	24,000	32,000	40,000
	Prime Cost		i)	**5,04,000**	**6,72,000**	**8,40,000**
Add :	Factory Overheads					
	i) Variable Works Overheads			1,20,000	1,60,000	2,00,000
	ii) Fixed Production Overheads		(+)	80,000	80,000	80,000
	Works Cost		ii)	**7,04,000**	**9,12,000**	**11,20,000**
Add :	Administrative Expenses – Rigid		(+)	40,000	40,000	40,000
	Cost of Production		iii)	**7,44,000**	**9,52,000**	**11,60,000**
Add :	Selling and Distribution Overheads					
	i) Selling Overheads –	1,20,000				
	F) Fixed – 10%	12,000		12,000	12,000	12,000
	V) Variable – 90%	(+) 1,08,000		64,800	86,400	1,08,000
	ii) Distribution on Cost –	60,000				
	F) Fixed – 20%	12,000		12,000	12,000	12,000
	V) Variable – 80%	(+) 48,000	(+)	28,800	38,400	48,000
	Cost of Turnover		iv)	**8,61,600**	**11,00,800**	**13,40,000**

ILLUSTRATION 2

From the following information relating to Castrol Ltd., Cochi prepare a Flexible Budget at 60% and 80% capacity.

Particulars	70% Capacity ₹
A) Variable Overheads :	
• Indirect Material	5,000
• Indirect Labour	15,000
B) Semi-variable Overheads :	
• Electricity	50,000
Variable – 60%	
Fixed – 40%	
• Repairs and Maintenance	5,000
Variable – 65%	
Fixed – 35%	
C) Fixed Overhead :	
• Salaries to Staff	10,000
• Depreciation on Machines	14,000
• Insurance on Machines	(+) 6,000
∴ Total	**1,05,000**

The company estimated the direct labour hours to be worked at 70% capacity as 70,000 hours. Also calculate the overhead recovery rate at 60%, 70% and 80% capacities.

SOLUTION

In the Books of Castrol Ltd., Cochin
Flexible Budget

Normal Activity : Units
Capacity : 70%

Production Capacity		Units %	– 60	– 70	– 80
Particulars			Total Cost ₹	Total Cost ₹	Total Cost ₹
A) Variable Overheads :					
i) Indirect Material			4,286	5,000	5,714
ii) Indirect Labour			12,857	15,000	17,143
B) Semi-variable Overheads :					
i) Electricity		50,000			
V) Variable - 60%	30,000		25,714	30,000	34,286
F) Fixed - 40%	20,000		20,000	20,000	20,000
ii) Repairs and Maintenance		5,000			
V) Variable - 65%	3,250		2,786	3,250	3,714
F) Fixed - 35%	1,750		1,750	1,750	1,750
C) Fixed Overheads :					
i) Salaries to Staff			10,000	10,000	10,000
ii) Depreciation on Machines			14,000	14,000	14,000
iii) Insurance on Machines		(+)	6,000	6,000	6,000
∴ Total			**97,393**	**1,05,000**	**1,12,607**
Calculation of Overhead Recovery Rate on the basis of Direct Labour Hours : $= \dfrac{\text{Total Overheads}}{\text{Direct Labour Hours}}$			$= \dfrac{₹\,97,393}{60,000\ \text{Hrs.}}$ $= ₹\,1.62$	$= \dfrac{₹\,1,05,000}{70,000\ \text{Hrs.}}$ $= ₹\,1.50$	$= \dfrac{₹\,1,12,607}{80,000\ \text{Hrs.}}$ $= ₹\,1.41$

ILLUSTRATION 3

Dupont Chemicals Ltd., Delhi has submitted the actual cost data working on two capacity levels as follows :

Particulars	Capacity – Cost –	60% Total ₹	70% Total ₹
Distribution on Cost		30,000	40,000
Prime Cost Labour		3,00,000	3,50,000
Factory Overheads		2,00,000	2,20,000
Chargeable Expenses		1,20,000	1,40,000
Raw Materials		3,60,000	4,20,000
Selling Expenses		60,000	70,000
Office on Cost (Rigid)		1,00,000	1,00,000

Prepare a Flexible Budget at 80%, 90% and 100% capacity showing clearly i) Direct Cost, ii) Works Cost, iii) Cost of Production, and iv) Total Cost.

The costs have a rising tendency according to change in the capacity levels.

SOLUTION

Working Notes :

  i)   Raw Materials Cost increases by ₹ 60,000 per 10% increase in capacity.

  ii) Prime Cost Labour increases by ₹ 50,000 per 10% increase in capacity.

  iii) Factory Overheads increases by ₹ 20,000 per 10% increase in capacity.

  iv) Office on Cost are rigid hence remain fixed at various capacity levels.

  v)   Selling Expenses and Distribution on Cost increases by ₹ 10,000 per 10% increase in capacity.

In the books of Dupont Chemicals Ltd., Delhi
Flexible Budget

Normal Activity :   Units
Capacity : 60% to 100%

Production Capacity	Units %	– 60 Total Cost ₹	– 70 Total Cost ₹	– 80 Total Cost ₹	– 90 Total Cost ₹	– 100 Total Cost ₹
Particulars						
Raw Materials		3,60,000	4,20,000	4,80,000	5,40,000	6,00,000
Add : Prime Cost Labour		3,00,000	3,50,000	4,00,000	4,50,000	5,00,000
Add : Chargeable Expenses	(+)	1,20,000	1,40,000	1,60,000	1,80,000	2,00,000
∴ **Direct Cost**	i)	**7,80,000**	**9,10,000**	**10,40,000**	**11,70,000**	**13,00,000**
Add : Factory Overheads	(+)	2,00,000	2,20,000	2,40,000	2,60,000	2,80,000
∴ **Works Cost**	ii)	**9,80,000**	**11,30,000**	**12,80,000**	**14,30,000**	**15,80,000**
Add : Office-on-Cost	(+)	1,00,000	1,00,000	1,00,000	1,00,000	1,00,000
∴ **Cost of Production**	iii)	**10,80,000**	**12,30,000**	**13,80,000**	**15,30,000**	**16,80,000**
Add : Selling Expenses		60,000	70,000	80,000	90,000	1,00,000
Add : Distribution on Cost	(+)	30,000	40,000	50,000	60,000	70,000
∴ **Total Cost**	iv)	**11,70,000**	**13,40,000**	**15,10,000**	**16,80,000**	**18,50,000**

ILLUSTRATION 4

From the following cost data made available by Ambuja Metals Co. Ltd., Ahmednagar for a quarterly period, forecast the results by preparing a Flexible Budget at 70%, 80% and 90% capacity level where the estimated turnover amounted to ₹ 1,26,000, ₹ 1,34,000 and ₹ 1,42,000 respectively. It is assumed that,

   i)   Marginal expenses vary due to change in production capacity level,
   ii) Rigid expenses remain constant at various production capacity levels and
   iii) Semi-fixed expenses are constant between 55% and 75% capacity, increase by 10% between 75% and 85% capacity and increase by 20% between 85% and 90% capacity.

The expenses and sales at 60% capacity level are as under :

Particulars		₹
A) Fixed Expenses :		
i) Workshop Salary	...	9,300
ii) Office Rent	...	6,100
iii) Machinery Depreciation	...	8,600
B) Variable Expenses :		
i) Basic Materials	...	24,000
ii) Direct Labour	...	9,000
iii) Productive Expenses	...	3,000
C) Semi-Variable Expenses :		
i) Repairs and Maintenance	...	10,000
ii) Telephone Charges	...	6,000
iii) Indirect Labour	...	(+) 4,000
∴ **Total Cost of Sales**		**80,000**
Value of Sales		**1,10,000**

Also find out the percentage of profit to sales and submit a report to the management indicating your critical comments on the position at various production capacity level.

In the books of Ambuja Metals Co. Ltd.; Ahmednagar
Flexible Budget

Normal Activity : – Units

Capacity :   60%

SOLUTION

Production	Units	–	–	–	–
Capacity	%	**60**	**70**	**80**	**90**
Particulars		Total Cost ₹	Total Cost ₹	Total Cost ₹	Total Cost ₹
A) Fixed Expenses :		9,300	9,300	9,300	9,300
i) Workshop Salary		6,100	6,100	6,100	6,100
ii) Office Rent		8,600	8,600	8,600	8,600
iii) Machinery Depreciation					

contd. ...

Production	Units	–	–	–	–
Capacity	%	**60**	**70**	**80**	**90**
Particulars		**Total Cost ₹**	**Total Cost ₹**	**Total Cost ₹**	**Total Cost ₹**
B) Variable Expenses					
i) Basic Materials		24,000	28,000	32,000	36,000
ii) Direct Labour		9,000	10,500	12,000	13,500
iii) Productive Expenses		3,000	3,500	4,000	4,500
C) Semi-Variable Expenses :					
i) Repairs and Maintenance		10,000	10,000 (constant)	11,000 (increases by 10%)	12,000 (increases by 20%)
ii) Telephone Charges		6,000	6,000 (constant)	6,600 (increases by 10%)	7,200 (increases by 20%)
iii) Indirect Labour	(+)	4,000	4,000 (constant)	4,400 (increases by 10%)	4,800 (increases by 20%)
∴ **Total Cost of Sales**	i)	80,000	86,000	94,000	1,02,000
Add : Forecasted Profits	ii) (+)	30,000	40,000	40,000	40,000
Total Turnover		**1,10,000**	**1,26,000**	**1,34,000**	**1,42,000**
Percentage of Profit to Sales	**iii)**	27.27%	31.75%	29.85%	28.17%

Reporting to the Management :

A critical analysis of the forecasted results as shown above in the flexible budgets reveals that at 70% production capacity level the percentage of profit to sales (i.e. 31.75%) is more as compared to other production levels. Hence, it is suggested to the management that,

- the company should increase their production from 60% to 70% capacity level.
- additional efforts are necessary to reduce the cost substantially by introducing effective technique to control variable cost.
- the company should concentrate on increasing the turnover sizably.

ILLUSTRATION 5

In Burma Plastics Co., Badalpur the cost of an article at a capacity level of 5,000 units is given under 'A' below. For a variation of 25% in capacity above or below this level, the individual items vary as indicated under 'B' below.

Particulars	A ₹	B Variation
Raw Materials	25,000	100% varying
Direct Labour	15,000	100% varying
Stores Overhead	1,000	100% varying
Productive Expenses	10,000	100% varying
Repairs and Maintenance	2,000	75% varying
Power	1,250	80% varying
Inspection	500	20% varying
Office Overheads	5,000	25% varying
Selling on Cost	3,000	25% varying

Prepare a flexible budget at production levels of 4,000 units and 6,000 units.

SOLUTION

In the books of Burma Plastic Co., Badalpur
Flexible Budget

Normal Activity : Units 5,000
Capacity : –

Production	Units		4,000		5,000		6,000	
Capacity	%		–		–		–	
Particulars		Nature of Cost	Unit Cost ₹	Total Cost ₹	Unit Cost ₹	Total Cost ₹	Unit Cost ₹	Total Cost ₹
A) Variable Expenses :								
i) Raw Materials		Variable	5.00	20,000	5.00	25,000	5.00	30,000
ii) Direct Labour		Variable	3.00	12,000	3.00	15,000	3.00	18,000
iii) Stores Overhead		Variable	0.20	800	0.20	1,000	0.20	1,200
iv) Productive Expenses		Variable	2.00	8,000	2.00	10,000	2.00	12,000
B) Semi-Variable Expenses :		Semi-variable						
i) Repairs and Maintenance	2,000							
F) Fixed : 25%	500		0.13	500	0.10	500	0.08	500
V) Variable : 75%	(+) 1,500		0.30	1,200	0.30	1,500	0.30	1,800
II) Power	1,250	Semi-variable						
F) Fixed : 20%	250		0.06	250	0.05	250	0.04	250
V) Variable : 80%	(+) 1,000		0.20	800	0.20	1,000	0.20	1,200
III) Inspection	500	Semi-variable						
F) Fixed : 80%	400		0.10	400	0.08	400	0.07	400
V) Variable : 20%	(+) 100		0.02	80	0.02	100	0.02	120
iv) Office Overheads,	5,000	Semi-variable						
F) Fixed : 75%	3,750		0.94	3,750	0.75	3,750	0.63	3,750
V) Variable : 25%	(+) 1,250		0.25	1,000	0.25	1,250	0.25	1,500
v) Selling on Cost	3,000	Semi-variable						
F) Fixed : 75%	2,250		0.56	2,250	0.45	2,250	0.38	2,250
V) Variable : 25%	(+) 750	(+)	0.15	600	0.15	750	0.15	900
∴ Total			**12.91**	**51,630**	**12.55**	**62,750**	**12.32**	**73,870**

ILLUSTRATION 6

Thomas Cook Ltd., Talegaon provides the following cost data for a 60% working capacity, from which you are required to prepare a Flexible Budget for the production at 80% and 100% capacity level.

Current Production	Units 600
Selling Price (Fixed) per unit	₹ 300
Process Material Cost per unit	₹ 100
Productive Wages per unit	₹ 40
Prime Cost Expenses	₹ 10
Total Works Overheads (40% Fixed)	₹ 40,000
Total Office, Selling and Distribution Overheads ₹ 30,000 (50% Variable)	

SOLUTION

In the books of Thomas Cook Ltd., Talegaon
Flexible Budget

Normal Activity : Units 600
Capacity : 60%

Poduction — Units		600		800		1,000	
Capacity — %		60		80		100	
Particulars		Unit Cost ₹	Total Cost ₹	Unit Cost ₹	Total Cost ₹	Unit Cost ₹	Total Cost ₹
Process Material Cost		100.00	60,000	100.00	80,000	10.00	1,00,000
Add : Productive Wages		40.00	24,000	40.00	32,000	40.00	40,000
Add : Prime Cost Expenses	(+)	10.00	6,000	10.00	8,000	10.00	10,000
∴ **Prime Cost**	i)	150.00	90,000	150.00	1,20,000	150.00	1,50,000
Add : Works Overheads 40,000							
F) Fixed : 40% 16,000		26.67	16,000	20.00	16,000	16.00	16,000
V) Variable : 60% (+) 24,000	(+)	40.00	24,000	40.00	32,000	40.00	40,000
∴ **Works Cost**	ii)	216.67	1,30,000	210.00	1,68,000	206.00	2,06,000
Add : Office, Selling & Distribution Overheads 30,000							
F) Fixed : 50% 15,000		25.00	15,000	18.75	15,000	15.00	15,000
V) Variable : 50% (+) 15,000	(+)	25.00	15,000	25.00	20,000	25.00	25,000
∴ **Total Cost**	iii)	266.67	1,60,000	253.75	2,03,000	246.00	2,46,000
Add : Profit	iv) (+)	33.33	20,000	46.25	37,000	54,000	54,000
∴ **Selling Price**		**300.00**	**1,80,000**	**300.00**	**2,40,000**	**300.00**	**3,00,000**

ILLUSTRATION 7

Activa Co. Ltd., Anand produces computer hardware. The estimated unit cost is as under :

Particulars	₹
Direct Material	15
Direct Wages	10
Direct Expenses	4
Variable Overheads	(+) 6
∴ Total	35

The Fixed Overheads are estimated at ₹ 1,00,000. The Semi-Vaiable Overheads are ₹ 50,000 at 100% capacity i.e. 10,000 units. The semi-variable expenses vary in stages of ₹ 4,000 for each change in output of 1,000 units. Selling Price per unit is ₹ 70.

You are required to prepare a Flexible Budget at 50%, 70%, 90% and 100% capacities and determine the profit at each level.

SOLUTION

In the Books of Activa Co. Ltd., Anand
Flexible Budget

Normal Activity : 10,000 units
Capacity : 100%

| Production Units | | 5,000 | | 7,000 | | 9,000 | | 10,000 | |
| Capacity % | | 50 | | 70 | | 90 | | 100 | |
Particulars		Unit Cost ₹	Total Cost ₹	Unit Cost ₹	Total Cost ₹	Unit Cost ₹	Total Cost ₹	Unit Cost ₹	Total Cost ₹
Direct Material		15.00	75,000	15.00	1,05,000	15.00	1,35,000	15.00	1,50,000
Add : Direct Wages		10.00	50,000	10.00	70,000	10.00	90,000	10.00	1,00,000
Add : Direct Expenses (+)		4.00	20,000	4.00	28,000	4.00	36,000	4.00	40,000
∴ Prime Cost i)		29.00	1,45,000	29.00	2,03,000	29.00	2,61,000	29.00	2,90,000
Add : Variable Overheads		6.00	30,000	6.00	42,000	6.00	54,000	6.00	60,000
Add : Fixed Overheads		20.00	1,00,000	14.29	1,00,000	11.11	1,00,000	10.00	1,00,000
Add : Semi-Variable Overheads (+)		6.00	30,000	5.43	38,000	5.11	46,000	5.00	50,000
∴ Total Cost ii)		61.00	3,05,000	54.72	3,83,000	51.22	4,61,000	50.00	5,00,000
Add : Profit iii) (+)		9.00	45,000	15.28	1,07,000	18.78	1,69,000	20.00	2,00,000
∴ Selling Price iv)		70.00	3,50,000	70.00	4,90,000	70.00	6,30,000	70.00	7,00,000

ILLUSTRATION 8

The expenses for the production at 5,000 units at 50% capacity in Baroda Chemicals Ltd., Bhavnagar are given as follows :

	Unit Cost ₹
Materials	50
Labour	20
Variable Overheads	15
Fixed Overheads (₹ 50,000)	10
Administrative Expenses (5% Variable)	10
Selling Expenses (20% Fixed)	6
Distribution Expenses (10% Fixed)	(+) 5
∴ Total Cost of Sales	116

You are required to prepare a budget for 70% and 90% production capacity, assuming that 90% capacity cost of materials will increase by 10% where as labour cost will decrease by 5%.

SOLUTION

In the Books of Baroda Chemicals Ltd., Bhavnagar
Flexible Budget

Normal Activity : 5,000 units
Capacity   : 50%

Production Capacity	Units %	5,000 50 Unit Cost ₹	5,000 50 Total Cost ₹	7,000 70 Unit Cost ₹	7,000 70 Total Cost ₹	9,000 90 Unit Cost ₹	9,000 90 Total Cost ₹
Particulars							
A) Fixed Expenses :							
i) Fixed Overheads		10.00	50,000	7.14	50,000	5.56	50,000
B) Variable Expenses :							
i) Materials		50.00	2,50,000	50.00	3,50,000	55.00 (50 + 10% i.e. ₹ 5)	4,95,000
ii) Labour		20.00	1,00,000	20.00	1,40,000	19.00 (20 – 5% i.e. ₹ 1)	1,71,000
iii) Variable Overheads		15.00	75,000	15.00	1,05,000	15.00	1,35,000
C) Semi-Variable Expenses :							
i) Administrative Expenses 10.							
F) Fixed 95% 9.50		9.50	47,500	6.79	47,500	5.28	47,500
V) Variable 5% (+) 0.50		0.50	2,500	0.50	3,500	0.50	4,500
ii) Selling Expenses 6.							
F) Fixed 20% 1.20		1.20	6,000	0.86	6,000	0.67	6,000
V) Variable 80% (+) 4.80		4.80	24,000	4.80	33,600	4.80	43,200
iii) Distribution Expenses 5.							
F) Fixed 10% 0.50		0.50	2,500	0.36	2,500	0.28	2,500
V) Variable 90% (+) 4.50		4.50	22,500	4.50	31,500	4.50	40,500
∴ **Total Cost of Sales**		**116.00**	**5,80,000**	**109.95**	**7,69,600**	**110.59**	**9,95,200**

ILLUSTRATION 9

Dabur Chemicals Ltd., Delhi has given you the following information at 50% capacity of the production of 5,000 units during the month of March, 2013.

Particulars	Unit Cost ₹
Materials	50
Labour	30
Variable Overheads	20
Fixed Overheads (₹ 50,000)	10
Administrative Overheads	10
Selling Expenses (25% Fixed)	08
Distribution Expenses (20% Fixed)	(+) 05
∴ **Total**	**133**

You are required to prepare Flexible Budgets at 60%, 70% and 80% capacity presuming that at 80% capacity material cost will be less by 5% and variable selling expenses will increase by 10%.

SOLUTION

In the Books of Dabur Chemicals Ltd., Delhi
Flexible Budget

Normal Activity : 5,000 units
Capacity : 50%

| Production | Units | | 5,000 | | 6,000 | | 7,000 | | 8,000 | |
| Capacity | % | | 50 | | 60 | | 70 | | 80 | |
Particulars		Unit Cost ₹	Total Cost ₹	Unit Cost ₹	Total Cost ₹	Unit Cost ₹	Total Cost ₹	Unit Cost ₹	Total Cost ₹
A) Fixed Expenses									
i) Fixed Overheads		10.00	50,000	8.33	50,000	7.14	50,000	6.25	50,000
B) Variable Expenses									
i) Materials		50.00	2,50,000	50.00	3,00,000	50.00	3,50,000	47.50	3,80,000
ii) Labour		30.00	1,50,000	30.00	1,80,000	30.00	2,10,000	30.00 (₹ 50 – 5% i.e. ₹ 2.50)	2,40,000
iii) Variable Overheads		20.00	1,00,000	20.00	1,20,000	20.00	1,40,000	20.00	1,60,000
C) Semi-Variable Expenses :									
i) Administration Overheads 10.									
F) Fixed 90% 9.		9.00	45,000	7.50	45,000	6.43	45,000	5.62	45,000
V) Variable 10% (+) 1.		1.00	5,000	1.00	6,000	1.00	7,000	1.00	8,000
ii) Selling Expenses 8.									
F) Fixed 25% 2.		2.00	10,000	1.67	10,000	1.43	10,000	1.25	10,000
V) Variable 75% (+) 6.		6.00	30,000	6.00	36,000	6.00	42,000	6.60 (₹ 6 + 10% i.e. .60)	52,800
iii) Distribution Expenses 5.									
F) Fixed 20% 1.		1.00	5,000	0.83	5,000	0.71	5,000	0.62	5,000
V) Variable 80% (+) 4.		4.00	20,000	4.00	24,000	4.00	28,000	4.00	32,000
Total Cost		133.00	6,65,000	129.33	7,76,000	126.71	8,87,000	122.84	9,82,800

ILLUSTRATION 10

Crysta Ltd., Cochin is currently working at 50% capacity and produces 1,000 units at a cost of ₹ 180 per unit as per the details shown below.

Particulars	Unit Cost ₹
Direct Material	100
Direct Labour	30
Factory Overhead (40% Fixed)	30
Administrative Overhead (50% Fixed)	20

The current selling price is ₹ 200 per unit. At 60% capacity working, raw material cost increases by 2% and selling price falls by 20%. At 80% capacity working, material cost increases by 5% and selling price falls by 5%. Estimate profits of the company at 60% and 80% capacity by preparing Flexible Budgets and offer your critical comments.

SOLUTION

In the Books of Crysta Ltd., Cochin
Flexible Budget

Normal Activity : **1,000 units**
Capacity   : **50%**

Production	Units		1,000		1,200		1,600	
Capacity	%		50		60		80	
Particulars			Unit Cost ₹	Total Cost ₹	Unit Cost ₹	Total Cost ₹	Unit Cost ₹	Total Cost ₹
Direct Material			100.00	1,00,000	102.00 (100 + 2% i.e. ₹ 2)	1,22,400	105.00 (100 + 5% i.e. ₹ 5)	1,68,000
Add : Direct Labour			30.00	30,000	30.00	36,000	30.00	48,000
		(+)						
∴ Prime Cost		i)	130.00	1,30,000	132.00	1,58,400	135.00	2,16,000
Add : Factory Overheads	30							
F) Fixed 40% 12			12.00	12,000	10.00	12,000	7.50	12,000
V) Variable 60% (+) 18			18.00	18,000	18.00	21,600	18.00	28,800
Add : Administrative Overhead	20							
F) Fixed 50% 10			10.00	10,000	8.33	10,000	6.25	10,000
V) Variable 50% (+) 10			10.00	10,000	10.00	12,000	10.00	16,000
		(+)						
∴ Total Cost		ii)	180.00	1,80,000	178.33	2,14,000	176.75	2,82,800
Add : Profits		iii)	20.00	20,000	17.67	21,200	13.25	21,200
		(+)						
∴ Selling Price		iv)	**200.00**	**2,00,000**	**196.00** (200 – 2% i.e. ` 4)	**2,35,200**	**190.00** (200 – 5% i.e. ` 10)	**3,04,000**

Comment :

After making critical anlaysis, it is suggested that production capacity should not be increased as profit remains constant at 60% and 80% capacity level.

ILLUSTRATION 11

Sudarshan Co., Satara is engaged in manufacturing Foolscap Note Books is working currently at 40% capacity and produces 10,000 note books per month. The cost and price details for one note book is as under :

Particulars	Unit Cost and Price ₹
On Cost (40% Variable)	5
Productive Expenses	1
Direct Labour Cost	2
Basic Materials Cost	10
Market Price	20

You are required to prepare a Flexible Budget showing separately the profit at 50% and 90% capacities and the break-even-points at the production capacity levels assuming that –

a)   at 50% capacity the invoice price falls by 3% and

b)   at 90% capacity the selling price falls by 5% accompanied by a similar fall in the price of Direct Material.

SOLUTION

In the books of Sudarshan Co., Satara
Flexible Budget

Normal Activity : Units 10,000
Capacity : 40%

Production Capacity	Units	10,000 40		12,500 50		22,500 90	
Particulars		Per Unit ₹	Total ₹	Per Unit ₹	Total ₹	Per Unit ₹	Total ₹
Sales		20.00	2,00,000	19.40 (fall by 3%)	2,42,500	19.00 (fall by 5%)	4,27,500
Less : Variable Cost							
i) Basic Material Cost		10.00	1,00,000	10.00	1,25,000	9.50 (fall by 5%)	2,13,750
ii) Direct Labour Cost		2.00	20,000	2.00	25,000	2.00	45,000
iii) Productive Expenses		1.00	10,000	1.00	12,500	1.00	22,500
iv) On Cost (40% of ₹ 5.00)	(–)	2.00	20,000	2.00	25,000	2.00	45,000
∴ Contribution where, (C = S – V)		5.00	50,000	4.40	55,000	4.50	1,01,250
Less : Fixed Cost							
i) On Cost (60% of ₹ 5.00)	(–)	3.00	30,000	2.40	30,000	1.33	30,000
∴ **Profit** where, (P = C – F)		**2.00**	**20,000**	**2.00**	**25,000**	**3.17**	**71,250**
∴ Break-Even Point (Units) = Total Fixed Cost / Contribution per unit		= ₹ 30,000 / ₹ 5.00 = 6,000 units		= ₹ 30,000 / ₹ 4.40 = 6,818 units		= ₹ 30,000 / ₹ 4.50 = 6,667 units	

5.3.4 CAPITAL BUDGET

It is also known as 'Capital Expenditure Budget'. It shows the estimated expenditure on fixed assets during the budget period. As the amount involved in capital expenditure is usually very high, it requires careful attention and critical judgement of the top management. This budget is based on the requisition for capital expenditure from various departments and after understanding their profitability. Capital expenditure is sanctioned and incorporates in the budget accordingly.

QUESTIONS FOR SELF-STUDY

I. Theory Questions :

i) Clearly bring out the meaning of Budget, Budgeting and Budgetary Control.

ii) What do you mean by Budgetary Control ? Suggest a suitable organisation for efficient Budgetary Control System.

iii) Discuss the objective, advantages and limitations of Budgetary Control System.

iv) What are the different types of functional budgets which are prepared by a large scale manufacturing concern ?

v) What do you understand by a Flexible Budget ? How does fixed cost per unit vary in case of a budget for varying levels of activity ?

vi) Define Cash Budget. Show neatly with the help of a proforma how it is prepared ?

vii) Write short notes on :

a) Cash Budget

b) Flexible Budget

c) Types of Budget

d) Objectives of Budgetary Control

II. Practical Problems :

i) The following budget estimates are available from Akash Ltd., Akurdi working at 50% capacity.

Variable Costs   ₹ 50,000

Semi-variable Costs   ₹ 25,000

Fixed Costs   ₹ 10,000

You are required to prepare a flexible budget for 80% capacity assuming that semi-variable expenses increases by 10% for every 20% increases in capacity.

ii) In a Bokaro Ltd., Baroda a cost centre works at 60% capacity and the following overhead expenses are incurred.

Particulars	₹
Salary of Supervisor	2,000
Salary of Assistant Supervisor	1,000
Wages of Workers	5,000
Repairs of Machines	8,000
Spoiled Work	2,500
Spoiled Work	2,500
Oils and Lubricants	2,000
Depreciation of Machine	10,000
∴ Total	33,000

Prepare a Flexible Budget for 75%, 100% and 125% capacities.

iii) Charlie Ltd., Chembur produces a consumer product. The estimated costs per unit are given below :

	₹
Raw Material	500
Direct Labour	300
Factory Overhead	400 (30% fixed)
Administrative Overheads	200 (60% fixed)
Cost per unit	1,400

The selling price per unit is ₹ 1,800. At 50% capacity it produces 5,000 units. Find out the profits when it works at 60% and 80% capacity.

Notes :

a)   The cost per unit of ₹ 1,400 is at 50% capacity.

b)   At 60% capacity raw material cost increases by 3% and selling price falls by 3%.

c)   At 80% capacity raw material cost increases by 4% and selling price falls by 5%. Draw a proforma of a Flexible Budget using imaginary figures for 50%, 60% and 70% capacity levels.

iv) Prepare a Production Budget for 3,000 Units and 2,000 Units capacities assuming that administration expenses remain constant at all levels of output. The budgeted expenses for production of 4,000 units are :

Particulars	Per Unit ₹
Raw Materials	80
Direct Labour	30
Variable Overheads	20
Fixed Overheads (₹ 80,000)	10
Variable Overheads (Direct)	4
Selling Expenses (10% Fixed)	15
Administration Expenses (₹ 40,000)	5
Distribution Expenses (25% Fixed)	6
∴ Total Cost	170

v) From the following particulars prepare a Cash Budget for January, February and March 2013 in a tabular form.

2012-2013 Months	Sales ₹	Purchases ₹	Wages ₹	Expenses ₹
October	1,00,000	50,000	15,000	6,000
November	90,000	45,000	19,000	5,000
December	80,000	40,000	24,000	7,000
January	85,000	42,500	22,000	5,000
February	95,000	50,000	18,000	6,000
March	90,000	45,000	20,000	5,000

Further information :

a) 5% of the purchases and 10% of the sales are for cash.
b) Creditors allowed to customers is 1/2 months.
c) Creditors for purchases are paid following the month of purchases.
d) Wages are paid every 15 days.
d) Opening Balance of cash as on January 2013 is ₹ 15,000.

vi) From the following particulars prepare a Cash Budget for the quarter ended 30th June 2013.

Particulars	Actual			Budgeted		
	January ₹	February ₹	March ₹	April ₹	May ₹	June ₹
Sales	1,00,000	1,00,000	95,000	1,20,000	1,15,000	1,10,000
Purchases	50,000	45,000	48,000	50,000	45,000	30,000
Wages	30,000	25,000	28,000	30,000	25,000	20,000
Expenses	4,000	5,000	5,000	8,000	6,000	40,000

Further Information :

a) 50% of the purchases and sales are for cash.
b) Debtors realised after one month.
c) Creditors paid after two months.
d) Payment of wages made after one week.
e) Expenses are paid after one month.
f) Rent of ₹ 5,000 per month not considered in expenses.
g) Income-tax payable in April ₹ 1,500.
h) Cash balance as on 1st April, 2008 was ₹ 1,500.

vii) The following is the estimated data for six months - March 2013 to August 2013 of a company.

Months 2013	Credit Sales ₹	Credit Purchases ₹	Wages ₹	Manufacturing Expenses ₹	Office Expenses ₹	Selling Expenses ₹
March	50,000	35,000	9,000	5,000	1,500	1,500
April	54,000	39,000	8,500	4,000	2,000	4,000
May	58,000	32,000	9,500	4,500	3,500	4,500
June	50,000	35,000	8,000	3,000	1,000	3,500
July	55,000	38,000	7,900	5,500	1,500	4,500
August	60,000	36,000	8,200	4,400	2,500	4,000

Other Information :

a) A machine valued at ₹ 20,000 will be supplied in June 2013 when 20% will have to be paid against delivery and the remaining balance to be paid after 4 months.
b) Credit Period ……….   Allowed to customers ……..   1 month
                             Allowed by suppliers ……..   2 month
c) Tax to be paid in advance   ₹ 10,000 in March 2013
d) Lag in payments ……….   Manufacturing expenses 15 days
                   ……….   All other expenses 30 days

Prepare a Cash Budget for the six months ended 31st August, 2013.

■■■

Chapter **6**...

Standard Costing

Synopsis...

Control is any specific action that guides the activity towards some predetermined unfaovurable events. It is exercised more effectively through goal setting and evaluation of performance. It is a continuous process which aims at ensuring that corrective actions conform to well designed plans. **Cost Control** is the most important objective of cost accounting and cannot be achieved without some standard against which the actuals can be compared. **Standard** is the desired level of performance for evaluating whether the actual performance is upto the expected level.

All management officials are interested not only in understanding what costs are but also how satisfactory and productive they are. The **standards** provide incentive and motivation to work with greater effort and vigilance for achieving the standard, which increases ultimate efficiency and productivity too. **Standard Costs** are the pre-determined costs calculated in advance of production on the basis of specification of all the factors affecting costs.

6.1 CONCEPT

Standard Costing is a useful technique of exercising control in the areas of cost of production by comparing actual cost with the standard cost ascertainment variances, finding out the causes of variances and taking corrective actions under the techniques of standard costing, the effective use of standard cost, increases cost consciousness among management and employees and business profits by providing a suitable base for performance evaluation. Thus, standard costing helps managerial planning and control in a significant manner. In twenty-first century of global market every manufacturing undertaking uses the technique of standard costing, which serves as an effective tool for management control.

A) Standard Cost :

Meaning :

The word **'Standard'** means a criterion. Thus, a **Standard Cost** is one which is pre-determined and used as a criterion for measuring the efficiency with which actual cost has been incurred. Standard costs represent 'planned' cost of a product. They are expected to be achieved in a particular production process under normal conditions.

Definitions :

The following definitions crystallise the concept of 'Standard Cost'.

i) **Standard Cost** is defined in the **CIMA** Official terminology as,

"a predetermined calculation of how much costs should be under specified working conditions. It is built-up from an assessment of the value of cost elements and correlates technical specifications and the qualification of materials, labour and other costs to the prices and/or usage rates expected to apply during the period in which the Standard Cost is intended to be used. Its main purpose is to provide basis for control through variance accounting for the valuation of stock and work-in-progress and in some cases for fixing selling prices".

ii) **The Institute of Cost and Management Accountants** (U.K.) defines **Standard Costs** as,

"a predetermined cost which is calculated from management's standards of efficient operation and the relevant necessary expenditure. It may be used as a basis for price fixing and for cost control through variance analysis".

Thus, a **Standard Cost** is a planned cost for a unit of product or service rendered. Standard costs are highly detailed scientifically predetermined costs of material, labour and overhead chargeable to a product or service. Standard costs represent excellent target costs that should be obtained.

Standard Cost expresses what costs should be under attainable good performance. They are projections of what actual cost should be under an assumed set of conditions. The term "standard", has been called by different names in accounting e.g., "a norm", "a model or example or comparison", "a measure of comparison", "a criterion of excellence", "a yardstick", "a benchmark", "an index of waste or potential savings", "a sea level from which to measure cost attitudes", "a guage". A **standard** may be a normal or a measure of comparison in terms of specific items such, as pounds or kilograms of materials, labour hours required, hours of plant capacity used etc.

From the above definitions, it is observed that,

i) **Standard Cost** is a target cost which must be attained.

ii) It is based on technical and engineering studies, production method, material specifications, material and labour price projections.

Thus, **Standard Costs** are the normal costs, for nomal production efficiency, at a normal level of output.

B) Standard Costing :

Meaning :

It is a scientific procedure under which predetermined costs are used to measure the efficiency of production. It simply refers to the determination of standard costs and their application to managerial problems particularly to production costs. Standard Costing is a technique which uses predetermined standards for costs and revenues for the purpose of control through variance analysis.

Definitions :

The following definitions crystallise the concept of 'Standard Costing'.

i) According to **CIMA, London, Standard Costing** is,

"the preparation and use of standard costs, their comparison with actual cost and the analysis of variance to their causes and points of incidence".

ii) **Brown and Harward** defines Standard Costing as,

"a technique of cost accounting which compares the standard cost of each product or service with the actual costs to determine the efficiency of the operation so that any remedial action may be taken immediately".

Thus, **Standard Costing** involves the setting of pre-determined cost estimates in order to provide a basis for comparison with actual costs. A **Standard Cost** is a planned cost for a unit of product or service rendered. **Standard Costing** is universally accepted as an effective instrument for cost control in industries. It can be used in conjunction with any method of costing. However, it is specially suitable where the manufacturing method involves production of standardised goods of repetitive nature.

From the above definitions, it is observed that,

i) In Standard Costing all costs are pre-determined in advance. These pre-determined costs are compared with the actual costs incurred. The difference between the standard cost and the actual cost is known as the Variance. These variances are then analysed and reasons found out for taking corrective actions.

ii) The standards are set based on the past records and performances.

iii) Comparison between actual performance and standard performance is shown by way of reports which are presented to the top management.

iv) Analysis of variances are made for taking appropriate action according to the nature of expenses, i.e. controllable and uncontrollable.

v) In case of controllable costs if there is adverse variance, efforts are taken to prevent its recurrence. But in case of uncontrollable costs, the standards are revised.

vi) Standard Costing may be applied to any industry.

Objectives of Standard Costing :

Standard costing system establishes yard-sticks against which efficiency or inefficiency of actual performances are measured.

The **basic objectives of Standard Costing technique can be** outlined as follows :

 i) To provide a formal basis for assessing performance and efficiency.

 ii) To control costs by establishing standards and analysis of variances.

 iii) To enable the principle of "Management by Exception" to be practised at a detailed operational level.

 iv) To assist in setting budgets.

 v) To assist in assigning responsibility for non-standard performance in order to correct deficiencies or to capitalise on benefits.

 vi) To provide a basis for estimating.

 vii) To provide guidance on possible ways of improving performance.

Standard Costing is not a method of costing

Standard Costing is not a distinct method of costing but is only a technique which can be applied to all methods of costing such as job costing or process costing, marginal costing or absorption costing. Standard costing is often used in conjunction with budgetary control. Both techniques use variance analysis as a means of management control. Standard costs are useful for cost estimates and price quotations.

6.2 ADVANTAGES

The advantages to be derived from a system of standard costing will vary from one business to another. It depends upon the degree of sophistication achieved and the acceptance by the management of utility of the system. **Possible Advantages of Standard Costing technique** are as follows :

i) **Effective Cost Control :**

The most important advantage of standard costing is that it facilitates the control of cost. Control is exercised by comparing actual performance with standards and taking action on the basis of variances so revealed.

ii) **Help in Planning :**

Establishing standards is a very useful exercise in business planning which instils in the management a habit of thinking in advance.

iii) **Provides Incentives :**

The standards provide incentives and motivate to work with greater effort. Schemes may be formulated to reward those who achieve or surpass the standard. This increases efficiency and productivity.

iv) **Fixing Prices and Formulating Policies :**

Standard costs are a valuable aid to management in determining prices and formulating production policies. For example, prices may be fixed by adding a standard margin of profit in standard cost. Similarly, standard costing furnishes cost estimates while planning production of new products.

v) **Facilitates Delegation of Authority :**

In order that responsibility for off standard performance may be identified directly with the persons concerned, an organisation chart is prepared which shows delegated authority and establishes responsibility of each executive.

vi) Facilitates Co-ordination :
While establishing standards, the performance of different departments such as production, sales, purchases etc. is taken into account. Thus, standard costing facilitate co-ordination between different functions of different departments.

vii) Eliminates Wastes :
By fixing standards, certain wastages, such as materials wastage, idle time, lost machine hours, etc. are reduced.

viii) Valuation of Stocks :
Standard costing simplifies the valuation of stock because the stock is valued at standard cost. The difference between standard and actual cost is transferred to a variance account. This ensures a uniform pricing of stocks in the form of raw materials, work-in-progress and finished goods.

ix) Management by Exception :
Reporting of variances is based on the principle of management by exception. Only variances beyond a predetermined limit may be considered by the management for corrective action. This also reduces the cost of preparing reports.

x) Economical and Simple :
Standard costing is an economical and simple means of cost accounting and generally results in a saving in the cost of costing system. It results in reduction in paper work in accounting and needs lesser number of forms and records. This leads to considerable saving in clerical labour.

xi) Facilitates Cost Audit :
Standard costing facilitates cost audit since it variances are satisfactorily explained, the accuracy of costing can be safely assumed.

xii) Provides Forward Looking Approach :
By adoption of standard costing system, the whole concern is imbued with a dynamic forward looking mentality.

xiii) Provides Objective Measurement of Operational Efficiency :
Standard costing through setting of standards, enables to measure the operational efficiency of workers and other materials of the staff objectively against those standards.

xiv) Creates Cost Consciousness :
Standard costing creates cost consciousness among executives which increases efficiency and productivity.

Hence, the entire success of a standard cost accounting system is dependent on the extent of responsibility which the top management assumes in correcting the conditions which cause variances from standards.

Techniques of Standard Costing :
    i)   Pre-determination of technical data related to manufacturing operations, processes, products and their efficiencies, wastage, losses, machine utilisation etc.

    ii)   Pre-determination of standard costs in full details under each element of cost, i.e., Material, Labour, overheads.

iii) Pre-determination of standard selling prices.

iv) Pre-determination of standard profit margins.

v) Comparison of actual performance and costs with standards.

vi) Analysis of variances-cost, sales and profit along with reasons for deviations of actuals from the standards.

vii) Presentation of variances to management for taking appropriate action and remedial measures.

viii) Revision of standards where necessary.

Logical dissimilarity between Estimated Costs and Standard Cost :

Even it might appear that standard and estimated costs are the same, some dissimilarity exists. An **estimated cost** is determined on the basis of average past performance and therefore, can be regarded as a reasonable assessment of what a cost "will be".

On the other hand, **standard costs** are the costs that would be incurred under the most efficient operating conditions and are forecast before the manufacturing process begins. Thus, it is carefully predetermined costs used as performance criteria - a measure what a cost should be. Whereas budgeted costs are viewed as future costs (prediction, estimates, forecasts) that are formally combined into an integrated plan of action. It is the standard cost per unit of the budgeted quantity to be produced during a particular period. Thus, both standard costs and estimated costs are pre-determined costs, but their basic purposes are quite different from each other.

Features of Standard Costing :

The **Features of Standard Costing** are shown below in Figure 6.1.

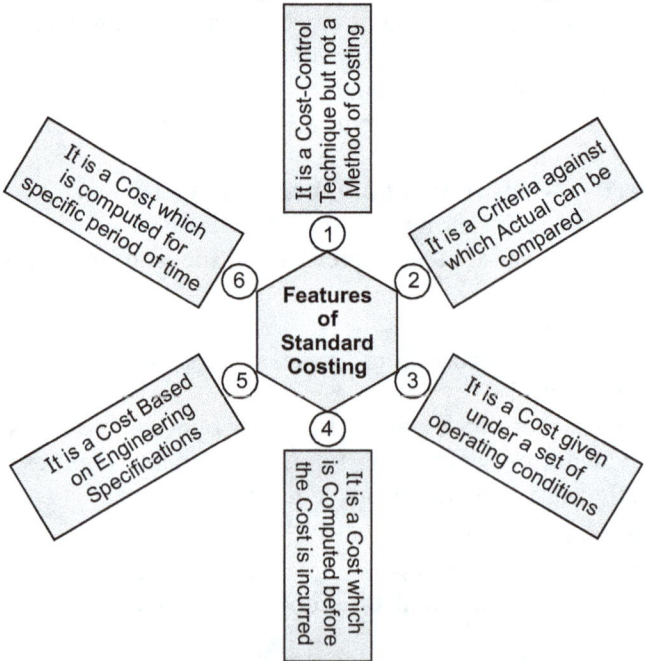

Fig. 6.1 : Features of Standard Costing

1) Standard Costing is one of the cost control techniques and not a method of costing like job costing, process costing.

2) Standard means a criterion or a yardstick against which actual activity can be compared to determine the difference between the two.

3) Standard cost is the cost what should have been under a given set of operating conditions.

4) It is a pre-determined cost which is computed before the cost is incurred (i.e. in advance of production).

5) It is based on engineering specification of all the factors affecting cost.

6) It is computed for a specific period of time.

Establishment of Cost Standards :

Setting up of standards and the comparison of actuals with the standards are the essentials of standard costing. The effectiveness of standard cost as a technique wholly depends upon the establishment of the accurate cost standards. Care should be taken in setting the standards considering all relevant factors such as the employees, their attitudes and abilities, the extent of control exercised over their operations and so on.

There are several methods adopted for fixing the standards such as engineering estimates, observed behaviour, predicted behaviour and desired behaviour. The standard cost in a particular situation is based on two or more of these bases.

When cost standards are determined on the basis of engineering estimates, it is but proper to consider the specifications of the machinery for accurately ascertaining the standard relationship between a given unit of output and a given unit of input. On the basis of such technical specifications cost standards can be fixed. The cost standards so fixed, represent only what can be accomplished.

Another technique employed for establishing cost standards is the past experience. Here, the principle involved is to consider the past achievement as standard for the future. Of course, the past can provide a reliable guide for the future as long as the processes and procedures of the past remain unchanged. If changes occur in the processes and procedures, the observed behaviour can no longer provide a reliable basis for establishing cost standards.

When certain technological changes are expected to take place they are likely to have profound influence on the cost estimates. In such cases, the predicted behaviour which represents what is most likely to happen, can be used for setting cost standards. This calls for a minor adjustment to historical standard cost. Hence, standards may need to be revised to accommodate necessary changes in the organisation or its environment.

Desired Behaviour :

The desired behaviour can also be taken as the basis for setting cost standards. The term **"desired behaviour"** represents what the management actually desires. Again, the desire of the management in turn, reflects the experience of similar concerns or the industry as a whole.

It is clear that there are several techniques available for establishing cost standards. But, the final basis adopted for the purpose depends on the management's judgement. The management should be careful while setting the standards. The standards so set are very attainable with reasonable efforts. When standards set are very high, they will be difficult to achieve resulting in all round demoralisation. On the other hand, if the standards set are very low, there may not be adequate motivation to achieve them. Hence, it is essential that the standards set in manufacturing organisation should be easily attainable standards.

Steps involved in Standard Costing :

Standard Costing system involves the following important steps :

i)   Determination of standard cost for each element of cost - direct material, direct labour, and overhead;

ii)   Recording of both standard and actual costs in appropriate books of accounts;

iii) Computation of variance between standard cost and actual cost;

iv)   Analysis and investigation of the variances; and

v)   Feed correction and suggest modification where required. Corrective actions are taken to ensure that future performance will be in accordance with pre-determined-standards.

The standard cost of a product consists of :

i)   Quantitative Factors :

Standard quantity of given material, standard labour hours for specified operations, and standard machine hours for the stated machines to be used; and

ii)   Price Factors :

Standard cost per rupee and per hour, by which the standard quantities are converted to the standard product costs.

The quantitative factors are based on engineered specifications tempered by experience, and vice-versa whereas prices used are typically those which are expected to be representative of actual prices during the period for which the standard are established.

For control purposes, the various actual activities of a period; such as quantity of each type of material used, labour hours worked, and machine hours involved, as well as units of goods produced, are multiplied by appropriate unit standard cost to establish standard cost totals for work performed by job or process, and by department. The actual costs of these activities are then compared with the standard costs and the resulting variances are examined;

i)   to aid the interpretation of financial results for the period;

ii)   to fix the responsibility for non-standard performance; and

iii) to focus attention on areas in which cost improvement should be sought.

6.3 TYPES OF STANDARDS

The various **Types of Standards** are shown in Figure 6.2 as follows :

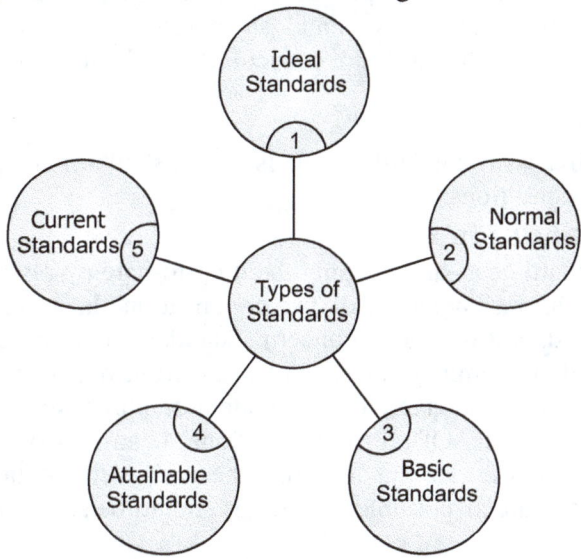

Fig. 6.2 : Types of Standards

1) **Ideal Standards :**

   Ideal Standards are set at the level of maximum efficiency, representing conditions that can seldom if-ever be attainable. Such a standard fails to pay any attention to normal materials, spoilage and idle labour time. This type of standard can be used as standard of perfection rather than a standard for the measurement of practical results because conditions that satisfy ideal standards are extremely rare. Ideal standards are more effective for direct material costs and usage. The application of ideal standard makes variance accounts less significant for control purposes.

2) **Normal Standards :**

   Normal Standards are the standards that can be achieved by efficient working and efficient management. Such standards are set after taking into consideration the conditions that are expected to prevail over a long period of time sufficient to reflect the effects of seasonal and cyclical fluctuations. These standards are of great significance for manufacturing overhead expenses.

3) **Basic Standards :**

   Basic Standards provide a measuring scale for performance over a long period of time. Such standards are not influenced by any change in material prices and labour rates and therefore, remain unchanged for a number of years. Basic standards are useful for such items of expenditure that are fixed in nature.

4) **Attainable Standards :**

   Attainable Standards based on past performance, can be achieved with reasonable effort. Perhaps the standards should be somewhat lower than what can be achieved by earnest effort. Such standards are set as closely as possible to that level which represents anticipated conditions. They allow for usual production problems, such as down time for maintenance, employee errors, or occasional inventory shortages. These standards are more realistic and satisfactory and thus represent desirable performance. Attainable standards are particularly useful in setting price standards for materials and labour.

5) **Current Standards :**

Current Standard is a standard which is established for a limited period and is related to current conditions.

Setting up of Standards :

Establishing standard costs and keeping them up-to-date involves considerable effort and co-operation of various members of the organisation. In a small concern a single person sets the standard. But in a large concern a standards committee is appointed to do this job. The Standards Committee consists of production manager, personnel manager, production engineer, sales manager, cost accountant, purchasing manager, marketing manager, finance manager etc. Of all these functional heads, Cost Accountant will have to play a very important role. He has to supply necessary cost data and ensure that the standards set are as accurate as possible. Standards should be set for each demand of cost separately.

A Standard Cost is a measure in quantities, hours and value of the input factors. It consists of three elements viz. direct material, direct labour and overhead. The setting up of standards for direct material and direct labour involves the establishment of physical standards and price standards. **Physical standards** refer to product specifications material specification, method of manufacture and equipment to be used. As such, these should be in terms of kg. of materials, unit of time and hours of plant capacity. **Price standards** are set on the basis of actual average price expected to prevail during the next period or normal prices expected to prevail during a cycle of reasons which may be of a number of years.

After the standards have been fixed, the management is interested in calculation of variance from the standards with the purpose of making the members of various management levels to know what the variances are and who is responsible for it. Thus, the purpose of setting standards is to help in responsibility accounting.

Organisation of Standard Costing :

The efficiency of a standard costing system largely depends upon the accuracy and reliability of the standards. In the past the job of standard setting was the responsibility of the cost accountant. However, keeping in view the dynamic conditions of the present business, it requires the combined thinking and expertise of all persons who have responsibility over prices and quantities of inputs against this background, almost in every big organisation. At present, this function is discharged by a standard committee comprising of representatives from various concerned departments of the organisation. The said committee establishes and monitors standards for various costs and activities and is also responsible for changing and updating the standards when requires. Revision of standards is definitely a costly affair and may create a number of other problems, hence some of the manufacturing firms simply ignore such revision.

> **Inaccurate, unreliable and outdated standards do more harm than benefit.**

The important component of standard costing system is the setting of standards to be used for evaluation of actual results. The term standard cost refers to cost that should reasonably be incurred in the manufacture of a product. **The components of standard costs** are Standard Direct Material Cost, Standard Direct Labour Cost and Manufacturing Overheads which are shown in Figure 6.3 as follows :

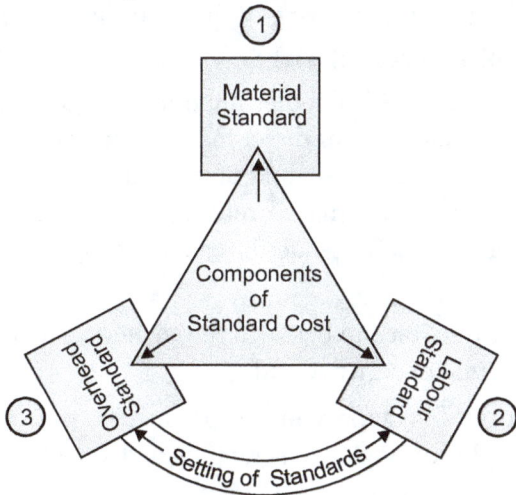

Fig. 6.3 : Components of Standard Cost

1) Material Standard :

The standard direct materials cost of a product incurred depends on price and quantity standards. It can be ascertained by application of the following formula :

Standard Direct Material Cost = Standard price of direct material × Standard quantity of direct material

i) Standard Price of Direct Material :

One of the important ingredient of cost is the cost of direct material used in the manufacture of goods. An important element of cost control is the price paid for the purchase of material. Another essential of cost control is that the price paid should be reasonable. The material price standard refers to the price which should be reasonably paid for a particular direct raw material under the most favourable possible conditions. But the most favourable possible conditions will differ from firm to firm depending upon the circumstances of each case. It implies, therefore, that direct material price standard should be set for each firm and not for the industry as a whole.

The standard price of the direct material should include all the components of the amount spent in the acquisition of a particular material. Where the prices differ for the goods of the same quality, the standard should be set based on the lowest price. Again, where the supplier who is prepared to sell the material at the lowest price, is not a reliable one, there is no real savings to the firm. In such cases, higher prices charged by more reliable suppliers will form the basis for fixing the standard price. While fixing the standard price of direct material, freight charges and import duties should be considered wherever applicable. Another related aspect to be considered is that of the discounts available for the purchase of materials. This includes quantity discounts which are granted for purchase of goods in bulk and cash discounts which are allowed for prompt payment. The effect of discounts is lowering of the costs and hence, the standard price.

ii) Standard Quantity of Direct Material :

The quantity of direct material is another important factor affecting the cost of direct material. For setting the standard cost of direct material, the quantity of materials used for the production of a particular product should also be standardised. The standards of the quantity of consumption of raw materials is referred to as standard quantity of materials or material usage standards. Such standards can be determined on the basis of the following factors :

- The input-output relationship between raw-materials and final products based on observation of actual experience and

- The inherent loss of materials in the productive processes such as shrinkage, evaporation, weight losses due to scrapping and smoothing etc.

The total standard direct material cost is computed by multiplying the standard price with the standard quantity of direct material.

2) Labour Standard :

The second component of the total standard cost is standard direct labour cost. It is calculated by multiplying the labour standard rate by the labour standard time.

i) Standard Rate of Direct Labour :

The payment made to labour for carrying out production represents wages. The wages are calculated either on time basis (monthly, weekly or daily) or on piece basis (per piece of production). The term standard labour rate refers to the conventional standard wage rate only, i.e. in case of the time wage payment only. In fact, these standard labour rates come into force either as a result of the management policy or due to negotiation between management and trade unions. Moreover, there will be several wage rates depending upon the degree of skill, the inherent risk involved, seniority and so on. Thus, it is clear that the labour standard rates are quite different from material standard price. It should be remembered that the standard labour rates are not under the control of the management.

ii) Standard Time of Direct Labour :

The quantum of labour is measured in terms of the time consumed for the completion of the particular piece of work. Hence, labour standard time refers to the total time which particular operation should take. This is based on the observation of actual operation and critical evolution of the whole performance. Time and motion studies provide a popular example of this type. It is on this basis the labour standard time is determined. While doing so some allowance must be given, since human beings are not mechanical devices and cannot utilise the entire time for production purpose. At the same time, it should also be remembered that while setting the standards no allowance is made for prolonged periods of illness of the workers.

3) Overhead Standard :

Another component of cost standard is overhead. There is a basic difference between the material and labour standards and overhead standards. For the material and labour, standards are set on the basis of price and quantity standards. This only establishes the functional relationship that exists between the number of units of a product and the quantities of material and labour required for producing the same with the underlying fact that each material has its standard price and each worker has a standard wage rate. But no such functional relationship exists between the units produced and the total overhead cost. Even that part of the manufacturing overhead which varies with the volume of production cannot be directly related to production in the same way as direct material and direct labour. Therefore, the determination of overhead standards is completely different from that of direct material and direct labour.

The overheads are classified into (a) variable and (b) fixed. The standard variable overhead is fixed directly per unit of volume. The volume of measure refers to some measure of input such as direct labour cost or hours. Standard fixed rates, on the other hand are usually fixed at some volume representative of the firm's operations over a longer period.

Such standards are set after careful study of cost volume analysis.

Actual Costs Accumulation :

The establishment of standards is followed by the accumulation of actual costs which are then compared with standards in performance reports. For accumulating actual manufacturing costs, firms use either a job order system or a process cost system. The application of standard costing gets much information from the cost data than is possible with just actual costs. A sound system of standard costing will help management in determining the type of required cost data and in reporting such data.

In short, 'Standard Cost' is the key to the system of standard costing. Extreme care is required to be taken in the establishment of standards because the success of standard cost system depends on the accuracy and reliability of these standards. Standards are set for each element of cost, i.e. Material, Labour and Overhead.

Key Factors to be considered for setting up Standards :

The following table indicates how standards are set for each element of cost and what key factors should be consider for the same :

Element of Cost and Standards	Department Concerned	Key Factors for Setting of Standards
A) Direct Material Standards i) **Material Price Standard**	• Purchase Department or Marketing Department	• Current Market price. • Market Conditions • Forecasts of Price • Discount Rebate Packing and Delivery Charges etc.
ii) **Material Usage Standard**	• Engineering Department and Production Department	• Quality of Material. • Quantity of Material. • Normal Material • Losses like evaporation, shrinkage, breakage, etc.
B) Direct Labour Standards i) **Labour Rate Standard**	• Human Resource Department	• Current rates of pay. • Current method of wage payment. • Forecast of wage trends. • Wage structure and designated posts.
ii) **Labour Efficiency Standard**	• Engineering Department	• Grade of Labour (Skilled /semi-skilled/un-skilled). • Standard time for each operation. • Most efficient method of working/operation. • Normal Idle time like fatigue, tool setting etc.
C) Standard for Overhead	• Engineering Department, Human Resource Department, Purchase Department, Administrative Department, Selling and Distribution Department, Marketing Department	• Standard Indirect Material Costs. • Standard Indirect Labour Costs. • Standard Indirect Expenses. • Standard level of activity such as Standard Hours, Standard Production (in units) • Fixed Overheads • Variable Overheads

6.4 VARIANCE ANALYSIS

The basic function of standard costing is to find out the variances between standard costs allowed and the actual costs incurred. **Variance** is the difference between the actual cost and the standard cost. **Variance Analysis** is the process of analysis of variance of sub-dividing the total variance in such a way that management can fix the responsibility for the divergence from the standard performance. If actual cost is less than standard cost, it is considered to be a sign of efficiency and the difference is termed as **favourable variance**. On the other hand, if actual cost is more than standard cost, it is considered to be a sign of inefficiency and the difference is termed as **unfavourable variance**. Favourable variance is also referred to as positive variance while unfavourable variance is also known as negative variance.

It should also be borne in mind that the words favourable or positive and unfavourable or negative merely indicate the direction of variance from the standard cost, they need not be construed as good or bad from the point of view of the firm. A real quantitative evaluation can be effected only after determining the causes for the variance. Again, the final result is also affected by the type of standards predetermined by the firm. If the set standards are reasonable and accurate and are revised from time to time, according to the changed circumstances, any deviation would reflect true deviation. On the other hand, if the expected standards are not reasonable and accurate, the deviations will be distorted. Thus, pre-determined standards, function as a indicators of variances between standard costs and actual costs incurred. Variance analysis indicates the areas of strengths and weaknesses but does not indicate what the action, if any, should be taken.

1) Variance :

Meaning :

The difference between pre-determined standard costs and the actual costs is known as a **Variance.** Variances indicate the difference between planned performance and actual performance. Planned performances, usually are indicated in the form of standards or budgeted costs whereas actual performances, are indicated in the form of actual costs. Hence, variance is the extent of deviation of the actual cost from the standard cost.

Definitions :

The term **'Variance'** has been defined by different experts and professional institutes in the manner stated below :

i) **The Terminology of CIMA, defines variance as,**
   "the difference between the planned, budgeted or standard costs and actual costs".

ii) **The Institute of Cost and Management Accountants, U.K. defines Variance as,**
   "the difference between standard cost and the comparable actual cost incurred during a period".

Thus, **Variances** are the deviations between standard performances set and actual performances recorded. When actual results are better than the standard, a favourable or positive variance arises and where they are not upto the standard an unfavourable or negative variance occurs. Variances indicate different situations where actual performances are not as pre-determined, whether good or bad. Variance assists managers at different levels in their planning and control decisions.

2) Variance Analysis :

Meaning :

The difference between actual cost and standard cost is termed as 'Variance' which is composed of variances arising from a number of causes. Hence, it is necessary to analyse the cost variances into different components and the detailed explanation of the causes of variances. The systematic process of computation of individual variances, determination of the causes of each variance and reporting of the same to the responsible manager, it is known as **'Variance Analysis'**. Variance analysis and reporting to management is based on the principles by exception. Thus, variance analysis is a cost accounting process that helps to calculate the influence upon the cost of each cause of deviation. It provides a readymade well classified and interpreted valuable cost data to the management for the purposes of effective planning, efficient control and appropriate decision making.

Definitions :

The term **'Variance Analysis'** has been defined by different experts and professional institutes in the manner stated below.

i) **The Terminology of CIMA, defines Variance Analysis** as,

"the analysis of variances arising in a standard costing system into their constituent parts".

ii) **The Institute of Cost and Management Accountants, U.K. defines 'Variance Analysis as,**

"the process of computing the amount of, and isolating the cause of variances between actual costs and standard costs".

Thus, **Variance Analysis**, indicates the calculation of variances according to the important elements of cost and the detailed analysis of the cause and incidence of each variance separately. It helps the management to identify the responsibility for negative variance to executives and remove inefficiency.

> **Variance Analysis is an integral part of the Standard Costing System.**

3) Variance Accounting :

Meaning :

The systematic and accurate accounting of variance is of obsolute importance. Standard costing is the control technique more useful to investigate the reasons for important variances so as to identify the basic problems and take necessary corrective action. Thus, standard costing makes appropriate use of **Variance Accounting** as a modern technique for controlling the ultimate costs.

Definitions :

The term **'Variance Accounting'** has been defined by different experts and professional institutes in the manner stated below.

i) **The Terminology of CIMA, defines Variance Accounting** as,

"a technique whereby the planned activities of an undertaking are quantified in budgets, standard cost, standard selling prices and standard profit margins and the difference between these and the actual costs are compared. The procedure is to collect, compare, comment and correct".

Variance Accounting is thus, a systematic method of cost accounting which includes a number of steps to be followed which are as follows :

    i) preparation of well designed plans,

    ii) fixation of achievable standards,

    iii) computation of actual performance,

iv) continuous comparison of standard set and actuals achieved,

v   scientific analysis of variances into their constituents parts,

vi) finding out the causes of variances and fixation of responsibility and

vii) taking corrective actions.

Variance Accounting, will be a very useful method if the pre-determined standards are revised periodically, investigations are made more effectively and efficiently, and follow-up actions are taken immediately.

Types of Variances :

Variances may be segregated by department, by cost and by elements of cost, e.g. price and quantity. It is common experience that different industries make use of different variances. Despite the existence of a number of variances the following are some basic variances found in actual practice.

i)   Direct Material Variance,

ii) Direct Labour Variance,

iii) Variable Overhead Variance,

iv) Fixed Overhead Variance,

    • Based on units and

    • Based on standard hours.

Basically, there are two different types of variances, Price variance and Volume variance. The price variance is closely related to the price of materials, rates of labour, expenditure on overheads or selling price of products. The volume variance has some thing to do with quantity and is related to quantity of units in terms of raw materials consumed, number of hours worked or number of products sold.

Classification of Variances :

Classification of Variances based on price variance are :

i)   Material Price Variance,

ii) Labour Price Variance,

iii) Variable Overhead Expenditure Variance,

iv) Fixed Overhead Expenditure Variance,

v)   Sales Price Variance.

Classification of Variances based on quantity are,

i)   Materials Usage Variance,

ii) Labour Efficiency Variance,

iii) Fixed Overhead Volume Variance,

iv) Sales Volume Variance.

Thus, the cost variance comprises both price variance as well as volume variance. Again, for sales there is a total variance called sales value variance comprising the total of price variance and volume variance.

The needs of the management cannot be met fully by the basic variances which merely provide information regarding the extent of change in the volume. The management should also ascertain the causes for such changes, so that they can initiate corrective action whenever needed. The **Total Cost Variance Analysis** is shown below in Figure 6.4.

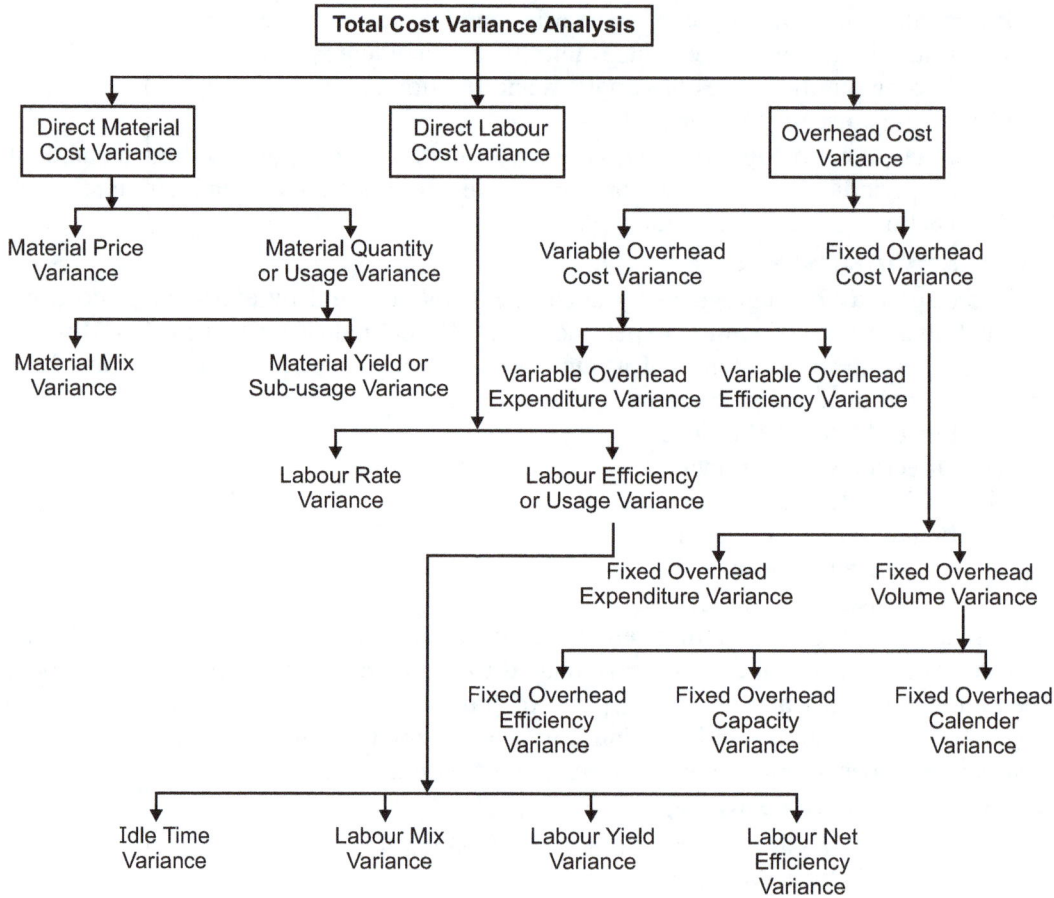

Fig. 6.4 : Total Cost Variance Analysis

6.4.1 MATERIALS VARIANCE

Material Variances are commonly referred to as Material Cost Variance (MCV). The MCV represents the difference between the standard cost of standard quantity of materials of actual output and the actual cost of materials consumed.

Symbolically :

Material Cost Variance (MCV) = Standard Cost (SC) − Actual Cost (AC)

From the above, it is clear that the MCV depends on two factors, viz., the price paid for material and the actual quantity of materials used. Accordingly, the MCV which represents a total variance can be divided into two sub-variances:

a)   Material Price Variance (MPV)

b)   Material Usage/Quantity Variance (MUV)

a)   Material Price Variance (MPV) :

MPV occurs when the actual price paid for the materials used is different from the standard price. The MPV is calculated by multiplying the difference between the standard unit price and the actual unit price paid for the materials used by the actual number of units or quantity of materials used in production.

Symbolically :

Material Price Variance = Actual Quantity / Number of Units Purchased (Standard Price – Actual Price)

$$MPV = AQ\,(SP - AP)$$

It should be remembered that, in the absence of specific information, the actual number of units purchased can be considered synonymous with those used in production.

MPV is caused by any one or combination of the factors such as changes in the price of materials, excessive freight charges, increase in the rates of taxes and customs duty, failure to avail cash discount or off-season low price, buying uneconomic quantities and the like. From the above, it is clear that the purchasing department may not always be held responsible for paying higher or lower than the standard price, since some of the factors devolve on persons outside the purchase department. It is but proper to institute a detailed analysis for the MPV and then attribute the responsibility for such variance to the concerned department / departments other than purchasing.

b)   Material Usage/Quantity Variance (MUV) :

The material usage/quantity variance (MUV), the second component of MCV, measures the extent of utilisation of materials in production. The Mi 1V represents the difference between the actual quantity consumed in production and the standard quantity that should have been used for actual output. The MUV is calculated by multiplying the standard unit price of materials with the difference between the actual quantity of material and the standard quantity.

Symbolically :

Material Usage Variance (MUV) = Standard Price × (SP) (Standard Quantity (SQ) – Actual Quantity – AQ)

The MUV arises due to any one or combination of the factors such as carelessness in the handling of materials by workers, wastage due to inefficient production methods or unskilled/untrained employees, low quality of materials used, pilferage and spoilage due to poor storage, maintenance, use of defective materials causing excessive consumption and the like. The overall responsibility for the MUV lies with the production personnel. But this should not be taken as a general rule always, as in the case of MPV. For instance, a favourable MUV may arise solely on account of substitution of above standard materials resulting in less wastage than was anticipated. Viewed from another angle, the purchase of above standard materials will definitely result in unfavourable MPV, since higher quality materials will cost more.

Classification of Material Usage Variance :

Where more than one type of material is used in the manufacture of products in a factory, MUV can be further sub-divided into i) "Material Mix Variance" (MMV) and ii) "Material Yield Variance" (MYV).

i) Material Mix Variance (MMV) :

This is component of material usage/quantity variance and hence, it is also called material mix sub-variance. This arises due to difference between the standard and actual composition of mix. The MMV occurs only where more than one type/grade of raw materials or combination of materials is used and when quantities issued to production differ from pre-determined standard mix. MMV is calculated by multiplying the standard price per unit of materials with the difference between actual proportion of those materials in actual quantity used and the standard proportions of those materials in actual quantity used. The standard proportions of materials in the actual total quantity used are referred to as "Revised Standard Quantity" (RSQ).

Symbolically :

Material Mix Variance (MMV) = Standard Unit Price (SP) × (Revised Standard Quantity (RSQ) – Actual Quantity) – AQ

A favourable variance would arise, when the Revised Standard Quality (RSQ) is more than the Actual Quantity (AQ) and vice versa.

Material Revised Usage Variance (MRUV) :

The word "Revised" is prefixed to `usage variance' only to denote the residue left after segregating material mix variance. In other words, it represents that portion of material total usage variance which is attributable to causes other than the difference between the standard and actual proportion of actual quantity used. MRUV is calculated by multiplying the standard price per unit of material with the difference between the standard proportion of different types of materials in the standard quantity and the standard proportion of those materials in actual quantity used.

Symbolically :

Material Revised Usage Variance (MRUV) = Sandard Unit Price SP × (Standard Quantity (SQ) – Revised Standard Quantity – (RSQ)

A favourable variance would arise, if the standard quantity is more than the Revised Standard Quantity and vice-versa.

ii) Material Yield Variance (MYV) :

In all process industries, "loss in production" is usually inevitable. This loss is classified into two types as 'normal' and 'abnormal'. The normal loss is taken into consideration while determining the standard for normal expected output or yield. Quite frequently, the actual yield differs from the standard yield due to abnormal loss sustained in the different processes of production. This difference is designated as "Yield Variance".

The yield variance represents that portion of the Material. Total Usage Variance which arises as a result of difference between the standard yield and the actual yield obtained. Again, the standard yield represents that output which should have resulted from the actual input of materials based on the standard expectations. It should also be remembered that while yield variance represents output variance other variances like price, usage and mix variances are input variances. MYV is calculated by multiplying the standard material; cost per unit of output with the difference between the standard yield and the actual yield.

Symbolically :

Material Yield Variance MYV = Standard Material Cost (SMC) per unit of output
(Standard Yield – (SY) Actual Yield (AY))

Diagrammatic Representation of Material Variance :

I.   Here one type of material is used.

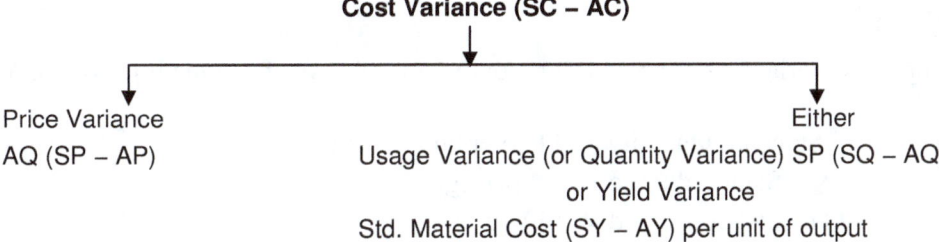

Cost Variance (SC – AC)

Price Variance
AQ (SP – AP)

Either
Usage Variance (or Quantity Variance) SP (SQ – AQ)
or Yield Variance
Std. Material Cost (SY – AY) per unit of output

Verification :

Cost Variance = Price Variance + Either Usage or Yield Variance

II. Where more than one type of material is used.

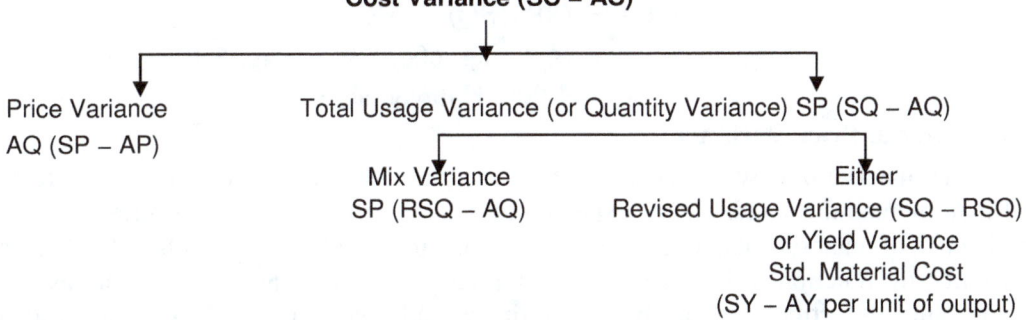

Cost Variance (SC – AC)

Price Variance
AQ (SP – AP)

Total Usage Variance (or Quantity Variance) SP (SQ – AQ)

Mix Variance
SP (RSQ – AQ)

Either
Revised Usage Variance (SQ – RSQ)
or Yield Variance
Std. Material Cost
(SY – AY per unit of output)

Verification :

Cost Variance = Price Variance + Mix Variance + Either Revised
Usage Variance or Yield Variance

Let us understand now the actual calculations of various types of material variances with the help of simple examples as shown below:

1) Material Cost Variance :

Material cost variance represents the differences between the actual costs and the standard costs of materials for a specified output. The actual cost is computed by multiplying actual price with the actual quantity of material and in the same way standard cost is computed by multiplying the standard price with the standard quantity of material. Cost analysts can also develop other variances of material cost to meet specialised purposes of management. However such variance may either be related to price, quantity or to the combination of price and quantity. Material cost variance can be expressed in abbreviated form as shown below.

$$MCV = (SP \times SQ) - (AP \times AQ)$$

where, SP = Standard price

SQ = Standard Quantity

AP = Actual Price

AQ = Actual Quantity

Note : Standard quantity should be taken for actual output.

EXAMPLE

Compute Material Cost Variance for a output of 200 units from the information given below:

Standard Quantity = 3 kg per unit of output

Standard Price = ₹ 4 per kg

Actual Quantity Consumed = 550 kg

Actual Price = ₹ 6 per kg

ANSWER

Material Cost Variance = (Total Standard Cost – Total Actual Cost)

$$MCV = (SP \times SQ) - (AP - AQ)$$

$$= (₹\ 4 \times kg.\ 600) - (₹\ 6 \times kg.\ 550)$$

$$= ₹\ 900\ (Unfavourable)$$

2) Material Price Variance :

The material price variance attempts to measure the variation between the actual cost of material and the standard cost expected to be paid for the material. It reflects the actual unit cost of material above or below the standard unit cost, multiplied by the actual quantity of function will attain standard price. The payment of lower prices by the purchasing department for a given quantity would results in favourable material price variance and thereby maintaining the required standard; whereas purchasing department will fail to meet the standard if it pays higher prices that will reflect an unfavourable material price variance. The material price variance is computed as follows :

Material Price Variance (MPV) = (Standard Price (SP) – Actual Price (AP)) × Actual Quantity (AQ)

EXAMPLE

Calculate Material Variance from the information as given in above example.

ANSWER

Material Price Variance = (Standard Price – Actual Price) × Actual Quantity

$$MPV = (₹\ 4 - ₹\ 6) \times 550\ kg.$$

$$= ₹\ 1100\ (Unfavourable)$$

Material Usage Variance (MUV) :

Material usage variance is deviation caused from the standard due to difference in quantities used. It indicates the actual quantity of direct materials used above or below the standard price.

  Material Usage Variance (MUV) = (Standard Quantity (SQ) – Actual Quantity (AQ))
             × Standard Price (SP)

This variance can also be calculated as follows :

  Material Usage Variance (MUV) = (Standard Price of Standard Quantity (SPSQ) –
             Standard Price of Actual Quantity (SPAC))

| EXAMPLE |

With the help of information as given in above example, calculate Material Usage Variance.

| ANSWER |

    Material Usage Variance = (Standard Quantity – Actual Quantity) × Standard Price

      MUV = (600 kg – 550 kg) × ₹ 4

        = ₹ 200 (Favourable)

or   MUV = (Standard Price of Standard Quantity – Standard Price of Actual Quantity)

        = ₹ 2400 – ₹ 2200

        = ₹ 200 (Favourable)

| EXAMPLE |

Suba an engineering industrial enterprise manufactured 100 items of product 'MCC' compute material cost variances from the information given below :

Standard quantity : 2 kg per item   Actual quantity : 3 kg per item
Standard price : ₹ 10 per kg   Actual price : ₹ 8 per kg

| ANSWER |

    Material Cost Variance = (Standard Cost – Actual Cost)

      MCV = (SQ × SP) – (AQ × AP)

        = (200 kg. × ₹ 10) – (300 kg. × ₹ 8)

        = ₹400 (Unfavourable)

    Material Price Variance = (Standard Price – Actual Price) × Actual Quantity

      MPV = (₹ 10 – ₹ 8) × 300 kg.

        = ₹ 600 (Favourable)

    Material Usage Variance = (Standard Quantity – Actual Quantity) × Standard Price

      MUV = (200 kg. – 300 kg.) × ₹ 10

        = ₹1,000 (Unfavourable)

Verification :

$$MCV = MPV + MUV$$
$$₹\ 400\ (U) = ₹\ 600\ (F) + ₹\ 1000\ (U)$$
$$₹\ 400\ (U) = ₹\ 400\ (U)$$

Presentation of Material Cost Variance by Graphical Method :

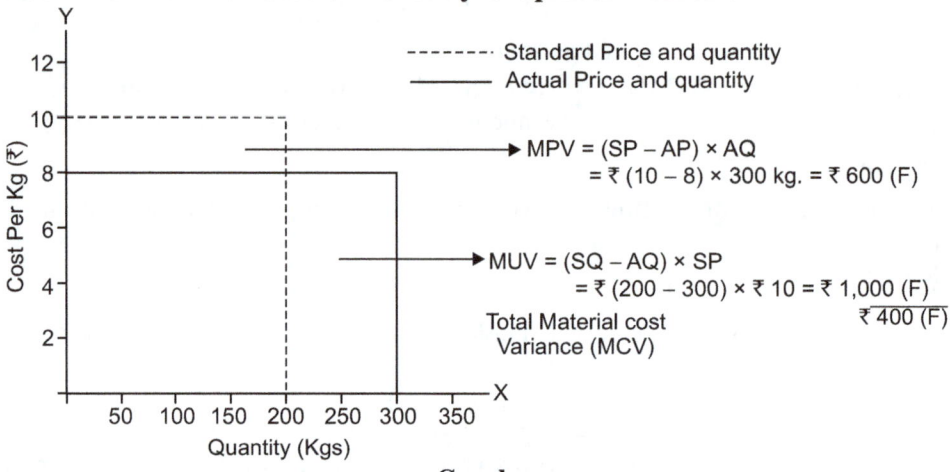

Graph

4) Material Mix Variance

The difference in material mix is the only cause responsible for material usage variance. However when standard weight and actual weight of material mix varies, the quantity variance shall be due to mix accompanied by other reasons. Under such a situation. Material Usage Variance (MUV) would be equal to Material Mix Variance (MMV) and Revised Material Usage Variance (RMUV).

Revised Material Usage Variance (RMUV) = (Standard Quantity (SQ) – Revised Standard Quantity (RSQ)) × Standard Price (SP)

The variance will be favourable if standard quantity is greater than Revised Standard Quantity and vice-versa.

Note : Generally Revised Material Usage Variance is calculated only when question is silent about the output because under such a situation it is not possible to calculate Material Yield Variance. Other wise Revised Material Usage Variance is not usually calculated.

EXAMPLE

Calculate, a) Material Usage Variance, b) Material Mix Variance and c) Material Revised Usage variance from the following information.

Material	Standard			Actual		
	Quantity (Kg.)	Price (₹)	Value (₹)	Quantity (Kg.)	Price (₹)	Value (₹)
EXX	70	15	350	80	12	320
YA	30	18	180	40	21	280

ANSWER

a) Material Usage Variance (MUV) = (SQ – AQ) × SP

For material EXX =	(70 kg. – 80 kg.) × ₹ 15	=	₹	150 (UF)
For material YA =	(30 kg. – 40 kg.) × ₹ 8	=	₹	180 (UF)
Total MUV =			₹	330 (UF)

b) Material Mix Variance (MMV) = (RSQ – AQ) × SP

For material EXX =	(70 kg. – 84 kg.) × ₹ 15	=	₹	210 (UF)
For material YA =	(30 kg. – 36 kg.) × ₹ 18	=	₹	108 (UF)
Total RUV =		=	₹	318 (UF)

Verification :

Material Usage Variance = Material Mix Variance + Material Revised Usage Variance

₹ 330 (UF) = ₹ 12 (UF) + ₹ 318 (UF)

₹ 330 (UF) = ₹ 330 (UF)

5) Material Yield Variance :

Material Yield Variance is calculated with the help of the following formula :

Material Yield Variance (MYV) = (Standard Yield – Actual Yield) × Standard Rate*

MYV = (Standard Loss of Actual Mix – Actual Loss of Actual Mix) × Standard Cost per unit

$$* \text{ Standard Rate} = \frac{\text{Standard Cost of Standard Mix}}{\text{Net Standard Output}}$$

EXAMPLE

ABC Ltd. which has adopted standard costing furnishes the following information.

Material	Standard			Actual		
	Quantity Kg.	Price ₹	Value ₹	Quantity (Kg.)	Price ₹	Value ₹
XY	60	15	900	55	18	990
AB	40	12	480	45	12	540
	100		1,380	100		1,530
Loss	10			20		
	90		1,380	80		1,530

Calculate Material Yield Variance.

ANSWER

Material Yield Variance (MYV) = (Standard Yield – Actual Yield) × Standard Rate

$$\text{MYV} = (90 \text{ kg} - 80 \text{ kg.}) \times ₹ \, 15.33 = 15.3 \text{ (Unfavourable)}$$

As mentioned earlier, Material Yield Variance can also be calculated on the basis of Standard Loss and Actual Loss like :

MYV = (Standard Loss of Actual Mix – Actual Loss on Actual Mix) × (Standard Cost per unit)

$$\text{MYV} = (10 \text{ kg.} - 20 \text{ kg.}) \times ₹ \, 15.33$$
$$= ₹ \, 153.3 \text{ Unfavourable}$$

Calculation of Standard Rate :

$$\text{Standard Rate} = \frac{\text{Standard Cost of Standard Mix}}{\text{Net Standard Output}}$$
$$= \frac{₹ \, 1,380}{90 \text{ kg.}}$$
$$= ₹ \, 15.33$$

EXAMPLE

The standard cost shows the following details relating to the materials needed to produce 1 kg of groundnut oil :

Quantity of groundnut required	:	3 kg.
Price of groundnut	:	₹ 2.50 per kg.
Actual production data		
Production during the week	:	1,000 kg.
Quantity used	:	3,500 kg.
Price of groundnut per kg.	:	₹ 3

Calculate :

a) Material Cost Variance;

b) Material Price Variance; and

c) Material Usage Variance

ANSWER

a) Material Cost Variance = (Standard Quantity for Actual Output × Standard Price) – (Actual Quantity × Actual Price)

$$= (3,000 \text{ kg.} \times ₹ \, 2.50) - (3,500 \text{ kg.} \times ₹ \, 3)$$
$$= ₹ \, 3,000 \text{ (Adverse)}$$

b) Material Price Variance = (Standard Price – Actual Price) × Actual Quantity

$$= (₹ \, 2.50 - ₹ \, 3) \times 3,500 \text{ kg.}$$
$$= ₹ \, 1,750 \text{ (Adverse)}$$

c)   Material Usage Variance = (Standard Quantity for Actual Output – Actual Quantity) × Standard Price

$$= (3,000 \text{ Kg.} - 3,500 \text{ Kg.}) \times ₹ 2.50$$

$$= ₹ 1,250 \text{ (Adverse)}$$

Alternative Method :

Answer by the Worksheet Method :

(1)	(2)	(3)
Applied input at Std. Price and Std. Quantity	Flexible budget input a Std. Price and Actual Quantity	Actual input incurred (Actual Quantity Actual Price)
(₹ 2.5 × 3,000 kg.)	(₹ 2.50 × 3,500 kg.)	(₹ 300 × 3,500 kg.)
= ₹ 7,500	= ₹ 8,750	= ₹ 10,500

Material Usage Variance	Material Price Variance
₹ 1,250 (A)	₹ 1,750 (A)

Total Material Cost Variance ₹ 3,000 (A)

EXAMPLE

From the following, you are required to calculate :

a)   Material Price Variance

b)   Material Usage Variance

c)   Material Cost Variance

Quantity of material purchased	:	3,000 units
Value of material purchased for	:	₹ 9,000

Standard of quantity of material required for one tonne of finished product : 25 units.

Standard rate of material	:	₹ 2 per unit
Opening Stock of material	:	100 units
Closing Stock of material	:	600 units
Finished production during the period	:	80 tonnes

ANSWER

Standard quantity of material required for actual production $= 80 \text{ ton} \times 25 \text{ units}$

$$= 2,000 \text{ units}$$

Actual quantity of material used = Opening Stock + Material Purchased – Closing Stock

$$= 100 \text{ units} + 3,000 \text{ units} - 600 \text{ units}$$

$$= 2,500 \text{ units}$$

Standard Price per unit $= ₹ 2$

Actual Price per unit $= ₹ 9,000/3,000 \text{ units}$

$$= ₹ 3$$

a)   Material Price Variance = (Std. Price – Actual Price) Actual Qty.

$$= (₹\ 2 - ₹\ 3) \times 2,500\ \text{units}$$
$$= ₹\ 2,500\ (A)$$

b)   Material Usage Variance = (Std. Qty. – Actual Qty.) Std. Rate

$$= (2,000\ \text{units} - 2,500\ \text{units}) \times ₹\ 2$$
$$= ₹\ 1,000\ (A)$$

c)   Material Cost Variance = (Total Std. Cost – Total Actual Cost)

$$= (\text{Std. Price} \times \text{Std. Qty.}) - (\text{Actual Price} \times \text{Actual Qty.})$$
$$= (₹\ 2 \times 2,000\ \text{units}) - {}^*₹\ 3 \times 2,500\ \text{units})$$
$$= ₹\ 3,500\ (A)$$

Verification :

$$MCV = MUV + MPV$$
$$₹\ 3,500\ (A) = ₹\ 2,500\ (A) + ₹\ 1,000\ (A)$$
$$₹\ 3,500\ (A) = ₹\ 3,500\ (A)$$

EXAMPLE

Modi Ltd., Mysore Ltd. manufacturing a simple product, the standard mix of which is,

Material A :   60% at ₹ 20 per kg.

Material B :   40% at ₹ 10 per kg.

Normal loss in production is 20% of input. Due to shortage of Material A, the standard mix was changed. Actual results for March 2013 were :

Material A :   105 kg. at ₹ 20 per kg.

Material B :   kg. at ₹ 9 per kg.

Input :   200 kg.

Loss :   35 kg.

Output :   165 kg.

Calculate :

a)   Material Price Variance

b)   Material Usage Variance

c)   Material Mix Variance

d)   Material Yield Variance

ANSWER

a)   Material Price Variance = (Standard Price – Actual Price) × Actual Quantity

$$A = (₹\ 20 - ₹\ 20) \times 105\ \text{kg.}$$
$$= \text{NIL}$$
$$B = (₹\ 10 - ₹\ 9) \times 95\ \text{kg.}$$
$$= ₹\ 95\ (\text{Favourable})$$

b)   Material Usage Variance = (Standard Quantity for Actual Output – Actual Quantity) × Standard Price

$$A = (123.75 \text{ kg.} – 105 \text{ kg.}) × ₹\ 20$$
$$= ₹\ 375 \text{ (Favourable)}$$
$$B = (82.50 \text{ kg.} – 95 \text{ kg.}) × ₹\ 10$$
$$= ₹\ 125 \text{ (Adverse)}$$
$$\text{Total } ₹\ 250 \text{ (Favourable)}$$

c)   Material Mix Variance = (Standard proportion of Actual Input – Actual Proportion) × Standard Price

$$\frac{\text{Standard proportion}}{\text{of Actual Input}} = \frac{\text{Standard Proportion} × \text{Total Actual Input}}{\text{Total Standard Quantity}}$$

$$\text{For A} = \frac{120 \text{ kg.} × 200 \text{ kg.}}{200 \text{ kg.}} = 120 \text{ kg.}$$

$$\text{For B} = \frac{80 \text{ kg.} × 200 \text{ kg.}}{200 \text{ kg.}} = 80 \text{ kg.}$$

For A : $(120 \text{ kg.} – 105 \text{ kg.}) × ₹\ 20 = ₹\ 300$ (Favourable)
For B : $(80 \text{ kg.} – 95 \text{ kg.}) × ₹\ 10 = ₹\ 150$ (Adverse)
                            Total = ₹ 150 (Favourable)

d)   Material Yield Variance = (Standard Yield – Actual Yield) × Standard cost per unit

            Actual Input   200 kg.
Less :   Normal Loss @ 20% of Input   40 kg.
            Standard Yield   160 kg

$$\text{MYV} = (160 \text{ kg.} – 165 \text{ kg.}) × \frac{₹\ 3,200}{160 \text{ kg}}$$

$$= 5 \text{ kg} × ₹\ 20 = ₹\ 100 \text{ (Favourable)}$$

Verification :

Particulars	₹	₹
Material Price Variance		95 Fav.
Material Mix Variance	150 Fav.	
Material Yield Variance	100 Fav.	
Material Usage Variance	250 Fav.	250 Fav.
Material Cost Variance		345 Fav.

6.4.2 LABOUR VARIANCE

The direct labour or wage variance is similar to direct material variance. But for the change of name, they parallel the material variances in concept and calculation. Whenever difference occurs between the standards specified for direct labour and the actual, labour variances arise necessitating their investigation and remedy. The following are the principal labour variances calculated in practice :

1) Labour Rate Variance
2) Labour Efficiency Variance
3) Labour Cost Variance
4) Labour Mixture Variance
5) Labour Yield Variance
6) Labour Idle Time Variance

1) Labour Rate Variance :

Labour rate variance is similar to the material price variance, and is the cost of having paid and actual wage higher or lower than standard rate. It is the difference between the standard rate of pay and the rate paid for the actual hours worked. Since labour rate variance equals the time taken multiplied by the difference between the standard and actual wage rate, the following formula emerges :

$$LRV = (SR - AR) \times AH$$

where,
SR = Standard wage rate per hour,
AR = Actual wage rate per hour,
AH = Actual direct labour hours worked.

If the standard rate is higher than the rate, it shall result in favourable variance and vice-versa.

EXAMPLE

Standard wage rate	:	₹ 4 per hour
Standard hours	:	400 Hrs.
Actual hours	:	380 Hrs.
Actual wage rate	:	₹ 5 per hour

Calculate wage rate variance.

ANSWER

$$\begin{aligned}\text{Labour Rate Variance} &= (\text{Standard Rate} - \text{Actual Rate}) \times \text{Actual Time}\\ &= (₹\ 4 - ₹\ 5) \times 380 \text{ Hrs.}\\ &= ₹\ 380 \text{ (Adverse)}\end{aligned}$$

2) Labour Efficiency Variance :

Labour efficiency variance, also called the labour usage or quantity variance, if the difference between the standard hours and the actual hours worked time the standard wage rate. It is the cost of using excess or less hours over the standard hours allowed for the units of products produced. Since labour efficiency variance equals standard wage rate multiplied by the difference between the standard labour hours specified and the actual labour hours expended, the formula is :

$$\begin{aligned}\text{Labour Efficiency Variance} &= (\text{Standard time for Actual Output} - \text{Actual Time})\\ &= (SH - AH) \times SR\end{aligned}$$

where,
SH = Standard hours
AH = Actual hours
SR = Standard wage rate per hour.

EXAMPLE

Using the figures contained in above Example, this variance will be as under :

ANSWER

$$= (400 \text{ Hrs.} - 380 \text{ Hrs.}) \times ₹ 4$$
$$= ₹ 80 \text{ (Favourable)}$$

The labour efficiency variance may be due to the following reasons :

i) Inaccurate selection of employees,

ii) Inadequately trained operatives,

iii) Labour turnover, i.e. constant training and breaking-in of new employees,

iv) Inferior working conditions,

v) Overtime hours,

vi) Length of production run,

vii) Interruptions or delays in work,

viii) Changes in method of production,

ix) Inaccurate recording of time or output,

x) Higher rates of wages during seasonal or emergency operations.

3) **Labour Cost Variance :**

Total direct labour costs depend on the wage rate paid and the number of hours worked. Similar to the material cost, labour cost variance is the difference between the total standard amount of labour and the actual amount of labour times the respective wage rates. In simple words, it is the difference between the standard cost of direct labour and the actual cost expended for it. The formula for the purpose is:

Labour Cost Variance (LCV) = (Std. Rate × Std. Time for Actual Output) −
(Actual Rate × Actual Time)
Or
= Standard Cost for Actual Output − Actual Cost

It should be noted that the labour rate and labour efficiency variances must equal the total labour cost variance.

EXAMPLE

Using the figures contained in above Example, labour cost variance would be :

ANSWER

$$= (₹ 4 \times 400 \text{ Hrs.}) - (₹ 5 \times 380 \text{ Hrs.})$$
$$= ₹ 300 \text{ (Adverse)}$$

Verification :

Labour Cost Variance = Labour Rate Variance + Labour Efficiency Variance
₹ 300 (A) = ₹ 380 (A)   + ₹ 80 (F)

4) Labour Mix Variance :

Labour mix variance is like materials mix variance and is a part of labour efficiency variance. It arises when there is a change in the labour composition during a particular period. It is calculated in the same manner as the material mix variance and, hence, also called gang composition variance. The following formulae are applicable.

Labour Mix Variance = Standard Cost of Std. Composition – Standard Cost of Actual Composition

In case there is a change in the labour composition due to shortage of one category of labour, but there is no change in the total standard time and actual time spent, then :

Labour Mix Variance = Std. Cost of Revised Std. Composition – Standard Cost of Actual Composition

In case standard are revised and total standard time of labour differs from the actual time of labour.

Labour Mix Variance = (Revised Standard Time – Actual Time) × Standard Rate

where,

$$\text{Revised Standard Time} = \frac{\text{Total time of actual workers}}{\text{Total time of Std. workers}} \times \text{Standard Time}$$

EXAMPLE

The standard time for unit component X are given below :

| Standard hours per unit | : | 15 Hours |
| Standard rate | : | ₹ 4 per hour |

The actual data and related information are as under :

Actual production	:	1,000 units
Actual hours	:	15,300 hours
Actual rate	:	₹ 3,90 per hour

Calculate :

i)   Labour Cost Variance
ii) Labour Efficiency Variance, and
iii) Labour Rate Variance

ANSWER

i)   Labour Cost Variance = (SR × SH – AR × AH)
$$= (₹\ 4 \times 15,000\ \text{Hrs.}) - (₹\ 3.90 \times 15,300\ \text{Hrs.})$$
$$= ₹\ 330\ (F)$$

ii) Labour Efficiency Variance = (SH – AH) × SR
$$= (15,000\ \text{Hrs.} - 15,300\ \text{Hrs.}) \times ₹\ 4$$
$$= ₹\ 1,200\ (A)$$

iii)   Labour Rate Variance = $(SR - AR) \times AH$
$$= (₹\ 4 - ₹\ 3.90) \times 15,300\ \text{Hrs.}$$
$$= ₹\ 1,530\ (F)$$

Verification :

$$\underset{₹\ 1,200\ (A)}{\text{Labour Efficiency Variance}} + \underset{₹\ 1,530\ (F)}{\text{Labour Rate Variance}} = \underset{₹\ 330\ (F)}{\text{Labour Cost Variance}}$$

Alternative Method :
Answer by the Worksheet Method

(1)	(2)	(3)
Applied inputs Standard Labour Rate (SR) allowed for actual output times Standard Hours (SH)	Flexible budget inputs Standard Labour Rate (SR) Times Actual Hours (AH) used	Actual inputs Actual Labour Rate (AR) Times Actual Hours (AH) used
(SR × SH)	(SR × AH)	(AR × AH)
(₹ 4 × 15,000 Hrs.)	(₹ 4 × 15,200 Hrs.)	(₹ 3.90 × 15,300 Hrs.)
= ₹ 60,000	= ₹ 61,200	= ₹ 59,670

Labour Efficiency Variance	Labour Rate Variance
₹ 1,200 (A)	₹ 1,530 (A)

Total Labour Cost Variance ₹ 330 (A)

EXAMPLE

A gang of workers normally consists of 30 men, 15 women and 10 boys. They are paid at standard rates as under :

Men : ₹ 0.80

Women : ₹ 0.60

Boy : ₹ 0.40

In normal working week of 40 hours, the gang is expected to produce 2,000 units of output.

During the week ended 31st December, the gang consisted of 40 men, 10 women and 5 boys. The actual wages paid were @ ₹ 0.70, ₹ 0.65 and 0.30 respectively and 1,600 units were produced.

Calculate :

i)   Labour Cost Variance

ii)   Labour Rate Variance

iii)   Labour Efficiency Variance

iv)   Gang Composition Variance, i.e. Labour Mix Variance and

v)   Labour Revised Efficiency Variance.

ANSWER

Type of Worker	Standard			Actual		
	Hours	Rate ₹	Amount ₹	Hours	Rate ₹	Amount ₹
Men	30 × 40 Hrs. = 1,200 Hrs.	0.80	960	40 × 40 Hrs. = 1,600 Hrs.	0.70	1,120
Women	15 × 40 Hrs. = 600 Hrs.	0.60	360	10 × 40 Hrs. = 400 Hrs.	0.65	260
Boys	10 × 40 Hrs. = 400 Hrs.	0.40	160	5 × 40 Hrs. = 200 Hrs.	0.30	60
Total	2,200 Hrs.		1,480	2,200 Hrs.		1,440

Hours = Number of Workers × Weekly Hours

i) Labour Cost Variance = (Standard Cost of Actual Output) − (Actual Cost of Actual Output)

= ₹ 1,184 − ₹ 1,440 = ₹ 256 (Adverse)

$$\text{SC of Actual Output} = \frac{1,600 \text{ units}}{2,000 \text{ units}} \times ₹\, 1,480 = ₹\, 1,184$$

ii) Labour Rate Variance = (SR − AR) × AH

Men = (₹ 0.80 − ₹ 0.70) × 1,600 Hrs.

= ₹ 160 (Favourable)

Women = (₹ 0.60 − ₹ 0.65) × 400 Hrs.

= ₹ 20 (Adverse)

Boys = (₹ 0.40 − ₹ 0.30) × 200 Hrs.

= ₹ 200 (Favourable)

LRV = ₹ 160 (Favourable)

iii) Labour Efficiency Variance = (SH − for Actual Output − AH) × SR

Men = (960 Hrs. − 1,600 Hrs.) × ₹ 0.80

= ₹ 512 (A)

Women = (480 Hrs. − 400 Hrs.) × ₹ 0.60

= ₹ 48 (F)

Boys = (320 Hrs. − 200 Hrs.) × ₹ 0.40

= ₹ 48 (F)

LEV = ₹ 416 (F)

Standard hours for actual output are calculated as follows :

$$\text{Men} = \frac{1,200 \text{ Hrs}}{2,000 \text{ Units}} \times 1,600 \text{ Hrs.} = 960 \text{ Hrs.}$$

$$\text{Women} = \frac{600 \text{ Hrs.}}{2,000 \text{ Units}} \times 1,600 \text{ Hrs.} = 480 \text{ Hrs.}$$

$$\text{Boys} = \frac{400 \text{ Hrs.}}{2,000 \text{ Units}} \times 1,600 \text{ Hrs.} = 320 \text{ Hrs.}$$

iv) Labour Mix Variance i.e. (Gang Composition Variance):

$$= \text{(Revised Standard Hours} - \text{Actual Hours)}$$
$$\times \text{Standard Rate}$$

$$\text{Men} = (1,200 \text{ Hrs.} - 1,600 \text{ Hrs.}) \times ₹ \, 0.80$$
$$= ₹ \, 320 \, (A)$$

$$\text{Women} = (600 \text{ Hrs.} - 400 \text{ Hrs.}) \times ₹ \, 0.60$$
$$= ₹ \, 120 \, (F)$$

$$\text{Boys} = (400 \text{ Hrs.} - 200 \text{ Hrs.}) \times ₹ \, 0.40$$
$$= ₹ \, 80 \, (F)$$

$$\text{LMV} = ₹ \, 120 \, (A)$$

Revised Standard hours are total actual hours i.e. 2,200 hrs. in the standard proportion for men, women and boys. This is given in the table above.

v) Labour Revised Efficiency Variance

$$= \text{(Std. hours for actual output} - \text{Revised Std. hrs.)}$$
$$\times \text{Std. Rate}$$

$$\text{Men} = (960 \text{ Hrs.} - 1,200 \text{ Hrs.}) \times ₹ \, 0.80$$
$$= ₹ \, 192 \, (A)$$

$$\text{Women} = (480 \text{ Hrs.} \times 600 \text{ Hrs.}) \times ₹ \, 0.60$$
$$= ₹ \, 72 \, (A)$$

$$\text{Boys} = (320 \text{ Hrs.} - 400 \text{ Hrs.}) \times ₹ \, 0.40$$
$$= ₹ \, 32 \, (A)$$

$$\text{LREV} = ₹ \, 296 \, (A)$$

Verification :

$$\text{Wage Variance} = \text{Rate Variance} + \text{Efficiency Variance}$$
$$₹ \, 256 \, (A) = ₹ \, 160 \, (F) + ₹ \, 416 \, (A)$$
$$\text{Efficiency Variance} = \text{Mix Variance} + \text{Revised Efficiency Variance}$$
$$₹ \, 416 \, (A) = ₹ \, 120 \, (A) + ₹ \, 296 \, (A)$$

5) Labour Yield Variance :

It is just like Material Yield Variance. It is the difference between the standard labour output and actual output or yield. It is calculated as below :

$$\text{Labour Yield Variance} = \text{(Std. Production for Actual Mix} - \text{Actual Production)}$$
$$\times \text{Std. cost per unit}$$

If the actual production is more than standard production, the difference would be a favourable variance and vice-versa. However, it should be noted that the figure would be negative.

EXAMPLE

Standard production	:	200 units
Actual production	:	180 units
Standard wage rate	:	₹ 15 per hour
Standard time	:	2 Hrs. per unit

ANSWER

Labour yield would be :

Standard cost per unit $= 2$ Hrs. $\times ₹ 15$

$= ₹ 30$

Labour Yield Variance $= (200 \text{ units} - 180 \text{ units}) \times ₹ 30$

$= ₹ 600 \text{ (A)}$

6) Labour Idle Time Variance :

It arises due to abnormal circumstances like strike, lock-outs, power failures, etc. and is calculated as under :

Idle Time Variance = Idle Hours × Standard Hourly Rate

EXAMPLE

In a factory's idle time recorded was 40 hours and workers were paid ₹ 15 per hour. Calculate Labour Idle Time Variance.

ANSWER

Variance would be 40 Hrs. × ₹ 15 = ₹ 600.

This variance will be always unfavourable.

EXAMPLE

From the following records of Apollo Bolt Nut Manufacturing Company, you are required to compute material and labour variances :

An input of 100 kg. of material yield to a standard output of 10,00,000 units.

Standard price per kg. of material = ₹ 20.

Actual quantity of material issued and used by production department 10,000 kg.

Actual price per kg of material	:	₹ 21 per kg
Actual output	:	9,00,000 units
Number of employees	:	200
Standard wage rate per employee per day	:	₹ 40
Standard daily output per employee	:	100 units
Total number of days worked	:	50 days

(Idle time paid for and included in the above half day for each employee).

Actual wage rate per day	:	₹ 45

ANSWER

i) Material Cost Variance $= (SQ \times SP) - (AQ \times AP)$

$= (9{,}000 \text{ units} \times ₹\ 20) - (10{,}000 \text{ units} \times ₹\ 21)$

$= ₹\ 30{,}000 \text{ (A)}$

$$SQ = \frac{100 \text{ kg}}{10{,}000 \text{ kg.}} \times 9{,}00{,}000 \text{ units}$$

$= 9{,}000 \text{ kg.}$

ii) Material Price Variance $= (SP - AP) \times AQ$

$= (₹\ 20 - ₹\ 21) \times 10{,}000 \quad \text{kg.}$

$= ₹\ 10{,}000 \text{ (A)}$

iii) Material Quantity Variance $= (SQ - AQ) \times SP$

$= (9{,}000 \text{ kg.} - 10{,}000 \text{ kg.}) \times ₹\ 20$

$= ₹\ 20{,}000 \text{ (A)}$

Man-days required for actual output $= \dfrac{9{,}00{,}000 \text{ units}}{100 \text{ units}}$

$= 9{,}000 \text{ man-days}$

Idle time $= \dfrac{1}{2} \text{ of } 200$

$= 100 \text{ Days}$

Actual Man-days $= 200 \times 50 \text{ Days}$

$= 10{,}000$

iv) Labour Cost Variance $= \text{Standard Cost} - \text{Actual Cost}$

$= (9{,}000 \text{ kg.} \times ₹\ 40) - (10{,}000 \text{ kg.} \times ₹\ 45)$

$= ₹\ 90{,}000 \text{ (A)}$

v) Labour Rate Variance $= (SR - AR) \times \text{Actual Days}$

$= (₹\ 40 - ₹\ 45) \times 10{,}000 \text{ kg.}$

$= ₹\ 50{,}000 \text{ (A)}$

vi) Labour Efficiency Variance $= (\text{Std. Days} - \text{Actual Days}) \times SR$

$= (9{,}000 \text{ kg} - 10{,}000 \text{ kg}) \times ₹\ 40$

$= ₹\ 40{,}000 \text{ (A)}$

vii) Idle Time Variance $= \text{Idle Time} \times SR$

$= 100 \text{ Days} \times ₹\ 40$

$= ₹\ 4{,}000 \text{ (A)}$

6.4.3 OVERHEAD VARIANCES

Standard costs for factory overhead provide the third final cost element. Special attention is given to them because they are different from direct materials and direct labour costs. Factory overhead costs cannot be traced to individual units of production, and then these are not strictly variable costs. Hence, the budgetary and variance analysis procedures here are different.

Overhead costs are indirect costs of material, labour and other overhead that contain both fixed and variable components. The analysis of overhead variances are somewhat difficult than direct cost variances. The purposes of overhead variance analysis is to see whether the price paid for and the quantity used of indirect elements of cost vary or not as compared specified standard figures. Thus, overhead variance represents the difference between the amount of overhead applied to production during the period and the amount of actual overhead cost incurred during the period. It is the difference between the standard overhead and the actual overhead assigned to the products.

Specific Terms used in computing overhead variances :

While computing overhead variances, some specific terms are used, these terms are as follows :

i) Hourly Rate $= \dfrac{\text{Budgeted Overheads}}{\text{Budgeted Overheads}}$

ii) Unit Rate $= \dfrac{\text{Budgeted Hours}}{\text{Budgeted Output in units}}$

iii) Standard Hours for Actual Output $= \dfrac{\text{Budgeted Hours}}{\text{Budgeted Output}} \times \text{Actual Output}$

iv) Standard Output for Actual Time $= \dfrac{\text{Budgeted Output}}{\text{Budgted Hours}} \times \text{Actual Output}$

v) Recovered or Absorbed Overheads $=$ Actual Output $\times$ Standard Rate per hour

or

Standard Hours for Actual Output $\times$ Standard Rate per hour

vi) Budgeted Overheads $=$ Budgeted Output $\times$ Standard Rate per unit

or

Budgeted Hours $\times$ Standard Rate per hour

vii) Standard Overheads $=$ Actual Hours $\times$ Standard Rate per hour

or

viii) Standard Output for Actual Time $\times$ Standard Rate per unit

ix) Actual Overheads $=$ Actual Hours $\times$ Actual Rate per hour

or

Actual Output $\times$ Actual Rate per unit

Important points to be noted :

i) Overhead cost variances can be calculated using standard overhead rate per hour or standard rate per unit or both, depending upon the availability of information.

ii) It would also be seen that 'Budgeted Overheads' are used for budgeted output or budgeted time while 'Standard Overheads' are used for actual time or budgeted output in actual time.

iii) Words like budgeted overhead rate per unit and standard overhead rate unit, budgeted overhead rate per hour and standard overhead rate per hour, budgeted output and standard output, budgeted hours and standard hours have been used interchangeably.

Classification of Overhead Variances :

Overheads are classified into fixed variable. Fixed overheads are those which do not change with the level of operation and remain fixed for a given period. Variable overheads are those which change directly with the level of operation. But this should be noted that in most circumstances, the largest proportion or overhead incurred will be fixed and only a small proportion variable. Because of the difference in the nature of variability, overhead costs are analysed separately for fixed and variable overheads, and so are the variance.

Overhead Cost Variance

It is the difference between standard overhead cost specified for the actual production and actual overhead cost incurred. It is the total of both variable and fixed overhead variances. The formula is given as follows.

$$\text{Overhead Cost Variance} = \text{Actual Output} \times \text{Std. Overhead Rate} - \text{Actual Output} \times \text{Actual Overhead per unit}$$
$$= (\text{Std. Hours for Actual output} \times \text{Std. Overhead Rate})$$
$$= (\text{Actual Hours} \times \text{Actual Overheads Rate per hour})$$
$$= \text{Recovered Overheads} - \text{Actual Overheads}$$

EXAMPLE

Particulars		Budgeted	Actual
Production	Units	10,000	8,000
Standard hours	Hrs.	5,000	4,500
Overheads	₹	10,000	12,000
Fixed	₹	6,000	6,000
Variable	₹	4,000	6000

Calculate Overhead Cost Variance.

ANSWER

$$\text{Unit Rate} = \frac{₹\,10,000}{5,000\ \text{Units}} = ₹\,1$$

$$\text{Standard Hourly Rate} = \frac{₹\,10,000}{10,000\ \text{Hrs.}} = ₹\,2$$

i)   Overhead Cost Variance = Actual Output × Standard Rate – Actual Overhead)
(If unit rate)
$$= 8,000\ \text{Units} \times ₹\,1 - ₹\,12,000$$
$$= ₹\,8,000 - ₹\,12,000$$
$$= ₹\,4,000\ (A)$$

(If hourly rate) = (Standard hour for Actual Output) × Standard hourly rate) – Actual Overhead
$$= \frac{8,000\ \text{Units} \times 5,000\ \text{Hrs.}}{10,000\ \text{Units}} \times ₹\,2 - ₹\,12,000$$
$$= ₹\,8,000 - ₹\,12,000$$
$$= ₹\,4,000\ (A)$$

or

ii) Overhead Cost Variance = Recovered Overheads – Actual Overheads

= (8,000 Units × ₹ 1) – ₹ 12,000

= ₹ 4,000 (A)

or

= Recovered Overheads – Actual Overheads

= (4,000 Units × ₹ 2) – ₹ 12,000

= ₹ 4,000 (A)

It may be noted from the above example that overhead variances can be calculated either by using standard hourly rate or by standard unit rate.

The two major categories of overhead cost variance are, Variable overhead variances, and Fixed overhead variance

A) Variable Overhead Variance :

The variable overheads may be manufacturing, administration, selling and distribution. The total variable overhead variance is the difference between the standard variable overhead variance/charged to production (SC) and the actual variable overheads incurred (AC).

$$= SC - AC$$

The actual cost per unit or output may vary from standard cost unit due to : i) Actual overhead incurred may be more or less than the standard overheads on the basis of actual operation. ii) Change in output per hour. Due to the two situations, variable overhead variances are classified into :

1) Variable Overhead Expenditure Variance :

This variance occurs due to actual expenditure being in excess or short of standard overhead. It is the difference between the standard overhead allowed and actual overhead incurred for the actual time taken. The formula is :

Recovered Variable Overheads – Actual Overheads

= Standard Variable Overheads on actual production – Actual Variable Overheads

Standard variable overhead on actual production in the product of actual production for the period multiplied by the stand rate per unit.

If hourly rate is used, then it as (Actual Hours × Standard Rate – Actual Overhead)

2) Variable Overhead Efficiency Variance :

The variable overhead efficiency variance is the difference between the standard hours of output (SH) and the actual of input (AH) for the period multiplied by the standard variable overhead rate (SR). Symbolically, it is :

$$(SH - AH) \times SR$$

The variance arise from the efficiency of labour. Consequently, the reasons for the variance are the same as those which have been explained previously for labour efficiency variance.

EXAMPLE

Budgeted production for the month	:	2,500 Units
Actual production	:	2,200 Units
Budgeted Variable Overheads	:	₹ 10,000
Actual Variable Overheads	:	₹ 9,000
Budgeted Man Hours	:	1,250 Hrs.
Actual Hours Worked	:	1,150 Hrs.

Calculate :

i)   Variable Overhead Expenditure Variance

ii)   Variable Overhead Efficiency Variance and

iii) Variable Overhead Cost Variance

ANSWER

Working Notes:

a) Standard Hourly Rate $= \dfrac{\text{Budgeted Overheads}}{\text{Budgeted Hours}} = \dfrac{₹ 10,000}{1,250 \text{ Hrs.}}$

$= ₹ 8$

b) Standard Unit Rate $= \dfrac{\text{Budgeted Overheads}}{\text{Budgeted Output in units}}$

$= \dfrac{₹ 10,000}{2,500 \text{ Hrs.}}$

$= ₹ 4$

c) Variable Overhead Expenditure Variance (if hourly rate is used) $=$ Actual Hours × Standard Rate – Actual Overheads

$= 1,150 \text{ Hrs.} × ₹ 8 – ₹ 9,000$

$= ₹ 200 \text{ (Favourable)}$

i) Variable Overhead Expenditure Variance (if unit rate is used) $=$ (Standard Production at actual hours × Standard Rate) – Actual Overheads

$= \dfrac{1,150 \text{ Hrs.} × 2,500 \text{ Units}}{1,250 \text{ Hrs.}} × ₹ 4 – ₹ 9,000$

$= ₹ 200 \text{ (Favourable)}$

ii) Variable Overhead Efficiency Variance (if hourly rate is used) $=$ Standard Hours for Actual Hours × Standard Rate

Actual Production

$= \left\{ \dfrac{2,200 \text{ Units} × 1,250 \text{ Hrs.}}{2,500 \text{ Units}} × \text{Hrs. } 1,150 \right\} × ₹ 8$

$= ₹ 400 \text{ (Adverse)}$

or

iii) Variable Overhead Efficiency Variance if unit rate is used = (Actual Production − Standard Production at Actual Hours) × Standard Rate

$$= 2,200 \text{ Units} - \frac{1,150 \text{ Hrs.} \times 2,250 \text{ Units}}{1,250 \text{ Hrs.}} \times ₹\, 4$$

= ₹ 400 (Adverse)

iv) Variable Overhead Cost Variance = Recovered Variable Overhead − Actual Variable Overhead

= 2,200 Units × ₹ 8 − ₹ 9,000

= ₹ 200 (Adverse)

Verification :

Overhead Cost Variance ₹ 200 (Adverse) = Overhead Expenditure Variance + Overhead Efficiency

= ₹ 200 (Favourable) + ₹ 400 (Adverse)

B) Fixed Overhead Variance :

The term 'fixed overhead' related to all items of expenditure which are more or less constant, irrespective of fluctuations in the level of output. The standard overhead rates are set according to rate per hour or rate per unit of output. The actual fixed overhead cost per unit may vary from standard cost per unit due to, i) Change in total actual overhead from budgeted overhead; ii) Change in actual level of operation from budgeted level which may be expressed in outputs or hours. iii) Change in production per hours.

1) Total Fixed Overhead Cost Variance :

It is the difference between the standard overheads recovered or absorbed for actual output and the actual fixed overheads incurred. In other words, it is the difference between the standard overhead charged to production in a period and the overhead incurred. While computing the standard cost, it is always necessary to take standard cost for the production actually achieved. For this purpose, the standard hours for actual production should be multiplied by the standard overhead rate per unit or per hour. The formula is:

Overhead Cost Variance = Recovered or Absorbed Overheads − Actual Overhead

OR

= Standard hours for actual output × Std. Overheads Rate − Actual Overhead

2. Fixed Overhead Expenditure Variance :

Also called fixed overhead spending variance, it is the difference between the budgeted overhead and actual overhead. In other words, it represents the difference between the budgeted fixed overhead for the period and the actual overhead which was incurred. Put in the shape of a formula, it would appear as :

Fixed Overhead Expenditure Variance = Total Budgeted Fixed Overhead –
                                          Total Actual Fixed Overhead.

It would be seen that both actual and budgeted overhead costs are shown as total amount, not as unit costs related to activity level. If standard overheads are more, it shall result in favourable and vice-versa.

3) Fixed Overhead Volume Variance :

It is the difference between budgeted and applied fixed overhead. It shows the difference in overhead recovery due to the budgeted quantity of products being greater or less than the actual production. The expenses being fixed for the period, hourly rate changes with the change in the level of operation. The higher the actual level of operation the lower will be cost per unit. Simply defined, fixed overhead volume variance is the difference between the budgeted and the actual output multiplied by the standard fixed overhead rate. Symbolically, this variance is :

$$= (BP - AP) \times SR$$

EXAMPLE

Standard Rate of fixed overheads	:	₹ 20 per unit
Budgeted Production for the month	:	250 units
Actual Production for the month	:	220 units
Actual Fixed Overheads	:	₹ 5,200

Calculate overhead Expenditure and Volume Variances.

ANSWER

Working Notes:

a) Recovered Overheads = Actual Output × Standard Rate
                        = 220 Units × ₹ 20
                        = ₹ 4,400

b) Budgeted Overheads = Budgeted Output × Standard Rate
                       = 250 Units × ₹ 20
                       = ₹ 5,000

i) Fixed Overhead Cost Variance = Recovered Overheads – Actual Overheads
                                 = ₹ 4,400 – ₹ 5,200 = ₹ 800 (Adverse)

ii) Fixed Overhead Expenditure Variance = Budgeted Overheads – Actual Overheads
                                        = ₹ 5,000 – ₹ 5,200 = ₹ 200 (Adverse)

iii) Fixed Overhead Volume Variance = Recovered Overheads – Budgeted Overheads
                                    = ₹ 4,400 – ₹ 5,000 = ₹ 600 (A)

Verification :

$$\text{Fixed Overhead Cost Variance} = \frac{\text{Fixed Overhead}}{\text{Expenditure Variance}} + \frac{\text{Fixed Overhead}}{\text{Volume Variance}}$$

₹ 800 (A) = ₹ 200 (A) + ₹ 600 (Adverse)

EXAMPLE

In the above problem, if the time budgeted is 500 hours and the standard rate overhead per hour ₹ 15, calculate overhead variances.

ANSWER

Working Note:

a) Budgeted Overheads = Budgeted hours × Std. Rate per hour

= 500 Hrs. × ₹ 15

= ₹ 7,500

b) Standard hours for actual production = $\dfrac{\text{Budgeted hours} \times \text{Actual output}}{\text{Budgeted output}}$

= $\dfrac{500 \text{ Hrs.} \times 220 \text{ Units}}{250 \text{ Units}}$ = 2 Hrs. × 220 units

= 440 Hours

c) Recovered Overheads = Standard Hours × Standard Hours rate for actual production

∴ Recovered Overheads = 440 Hrs. × ₹ 15

= ₹ 6,600

i) Fixed Overhead Expenditure Variance = Budgeted Overheads − Actual Overheads

= ₹ 7,500 − ₹ 5,200 − ₹ 2,300 (F)

ii) Fixed Overhead Volume Variance = Recovered Overheads − Budgeted Overheads

= ₹ 6,600 − ₹ 7,500 = ₹ 900 (A)

The volume variance can further be subdivided into Efficiency Variance, and Capacity Variance.

4) Fixed Overhead Efficiency Variance :

The actual output of quantity produced may be different from the standard quantity of output fixed for the period. This may be for a variety of reasons. This variance is the difference between the standard hours allowed for the actual production and the actual hours taken multiplied by speed with which the labour force has produced the output compared with the budgeted time allowed.

Symbolically it is : (SH − AH) × SR

Efficiency Variance = Standard Overheads − Recovered Overheads

5) Fixed Overhead Capacity Variance :

This variance relates to capacity utilisation of the plant and machinery. The actual capacity utilised may be less or more than the standard capacity. This variance is the difference between the budgeted hours of input and the actual hours of input multiplied by standard fixed overhead rate.

Symbolically it is : $(BH - AH) \times SR$

It would be seen that total of overhead efficiency and capacity variance would be equal to overhead volume variance.

EXAMPLE

From the following information, compute Fixed Overhead Cost, Expenditure and Volume Variances : Normal capacity is 5,000 hours. Budgeted fixed overhead rate is ₹ 10 per standard hour. Actual level of capacity utilised is 4,400 standard hours. Actual fixed overheads ₹ 5,200.

ANSWER

i) Fixed Overhead Cost Variance = (Recovered Fixed Overhead – Actual Fixed Overhead)

= ₹ 44,000 – ₹ 5,200 = ₹ 38,800 (F)

ii) Fixed Overhead Expenditure Variance = (Budgeted Fixed Overhead – Actual Fixed Overhead)

= ₹ 50,000 – ₹ 5,200 = ₹ 44,800 (F)

iii) Fixed Overhead Expenditure Variance = (Budgeted Fixed Overhead – Actual Fixed Overhead)

= ₹ 50,000 – ₹ 5,200 = ₹ 44,800 (F)

iv) Fixed Overhead Volume Variance = (Recovered Fixed Overhead – Budgeted Fixed Overhead)

= ₹ 44,000 – ₹ 50,000 = ₹ 6,000 (A)

6) Fixed Overhead Calendar Variance :

It is part of the capacity variance, and is attributed to the number of days in a period being less or more than those budgeted, it arises to the hours worked being more or less than the hours budgeted. As the number of hours worked are normally within the control of management, the calendar factor is not so controllable. Therefore, it is the difference between the number of working days anticipated in the budgeted period and the actual working days in the budgeted period. For calculating standard overhead recovery rate, the working days for the whole year are calculated, and the standard days so calculated are divided by 12, so as to give standard equal days per month. But the actual days in a month may be more or less than the standard day. The difference may be on account of holidays, and the different days in different months, as per calendar, e.g., January being 31, while February 28 or 29, and April 30, and so on.

It may be computed by applying the following formula :

Calendar Variance
- Possible Overheads = Budgeted Overhead
- Possible Overheads = Possible hours × Standard Rate per hour
- Possible hours = Actual number of days × Standard Hours per day

In actual scence calendar variance is a self adjusting variance.

EXAMPLE

a) The Budget for a period indicates :

Works Overhead Fixed : ₹ 50,000
Works Overhead Variable : ₹ 1,50,000
Normal Activity : 100 %

During the period the actual activity was only 70% of the normal load for a total expenditure of ₹ 1,50,000.

What are the overhead budget and overhead volume variances ?

b) Determine the overhead budget and overhead capacity variance from the following data :

Estimated Factory Overhead : ₹ 25,000
Estimated Direct Labour Hours : 5,000 Hrs.
Actual Overhead Expenses : ₹ 26,500
Applied Overhead Expenses : ₹ 22,500

ANSWER

Working Notes:

- Budgeted Overhead for actual activity ₹ 50,000
  Add: Fixed Overheads
  If 100% activity Standard Overhead ₹ 1,50,000
  ∴ 70% of actual activity :

  $$= \frac{₹\ 1,50,000 \times 70}{100}$$ (+) 1,05,000

  ∴ Budgeted Overheads 1,55,000

- Overhead recovered for actual activity :
  Variable Overhead 1,05,000

  Add: Fixed Overhead = ₹ 50,000 × $\frac{70}{100}$ (+) 35,000

  ∴ Recovered Overheads 1,40,000

a) i) Overhead Budget Variance = Budgeted Overhead – Actual Overhead
   = ₹ 1,55,000 – ₹ 1,50,000
   = ₹ 5,000 (F)

ii) Overhead Volume Variance = Recovered Overhead – Budgeted Overhead
   = ₹ 1,40,000 – ₹ 1,55,000
   = ₹ 15,000 (A)

b)   i)   Overhead Budget Variance = Budgeted Overhead – Actual Overhead

$$= ₹ 25,000 - ₹ 26,500$$

$$= ₹ 1,500 \text{ (A)}$$

ii) Overhead Capacity Variance = (Standard hours for actual output – Actual hours) × Standard Overhead rate per hour

$$= (4,500 \text{ Hrs.} - 5,000 \text{ Hrs.}) \times ₹ 5$$

$$= ₹ 2,500 \text{ (A)}$$

EXAMPLE

In a factory the standard units of production for the year were fixed at 1,20,000 units and overhead expenditures were estimated to be,

Fixed : 13,080   and   Variable : ₹ 6,720

Actual production during April of the year was 8,000 units. Each month has 20 working days.

During the month in question there was one statutory holiday.

The actual overheads amounted to Fixed : ₹ 1,305.20 and Variable : ₹ 556.80

Find out the overhead expenditure, overhead volume and overhead calendar variances.

ANSWER

Working Notes:

$$\text{Standard fixed overhead rate per unit} = \frac{₹ 13,080}{1,20,000 \text{ units}}$$

$$= ₹ 0.109$$

$$\text{Standard variable overhead rate per unit} = \frac{₹ 6,720}{1,20,000 \text{ units}}$$

$$= ₹ 0.056$$

$$\text{Budgeted fixed overhead per month} = \frac{₹ 13,080}{120 \text{ months}}$$

$$= ₹ 1,090$$

Absorbed Overhead : Fixed = 8,000 Units × ₹ 0.109 = ₹ 872

Variable = 8,000 Units × ₹ 0.056 = ₹ 448

Total   ₹ 1,320

Actual Overheads (Total) = ₹ 1,305.20 + ₹ 556.80

$$= ₹ 1,862$$

Calculations of Overhead Variances :

i)   Total Overhead Cost Variance = Absorbed Overhead – Actual Overhead

$$= ₹ 1,320 - ₹ 1,862$$

$$= ₹ 542 \text{ (A)}$$

ii) Overhead Volume Variance (Fixed Overhead) = (Actual Output – Standard Output)

$\times$ Standard Fixed Overhead Rate

= (8000 Units – 10,000 Units) $\times$ ₹ 0.019

= ₹ 218 (A)

iii) Overhead Expenditure Variance = Budgeted Overhead – Actual Overhead

- For Fixed Overhead = ₹ 1,090 – ₹ 1,302.20

= ₹ 215.20 (A)

- For Variable Overhead = (8,000 units $\times$ ₹ 0.056) – 556.80

= ₹ 215.20 (A) + ₹ 108.80 (A)

= ₹ 324 (A)

Verification,

Overhead Cost Variance = Overhead Volume Variance +

Overhead Expenditure Variance

₹ 542 (A) = ₹ 218 (A) + ₹ 324 (A)

Calendar Variance (Sub-variance of volume variance):

For Overhead absorbed per day = $\dfrac{₹\ 13,080}{240\ days}$

= ₹ 54.50

iv) Overhead Calendar Variance (Loss due to one holiday) = ₹ 54.50 (A)

6.5 MANAGERIAL USES OF VARIANCES

The main objective of variance analysis is to determine the persons responsible for each variance and to pinpoint the causes for incurrence of these variances. In practice, standard cost variances are useful tools in achieving effective cost control.

Variances, as a control technique, are computed only to fix the responsibility for the deviation from the standard cost and thus ensure perfect control over the standard cost. For purposes of control, variances are classified into "controllable" and "uncontrollable" variances.

If a variance can be located with the responsibility of a particular individual, it is considered to be a "controllable" variance. If variances arise from causes beyond the control of the responsible individuals, it is considered to be-uncontrollable". For instance an increase in the price of materials and increase in the wage rates, are often referred to as "uncontrollable" variance, whilst excessive inputs of material in production and more then standard hours taken by direct labourers provide example of "controllable" variance. This distinction between controllable and uncontrollable variance is important. This facilitates careful analysis of the controllable variance and reporting to the management so as to enable it to implement correction action as and when needed.

Analysis of Standard Cost Variances :

Analysis of standard cost variances is, therefore necessary by responsibilities and causes.

a) Analysis of Variance by Responsibilities :

Standard costs facilitates cost control by revealing exact degree of efficiency in various operations through comparison of actual figures with standard figures.

Control over cost must be applied at the place and time where the cost originates. Variances must be identified with the manager responsible for the costs incurred who should be held responsible for the cost. The cost factors which are directly controllable by operating supervision must be separated from those costs factors for which executive management is responsible.

Define titles of individuals who are responsible for each type of variance differ among business houses. But in general the following personnel are held responsible for variances noted against them. Following table indicate cost variances and personnel responsible for the same. Personnel responsible for Cost Variance are as shown below:

Sr. No.	Variance	Personnel Responsible
1)	Materials Price Variance	Purchasing agent or purchasing manager or purchase officer.
2)	Materials Quantity Variance	Plant superintendent, departmental supervisors, machine operators, quality control department and material handlers or R. D. Department / Engineering Dept.
3)	Labour Rate Variance	Personnel (employment) department manager, departmental supervisor and plant super-intendent or H.R. Dept.
4)	Labour Efficiency Variance	Plant superintendent, departmental supervisors, production scheduling department, quality control department, material handlers and machine operators.
5)	Overhead Expenditure Variance	Variable portion is the responsibility of the individual foreman or supervisor, they are expected to keep actual expenses within the budget. Fixed portion is the responsibility of top management or top executives.
6)	Overhead Efficiency Variance	Same personnel who are responsible for labour efficiency variance as mentioned above.
7)	Overhead Volume Variance	Top management and production schedulers and strategist.

b) Analysis of Variances by Causes :

Variances reflect the effect on costs which certain events or conditions have produced. Before management can take effective action for improving control over costs, it is necessary to know what caused the variances to arise. Therefore, causes for the variances should be determined and plans for necessary corrective action made either by look at carefully, underlying data and records or by discussing possible causes with supervisors.

In short, the analysis of variances by causes is therefore an important aspect of the use of standard costs to attain effective cost control. Following are some of practicable causes of standard cost variances.

1) Materials Price Variance :

i)   Recent changes in purchase price of materials or current market price.

ii) Failure to purchase anticipated quantities when standards were established in higher prices owing to non-availability of quantity purchase discounts.

iii) Not taking cash discount delivery changes / packing etc. anticipated at the time of setting standards resulting in higher prices.

iv) Substituting raw material differing from original materials specifications.

v)   Freight cost changes and changes in purchasing and storekeeping costs if these are debited to the materials cost.

2) Materials Quantity Variance :

i)   Poor or weak material handling.

ii) Inferior workmanship by machine operator.

iii) Faulty or defective equipment.

iv) Cheaper, defective or imperfect raw material causing excessive scrap.

v)   Inferior quality control inspection.

vi) Pilferage.

vii) Wastage due to inefficient production method or production process.

3) Labour Rate Variance :

i)   Recent labour rate change within industry.

ii) Employing a man of a grade different from the one laid down in the standard.

iii) Labour strike leading to utilisation of unskilled help.

iv) Labour layoff causing skilled labour to be retained at higher rates, so as to prevent resignations and job switching.

v)   Employee sickness and vacation time or gap between time keeping and time booking.

vi) Paying a higher overtime allowance than provided for in the standard.

4) Labour Efficiency Variance :

i) Machine breakdown, use of defective machinery and equipment or use of defective system.

ii) Inferior raw materials.

iii) Poor or weak supervision.

iv) Lack of timely material handling.

v) Poor employee performance.

vi) Inefficient production scheduling – delays in the routing work, materials, tools and instructions.

vii) Inferior engineering specifications.

viii) New inexperienced employees.

ix) Insufficient training of workers.

x) Poor working conditions – inadequate or excessive heating, lighting, ventilation etc.

5) Overhead Efficiency Variance :

All the included causes which are listed under labour efficiency variances as mentioned above.

6) Overhead Volume Variance :

(Factors causing either idle time or overtime of plant and facilities)

1. Failure to utilise usual capacity.
2. Lack of sales order.
3. Too much idle capacity.
4. Inefficient utilisation of existing capacity.
5. Machine breakdown or stopping of machine.
6. Defective materials.
7. Labour troubles or disturbances.
8. Power failures / Load shading.

Analysis of variances by product :

The concept of 'variance' which is the valuable contribution of standard costing to cost accounting literature, is the pillar or basis of the principle – "Management by Exception". The most common methods of management in the area of Financial Management are :

(a) Management by Exception and

(b) Management by Objective.

The different aspects of variance analysis is related to management by objective. The concept to variance analysis is the direct contribution to the idea of Responsibility Accounting.

Since management usually wants currents true costs when decisions are to be made with respect to pricing and related questions, variances are often analysed by products in order to arrive at current product costs. Companies producing non-standard goods according to customer's specification may also help analyse variances by job orders.

ILLUSTRATIONS

MATERIAL VARIANCES

ILLUSTRATION 1

From the following information calculate,

i) Material Cost Variance   ii) Material Price Variance and

iii) Material Usage Variance

Particulars		Standard	Actual
Quantity of Material	Units	5,000	5,500
Price Per unit	₹	2	3

Verify the results.

SOLUTION

Calculation of Material Variances :

i) **Material Cost Variance : $(SQ \times SP) - (AQ \times AP)$**

= (Standard Quantity × Standard Price) – (Actual Quantity × Actual Price)

= (5,000 units × ₹ 2) – (5,500 units × ₹ 3)

= ₹ 10,000 – ₹ 16,500

= ₹ 6,500 (Adverse)

ii) **Material Price Variance : $(SP - AP) \times AQ$**

= (Standard Price – Actual Price) × Actual Quantity

= (₹ 2 – ₹ 3) × 5,500 units

= ₹ 1 × 5,500 units

= ₹ 5,500 (Adverse)

iii) **Material Usage Variance : $(SQ - AQ) \times SP$**

= (Standard Quantity – Actual Quantity) × Standard Price

= (5,000 units – 5,500 units) × ₹ 2

= 500 units × ₹ 2

= ₹ 1,000 (Adverse)

Verification, MCV = MPV + MUV

Material Cost Variance = Material Price Variance + Material Usage Variance

∴   ₹ 6,500 (A) = ₹ 5,500 (A) + ₹ 1,000 (A)

∴   Total : ₹ 6,500 (A) = ₹ 6,500 (A)

ILLUSTRATION 2

From the following cost data, calculate,

i) Material Cost Variance

ii) Material Price Variance

iii) Material Usage Variance

Standard			Actual		
Material required	-	100 kgs	Output	-	2,10,000 kgs
For Finished product of	-	70 kgs	Materials used	-	2,80,000 kgs
Price of materials	-	₹ 1 per kg	Cost of Materials	-	₹ 2,52,000

Also verify your results.

SOLUTION

Working Notes :

i) **Calculation of standard quantity of material required for actual output :**

$\quad$ If 70 kgs output $=$ 100 kgs input

$\therefore \quad$ 2,10,000 kgs output $=$?

$$= \frac{2,10,000 \text{ kgs} \times 100 \text{ kgs}}{70 \text{ kgs}}$$

$$= 3,00,000 \text{ kgs}$$

ii) **Calculation of actual price per kg :**

$\quad$ If 2,80,000 kgs $=$ ₹ 2,52,000

$\therefore \quad$ 1 kg $=$?

$$= \frac{1 \text{ kg} \times ₹ 2,52,000}{2,80,000 \text{ kgs}}$$

$$= ₹ 0.90 \text{ per kg}$$

Calculation of Material Variances :

i) **Material Cost Variance :** $(SQ \times SP) - (AQ \times AP)$

$=$ (Standard Quantity $\times$ Standard Price) $-$ (Actual Quantity $\times$ Actual Price)

$=$ (3,00,000 kgs $\times$ ₹ 1) $-$ (2,80,000 kgs $\times$ ₹ 0.90)

$=$ ₹ 3,00,000 $-$ ₹ 2,52,000

$=$ ₹ 48,000 (Favourable)

ii) **Material Price Variance :** $(SP - AP) \times AQ$

$=$ (Standard Price $-$ Actual Price) $\times$ Actual Quantity

$=$ (₹ 1.00 $-$ ₹ 0.90) $\times$ 2,80,000 kgs

$=$ ₹ 28,000 (Favourable)

iii) **Material Usage Variance :** $(SQ - AQ) \times SP$

$=$ (Standard Quantity $-$ Actual Quantity) $\times$ Standard Price

$=$ (3,00,000 kgs $-$ 2,80,000 kgs) $\times$ ₹ 1

$=$ 20,000 kgs $\times$ ₹ 1

$=$ ₹ 20,000 (Favourable)

Verification,

$\qquad$ MCV $=$ MPV + MUV

Material Cost Variance $=$ Material Price Variance + Material Usage Variance

$\qquad$ ₹ 48,000 (F) $=$ ₹ 28,000 (F) + ₹ 20,000 (F)

$\qquad$ Total : ₹ 48,000 (F) $=$ ₹ 48,000 (F)

ILLUSTRATION 3

Ajanta Chemicals, Aurangabad are using standard costing technique to control their cost. A standard estimate for basic materials of 1,000 units of a commodity is 400 kgs. @ ₹ 2.50 per kgs. During March, 2013 when 2,000 units of a commodity are manufactured, it is ascertained that 850 kgs. of materials are actually consumed @ ₹ 2.20 per kg.

Calculate various material variances.

SOLUTION

Working Notes :

i) **Calculation of Standard Quantity of Material required for actual output :**

If 1,000 units = 400 kgs.

∴ 2,000 units = ?

$= \dfrac{2{,}000 \text{ units} \times 400 \text{ kgs.}}{1{,}000 \text{ units}}$

= 800 kgs.

Calculation of Material Variances :

i) **Material Cost Variance : (SQ × SP) – (AQ × AP)**

= (Standard Quantity × Standard Price) – (Actual Quantity × Actual Price)

= (800 kgs. × ₹ 2.50) – (850 kgs. × ₹ 2.20)

= ₹ 2,000 – ₹ 1,870

= ₹ 130 (Favourable)

ii) **Material Price Variance : (SP – AP) × AQ**

= (Standard Price – Actual Price) × Actual Quantity

= (₹ 2.50 – ₹ 2.20) × 850 kgs.

= ₹ 0.30 × 850 kgs.

= ₹ 255 (Favourable)

iii) **Material Usage Variance : (SQ – AQ) × SP**

= (Standard Quantity – Actual Quantity) × Standard Price

= (800 kgs. – 850 kgs.) × ₹ 2.50

= 50 kgs. × ₹ 2.50

= ₹ 125 (Adverse)

Verification,

MCV = MPV + MUV

Material Cost Variance = Material Price Variance + Material Usage Variance

₹ **130 (F)** = ₹ **255 (F)** + ₹ **125 (A)**

∴ **Total : ₹ 130 (F)** = ₹ **130 (F)**

ILLUSTRATION 4

In the manufacture of a Formica Table of four square feet, the standard rate of Formica is ₹ 40 per square feet. During December, 2013 Majestic Furnitures, Malad made 1,000 Tables by using actually 4,200 square feet of Formica @ ₹ 45 per square feet.

You are required to calculate Material Cost Variances and verify your results.

SOLUTION

Working Notes :

i) Calculation of Standard Quantity of Material required for Actual Output :

If 1 Table = 4 sq. ft.

∴   1,000 Tables = ?

$$= \frac{1,000 \text{ Tables} \times 4 \text{ sq. ft.}}{1 \text{ Table}}$$

=   4,000 sq. ft.

Calculation of Material Variances :

i) Material Cost Variance : (SQ × SP) – (AQ × AP)

= (Standard Quantity × Standard Price) – (Actual Quantity × Actual Price)

= (4,000 sq. ft. × ₹ 40) – (4,200 sq. ft. × ₹ 45)

= ₹ 1,60,000 – ₹ 1,89,000

= ₹ 29,000 (Adverse)

ii) Material Price Variance : (SP – AP) × AQ

= (Standard Price – Actual Price) × Actual Quantity

= (₹ 40 – ₹ 45) × 4,200 sq. ft.

= ₹ 5 × 4,200 sq. ft.

= ₹ 21,000 (Adverse)

iii) Material Usage Variance : (SQ – AQ) × SP

= (Standard Quantity – Actual Quantity) × (Standard Price)

= (4,000 sq. ft. – 4,200 sq. ft.) × ₹ 40

= 200 sq. ft. × ₹ 40

= ₹ 8,000 (Adverse)

Verification,

MCV = MPV + MUV

Material Cost Variance = Material Price Variance + Material Usage Variance

₹ 29,000 (A) = ₹ 21,000 (A) + ₹ 8,000 (A)

∴   **Total : ₹ 29,000 (A) = ₹ 29,000 (A)**

ILLUSTRATION 5

In Sudarshan Chemicals Ltd., Someshwarnagar for producing 10 kgs. of a product 'SANNY', the standard requirement is as follows :

Materials	Quantity kgs.	Rate per kg. ₹
C_2	8	6
D_1	4	4

During January, 2013, 1,000 kgs. of product 'SANNY' were produced. The actual consumption of material is as under :

Materials	Quantity ₹	Rate per kg. ₹
C_2	750	7
D_1	500	5

You are required to calculate,

i)   Material Cost Variance,

ii) Material Price Variance, and

iii) Material Usage Variance.

Also, verify the results.

SOLUTION

Working Notes :

i)   **Calculation of Standard Quantity of Material required for actual output of 1,000 kgs :**

Material C_2 :

If 10 kgs. output = 8 kgs. input

∴   1,000 kgs. output = ?

$$= \frac{1,000 \text{ kgs.} \times 8 \text{ kgs.}}{10 \text{ kgs.}}$$

=   800 kgs.

Material D_1 :

If 10 kgs. output = 4 kgs. input

∴   1,000 kgs. output = ?

$$= \frac{1,000 \text{ kgs.} \times 4 \text{ kgs.}}{10 \text{ kgs.}}$$

=   400 kgs.

Calculation of Material Variances :

i) **Material Cost Variance : $(SQ \times SP) - (AQ \times AP)$**

=   (Standard Quantity $\times$ Standard Price) – (Actual Quantity $\times$ Actual Price)

Material C_2 :

=   (800 kgs. $\times$ ₹ 6) – (750 kgs. $\times$ ₹ 7)

=   ₹ 4,800 – ₹ 5,250

=   ₹ 450 (Adverse)

Material D_1 :

=   (400 kgs. $\times$ ₹ 4) – (500 kgs. $\times$ ₹ 5)

=   ₹ 1,600 – ₹ 2,500

=   ₹ 900 (Adverse)

ii) **Material Price Variance : $(SP - AP) \times AQ$**

=   (Standard Price – Actual Price) $\times$ Actual Quantity

Material C_2 :

=   (₹ 6 – ₹ 7) $\times$ 750 kgs.

=   ₹ 1 $\times$ 750 kgs.

=   ₹ 750 (Adverse)

Material D_1 :

=   (₹ 4 – ₹ 5) $\times$ 500 kgs.

=   ₹ 1 $\times$ 500 kgs.

=   ₹ 500 (Adverse)

iii) **Material Usage Variance : $(SQ - AQ) \times SP$**

=   (Standard Quantity – Actual Quantity) $\times$ Standard Price

Material C_2 :

=   (800 kgs. – 750 kgs.) $\times$ ₹ 6

=   50 kgs. $\times$ ₹ 6

=   ₹ 300 (Favourable)

Material D_1 :

=   (400 kgs. – 500 kgs.) $\times$ ₹ 4

=   100 kgs. $\times$ ₹ 4

=   ₹ 400 (Adverse)

Verification,

MCV = MPV + MUV

Material Cost Variance = Material Price Variance + Material Usage Variance

C_2 :   ₹ 450 (A) = ₹ 750 (A) + ₹ 300 (F)

D_1 :   ₹ 900 (A) = ₹ 500 (A) + ₹ 400 (A)

              ₹ 1,350 (A) = ₹ 1,250 (A) + ₹ 100 (A)

∴   **Total : ₹ 1,350 (A) = ₹ 1,350 (A)**

ILLUSTRATION 6

The following particulars derived from the cost records are made available from which you are required to find out :

i) Material Cost Variance

ii) Material Price Variance

iii) Material Usage Variance

Opening Stock of Material	...	Nil
Closing Stock of Material	...	1,000 units
Standard quantity of material required per tonne of output	...	50 units
Standard price of material per unit	...	₹ 1.50
Quantity of materials purchased	...	5,000 units
Cost of materials purchased	...	₹ 10,000
Quantity produced	...	100 tonnes

Also verify your results.

SOLUTION

Working Notes :

i) **Calculation of standard quantity of materials required :**

$$\text{If 1 tonne} = 50 \text{ units}$$

$$\therefore \quad 100 \text{ tonnes} = ?$$

$$= \frac{100 \text{ tonnes} \times 50 \text{ units}}{1 \text{ tonne}}$$

$$= 5,000 \text{ units}$$

ii) **Calculation of actual quantity of materials consumed in units :**

$$= \text{Opening Stock} + \text{Purchases} - \text{Closing Stock}$$

$$= \text{Nil} + 5,000 \text{ units} - 1,000 \text{ units}$$

$$= 4,000 \text{ units.}$$

iii) **Calculation of actual price of material per unit :**

$$\text{If 5,000 units} = ₹ 10,000$$

$$\therefore \quad 1 \text{ unit} = ?$$

$$= \frac{1 \text{ unit} \times ₹ 10,000}{5,000 \text{ units}}$$

$$= ₹ 2 \text{ per unit}$$

Calculation of Material Variances :

i)   **Material Cost Variance :** $(SQ \times SP) - (AQ \times AP)$

     =   (Standard Quantity $\times$ Standard Price) – (Actual Quantity $\times$ Actual Price)

     =   (5,000 units $\times$ ₹ 1.50) – (4,000 units $\times$ ₹ 2)

     =   ₹ 7,500 – ₹ 8,000

     =   ₹ 500 (Adverse)

ii)   **Material Price Variance :** $(SP - AP) \times AQ$

     =   (Standard Price – Actual Price) $\times$ Actual Quantity

     =   (₹ 1.50 – ₹ 2) $\times$ 4,000 units

     =   ₹ 0.50 $\times$ 4,000 units

     =   ₹ 2,000 (Adverse)

iii)   **Material Usage Variance :** $(SQ - AQ) \times SP$

     =   (Standard Quantity – Actual Quantity) $\times$ Standard Price

     =   (5,000 units – 4,000 units) $\times$ ₹ 1.50

     =   1,000 units $\times$ ₹ 1.50

     =   ₹ 1,500 (Favourable)

Verification,

$$MCV = MPV + MUV$$

Material Cost Variance = Material Price Variance + Material Usage Variance

$$₹ 500 \text{ (A)} = ₹ 2,000 \text{ (A)} + ₹ 1,500 \text{ (F)}$$

∴   Total : ₹ 500 (A) = ₹ 500 (A)

ILLUSTRATION 7

From the following information calculate :

i)   Material Cost Variance

ii)   Material Price Variance

iii)   Material Usage Variance

iv)   Material Mix Variance

Material	Standard Mix	Actual Mix
X	70 kgs @ ₹ 2 per kg	60 kgs @ ₹ 2 per kg
Y	30 kgs @ ₹ 4 per kg	50 kgs @ ₹ 5 per kg

SOLUTION

Working Notes :

i)   **Calculation of Standard Mixing Proportion between Material X and Material Y in kgs.**

Material X : Material Y

70 kgs : 30 kgs

7 : 3

ii) **Calculation of total quantity of Actual Material Consumed :**

= Material X + Material Y

= 60 kgs + 50 kgs

= 110 kgs

iii) **Calculation of standard revised mix in kgs :**

= Actual quantity of material consumed × Standard mixing proportion

Material X = 110 kgs × 7/10 = 77 kgs

Material Y = 110 kgs × 3/10 = 33 kgs

Calculation of Material Variances :

i) **Material Cost Variance :** (SQ × SP) – (AQ × AP)

= (Standard Quantity × Standard Price) – (Actual Quantity × Actual Price)

Material X = (70 kgs × ₹ 2) – (60 kgs × ₹ 2)

= ₹ 140 – ₹ 120

= ₹ 20 (Favourable)

Material Y = (30 kgs × ₹ 4) – (50 kgs × ₹ 5)

= ₹ 120 – ₹ 250

= ₹ 130 (Adverse)

ii) **Material Price Variance :** (SP – AP) × AQ

= (Standard Price – Actual Price) × Actual Quantity

Material X = (₹ 2 – ₹ 2) × 60 kgs

= NIL × 60 kgs

= NIL

Material Y = (₹ 4 – ₹ 5) × 50 kgs

= ₹ 1 × 50 kgs

= ₹ 50 (Adverse)

iii) **Material Usage Variance :** (SQ – AQ) × SP

= (Standard Quantity – Actual Quantity) × Standard Price

Material X = (70 kgs – 60 kgs) × ₹ 2

= 10 kgs × ₹ 2

= ₹ 20 (Favourable)

Material Y = (30 kgs – 50 kgs) × ₹ 4

= 20 kgs × ₹ 4

= ₹ 80 (Adverse)

iv) Material Mix Variance : $(RSM - AM) \times SP$

=   (Revised Standard Mix – Actual Mix) × Standard Price

$$\text{Material X} = (77 \text{ kgs} - 60 \text{ kgs}) \times ₹\,2$$
$$= 17 \text{ kgs} \times ₹\,2$$
$$= ₹\,34 \text{ (Favourable)}$$
$$\text{Material Y} = (33 \text{ kgs} - 50 \text{ kgs}) \times ₹\,4$$
$$= 17 \text{ kgs} \times ₹\,4$$
$$= ₹\,68 \text{ (Adverse)}$$

Verification,

$$MCV = MPV + MUV$$

Material Cost Variance = Material Price Variance + Material Usage Variance

Material X : ₹ 20 (F) = NIL + ₹ 20 (F)

Material Y : ₹ 130 (A) = ₹ 50 (A) + ₹ 80 (A)

∴   ₹ 110 (A) = ₹ 50 (A) + ₹ 60 (A)

∴   Total : ₹ 110 (A) = ₹ 110 (A)

ILLUSTRATION 8

In Toshniwal Chemicals, Tulapur for the output of 'Tosha' chemical of 10 kgs. the actual mix differs from the standard mix with a change in output.

The cost details for a period of March, 2013 are given as follows.

Materials	Standard Mix			Actual Mix		
	Quantity kgs.	Price ₹	Cost ₹	Quantity kgs.	Price ₹	Cost ₹
'Bk'	60	20	1,200	75	22	1,650
'Pk'	40	10	400	30	08	240
Total	100		1,600	105		1,890

Calculate the following material variances :

i)   Material Cost Variance,

ii)   Material Price Variance,

iii)   Material Usage Variance and

iv)   Material Mix Variance.

Also verify your results.

SOLUTION

Working Notes :

i) Calculation of Standard Mixing Proportion between Material - 'Bk' and Material - 'Pk'.

$$\text{Material - 'Bk'} : \text{Material - 'Pk'}$$
$$60 \text{ kgs.} : 40 \text{ kgs.}$$
$$3 : 2$$

ii) Calculation of Total Quantity of actual material consumed :

= Material - 'Bk' + Material - 'Pk'

= 75 kgs. + 30 kgs.

= 105 kgs.

iii) Calculation of Revised Standard Mix in kgs. :

$$\text{Material - 'Bk'} = 105 \text{ kgs.} \times \frac{3}{5}$$
$$= 63 \text{ kgs.}$$
$$\text{Material - 'Pk'} = 105 \text{ kgs.} \times \frac{2}{5}$$
$$= 42 \text{ kgs.}$$

Calculation of Material Variances :

i) Material Cost Variance : $(SQ \times SP) - (AQ \times AP)$

= (Standard Quantity × Standard Price) – (Actual Quantity × Actual Price)

Material - 'Bk' :

= (60 kgs. × ₹ 20) – (75 kgs. × ₹ 22)

= ₹ 1,200 – ₹ 1,650

= ₹ 450 (Adverse)

Material - 'Pk' :

= (40 kgs. × ₹ 10) – (30 kgs. × ₹ 8)

= ₹ 400 – ₹ 240

= ₹ 160 (Favourable)

ii) Material Price Variance : $(SP - AP) \times AQ$

= (Standard Price – Actual Price) × Actual Quantity

Material - 'Bk' :

= (₹ 20 – ₹ 22) ×75 kgs.

= ₹ 2 × 75 kgs.

= ₹ 150 (Adverse)

Material - 'Pk' :

= $(₹ 10 – ₹ 8) \times 30$ kgs.

= $₹ 2 \times 30$ kgs.

= ₹ 60 (Favourable)

iii) **Material Usage Variance : (SQ – AQ) × SP**

= (Standard Quantity – Actual Quantity) × Standard Price

Material - 'Bk' :

= $(60 \text{ kgs.} – 75 \text{ kgs.}) \times ₹ 20$

= $15 \text{ kgs.} \times ₹ 20$

= ₹ 300 (Adverse)

Material - 'Pk' :

= $(40 \text{ kgs.} – 30 \text{ kgs.}) \times ₹ 10$

= $10 \text{ kgs.} \times ₹ 10$

= ₹ 100 (Favourable)

iv) **Material Mix Variance : (RSM – AM) × SP**

= (Revised Standard Mix – Actual Mix) × Standard Price

Material - 'Bk' :

= $(63 \text{ kgs.} – 75 \text{ kgs.}) \times 20$

= $12 \text{ kgs.} \times ₹ 20$

= ₹ 240 (Adverse)

Material - 'Pk' :

= $(42 \text{ kgs.} – 30 \text{ kgs.}) \times ₹ 10$

= $12 \text{ kgs.} \times ₹ 10$

= ₹ 120 (Favourable)

Verification,

$$MCV = MPV + MUV$$

'Bk' : ₹ 450 (A) = ₹ 150 (A) + ₹ 300 (A)

'Pk' : ₹ 160 (F) = ₹ 60 (F) + ₹ 100 (F)

₹ **290 (A)** = ₹ **90 (A)** + ₹ **200 (A)**

∴ **Total : ₹ 290 (A) = ₹ 290 (A)**

ILLUSTRATION 9

Godrej Co., Gurgaon manufacturers a product 'Bosin' by mixing three raw materials viz. A_1, B_2 and C_3. It is ascertained that 125 kgs. of raw materials input are used for every 100 kgs. of output. In January, 2013, there was an output of 5,600 kgs. of product 'Bosin'. The additional cost data relating to the period is as follows :

Raw Material	Standard		Actual	
	Mixing Proportion	Price per kg.	Mixing Proportion	Price per kg.
	%	₹	%	₹
A_1	50	40	60	45
B_2	30	25	20	20
C_3	20	10	20	15

During the period, the actual quantity of material consumed was 7,000 kgs.

You are required to compute the following material variances and verify the results.

i)   Material Cost Variance,

ii)   Material Price Variance,

iii) Material Usage Variance and

iv)   Material Mix Variance.

SOLUTION

Working Notes :

i)   **Calculation of Standard Quantity of Material required for actual output :**

If 100 kgs. output = 125 kgs. input

∴   5,600 kgs. ouptut = ?

$$= \frac{5{,}600 \text{ kgs.} \times 125 \text{ kgs}}{100 \text{ kgs.}}$$

=   7,000 kgs.

Apportionment of Total Standard Quantity (i.e. 7,000 kgs. among Raw Materials A_1, B_2 and C_3 in standard mixing proportion i.e. 5 : 3 : 2).

$$A_1 \ = \ 7{,}000 \text{ kgs.} \times \frac{5}{10} = 3{,}500 \text{ kgs.}$$

$$B_2 \ = \ 7{,}000 \text{ kgs.} \times \frac{3}{10} = 2{,}100 \text{ kgs.}$$

$$C_3 \ = \ 7{,}000 \text{ kgs.} \times \frac{2}{10} = 1{,}400 \text{ kgs.}$$

ii) **Apportionment of Total Actual Quantity (i.e. 7,000 kgs.) among Raw Materials A_1, B_2 and C_3 in actual mixing proportion (i.e. 6 : 2 : 2).**

$$A_1 = 7{,}000 \text{ kgs.} \times \frac{6}{10} = 4{,}200 \text{ kgs.}$$

$$B_2 = 7{,}000 \text{ kgs.} \times \frac{2}{10} = 1{,}400 \text{ kgs.}$$

$$C_3 = 7{,}000 \text{ kgs.} \times \frac{2}{10} = 1{,}400 \text{ kgs.}$$

iii) **Calculation of Revised Standard Mix in kgs.**

= Actual Quantity of Material consumed × Standard Mixing Proportion

$$\text{Material } A_1 = 7{,}000 \text{ kgs.} \times \frac{5}{10} = 3{,}500 \text{ kgs.}$$

$$\text{Material } B_2 = 7{,}000 \text{ kgs.} \times \frac{3}{10} = 2{,}100 \text{ kgs.}$$

$$\text{Material } C_3 = 7{,}000 \text{ kgs.} \times \frac{2}{10} = 1{,}400 \text{ kgs.}$$

Calculation of Material Variances :

i) **Material Cost Variance : $(SQ \times SP) - (AQ \times AP)$**

= (Standard Quantity × Standard Price) – (Actual Quantity × Actual Price)

Material A_1 :

= (3,500 kgs. × ₹ 40) – (4,200 kgs. × ₹ 45)

= ₹ 1,40,000 – ₹ 1,89,000

= ₹ 49,000 (Adverse)

Material B_2 :

= (2,100 kgs. × ₹ 25) – (1,400 kgs. × ₹ 20)

= ₹ 52,500 – ₹ 28,000

= ₹ 24,500 (Favourable)

Material C_3 :

= (1,400 kgs. × ₹ 10) – (1,400 kgs. × ₹ 15)

= ₹ 14,000 – ₹ 21,000

= ₹ 7,000 (Adverse)

ii) **Material Price Variance : $(SP - AP) \times AQ$**

= (Standard Price – Actual Price) × Actual Quantity

Material A_1 :

= (₹ 40 – ₹ 45) × 4,200 kgs.

= ₹ 5 × 4,200 kgs.

= ₹ 21,000 (Adverse)

Material B_2 :

=   (₹ 25 – ₹ 20) × 1,400 kgs.

=   ₹ 5 × 1,400 kgs.

=   ₹ 7,000 (Favourable)

Material C_3 :

=   (₹ 10 – ₹ 15) × 1,400 kgs.

=   ₹ 5 × 1,400 kgs.

=   ₹ 7,000 (Adverse)

iii) Material Usage Variance : (SQ – AQ) × SP

=   (Standard Quantity – Actual Quantity) × Standard Price

Material A_1 :

=   (3,500 kgs. – 4,200 kgs.) × ₹ 40

=   700 kgs. × ₹ 40

=   ₹ 28,000 (Adverse)

Material B_2 :

=   (2,100 kgs. – 1,400 kgs.) × ₹ 25

=   700 kgs. × ₹ 25

=   ₹ 17,500 (Favourable)

Material C_3 :

=   (1,400 kgs. – 1,400 kgs.) × ₹ 10

=   NIL × ₹ 10

=   NIL

iv) Material Mix Variance : (RSQ – AQ) × SP

=   (Revised Standard Quantity – Actual Quantity) × Standard Price

Material A_1 :

=   (3,500 kgs. – 4,200 kgs.) × ₹ 40

=   700 kgs. × ₹ 40

=   ₹ 28,000 (Adverse)

Material B_2 :

=   (2,100 kgs. – 1,400 kgs.) × ₹ 25

=   700 kgs. × ₹ 25

=   ₹ 17,500 (Favourable)

Material C_3 :

$\quad =\quad$ (1,400 kgs. – 1,400 kgs.) $\times$ ₹ 10

$\quad =\quad$ NIL $\times$ ₹ 10

$\quad =\quad$ NIL

Verification,

$$\text{MCV} = \text{MPV} + \text{MUV}$$

Material Cost Variance $=$ Material Price Variance + Material Usage Variance

A_1 : $\quad$ ₹ 49,000 (A) $=$ ₹ 21,000 (A) + ₹ 28,000 (A)

B_2 : $\quad$ ₹ 24,500 (F) $=$ ₹ 7,000 (F) + ₹ 17,500 (F)

C_3 : $\quad\quad$ ₹ 7,000 (A) $=$ ₹ 7,000 (A) + NIL

$\quad\quad$ **₹ 31,500 (A)** $=$ **₹ 21,000 (A) + ₹ 10,500 (A)**

$\therefore$ $\quad$ **Total : ₹ 31,500 (A)** $=$ **₹ 31,500**

ILLUSTRATION 10

The standard, materials cost to produce one tonne of chemical 'Sulpha' is –

- Material A_3 : 300 kgs. @ ₹ 10 per kg.
- Material B_2 : 400 kgs. @ ₹ 5 per kg.
- Material C_1 : 500kgs. @ ₹ 6 per kg.

During January, 2013, in Alembic Chemicals Ltd., Ahmednagar 100 tonnes of chemical Sulpha was produced from the usage of,

- Material A_3 : 35 Tonnes @ ₹ 9,000 per tonne.
- Material B_2 : 42 Tonnes @ ₹ 6,000 per tonne.
- Material C_3 : 53 Tonnes @ ₹ 7,000 per tonne.

You are required to calculate,

i) Material Cost Variance,

ii) Material Price Variance,

iii) Material Usage Variance and

iv) Material Mix Variance.

Also verify the results.

SOLUTION

Working Notes :

i) **Calculation of standard quantity of material required for actual output of 100 tonnes :**

Material A_3 :

$\quad\quad$ If 1 Tonne $=$ 300 kgs.

$\therefore$ $\quad\quad$ 100 Tonnes $=$?

$\quad =\quad \dfrac{\text{100 Tonnes} \times \text{300kgs.}}{\text{1 Tonne}}$

$\quad =\quad$ 30,000 kgs.

Material B_2 :

$$\text{If 1 Tonne} = 400 \text{ kgs.}$$
$$\therefore \quad 100 \text{ Tonnes} = ?$$
$$= \frac{100 \text{ Tonnes} \times 400 \text{kgs.}}{1 \text{ Tonne}}$$
$$= 40,000 \text{ kgs.}$$

Material C_1 :

$$\text{If 1 Tonne} = 500 \text{ kgs.}$$
$$\therefore \quad 100 \text{ Tonnes} = ?$$
$$= \frac{100 \text{ Tonnes} \times 500 \text{ kgs}}{1 \text{ Tonne}}$$
$$= 50,000 \text{ kgs.}$$

ii) **Calculation of actual quantity of materials used for actual output of 100 tonnes in kgs.**

(Base 1 Tonne = 1,000 kgs.)

Material A_3 :

$$\text{If 1 Tonne} = 1,000 \text{ kgs.}$$
$$\therefore \quad 35 \text{ Tonnes} = ?$$
$$= \frac{35 \text{ Tonnes} \times 1,000 \text{ kgs}}{1 \text{ Tonne}}$$
$$= 35,000 \text{ kgs.}$$

Material B_2 :

$$\text{If 1 Tonne} = 1,000 \text{ kgs.}$$
$$\therefore \quad 42 \text{ Tonnes} = ?$$
$$= \frac{42 \text{ Tonnes} \times 1,000 \text{ kgs.}}{1 \text{ Tonne}}$$
$$= 42,000 \text{ kgs.}$$

Material C_1 :

$$\text{If 1 Tonne} = 1,000 \text{ kgs.}$$
$$\therefore \quad 53 \text{ Tonnes} = ?$$
$$= \frac{53 \text{ Tonnes} \times 1,000 \text{ kgs.}}{1 \text{ Tonne}}$$
$$= 53,000 \text{ kgs.}$$

iii) **Calculation of actual rate of material per kg. :**

Material A_3 :

$$\text{If 1,000 kgs.} = ₹ 9,000$$
$$\therefore \quad 1 \text{ kg.} = ?$$
$$= \frac{1 \text{ kg.} \times ₹ 9,000}{1,000 \text{ kgs.}}$$
$$= ₹ 9 \text{ per kg.}$$

Material B_2 :

$$\text{If } 1,000 \text{ kgs.} = ₹ 6,000$$

$$\therefore \qquad 1 \text{ kg.} = ?$$

$$= \frac{1 \text{ kg.} \times ₹ 6,000}{1,000 \text{ kgs.}}$$

$$= ₹ 6 \text{ per kg.}$$

Material C_1 :

$$\text{If } 1,000 \text{ kgs.} = ₹ 7,000$$

$$\therefore \qquad 1 \text{ kg.} = ?$$

$$= \frac{1 \text{ kg.} \times ₹ 7,000}{1,000 \text{ kgs.}}$$

$$= ₹ 7 \text{ per kg.}$$

iv) **Calculation of Standard mixing proportion between materials A_3, B_2 and C_1 in kgs. :**

A_3	:	B_2	:	C_1
30,000 kgs.	:	40,000 kgs.	:	50,000 kgs.

$$\therefore \quad 3 : 4 : 5$$

v) **Calculation of Total Quantity of actual material consumed in kgs. :**

Material - A_3 – 35,000 kgs.

Add : Material - B_2 – 42,000 kgs.

Add : Material - C_1 – (+) 53,000 kgs.

$$\therefore \text{ Total} \qquad \underline{1,30,000 \text{ kgs.}}$$

vi) **Calculation of Revised Standard Mix in kgs. :**

= Actual Total Quantity of Materials consumed × Standard Mixing Proportion

$$\text{Material } A_3 = 1,30,000 \text{ kgs.} \times \frac{3}{12} = 32,500 \text{ kgs.}$$

$$\text{Material } B_2 = 1,30,000 \text{ kgs.} \times \frac{4}{12} = 43,333 \text{ kgs.}$$

$$\text{Material } C_1 = 1,30,000 \text{ kgs.} \times \frac{5}{12} = 54,167 \text{ kgs.}$$

Calculation of Material Variances :

i) **Material Cost Variance : $(SQ \times SP) - (AQ \times AP)$**

= (Standard Quantity × Standard Price) – (Actual Quantity × Actual Price)

Material A_3 :

= (30,000 kgs. × ₹ 10) – (35,000 kgs. × ₹ 9)

= ₹ 3,00,000 – ₹ 3,15,000

= ₹ 15,000 (Adverse)

Material B_2 :

= (40,000 kgs. $\times$ ₹ 5) – (42,000 kgs. $\times$ ₹ 6)

= ₹ 2,00,000 – ₹ 2,52,000

= ₹ 52,000 (Adverse)

Material C_1 :

= (50,000 kgs. $\times$ ₹ 6) – (53,000 kgs. $\times$ ₹ 7)

= ₹ 3,00,000 – ₹ 3,71,000

= ₹ 71,000 (Adverse)

ii) Material Price Variance : $(SP – AP) \times AQ$

= (Standard Price – Actual Price) $\times$ Actual Quantity

Material A_3 :

= (₹ 10 – ₹ 9) $\times$ 35,000 kgs.

= ₹ 1 $\times$ 35,000 kgs.

= ₹ 35,000 (Favourable)

Material B_2 :

= (₹ 5 – ₹ 6) $\times$ 42,000 kgs.

= ₹ 1 $\times$ 42,000 kgs.

= ₹ 42,000 (Adverse)

Material C_1 :

= (₹ 6 – ₹ 7) $\times$ 53,000 kgs.

= ₹ 1 $\times$ 53,000 kgs.

= ₹ 53,000 (Adverse)

iii) Material Usage Variance : $(SQ – AQ) \times SP$

= (Standard Quantity – Actual Quantity) $\times$ Standard Price

Material A_3 :

= (30,000 kgs. – 35,000 kgs.) $\times$ ₹ 10

= 5,000 kgs. $\times$ ₹ 10

= ₹ 50,000 (Adverse)

Material B_2 :

= (40,000 kgs. – 42,000 kgs.) $\times$ ₹ 5

= 2,000 kgs. $\times$ ₹ 5

= ₹ 10,000 (Adverse)

Material C_1 :

=   (50,000 kgs. – 53,000 kgs.) $\times$ ₹ 6

=   3,000 kgs. $\times$ ₹ 6

=   ₹ 18,000 (Adverse)

iv) Material Mix Variance : (RSM – AM) $\times$ SP

=   (Revised Standard Mix – Actual Mix) $\times$ Standard Price

Material A_3 :

=   (32,500 kgs. – 35,000 kgs.) $\times$ ₹ 10

=   2,500 kgs. $\times$ ₹ 10

=   ₹ 25,000 (Adverse)

Material B_2 :

=   (43,333 kgs. – 42,000 kgs.) $\times$ ₹ 5

=   1,333 kgs. $\times$ ₹ 5

=   ₹ 6,665 (Favourable)

Material C_1 :

=   (54,167 kgs. – 53,000 kgs.) $\times$ ₹ 6

=   1,167 kgs. $\times$ ₹ 6

=   ₹ 7,002 (Favourable)

Verification,

MCV = MPV + MUV

Material Cost Variance = Material Price Variance + Material Usage Variance

A_3 :   ₹ 15,000 (A) = ₹ 35,000 (F) + ₹ 50,000 (A)

B_2 :   ₹ 52,000 (A) = ₹ 42,000 (A) + ₹ 10,000 (A)

C_1 :   **₹ 71,000 (A) = ₹ 53,000 (A) + ₹ 18,000 (A)**

∴ **Total : ₹ 1,38,000 (A) = ₹ 1,38,000 (A)**

ILLUSTRATION 11

Barua Chemicals Ltd., Badalapur produces certain chemicals, the standard material cost of the same is as follows :

Material 'Alfa' : 40% @ ₹ 20 per tonne

Material 'Bita' : 60% @ ₹ 30 per tonne

A standard production loss of 10% is normally expected in the manufacturing processes. During February, 2013 the results of chemical production are as follows :

	Units Tonnes
Material 'Alfa' : @ ₹ 18 per tonne	90
Material 'Bita' : @ ₹ 34 per tonne	(+) 110
∴ Input	200
Less : Production Loss	(–) 29
∴ Output	171

You are required to calculate :
i)   Material Price Variance and
ii) Material Yield Variance.

SOLUTION

i)   **Calculation of Standard Quantity of material required for actual output :**

	Units Tonnes
Material 'Alfa'	90
Material 'Bita'	(+) 110
∴ Standard Input	200
Less : Standard Loss - 10% of 20 tons	(−) 20
∴ Standard Output	180

If 180 Tonnes - Output = 200 Tonnes - Input

∴   171 Tonnes - Output = ?

$$= \frac{171 \text{ Tonnes} \times 200 \text{ Tonnes}}{180 \text{ Tonnes}}$$

=   190 Tonnes

Apportionment of Standard Quantity (i.e. 190 Tonnes) in standard mixing proportion (i.e. 4 : 6)

Material 'Alfa' :

$$190 \text{ Tonnes} \times \frac{4}{10} = 76 \text{ tonnes}$$

Material 'Bita' :

$$190 \text{ Tonnes} \times \frac{6}{10} = 114 \text{ Tonnes}$$

ii) **Calculation of standard cost per unit of output :**   ₹

Material 'Alfa' : 76 Tonnes × ₹ 20	1,520
Material 'Bita' : 114 Tonnes × ₹ 30	(+) 3,420
∴ Total Standard Cost	4,940

$$= \frac{\text{Total Standard Cost of Material}}{\text{Actual Output}}$$

$$= \frac{₹ 4,940}{\text{Tonnes } 171}$$

=   ₹ 28.89

Calculation of Material Variances :

1.   **Material Price Variance : (SP − AP) × AQ**
     Material 'Alfa' : (₹ 20 − ₹ 18) × 90 Tonnes
     =   ₹ 180 (Favourable)
     Material 'Bita' : (₹ 30 − ₹ 34) × 110 Tonnes
     =   ₹ 440 (Adverse)

Total Material Price Variance :

Material 'Alfa' : ₹ 180 (Favourable)

Material 'Bita' : ₹ 440 (Adverse)

∴   **Total** : **₹ 260 (Adverse)**

2.   **Material Yield Variance : (AY – RSY) × SC**

=   (Actual Yield – Revised Standard Yield) × Standard Cost per unit of output

=   (171 Tonnes – 180 Tonnes) × ₹ 28.89

=   9 Tonnes × ₹ 28.89

=   ₹ 260 (Adverse)

ILLUSTRATION 12

Sudarshan Ltd., Surat manufactures a single product, the standard mix of which is as follows :

Material Aey : 60% @ ₹ 10 per kg.

Material Bee : 40% @ ₹ 6 per kg.

Normal loss in production is 20% of input. Due to acute shortage of Material Aey, the standard mix was revised accordingly. The cost data relating to the actual results for January, 2013 are as follows :

		Units kgs.
Material Aey @ ₹ 10 per kg.		200
Material Bee @ ₹ 5 per kg.	(+)	100
∴ Input		300
Less : Loss	(–)	60
∴ Output		240

You are required to calculate,

i)   Material Cost Variance,

ii)   Material Price Variance,

iii) Material Usage Variance,

iv)   Material Mix Variance, and

v)   Material Yield Variance.

Also verify your results.

SOLUTION

Working Notes :

i)   **Calculation of Standard Quantity of material required for actual output :**

Normal loss in production is 20% of input

Input		Normal loss		Output
100	–	20	=	80

The standard mixing propotion of material Aey and Bee is 60%; 40% i.e. 3 : 2.

Material Aey :

$$\text{If 80 kg. Output} = 60 \text{ kgs.}$$

$$\therefore \quad 240 \text{ kgs. Output} = ?$$

$$= \frac{240 \text{ kgs.} \times 60 \text{ kgs.}}{80 \text{ kgs.}}$$

$$= 180 \text{ kgs.}$$

Material Bee :

$$\text{If 80 kgs. Output} = 40 \text{ kgs.}$$

$$\therefore \quad 240 \text{ kgs. Output} = ?$$

$$= \frac{240 \text{ kgs.} \times 40 \text{ kgs.}}{80 \text{ kgs.}}$$

$$= 120 \text{ kgs.}$$

ii) **Calculation of standard mixing proportion between Material Aey and Material Bee**

$$\text{Aey} \ : \ \text{Bee}$$
$$60\% \ : \ 40\%$$
$$3/5 \ : \ 2/5$$

iii) **Calculation of Total Quantity of actual material consumed in kgs. :**

Material Aey		200 kgs.
Add : Material Bee	(+)	100 kgs
$\therefore$ Total		300 kgs

iv) **Calculation of Revised Standard Mix in kgs. :**

$= $ Actual Total Quantity of Materials consumed $\times$ Standard Mixing Proportion

$$\text{Material Aey} = 300 \text{ kgs.} \times \frac{3}{5} = 180 \text{ kgs.}$$

$$\text{Material Bee} = 300 \text{ kgs.} \times \frac{2}{5} = 120 \text{ kgs.}$$

v) **Calculation of Standard Output :**

Total Standard Output	300 kgs.
Less : Normal Loss i.e. 20%	(–) 60 kgs.
$\therefore$ Total	240 kgs.

vi) Calculation of Standard Cost per unit of Output :

Material Aey : 60 kgs. × ₹ 10	₹ 600
Material Bee : 40 kgs. × ₹ 6	(+) ₹ 240
∴ Total Cost	₹ 840

$$\text{Input} - \text{Normal Loss} = \text{Output}$$
$$100 \quad - \quad 20 \quad = \quad 80$$

$$= \frac{\text{Total Standard Cost}}{\text{Net Output}}$$

$$= \frac{₹\ 840}{80\ \text{kgs.}}$$

$$= ₹\ 10.50\ \text{per kg.}$$

Calculation of Material Variances :

i) Material Cost Variances : (SQ × SP) – (AQ × AP)

= (Standard Quantity × Standard Price) – (Actual Quantity × Actual Price)

Material Aey :

= (180 kgs. × ₹ 10) – (200 kgs. × ₹ 10)

= ₹ 1,800 – ₹ 2,000

= ₹ 200 (Adverse)

Material Bee :

= (120 kgs. × ₹ 6) – (100 kgs. × ₹ 5)

= ₹ 720 – ₹ 500

= ₹ 220 (Favourable)

ii) Material Price Variance : (SP – AP) × AQ

= (Standard Price – Actual Price) × Actual Quantity

Material Aey :

= (₹ 10 – ₹ 10) × 200 kgs.

= NIL × 200 kgs.

= NIL

Material Bee :

= (₹ 6 – ₹ 5) × 100 kgs.

= ₹ 1 × 100 kgs.

= ₹ 100 (Favourable)

iii) Material Usage Variance : (SQ – AQ) × SP

= (Standard Quantity – Actual Quantity) × Standard Price

Material Aey :

= (180 kgs. – 200 kgs.) × ₹ 10

= 20 kgs. × ₹ 10

= ₹ 200 (Adverse)

Material Bee :

= (120 kgs. – 100 kgs.) $\times$ ₹ 6

= 20 kgs. $\times$ ₹ 6

= ₹ 120 (Favourable)

iv) Material Mix Variances : (RSQ – AQ) $\times$ SP

= (Revised Standard Quantity – Actual Quantity) $\times$ Standard Price

Material Aey :

= (180 kgs. – 200 kgs.) $\times$ ₹ 10

= 20 kgs. $\times$ ₹ 10

= ₹ 200 (Adverse)

Material Bee :

= (120 kgs. – 100 kgs.) $\times$ ₹ 6

= 20 kgs. $\times$ ₹ 6

= ₹ 120 (Favourable)

v) Material Yield Variance : (AY – RSY) $\times$ SC

= (Actual Yield – Revised Standard Yield) $\times$ Standard Cost per unit of output

= (240 kgs. – 240 kgs.) $\times$ ₹ 10.50

= NIL $\times$ ₹ 10.50

= NIL

Verification,

MCV = MPV + MUV

Material Cost Variance = Material Price Variance + Material Usage Variance

Aey : ₹ 200 (A) = NIL + ₹ 200 (A)

Bee : ₹ 220 (F) = ₹ 100 (F) + ₹ 120 (F)

₹ **20 (F)** = ₹ **100 (F)** + ₹ **80 (A)**

∴ **Total ₹ 20 (F)** = ₹ **20 (F)**

MUV = MMV + MYV

Material Usage Variance = Material Mix Variance + Material yield Variance

₹ 80 (A) = ₹ 80 (A) + NIL

∴ **Total : ₹ 80 (A)** = ₹ **80 (A)**

ILLUSTRATION 13

Zenith Co. Ltd., Nashik manufactures certain products. The cost data relating to a standard product for October, 2013 are given below :

Standard Cost Data				Actual Cost Data			
Raw Materials	Quantity Kgs.	Price ₹	Total ₹	Raw Materials	Quantity Kgs.	Price ₹	Total ₹
A	500	6.	3,000	A	400	6.	2,400
B	400	3.75	1,500	B	500	3.60	1,800
C (+)	300	3.	900	C (+)	400	2.80	1,120
	1,200				1,300		
Less : 10% Normal Loss (−)	120			Less : Actual Loss (−)	220		
	1,080		5,400		1,080		5,320

From the above mentioned cost data you are required to calculate :

i)   Material Cost Variance,

ii)   Material Price Variance,

iii) Material Usage Variance,

iv)   Material Mix Variance and

v)   Material Yield Variance.

SOLUTION

Working Notes :

i)   Calculation of Revised Standard Quantity :

$$RSQ = \frac{\text{Standard Quantity of each material}}{\text{Total Standard Quantity}} \times \text{Total Actual Quantity}$$

$$\text{Material A} = \frac{500 \text{ kgs}}{1,200 \text{ kgs}} \times 1,300 \text{ kgs}$$

$$= 541.67 \text{ kgs}$$

$$\text{Material B} = \frac{400 \text{ kgs}}{1,200 \text{ kgs}} \times 1,300 \text{ kgs}$$

$$= 433.33 \text{ kgs}$$

$$\text{Material C} = \frac{300 \text{ kgs}}{1,200 \text{ kgs}} \times 1,300 \text{ kgs}$$

$$= 325 \text{ kgs}$$

ii)   Calculation of Revised Standard Yield :

$$RSY = \frac{\text{Actual Output}}{\text{Total Standard Quantity}} \times \text{Total Actual Quantity}$$

$$= \frac{1,080 \text{ kgs}}{1,200 \text{ kgs}} \times 1,300 \text{ kgs}$$

$$= 1,170 \text{ kgs.}$$

iii) **Calculation of Standard Cost per unit of output :**

$$= \frac{\text{Total Standard Cost}}{\text{Net Output}}$$

$$= \frac{₹\,5,400}{1,080 \text{ kgs}}$$

$$= ₹\,5$$

Calculation of Material Variances :

i) **Material Cost Variance : $(SQ \times SP) - (AQ \times AP)$**

= (Standard Quantity × Standard Price) – (Actual Quantity × Actual Price)

Material A :

= $(500 \text{ kgs} \times ₹\,6) - (400 \text{ kgs} \times ₹\,6)$

= ₹ 3,000 – ₹ 2,400

= ₹ 600 (Favourable)

Material B :

= $(400 \text{ kgs} \times ₹\,3.75) - (500 \text{ kgs} \times ₹\,3.60)$

= ₹ 1,500 – ₹ 1,800)

= ₹ 300 (Adverse)

Material C :

= $(300 \text{ kgs.} \times ₹\,3) - (400 \text{ kgs} \times ₹\,2.80)$

= ₹ 900 – ₹ 1,120

= ₹ 220 (Adverse)

$$\underset{\text{(Net)}}{\text{MCV}} = \underset{₹\,600\,(F)}{\text{Material A}} + \underset{₹\,300\,(A)}{\text{Material B}} + \underset{₹\,220\,(A)}{\text{Material C}} = \underset{₹\,80\,(F)}{\text{MCV (Net)}}$$

ii) **Material Price Variance : $(SP - AP) \times AQ$:**

= Standard Price – Actual Price) × Actual Quantity

Material A :

= $(₹\,6 - ₹\,6) \times 400 \text{ kgs.}$

= NIL × 400 kgs.

= NIL

Material B :

= $(₹\,3.75 - ₹\,3.60) \times 500 \text{ kgs.}$

= ₹ 0.15 × 500 kgs.

= ₹ 75 (Favourable)

Material C :

= ($3 – $2.80) × 400 kgs.

= $0.20 × 400 kgs.

= $80 (Favourable)

$$\underset{\text{(Net)}}{\text{MPV}} = \underset{\text{NIL}}{\text{Material A}} + \underset{\text{$75 (F)}}{\text{Material B}} + \underset{\text{$80 (F)}}{\text{Material C}} = \underset{\text{$155 (F)}}{\text{MPV (Net)}}$$

iii) Material Usage Variance : (SQ – AQ) × SP :

= (Standard Quantity – Actual Quantity) × Standard Price

Material A :

= (500 kgs – 400 kgs) × $6

= 100 kgs × $6

= $600 (Favourable)

Material B :

= (400 kgs – 500 kgs) × $3.75

= 100 kgs × $3.75

= $375 (Adverse)

Material C :

= (300 kgs – 400 kgs.) × $3

= 100 kgs × $3

= $300 (Adverse)

$$\underset{\text{(Net)}}{\text{MUV}} = \underset{\text{$600 (F)}}{\text{Material A}} + \underset{\text{$375 (A)}}{\text{Material B}} + \underset{\text{$300 (A)}}{\text{Material C}} = \underset{\text{$75 (A)}}{\text{MUV (Net)}}$$

iv) Material Mix Variance : (RSQ – AQ) × SP

= (Revised Standard Quantity – Actual Quantity) × Standard Price

Material A :

= (541.67 kgs – 400 kgs) × $6

= 141.67 kgs × $6

= $850 (Favourable)

Material B :

= (433.33 kgs – 500 kgs) × $3.75

= 66.67 kgs × $3.75

= $250 (Adverse)

Material C :

= (325 kgs – 400 kgs) × ₹ 3

= 75 kgs × ₹ 3

= ₹ 225 (Adverse)

$$\frac{\text{MMV}}{\text{(Net)}} = \frac{\text{MaterialA}}{₹ 850 \text{ (F)}} + \frac{\text{Material B}}{₹ 250 \text{ (A)}} + \frac{\text{Material C}}{₹ 225 \text{ (A)}} = \frac{\text{MMV (Net)}}{₹ 375 \text{ (A)}}$$

v) Material Yield Variance : (AY – RSY) × SC

= (Actual Yield – Revised Standard Yield) × Standard Cost per unit of output

= (1,080 kgs – 1,170 kgs) × ₹ 5

= 90 kgs × ₹ 5

= ₹ 450 (Adverse)

Verification,

i) Material Cost Variance = Material Price Variance + Material Usage Variance

₹ 80 (F) = ₹ 155 (F) + ₹ 75 (A)

∴   Total : ₹ 80 (F) = ₹ 80 (F)

ii) Material Usage Variance = Material Mix Variance + Material Yield Variance

₹ 75 (A) = ₹ 375 (F) + ₹ 450 (A)

∴   **Total :** ₹ 75 (A) = ₹ 75 (A)

ILLUSTRATION 14

The standard material inputs required for 1,000 kgs of a finished product are given below :

Material	Quantity (kgs)	Standard Rate per kg (₹)
A	450	20
B	400	40
C	(+) 250	60
	1,100	
Less : Standard Loss	(–) 100	
∴ Standard Output	**1,000**	

Actual production in a period was 20,000 kgs of the finished product for which the actual quantities of material used and the prices thereof were as under :

Material	Quantity Used Kgs.	Actual Rate per kg ₹
A	10,000	19
B	8,500	42
C	4,500	65

Calculate,

     i)   Material Cost Variance,

     ii)   Material Price Variance,

     iii)   Material Usage Variance,

     iv)   Material Mix Variance and

     v)   Material Yield Variance

SOLUTION

Working Notes :

i)   **Calculation of Standard Quantity of Material required for actual production of 20,000 kgs.**

Material A :

$$\text{If } 1,000 \text{ kgs} = 450 \text{ kgs}$$

$$\therefore \qquad 20,000 \text{ kgs} = ?$$

$$= \frac{20,000 \text{ kgs} \times 450 \text{ kgs}}{1,000 \text{ kgs}}$$

$$= \quad 9,000 \text{ kgs.}$$

Material B :

$$\text{If } 1,000 \text{ kgs} = 400 \text{ kgs}$$

$$\therefore \qquad 20,000 \text{ kgs} = ?$$

$$= \frac{20,000 \text{ kgs} \times 400 \text{ kgs}}{1,000 \text{ kgs}}$$

$$= \quad 8,000 \text{ kgs.}$$

Material C :

$$\text{If } 1,000 = 250 \text{ kgs}$$

$$\therefore \qquad 20,000 \text{ kgs} = ?$$

$$= \frac{20,000 \text{ kgs} \times 250 \text{ kgs}}{1,000 \text{ kgs}}$$

$$= \quad 5,000 \text{ kgs.}$$

ii)   **Calculation of standard loss of material required for actual production of 20,000 kgs.**

$$\text{If } 1,000 \text{ kgs} = 100 \text{ kgs}$$

$$\therefore \qquad 20,000 \text{ kgs} = ?$$

$$= \frac{20,000 \text{ kgs} \times 100 \text{ kgs}}{1,000 \text{ kgs}}$$

$$= \quad 2,000 \text{ kgs.}$$

iii) When the actual weight of mix differs from standard weight of mix, the standard quantity of each material will be revised as follows :

Standard Material input for 20,000 kgs				Actual Material input for 20,00 kgs			
Material	Quantity Kgs.	Rate ₹	Amount ₹	Material	Quantity Kgs.	Rate ₹	Amount ₹
A	9,000	20	1,80,000	A	10,000	19	1,90,000
B	8,000	40	3,20,000	B	8,500	42	3,57,000
C (+)	5,000	60	3,00,000	C (+)	4,500	65	2,92,500
	22,000				23,000		
Less : Loss (−)	2,000			Less : Loss (−)	3,000		
∴ Output	20,000		8,00,000		20,000		8,39,500

v) Calculation of Revised Standard Quantity :

$$RSQ = \frac{\text{Standard Quantity of each material}}{\text{Total Standard Quantity}} \times \frac{\text{Total Actual}}{\text{Quantity}}$$

$$\text{Material A} = \frac{9,000 \text{ ks}}{22,000 \text{ kgs}} \times 23,000 \text{ kgs}$$

$$= 9,409.09 \text{ kgs}$$

$$\text{Material B} = \frac{8,000 \text{ kgs}}{22,000 \text{ kgs}} \times 23,000 \text{ kgs}$$

$$= 8,363.63 \text{ kgs}$$

$$\text{Material C} = \frac{5,000 \text{ kgs}}{22,000 \text{ kgs}} \times 23,000 \text{ kgs}$$

$$= 5,227.27 \text{ kgs.}$$

v) Calculation of Revised Standard Yield :

$$RSY = \frac{\text{Actual Output}}{\text{Total Standard Quantity}} \times \text{Total Actual Quantity}$$

$$= \frac{20,000 \text{ kgs}}{22,000 \text{ kgs}} \times 23,000 \text{ kgs}$$

$$= 20,909.09 \text{ kgs}$$

vi) Calculation of Standard Cost per unit of output :

$$SC = \frac{\text{Total Standard Cost}}{\text{Net Output}}$$

$$= \frac{₹ 8,00,000}{20,000 \text{ kgs}}$$

$$= ₹ 40$$

Calculation of Material Variances :

i) **Material Cost Variance : (SQ × SP) − (AQ × AP)**

=   (Standard Quantity × Standard Price) − (Actual Quantity × Actual Price)

Material A :

=   (9,000 kgs × ₹ 20) − (10,000 kgs × ₹ 19)

=   ₹ 1,80,000 − ₹ 1,90,000

=   ₹ 10,000 (Adverse)

Material B :

= (8,000 kgs × ₹ 40) − (8,500 kgs × ₹ 42)

= ₹ 3,20,000 − ₹ 3,57,000

= ₹ 37,000 (Adverse)

Material C :

= (5,000 kgs × ₹ 60) − (4,500 kgs × ₹ 65)

= ₹ 3,00,000 − ₹ 2,92,500

= ₹ 7,500 (Favourable)

$$\underset{\text{(Net)}}{\text{MCV}} = \underset{\text{₹ 10,000 (A)}}{\text{Material A}} + \underset{\text{₹ 37,000 (A)}}{\text{Material B}} + \underset{\text{₹ 7,500 (F)}}{\text{Material C}} = \underset{\text{₹ 39,500 (A)}}{\text{MCV (Net)}}$$

ii) Material Price Variance : (SP − AP) × AQ

= (Standard Price − Actual Price) × Actual Quantity

Material A :

= (₹ 20 − ₹ 19) × 10,000 kgs

= ₹ 1 × 10,000 kgs

= ₹ 10,000 (Favourable)

Material B :

= (₹ 40 − ₹ 42) × 8,500 kgs

= ₹ 2 × 8,500 kgs

= ₹ 17,000 (Adverse)

Material C :

= (₹ 60 − ₹ 65) × 4,500 kgs

= ₹ 5 × 4,500 kgs

= ₹ 22,500 (Adverse)

$$\underset{\text{(Net)}}{\text{MPV}} = \underset{\text{₹ 10,000 (F)}}{\text{Material A}} + \underset{\text{₹ 17,000 (A)}}{\text{Material B}} + \underset{\text{₹ 22,500 (A)}}{\text{Material C}} = \underset{\text{₹ 29,500 (A)}}{\text{MPV (Net)}}$$

iii) Material Usage Variance : (SQ − AQ) × SP :

= (Standard Quantity − Actual Quantity) × Standard Price

Material A :

= (9,000 kgs − 10,000 kgs) × ₹ 20

= 1,000 kgs × ₹ 20

= ₹ 20,000 (Adverse)

Material B :

= (8,000 kgs − 8,500 kgs) × ₹ 40

= 500 kgs × ₹ 40

= ₹ 20,000 (Adverse)

Material C :

=   (5,000 kgs − 4,500 kgs) × ₹ 60

=   500 kgs × ₹ 60

=   ₹ 30,000 (Favourable)

$$\underset{\text{(Net)}}{\text{MUV}} = \underset{\text{₹ 20,000 (A)}}{\text{Material A}} + \underset{\text{₹ 20,000 (A)}}{\text{Material B}} + \underset{\text{₹ 30,000 (F)}}{\text{Material C}} = \underset{\text{₹ 10,000 (A)}}{\text{MUV (Net)}}$$

iv) Material Mix Variance : (RSQ − AQ) SP

=   (Revised Standard Quantity − Actual Quantity) × Standard Price

Material A :

=   (9,409.09 kgs − 10,000 kgs) × ₹ 20

=   590.91 kgs × ₹ 20

=   ₹ 11,818.20 (Adverse)

Material B :

=   (8,363.63 kgs − 8,500 kgs) × ₹ 40

=   136.37 kgs × ₹ 40

=   ₹ 5454.80 (Adverse)

Material C :

=   (5,227.27 kgs − 4,500 kgs) × ₹ 60

=   727.27 kgs × ₹ 60

=   ₹ 43,636.20 (Favourable)

$$\underset{\text{(Net)}}{\text{MMV}} = \underset{\text{₹ 11,818.20 (A)}}{\text{Material A}} + \underset{\text{₹ 5,454.80 (A)}}{\text{Material B}} + \underset{\text{₹ 43,636.20 (F)}}{\text{Material C}} = \underset{\text{₹ 26,363 (F)}}{\text{MMV (Net)}}$$

v) Material Yield Variance : (AY − RSY) × SC

=   (Actual Yield − Revised Standard Yield) × Standard Cost per unit of output

=   (20,000 kgs − 20,909.09 kgs) × ₹ 40

=   909.09 kgs × ₹ 40

=   ₹ 36,363.60 (Adverse)

Verification,

i)   Material Cost Variance = Material Price Variance + Material Usage Variance

           ₹ 39,500 (A)   ₹ 29,500 (A) + ₹ 10,000 (A)

∴   Total : ₹ 39,500 (A) = ₹ 39,500 (A)

ii)   Material Usage Variance= Material Mix Variance + Material Yield Variance

           ₹ 10,000 (A) = ₹ 26,363 (F) + ₹ 36,363 (A)

     Total : ₹ 10,000 (A) = ₹ 10,000 (A)

ILLUSTRATION 15

From the data given below of a product 'ROBIN', calculate material variances.

Raw Material		Quantity Units	Rate per unit ₹	Total ₹	Raw Material		Quantity Units	Rate per unit ₹	Total ₹
X		30	20	600	X		34	18	612
Y	(+)	70	30 (+)	2,100	Y	(+)	66	36 (+)	2,376
Total		100		2,700			100		2,988
Less : Normal Loss 10% (−)		10	(+)	−	**Less** : Actual Loss 15% (−)		15	(−)	−
Total		**90**		**2,700**	**Total**		**85**		**2,988**

SOLUTION

Working Notes :

i) Calculation of Revised Standard Quantity :

$$RSQ = \frac{\text{Standard Quantity of each material}}{\text{Total Standard Quantity}} \times \text{Total Actual Quantity}$$

$$\text{Material X} = \frac{30 \text{ units}}{100 \text{ units}} \times 100 \text{ units}$$

$$= 30 \text{ units}$$

$$\text{Material Y} = \frac{70 \text{ units}}{100 \text{ units}} \times 100 \text{ units}$$

$$= 70 \text{ units}$$

ii) Calculation of Revised Standard Yield :

$$RSY = \frac{\text{Actual Output}}{\text{Total Standard Quantity}} \times \text{Total Actual Quantity}$$

$$= \frac{85 \text{ units}}{100 \text{ units}} \times 100 \text{ units}$$

$$= 85 \text{ units}$$

iii) Calculation of Standard Cost per unit of output :

$$= \frac{\text{Total Standard Cost}}{\text{Net Output}}$$

$$= \frac{₹ 2,700}{90 \text{ units}}$$

$$= ₹ 30$$

Calculation of Material Variances :

i) **Material Cost Variance :** $(SQ \times SR) - (AQ \times AR)$

    = (Standard Quantity Standard × Standard Rate) – (Actual Quantity × Actual Rate)

Material X :

    = (30 units × ₹ 20) – (34 units × ₹ 18)

    = ₹ 600 – ₹ 612

    = ₹ 12 (Adverse)

Material Y :

    = (70 units × ₹ 30) – (66 units × ₹ 36)

    = ₹ 2,100 – ₹ 2,376

    = ₹ 276 (Adverse)

ii) **Material Price Variance :** $(SP - AP) \times AQ$

    = (Standard Price – Actual Price) × Actual Quantity

Material X :

    = (₹ 20 – ₹ 18) × 34 units

    = ₹ 02 × 34 units

    = ₹ 68 (Favourable)

Material Y :

    = (₹ 30 × ₹ 36) × 66 units

    = ₹ 06 × 66 units

    = ₹ 396 (Adverse)

iii) **Material Usage Variance :** $(SQ - AQ) \times SR$

    = (Standard Quantity – Actual Quantity) × Standard Rate

Material X :

    = (30 units – 34 units) × ₹ 20

    = ₹ 04 units × ₹ 20

    = ₹ 80 (Adverse)

Material Y :

    = (70 units – 66 units) × ₹ 30

    = 04 units × ₹ 30

    = ₹ 120 (Favourable)

iv) **Material Mix Variance :** $(RSQ - AQ) \times SR$

    = (Revised Standard Quantity – Actual Quantity) × Standard Rate

Material Y :

=   (30 units – 34 units) × ₹ 20

=   04 units × ₹ 20

=   ₹ 80 (Adverse)

Material Y :

=   (70 units – 66 units) × ₹ 30

=   04 units × ₹ 30

=   ₹ 120 (Favourable)

v)   **Material Yield Variance :** (AY – RSY) × SC

=   (Actual Yield – Revised Standard Yield) × Standard Cost per unit of output

=   (85 units – 85 units) × ₹ 30

=   NIL × ₹ 30

=   NIL

Verification,

i)   MCV = MPV + MUV

Material Cost Variance = Material Price Variance + Material Usage Variance

Material X : ₹ 12 (A) = ₹ 68 (F) + ₹ 80 (A)

Material Y : ₹ 276 (A) = ₹ 396 (A) + ₹ 120 (F)

₹ 288 (A) = ₹ 328 (A) + ₹ 40 (F)

∴   **Total :** ₹ 288 (A) = ₹ 288 (A)

ii)   MUV = MMV + MYV

Material Usage Variance = Material Mix Variance + Material Yield Variance

Material X : ₹ 80 (A) = ₹ 80 (A) + NIL

Material Y : ₹ 120 (F) = ₹ 120 (F) + NIL

₹ 40 (F) = ₹ 40 (F) + NIL

∴   **Total :** ₹ 40 (F) = ₹ 40 (F)

LABOUR VARIANCES

ILLUSTRATION 1

Dynalog India Ltd., Durgapur provides following cost details from which you are required to calculate.

i) Labour Cost Variance, ii) Labour Rate Variance and iii) Labour Efficiency Variance.

Standard Hours per unit of output	20 Hours
Standard Rate per hour	₹ 5
Actual Production during October, 2013	2,000 units
Actual Hours	35,000 Hours
Actual Rate per hour	₹ 4

Also verify your results.

SOLUTION

Working Notes :

i) Calculation of standard labour hours for actual production :

If 1 unit = 20 Hours

∴ 2,000 units = ?

= $\dfrac{2,000 \text{ units} \times 20 \text{ Hours}}{1 \text{ Unit}}$

= 40,000 Hours.

Calculation of Labour Variances :

i) Labour Cost Variance : (SH × SR) – (AH × AR)

= (Standard Hours × Standard Rate) – (Actual Hours × Actual Rate)

= (40,000 Hours × ₹ 5) – (35,000 Hours × ₹ 4)

= ₹ 2,00,000 – ₹ 1,40,000

= ₹ 60,000 (Favourable)

ii) Labour Rate Variance : (SR – AR) × AH

= (Standard Rate – Actual Rate) × Actual Hours

= (₹ 5 – ₹ 4) × 35,000 Hours

= ₹ 1 × 35,000 Hours

= ₹ 35,000 (Favourable)

iii) Labour Efficiency Variance : (SH – AH) × SR

= (Standard Hours – Actual Hours) × Standard Rate

= (40,000 Hours – 35,000 Hours) × ₹ 5

= 5,000 Hours × ₹ 5

= ₹ 25,000 (Favourable)

Verification,

LCV = LRV + LEV

Labour Cost Variance = Labour Rate Variance + Labour Efficiency Variance

₹ **60,000 (F)** = ₹ **35,000 (F) +** ₹ **25,000 (F)**

∴ Total : ₹ **60,000 (F)** = ₹ **60,000 (F)**

ILLUSTRATION 2

Elite Co., Ernakulam produces a product and the standard cost card of the same discloses the following information :

- Standard Rate per hour   ₹ 26
- Standard Time for a unit of output   Hours 5

The actual cost data for a particular period are as follows :

- Total number of units produced   Units 200
- Actual hours worked   Hours 900
- Total Labour Cost   ₹ 27,000

You are required to calculate,

i) Labour Cost Variance,

ii) Labour Rate Variance and

iii) Labour Efficiency Variance.

Also verify your results.

SOLUTION

Working Notes :

i) Calculation of standard labour hours for actual production :

$$\text{If } 1 \text{ unit} = 5 \text{ Hours}$$

$$\therefore \qquad 200 \text{ units} = ?$$

$$= \frac{200 \text{ Units} \times 5 \text{ Hours}}{1 \text{ Unit}}$$

$$= 1{,}000 \text{ Hours.}$$

ii) Calculation of actual rate per hour :

$$\text{If } 900 \text{ Hours} = ₹\, 27{,}000$$

$$\therefore \qquad 1 \text{ Hour} = ?$$

$$= \frac{1 \text{ Hour} \times ₹\, 27{,}000}{900 \text{ Hours}}$$

$$= ₹\, 30 \text{ per hour}$$

Calculation of Labour Variances :

i) Labour Cost Variance : $(SH \times SR) - (AH \times AR)$

= (Standard Hours × Standard Rate) – (Actual Hours × Actual Rate)

= (1,000 Hours × ₹ 26) – (900 Hours × ₹ 30)

= ₹ 26,000 – ₹ 27,000

= ₹ 1,000 (Adverse)

ii) Labour Rate Variance : $(SR - AR) \times AH$

= (Standard Rate – Actual Rate) × Actual Hours

= (₹ 26 – ₹ 30) × 900 Hours

= ₹ 4 × 900 Hours

= ₹ 3,600 (Adverse)

iii) Labour Efficiency Variance : $(SH - AH) \times SR$

= (1,000 Hours – 900 Hours) × ₹ 26

= 100 Hours × ₹ 26

= ₹ 2,600 (Favourable)

Verification,

$$\text{LCV} = \text{LRV} + \text{LEV}$$

Labour Cost Variance = Labour Rate Variance + Labour Efficiency Variance

₹ 1,000 (A) = ₹ 3,600 (A) + ₹ 2,600 (F)

∴ **Total : ₹ 1,000 (A) = ₹ 1,000 (A)**

ILLUSTRATION 3

In Mangalam Industries, Malad the budgeted labour force employed in a welding process is as follows :

- Un-skilled Labour Force :
  200 workers @ ₹ 5 per hour for 40 hours.
- Semi-skilled Labour Force :
  300 workers @ ₹ 6 per hour for 50 hours. The actual labour force during a particular period was as follows :
- Un-skilled Labour Force :
  210 workers @ ₹ 4 per hour for 45 hours.
- Semi-skilled Labour Force :
  290 workers @ ₹ 7 per hour for 45 hours.

Compute the following labour variances,

i) Labour Cost Variance,
ii) Labour Rate Variance, and
iii) Labour Efficiency Variance.

SOLUTION

Calculation of Labour Variances :

i) **Labour Cost Variance : (SH × SR) – (AH × AR)**

= (Standard Hours × Standard Rate) – (Actual Hours × Actual Rate)

Unskilled Workers :

= ((200 workers × 40 Hours) × ₹ 5) – ((210 workers × 45 Hours) × ₹ 4)

= (8,000 Hrs. × ₹ 5) – (9,450 Hours × ₹ 4)

= ₹ 40,000 – ₹ 37,800

= ₹ 2,200 (Favourable)

Semi-skilled Workers :

= ((300 workers × 50 Hours) × ₹ 6) – ((290 workers × 45 Hours) × ₹ 7)

= (15,000 Hours × ₹ 6) – (13,050 Hours × ₹ 7)

= ₹ 90,000 – ₹ 91,350

= ₹ 1,350 (Adverse)

ii) **Labour Rate Variance : (SR – AR) × AH**

= (Standard Rate – Actual Rate) × Actual Hours

Unskilled Workers :

= (₹ 5 – ₹ 4) × 210 workers × 45 Hours

= ₹ 1 × 9,450 Hours.

= ₹ 9,450 (Favourable)

Semi-skilled Workers :

= $(₹6 – ₹7) × 290$ Workers $× 45$ Hours

= $₹1 × 13,050$ Hours

= $₹13,050$ (Adverse)

iii) Labour Efficiency Variance : (SH – AH) × SR

= (Standard Hours – Actual Hours) × Standard Rate

Un-skilled Workers :

= $(200$ workers $× 40$ Hours$) – (210$ workers $× 45$ Hours$) × ₹5$

= $(8,000$ Hours $– 9,450$ Hours$) × ₹5$

= $1,450$ Hours $× ₹5$

= $₹7,250$ (Adverse)

Semi-skilled Workers :

= $(300$ workers $× 50$ Hours$) – (290$ workers $× 45$ Hours$) × ₹6$

= $(15,000$ Hours $– 13,050$ Hours$) × ₹6$

= $1,950$ Hours $× ₹6$

= $₹11,700$ (Favourable)

Verification,

LCV = LRV + LEV

Labour Cost Variance = Labour Rate Variance + Labour Efficiency Variance

USW : ₹ 2,200 (F) = ₹ 9,450 (F) + ₹ 7,250 (A)

SSW : ₹ 1,350 (A) = ₹ 13,050 (A) + ₹ 11,700 (F)

₹ 850 (F) = ₹ 3,600 (A) + ₹ 4,450 (F)

∴ **Total : ₹ 850 (F) = ₹ 850 (F)**

ILLUSTRATION 4

From the following information calculate for each of the department,

i) Labour Cost Variance

ii) Labour Rate Variance

iii) Labour Efficiency Variance

Particulars		Dept. X	Dept. Y
Gross Direct Wages	₹	26,240	18,900
Standard Hours Produced	Hrs.	8,600	6,000
Standard Rate per hour	₹	3.00	3.40
Actual Hours Worked	Hrs.	8,200	6,300

SOLUTION

Working Notes :

i) **Calculation of actual rate per hour :**

Dept X :

$$\text{If } 8,200 \text{ Hours } = ₹ 26,240$$

$$\therefore \qquad 1 \text{ Hour } = ?$$

$$= \frac{1 \text{ Hour} \times ₹ 26,240}{8,200 \text{ Hours}}$$

$$= ₹ 3.20$$

Dept Y :

$$\text{If } 6,300 \text{ Hours } = ₹ 18,900$$

$$\therefore \qquad 1 \text{ Hour } = ?$$

$$= \frac{1 \text{ Hour} \times ₹ 18,900}{6,300 \text{ Hours}}$$

$$= ₹ 3.00$$

Calculation of Labour Variances :

i) **Labour Cost Variance :** $(SH \times SR) - (AH \times AR)$

= (Standard Hours × Standard Rate) – (Actual Hours × Actual Rate)

$$\text{Dept. X } = (8,600 \text{ Hours} \times ₹ 3.00) - (8,200 \text{ Hours} \times ₹ 3.20)$$

$$= ₹ 25,800 - ₹ 26,240$$

$$= ₹ 440 \text{ (Adverse)}$$

$$\text{Dept. Y } = (6,000 \text{ Hours} \times ₹ 3.40) - (6,300 \text{ Hours} \times ₹ 3.00)$$

$$= ₹ 20,400 - ₹ 18,900$$

$$= ₹ 1,500 \text{ (Favourable)}$$

ii) **Labour Rate Variance :** $(SR - AR) \times AH$

= (Standard Rate – Actual Rate) × Actual Hours

$$\text{Dept. X : } = (₹ 3.00 - ₹ 3.20) \times 8,200 \text{ Hours}$$

$$= ₹ 0.20 \times 8,200 \text{ Hours}$$

$$= ₹ 1,640 \text{ (Adverse)}$$

$$\text{Dept. Y : } = (₹ 3.40 - ₹ 3.00) \times 6,300 \text{ Hours}$$

$$= ₹ 0.40 \times 6,300 \text{ Hours}$$

$$= ₹ 2,520 \text{ (Favourable)}$$

iii) **Labour Efficiency Variance :** $(SH - AH) \times SR$

= (Standard Hours – Actual Hours) × Standard Rate

$\quad$ **Dept. X** = (8,600 Hours – 8,200 Hours) × ₹ 3.00

$\quad\quad\quad$ = 400 Hours × ₹ 3.00

$\quad\quad\quad$ = ₹ 1,200 (Favourable)

$\quad$ **Dept. Y :** = (6,000 Hours – 6,300 Hours) × ₹ 3.40

$\quad\quad\quad$ = 300 Hours × ₹ 3.40

$\quad\quad\quad$ = ₹ 1,020 (Adverse)

Verification,

$\quad\quad\quad$ LCV = LRV + LEV

$\quad$ Labour Cost Variance = Labour Rate Variance + Labour Efficiency Variance

Dept. X : $\quad$ ₹ 440 (A) = ₹ 1,640 (A) + ₹ 1,200 (F)

Dept. Y : $\quad$ ₹ 1,500 (F) = ₹ 2,520 (F) + ₹ 1,020 (A)

$\quad\quad$ **₹ 1,060 (F) = ₹ 880 (F) + ₹ 180 (F)**

∴ $\quad$ **Total : ₹ 1,060 (F) = ₹ 1,060 (F)**

ILLUSTRATION 5

Using the following cost data, calculate,

i)   Labour Cost Variance

ii) Labour Rate Variance

iii) Labour Efficiency Variance

iv) Idle Time Variance

and verify your results.

Gross Direct Wages	₹ 3,000
Standard hours produced	Hrs. 1,600
Standard rate per hour	₹ 1.50
Actual hours paid	Hrs. 1,500

(out of which hours not worked due to abnormality are 50 hours).

SOLUTION

Working Notes :

i)   **Calculation of actual rate per hour :**

$\quad\quad$ If 1,500 Hours = ₹ 3,000

∴ $\quad\quad$ 1 Hour = ?

$$= \frac{1 \text{ Hour} \times ₹ 3,000}{1,500 \text{ Hours}}$$

$\quad\quad\quad$ = ₹ 2 per hour

Calculation of Labour Variances :

i) Labour Cost Variance : (SH × SR) – (AH × AR)

= (Standard Hours × Standard Rate) – (Actual Hours × Actual Rate)

= (1,600 Hours × ₹ 1.50) – (1,500 Hours × ₹ 2.00)

= ₹ 2,400 – ₹ 3,000

= ₹ 600 (Adverse)

ii) Labour Rate Variance : (SR – AR) × AH

= (Standard Rate – Actual Rate) × Actual Hours

= (₹ 1.50 – ₹ 2.00) × 1,500 Hours

= ₹ 750 (Adverse)

iii) Labour Efficiency Variance : (SH – AH) × SR

= (Standard Hours – Actual Hours) × Standard Rate

= (1,600 Hours – 1,450 Hours) × ₹ 1.50

= 150 Hours × ₹ 1.50

= ₹ 225 (Favourable)

iv) Idle Time Variance : IT × SR

= Idle Time × Standard Rate

= 50 Hours × ₹ 1.50

= 75 (Adverse)

Verification,

$$LCV = LRV + LEV + ITV$$

Labour Cost Variance = Labour Rate Variance + Labour Efficiency Variance + Idle Time Variance

₹ 600 (A) = ₹ 750 (A) + ₹ 225 (F) + ₹ 75 (A)

∴   **Total : ₹ 600 (A) = ₹ 600 (A)**

ILLUSTRATION 6

Harison Electrical Ltd., Haridwar provides you the cost details regarding manufacture of certain products for June, 2013.

Standard Time per unit of output	10 Hours
Standard Rate per labour hour	₹ 8
Actual monthly production	1,100 units
Effective hours worked	11,500 Hours
Idle Time	500 Hours
Actual Total Hours paid	12,000 Hours
Total Wage payment for the month	₹ 1,20,000

You are required to find out various labour variances.

SOLUTION

Working Notes :

i) **Calculation of standard labour hours for actual production :**

$$\text{If } 1 \text{ unit } = 10 \text{ Hours}$$

$$\therefore \quad 1{,}100 \text{ units } = ?$$

$$= \frac{1{,}100 \text{ units} \times 10 \text{ Hours}}{1 \text{ Unit}}$$

$$= 11{,}000 \text{ Hours.}$$

ii) **Calculation of actual rate per hour :**

$$\text{If } 12{,}000 \text{ Hours } = ₹\,1{,}20{,}000 \text{ Total Wages}$$

$$\therefore \quad 1 \text{ Hour } = ?$$

$$= \frac{1 \text{ Hour} \times ₹\,1{,}20{,}000}{12{,}000 \text{ Hours}}$$

$$= ₹\,10 \text{ per labour hour}$$

Calculation of Labour Variances :

i) **Labour Cost Variance : (SH × SR) – (AH × AR)**

= (Standard Hours × Standard Rate) – (Actual Hours × Actual Rate)

= (11,000 Hours × ₹ 8) – (12,000 Hours × ₹ 10)

= ₹ 88,000 – ₹ 1,20,000

= ₹ 32,000 (Adverse)

ii) **Labour Rate Variance : (SR – AR) × AH**

= (Standard Rate – Actual Rate) × Actual Hours

= (₹ 8 – ₹ 10) × 12,000 Hours

= ₹ 2 × 12,000 Hours

= ₹ 24,000 (Adverse)

iii) **Labour Efficiency Variance : (SH – AH) × SR**

= (Standard Hours – Actual Hours) × Standard Rate

= (11,000 Hours – 11,500 Hours) × ₹ 8

= 500 Hours × ₹ 8

= ₹ 4,000 (Adverse)

iv) **Idle Time Variance : IT × SR**

= Idle Time × Standard Rate

= 500 Hours × ₹ 8

= ₹ 4,000 (Adverse)

Verification,

$$\text{LCV} = \text{LRV} + \text{LEV} + \text{ITV}$$

Labour Cost Variance = Labour Rate Variance + Labour Efficiency Variance + Idle Time Variance

₹ 32,000 (A) = **₹ 24,000 (A) + ₹ 4,000 (A) + ₹ 4,000 (A)**

∴ **Total : ₹ 32,000 (A)** = **₹ 32,000 (A)**

ILLUSTRATION 7

From the following details calculate,

i) Labour Cost Variance

ii) Labour Rate Variance

iii) Labour Efficiency Variance

iv) Labour Mix Variance

Workers	Standard			Actual		
	Hours	Rate ₹	Amount ₹	Hours	Rate ₹	Amount ₹
Skilled	30	5.00	150	32	5.00	160
Un-skilled	(+) 40	4.00	(+) 160	(+) 32	4.25	(+) 136
Total	70		310	64		296

SOLUTION

Working Notes :

i) Calculation of standard mixing proportion between Skilled and Unskilled workers in hours :

$$\text{Skilled Workers} \quad : \quad \text{Unskilled Workers}$$
$$30 \text{ Hours} \quad : \quad 40 \text{ Hours}$$
$$3 \quad : \quad 4$$

ii) Calculation of total actual hours worked for :

= Skilled workers + Unskilled workers

= 32 Hours + 32 Hours = 64 Hours.

iii) Calculation of revised standard mix in hours :

= Actual hours worked for × Standard mixing proportion

Skilled workers = 64 Hours × 3/7 = 27.42 i.e. 27 Hours

Unskilled workers = 64 Hours × 4/7 = 36.57 i.e. 37 Hours

Calculation of Labour Variances :

i) Labour Cost Variance : (SH × SR) – (AH × AR)

= (Standard Hours × Standard Rate) – (Actual Hours × Actual Rate)

Skilled workers = (30 Hours × ₹ 5.00) – (32 Hours × ₹ 5.00)

= ₹ 150 – ₹ 160

= ₹ 10 (Adverse)

Unskilled workers = (40 Hours × ₹ 4.00) – (32 Hours × ₹ 4.25)

= ₹ 160 – ₹ 136

= ₹ 24 (Favourable)

ii) **Labour Rate Variance : (SR – AR) × AH**

= (Standard Rate – Actual Rate) × Actual Hours

Skilled workers = (₹ 5.00 – ₹ 5.00) × 32 Hours

= NIL × 32 Hours

= NIL

Unskilled workers = (₹ 4.00 – ₹ 4.25) × 32 Hours

= ₹ 0.25 × 32 Hours

= ₹ 8 (Adverse)

iii) **Labour Efficiency Variance : (SH – AH) × SR**

= (Standard Hours – Actual Hours) × Standard Rate

Skilled workers = (30 Hours – 32 Hours) × ₹ 5

= 2 Hours × ₹ 5

= ₹ 10 (Adverse)

Unskilled workers = (40 Hours – 32 Hours) × ₹ 4

= 8 Hours × ₹ 4

= ₹ 32 (Favourable)

iv) **Labour Mix Variance : (RSM – AM) × SR**

= (Revised Standard Mix – Actual Mix) × Standard Rate

Skilled workers = (27 Hours – 32 Hours) × ₹ 5.00

= 5 Hours × ₹ 5.00

= ₹ 25 (Adverse)

Unskilled workers = (37 Hours – 32 Hours) × ₹ 4.00

= 5 Hours × ₹ 4.00

= ₹ 20 (Favourable)

Verification,

LCV = LRV + LEV

Labour Cost Variance = Labour Rate Variance + Labour Efficiency Variance

Skilled workers = ₹ 10 (A) = NIL + ₹ 10 (A)

Unskilled workers = ₹ 24 (F) – ₹ 8 (A) + ₹ 32 (F)

₹ 14 (F) = **₹ 8 (A)** = **₹ 22 (F)**

∴ **Total : ₹ 14 (F)** = **₹ 14 (F)**

ILLUSTRATION 8

Wipro Ltd., Wardha discloses the following cost details for a particular job which is to be completed within a span of fifty weeks.

Category of Workers	Standard Data		Actual Data	
	Total Number of Workers	Wage Rate (Per Worker per week) ₹	Total Number of Workers	Wage Rate (Per Worker per week) ₹
Skilled	80	75	70	80
Semi-skilled	40	50	40	60
Un-skilled	50	35	50	20

In actual practice, fifty-five weeks were taken up in total to complete the said job.

Calculate :

i) Labour Cost Variance,

ii) Labour Rate Variance,

iii) Labour Efficiency Variance and

iv) Labour Mix Variance.

Also verify your results.

SOLUTION

Working Notes :

i) **Calculation of Standard Labour Cost and Actual Labour Cost :**

Category of Workers	Standard			Actual		
	Weeks (Number of Workers × Number of weeks)	Rate (Per Worker per week) ₹	Amount ₹	Weeks (Number of Workers × Number of weeks)	Rate (Per Worker per week) ₹	Amount ₹
Skilled	80 × 50 = 4,000	75	3,00,000	70 × 55 = 3,850	80	3,08,000
Semi-skilled	40 × 50 = 2,000	50	1,00,000	40 × 55 = 2,200	60	1,32,000
Un-skilled	50 × 50 = 2,500	35 (+)	87,500	50 × 55 = 2,750	20 (+)	55,000
∴ Total	8,500		4,87,500	8,800		4,95,000

ii) **Calculation of standard mixing proportion of number of skilled, semi-silled and un-skilled workers in weeks :**

Skilled Workers	:	Semi-skilled Workers	:	Unskilled Workers
4,000 weeks	:	2,000 weeks	:	2,500 weeks
$\dfrac{8}{17}$	:	$\dfrac{4}{17}$	:	$\dfrac{5}{17}$

iii) Calculation of Total Actual Weeks worked :

$$= \quad \begin{array}{c} \text{Skilled Workers} \\ \text{3,850 weeks} \end{array} + \begin{array}{c} \text{Semi-skilled Workers} \\ \text{2,200 weeks} \end{array} + \begin{array}{c} \text{Unskilled Workers} \\ \text{2,750 weeks} \end{array}$$

= 8,800 weeks.

iv) Calculation of Standard Revised Mix in weeks :

= Actual weeks worked for × Standard mixing proportion

• **Skilled Workers :**

$$= \quad 8,800 \text{ weeks} \times \frac{8}{17}$$

= 4,141 weeks.

• **Semi-skilled Workers :**

$$= \quad 8,800 \text{ weeks} \times \frac{4}{17}$$

= 2,071 weeks

• **Unskilled Workers :**

$$= \quad 8,800 \text{ weeks} \times \frac{5}{17}$$

= 2,588 weeks

Calculation of Labour Variances :

i) Labour Cost Variance : (SW × SR) – (AW × AR)

= (Standard Weeks × Standard Rate) – (Actual Weeks × Actual Rate)

Skilled Workers :

= (4,000 weeks × ₹ 75) – (3,850 weeks × ₹ 80)

= ₹ 3,00,000 – ₹ 3,08,000

= ₹ 8,000 (Adverse)

Semi-skilled Workers :

= (2,000 weeks × ₹ 50) – (2,200 weeks × ₹ 60)

= ₹ 1,00,000 – ₹ 1,32,000

= ₹ 32,000 (Adverse)

Un-skilled Workers :

= (2,500 weeks × ₹ 35) – (2,750 weeks × ₹ 20)

= ₹ 87,500 – ₹ 55,000

= ₹ 32,500 (Favourable)

ii) Labour Rate Variance : (SR – AR) × AW

  =   (Standard Rate – Actual Rate) × Actual Weeks

Skilled Workers :

  =   (₹ 75 – ₹ 80) × 3,850 weeks

  =   ₹ 5 × 3,850 weeks

  =   ₹ 19,250 (Adverse)

Semi-skilled Workers :

  =   (₹ 50 – ₹ 60) × 2,200 weeks

  =   ₹ 10 × 2,200 weeks

  =   ₹ 22,000 (Adverse)

Un-skilled Workers :

  =   (₹ 35 – ₹ 20) × 2,750 weeks

  =   ₹ 15 × 2,750 weeks

  =   ₹ 41,250 (Favourable)

iii) Labour Efficiency Variance : (SW – AW) × SR

  =   (Standard Weeks – Actual Weeks) × Standard Rate

Skilled Workers :

  =   (4,000 weeks – 3,850 weeks) × ₹ 75

  =   150 weeks × ₹ 75

  =   ₹ 11,250 (Favourable)

Semi-skilled Workers :

  =   (2,000 weeks – 2,200 weeks) × ₹ 50

  =   200 weeks × ₹ 50

  =   ₹ 10,000 (Adverse)

Un-skilled Workers :

  =   (2,500 weeks – 2,750 weeks) × ₹ 35

  =   250 weeks × ₹ 35

  =   ₹ 8,750 (Adverse)

iv) Labour Mix Variance : (RSM – AM) × SR

  =   (Standard Revised Mix – Actual Mix) × Standard Rate

Skilled Workers :

  =   (4,141 weeks – 3,850 weeks) × ₹ 75

  =   291 weeks × ₹ 75

  =   ₹ 21,825 (Favourable)

Semi-skilled Workers :

= (2,071 weeks – 2,200 weeks) × ₹ 50

= 129 weeks × ₹ 50

= ₹ 6,450 (Adverse)

Un-skilled Workers :

= (2,588 weeks – 2,750 weeks) × ₹ 35

= 162 weeks × ₹ 35

= ₹ 5,670 (Adverse)

Verification,

$$LCV = LRV + LEV$$

Labour Cost Variance = Labour Rate Variance + Labour Efficiency Variance

Skilled Workers :

₹ 8,000 (A) = ₹ 19,250 (A) + ₹ 11,250 (F)

Semi-skilled Workers :

₹ 32,000 (A) = ₹ 22,000 (A) + ₹ 10,000 (A)

Un-skilled Workers :

₹ 32,500 (A) = ₹ 41,250 (F)+ ₹ 8,750 (A)

₹ 7,500 (A) = NIl + ₹ 7,500 (A)

∴ **Total : ₹ 7,500 (A) = ₹ 7,500 (A)**

ILLUSTRATION 9

From the following cost data made available by Glostar Ltd., Gulbarga, calculate –

i)   Labour Cost Variance,

ii)   Labour Rate Variance,

iii)   Labour Efficiency Variance,

iv)   Labour Mix Variance.

The standard labour force for manufacture of a Product 'Marshall' is as follows :

• 20 un-trained workers @ ₹ 0.75 per hour for 50 hours.

• 10 trained workers @ ₹ 1.25 per hour for 50 hours.

Whereas the actual labour force employed for manufacture of a product 'Marshall' is as follows :

• 22 un-trained workers @ ₹ 80 per hour for 50 hours.

• 8 trained workers @ ₹ 1.20 per hour for 50 hours.

Also verify your results.

SOLUTION

Working Notes :

i) **Calculation of Standard Labour Cost and Actual Labour Cost :**

Category of Workers	Standard			Actual		
	Weeks (Number of Workers × Number of Hours)	Rate (Per Worker per hour) ₹	Amount ₹	Weeks (Number of Workers × Number of Hours)	Rate (Per Worker per hour) ₹	Amount ₹
Un-trained	20 × 50 = 1,000	0.75	750	22 × 50 = 1,100	0.80	880
Trained	10 × 50 = 500	1.25	625	8 × 50 = 400	1.20	480
		(+)			(+)	
∴ Total	1,500		1,375	1,500		1,360

ii) **Calculation of standard mixing proportion of number of un-trained and trained workers in hours :**

Un-trained workers   :   Trained-workers

     1,000 Hours   :   500 Hours

      $\dfrac{2}{3}$: $\dfrac{1}{3}$

iii) **Calculation of Total Actual Hours worked :**

$$= \quad \underset{\text{1,100 Hours}}{\text{Un-trained workers}} \quad + \quad \underset{\text{400 Hours}}{\text{Trained workers}}$$

=   1,500 Hours

iv) **Calculation of Revised Standard Mix in hours :**

=   Actual Hours worked × Standard Mixing proportion

- **Untrained Workers :**

     =   1,500 Hours × $\dfrac{2}{3}$

     =   1,000 Hours

- **Trained Workers :**

     =   1,500 Hours × $\dfrac{1}{3}$

     =   500 Hours

Calculation of Labour Variances :

i) **Labour Cost Variance : (SH × SR) – (AH × AR)**

     =   (Standard Hours × Standard Rate) – (Actual Hours × Actual Rate)

Untrained Workers :

$=$ (1,000 Hours × ₹ 0.75) – (1,100 Hours × ₹ 0.80)

$=$ ₹ 750 – ₹ 880

$=$ ₹ 130 (Adverse)

Trained Workers :

$=$ (500 Hours × ₹ 1.25) – (400 Hours × ₹ 1.20)

$=$ ₹ 625 – ₹ 480

$=$ ₹ 145 (Favourable)

ii) Labour Rate Variance : (SR – AR) × AH

$=$ (Standard Rate – Actual Rate) × Actual Hours

Untrained Workers :

$=$ (₹ 0.75 – ₹ 0.80) × 1,100 Hours

$=$ ₹ 0.5 × 1,100 Hours

$=$ ₹ 55 (Adverse)

Trained Workers :

$=$ (₹ 1.25 – ₹ 1.20) × 400 Hours

$=$ ₹ 0.5 × 400 Hrs.

$=$ ₹ 20 (Favourable)

iii) Labour Efficiency Variance : (SH – AH) × SR

$=$ (Standard Hours – Actual Hours) × Standard Rate

Untrained Workers :

$=$ (1,000 Hours – 1,100 Hours) × ₹ 0.75

$=$ 100 Hours × ₹ 0.75

$=$ ₹ 75 (Adverse)

Trained Workers :

$=$ (500 Hours – 400 Hours) × ₹ 1.25

$=$ 100 Hours × ₹ 1.25

$=$ ₹ 125 (Favourable)

iv) Labour Mix Variance : (RSM – AM) × SR

$=$ (Revised Standard Mix – Actual mix) × Standard Rate

Untrained Workers :

$=$ (1,000 Hours – 1,100 Hours) × ₹ 0.75

$=$ 100 Hours × ₹ 0.75

$=$ ₹ 75 (Adverse)

Trained Workers :

= (500 Hours – 400 Hours) × ₹ 1.25

= 100 Hours × ₹ 1.25

= ₹ 125 (Favourable)

Verification,

i) LCV = LRV + LEV

Labour Cost Variance = Labour Rate Variance + Labour Efficiency Variance

Un-trained Workers :

₹ 130 (A) = ₹ 55 (A) + ₹ 75 (A)

Trained Workers :

₹ 145 (F) = ₹ 20 (F) + ₹ 125 (F)

₹ 15 (F) = ₹ 35 (A) + ₹ 50 (F)

∴ **Total : ₹ 15 (F) = ₹ 15 (F)**

ILLUSTRATION 10

The details regarding the composition and weekly wage rates of labour force engaged on a job scheduled to be completed in 30 weeks are as follows :

Type of Workers	Standard		Actual	
	Number of Workers	Weekly Rate ₹	Number of Workers	Weekly Rate ₹
Skilled	75	60	70	70
Semi-skilled	45	40	30	50
Unskilled	60	30	80	20

The work is actually completed in 32 weeks. Calculate various labour variances.

SOLUTION

Working Notes :

i) Calculation of Standard Labour Cost and Actual Labour Cost

Type of Workers	Standard			Actual		
	Week (Number of Workers × Number of Weeks)	Rate ₹	Amount ₹	Weeks (Number of Workers × Number of Weeks)	Rate ₹	Amount ₹
Skilled	75 × 30 = 2,250	60	1,35,000	70 × 32 = 2,240	70	1,56,800
Semi-skilled	45 × 30 = 1,350	40	54,000	30 × 32 = 960	50	48,000
Unskilled	60 × 30 = 1,800	30	54,000	80 × 32 = 2,560	20	51,200
	5,400		2,43,000	5,760		2,56,000

ii) **Calculation of Standard mixing proportion of number of skilled, semi-skilled and unskilled workers in weeks**

Skilled workers : Semi-skilled workers : Unskilled workers

$$2{,}250 \quad : \quad 1{,}350 \quad : \quad 1{,}800$$

$$\frac{45}{108} \quad : \quad \frac{27}{108} \quad : \quad \frac{36}{108}$$

iii) **Calculation of total actual weeks worked :**

Skilled workers + Semi-skilled workers + Unskilled workers

=   2,240 weeks   960 weeks   2,560 weeks

=   5,760 weeks

iv) **Calculation of Revised Standard Mix in weeks**

=   Actual weeks worked for × Standard mixing proportion

- **Skilled Workers :**

  = $5{,}760 \text{ weeks} \times \dfrac{45}{108}$

  =   2,400 weeks

- **Semi-skilled Workers :**

  = $5{,}760 \text{ weeks} \times \dfrac{27}{108}$

  =   1,440 weeks

- **Unskilled Workers :**

  = $5{,}760 \text{ weeks} \times \dfrac{36}{108}$

  =   1,920 weeks

Calculation of Labour Variances :

i) **Labour Cost Variances : (SW × SR) – (AW × AR)**

=   (Standard Weeks × Standard Rate) – (Actual Weeks × Actual Rate)

- **Skilled Workers :**

  =   (2,250 weeks × ₹ 60) – (2,240 weeks × ₹ 70)

  =   ₹ 1,35,000 – ₹ 1,56,800

  =   ₹ 21,800 (Adverse)

- **Semi-skilled Workers :**

  =   (1,350 weeks × ₹ 40) – (960 weeks × ₹ 50)

  =   ₹ 54,000 – ₹ 48,000

  =   ₹ 6,000 (Favourable)

- **Unskilled Workers :**
  - = (1,800 weeks × ₹ 30) – (2,560 weeks × ₹ 20)
  - = ₹ 54,000 – ₹ 51,200
  - = ₹ 2,800 (Favourable)

ii) **Labour Rate Variance : (SR – AR) × AW**
  - = (Standard Rate – Actual Rate) × Actual Weeks

- **Skilled Workers :**
  - = (₹ 60 – ₹ 70) × 2,240 weeks
  - = ₹ 10 × 2,240 weeks
  - = ₹ 22,400 (Adverse)

- **Semi-skilled Workers :**
  - = (₹ 40 – ₹ 50) × 960 weeks
  - = ₹ 10 × 960 weeks
  - = ₹ 9,600 Adverse

- **Unskilled Workers :**
  - = (₹ 30 – ₹ 20) × 2,560 weeks
  - = ₹ 10 × 2,560 weeks
  - = ₹ 25,600 (Favourable)

iii) **Labour Efficiency Variance : (SW – AW) × SR**
  - = (Standard Weeks – Actual Weeks) × Standard Rate

- **Skilled Workers :**
  - = (2,250 weeks – 2,240 weeks) × ₹ 60
  - = 10 weeks × ₹ 60
  - = ₹ 600 (Favourable)

- **Semi-skilled Workers :**
  - = (1,350 weeks – 960 weeks) × ₹ 40
  - = 390 weeks × ₹ 40
  - = ₹ 15,600 (Favourable)

- **Unskilled Workers :**
  - = (1,800 weeks – 2,560 weeks) × ₹ 30
  - = 760 weeks × ₹ 30
  - = ₹ 22,800 (Adverse)

iv) **Labour Mix Variance : (RSM – AM) × SR**

= (Revised Standard Mix – Actual Mix) × Standard Rate

- **Skilled Workers :**
  = (2,400 weeks – 2,240 weeks) × ₹ 60
  = 160 weeks × ₹ 60
  = ₹ 9,600 (Favourable)
- **Semi-skilled Workers :**
  = (1,440 weeks – 960 weeks) × ₹ 40
  = 480 weeks × ₹ 40
  = ₹ 19,200 (Favourable)
- **Unskilled Workers :**
  = (1,920 weeks – 2,560 weeks) × ₹ 30
  = 640 weeks × ₹ 30
  = ₹ 19,200 (Adverse)

Verification,

$$LCV = LRV + LEV$$

Labour Cost Variance = Labour Rate Variance + Labour Efficiency Variance

Skilled Workers : ₹ 21,800 (A) = ₹ 22,400 (A) + ₹ 600 (F)

Semi-skilled Workers : ₹ 6,000 (F) = ₹ 9,600 (A) + ₹ 15,600 (F)

Unskilled Workers : 2,800 (F) = ₹ 25,600 (F) + ₹ 22,800 (A)

₹ 13,000 (A) = ₹ 6,400 (A) + ₹ 6,600 (A)

∴ Total ₹ 13,000 (A) = ₹ 13,000 (A)

ILLUSTRATION 11

In Mafatlal Mills Ltd., Mumbai standard labour cost of producing 500 metre of cloth has been specified as follows :

- Men Workers : 20 Hours @ ₹ 15 per hour.
- Women Workers : 30 Hours @ ₹ 10 per hour.

The actual cost data for producing 500 metre of cloth is as follows :

- Men Workers : 30 Hours @ ₹ 17 per hour
- Women Workers : 30 Hours @ ₹ 10 per hour

You are required to calculate,

i)   Labour Cost Variance,
ii)   Labour Rate Variance,
iii) Labour Efficiency Variance,
iv) Labour Mix Variance,
v)   Labour Yield Variance.

Also verify your results.

SOLUTION

Calculation of Labour Variances :

i)   **Labour Cost Variance : (SH × SR) – (AH × AR)**

      =   (Standard Hours × Standard Rate) – (Actual Hours × Actual Rate)

- **Men Workers :**

      =   (20 Hours × ₹ 15) – (30 Hours × ₹ 17)

      =   ₹ 300 – ₹ 510

      =   ₹ 210 (Adverse)

- **Women Workers :**

      =   (30 Hours × ₹ 10) – (30 Hours × ₹ 10)

      =   ₹ 300 – ₹ 300

      =   NIL

ii)   **Labour Rate Variance : (SR – AR) × AH**

      =   (Standard Rate – Actual Rate) × Actual Hours

- **Men Workers :**

      =   (₹ 15 – ₹ 17) × 30 Hours

      =   ₹ 2 × 30 Hours

      =   ₹ 60 (Adverse)

- **Women Workers :**

      =   (₹ 10 – ₹ 10) × 30 Hours

      =   NIL × 30 Hours

      =   NIL

iii)   **Labour Efficiency Variance : (SH – AH) × SR**

      =   (Standard Hours – Actual Hours) × Standard Rate

- **Men Workers :**

      =   (20 Hours – 30 Hours) × ₹ 15

      =   10 Hours × ₹ 15

      =   ₹ 150 (Adverse)

- **Women Workers :**

      =   (30 Hours – 30 Hours) × ₹ 10

      =   NIL × ₹ 10

      =   NIL

iv) **Labour Mix Variance : (RSM – AM) × SR**

=   (Revised Standard Mix – Actual Mix) × Standard Rate

•   **Men Workers :**

=   (24 Hours – 30 Hours) × ₹ 15

=   6 Hours × ₹ 15

=   ₹ 90 (Adverse)

•   **Women Workers :**

=   (36 Hours – 30 Hours) × ₹ 10

=   6 Hours × ₹ 10

=   ₹ 60 (Favourable)

v)   **Labour Yield Variance : (AO – SO) × SC**

=   (Actual Output – Standard Output from Actual Hours Worked) × Standard Cost per metre

=   (500 metre – 600 metre) × ₹ 1.20

=   ₹ 120 (Adverse)

Verification,

i) LCV = LRV + LEV

Labour Cost Variance = Labour Rate Variance + Labour Efficinecy Variance

Men Workers :   ₹ 210 (A) = ₹ 60 (A) + ₹ 150(A)

Women Workers :   NIL = NIL + NIL

₹ **210 (A)** = ₹ **60 (A)** + ₹ **150 (A)**

∴   **Total : ₹ 210 (A)** = ₹ **210 (A)**

ii) LEV = LMV + LYV

Labour Efficiency Variance =Labour Mix Variance + Labour Yield Variance

₹ **150 (A)** = ₹ **30 (A)** + ₹ **120 (A)**

∴   **Total : ₹ 150 (A)** = ₹ **150 (A)**

Working Notes :

i)   **Calculation of Standard Mixing Proportion of men and women workers in hours :**

Men Workers : Women Workers

20 Hours : 30 Hours

$\dfrac{2}{5}$: $\dfrac{3}{5}$

ii) Calculation of Total Actual Hours Worked :

$$= \frac{\text{Men Workers}}{30 \text{ Hours}} + \frac{\text{Women Workers}}{30 \text{ Hours}}$$

= 60 Hours.

iii) Calculation of Revised Standard Mix in hours :

= Actual Hours worked for × Standard Mixing Proportion

• **Men Workers :**

$$= 60 \text{ Hours} \times \frac{2}{5}$$

= 24 Hours.

• **Women Workers :**

$$= 60 \text{ Hours} \times \frac{3}{5}$$

= 36 Hours

iv) Calculation of Standard Output i.e. expected output from actual hours worked :

If 50 Standard Hours = 500 metre output

∴ 60 Actual Hours = ?

$$= \frac{60 \text{ Hours} \times 500 \text{ Metre}}{50 \text{ Hours}}$$

= 600 Metre

v) Calculation of Standard Labour Cost per metre :

	₹
• Total Standard Labour Cost	
Men Workers : (20 Hours × ₹ 15)	300
Add : Women Workers : (30 Hours × ₹ 10)	(+) 300
∴ Total	600

If 500 Metre = ₹ 600 Labour Cost

∴ 1 Metre = ?

$$= \frac{1 \text{ Metre} \times ₹ 600}{500 \text{ Metre}}$$

= ₹ 1.20 per metre

QUESTIONS FOR SELF STUDY

I) **Theory Questions :**

i)   What do you mean by 'Standard Costing' ? What are its advantages ?

ii) Explain the concept of standard costing.

iii) Explain the main activities related to a sound standard costing system.

iv) What do you mean by Variances ? Explain the different catgories of Cost Variances.

v)   What do you mean by material cost variance ? Explain the classification of material cost variances into different categories with suitable illustrations.

vi) Distinguish between material price variance and material rate variance with suitable examples.

vii) Define labour cost variance and explain the possible reasons for labour rate variance, labour efficiency variance and idle time variance.

viii) What is overhead variance ? What are the different types of overhead variance ? How are they calculated and dealt with ?

ix) Write short notes on :

a) Concept of standard costing,	b) The standard costing system
c) Standard Direct Material cost	d) Standard Quantity of Direct Material
e) Over-head standard	f) Direct material variance
g) Standard costing	h) Direct labour variance
i) Labour price variance	j) Labour cost variance
k) Material mix variance	l) Material yield variance.

II) **Practical Problems :**

i)   Standard Price   : ₹ 6 per kg.

Actual Price   : ₹ 8 per kg.

Standard Quantity   : 1,000 kg.

Actual material price variance : 900 kg

ii) Calculate Material Cost, Material Price and Material Usage variances.

Calculate the material mix variance from the following particular :

Standard mix for product and actual mix of product

Standard	**Actual**
Product A : 60 kg @ 5	Product A : 80 kg @ ₹ 4
Product B : 40 kg @ ₹ 10	Product B : 20 kg @ ₹ 8
Total 100	Total 100

iii) From the following data, calculate the material variance :

Materials	Standard Qty.	Rate (₹)	Actual Qty.	Rate (₹)
A	160	10,000	128	9.50
B	80	8.00	112	9.00
	240		240	

Due to shortage of Material A, it was decided to reduce consumption of A by 15% and increase consumption of Material B by 30%.

iv) The standard mix and actual mix of producing an article is given below :

Standard Raw Material	Actual Raw Material
A 60 Units @ ₹ 10	80 Units @ ₹ 12
B 90 Units @ ₹ 20	60 Units @ ₹ 25
150 Units	140 Units

Calculate the material price variance, material usage variance and material mix variance.

v) From the following data of a factory, calculate,

a) Material Cost Variance, b) Material Price Variance and c) Material Usage Variance.

Material	Standard Units	Rate ₹	Actual Units	Rate ₹
A	300	1.00	300	0.80
B	600	0.50	340	0.60
C	900	0.80	900	1.00

vi) The standard cost of chemical mixture is,

40% material A at ₹ 20 per kg. and 60% material B at ₹ 30 per kg.

A standard loss of 10% is expected in production. During a period there is used :

90 kg. material A at a cost of ₹ 18 per kg.

110 kg. material B at a cost of ₹ 34 per kg.

The weight produced is 182f kg. of good product.

Calculate :

a) Material Price Variance

b) Material Mix Variance

c) Material Yield Variance

d) Material Cost Variance

vii) ABC Ltd. manufacturing LXE by mixing three raw materials for every batch of 100 kg. LXE, 125 kgs of raw materials are used. In March 2013, 60 batchs were prepared to produce output of 5,000 kgs. of LXE. The standard and actual particulars for March, 2007 are as under :

Raw Material	Standard		Actual		Quantity of Raw Materials Purchased kg.
	Mix %	Price per kg. (₹)	Mix %	Price per kg. (₹)	
A	50	20	60	21	5,000
B	30	10	20	8	2,000
C	20	5	20	6	1,200

Calculate :

a) Material Cost Variance

b) Material Price Variance

c) Material Mix Variance

d) Material Yield Variance

viii) The following information is received from a manufacturing company for the month of March 2013.

Particulars	Budgeted	Actual
Variable Overheads	₹ 25,200	₹ 27,500
Labour Hours	₹ 11,200	₹ 11,000
Production Units	5,600	5,400

Calculate :

a) Variable Overhead Expenditure, b) Variable Overhead Efficiency, c) Variable Overhead Cost Variance.

ix) ABC Company set 30 hours at a wage rate of ₹ 4 per hours for a given task. The given task was completed with 7 days with daily working of 4 hours.

Compute labour efficiency variance.

x) CTBT engaged 75 workers at an average rate of ₹ 3 per day. The work was completed within 4 days. The standard cost set for the specified work amount to ₹ 850.

Compute Labour Cost Variance.

xi) ABC Co. Ltd sets five hours as labour time standard for processing one unit of product XX at a standard direct labour rate of ₹ 5 per hour. During the month of May, the company used 6,000 actual direct labour hours at ₹ 4 per hours to process 1,000 units of product VX.

Compute Labour Cost Variances.

xii) Calculate Labour Mix Variance from the following :

	Standard			Actual		
	Hours	Rate ₹	Amount ₹	Hours	Rate ₹	Amount ₹
Men	600	3	1,800	550	4	2,200
Women	800	2	1,600	850	1.50	1,275
	1,400		3,400	1,400		3,475

xiii) From the information given below compute Overhead Cost Variance :

Particulars	Budgeted	Actual
Variable Overheads	₹ 3,000	₹ 3,000
Variable Overheads	₹ 1,500	₹ 3,000
Output : Unit	3,000	2,500

xiv) From the following data calculate Fixed Overhead Variances :

Budgeted Fixed Overhead	:	₹ 10,000
Actual Fixed Overhead	:	₹ 10,200
Budgeted Output	:	5,000 Units
Actual Output	:	5,200 Units
Budgeted Hours	:	10,400 Hours
Actual Hours	:	10,050 Hours

■■■

Bibliography

1. R. N. Anthony, G. A. Walsh : Management Accounting

2. M. Y. Khan, K. P. Jain : Management Accounting

3. I. M. Pandey : Management Accounting

4. J. Betty : Management Accounting

5. Dr. Kishor N. Jagtap : Management Accounting

6. Sr. K. Paul : Management Accounting

7. Dr. Jawaharlal : Management Accounting

■■■

Time: 3 Hours   April 2013   Max. Marks: 100

Instructions:

    (1) **All** *questions are* **compulsory**.

    (2) *Figures to the* **right** *indicate* **full** *marks.*

1. An Enterprise having the following two proposals of investment.

Particulars	Proposal A	Proposal B
Cost of Investments (₹)	20,000	28,000
Life of the Assets (Years)	4	5
Scrap Value	Nil	Nil

Net income after depreciation and tax.

Year	₹ Proposal 'A'	₹ Proposal 'B'
2008	500	Nil
2009	2,000	3,400
2010	3,500	3,400
2011	2,500	3,400
2012	–	3,400

It is estimated that each of the project will require an additional working capital of ₹ 2,000 which will be received back in full after the expiry of each project life. Depreciation is to be provided under straight line method.

The present value of Re.1 to be received at the end of each year at 10% per annum is given below.

Year	Present value ₹
1	0.91
2	0.83
3	0.75
4	0.68
5	0.62

You are required to assess the profitability of the projects on the basis of the following methods.

1. Return on Investment

2. Payback period

3. Discounted payback period

4. Profitability index.   **(20)**

2. Explain how the cost is determined in respect of the following?

   1. Cost of preference shares

   2. Cost of equity shares

   3. Cost of debentures. **(20)**

OR

A factory is currently working at 60% capacity and produces 1,200 units, at a cost of ₹ 250 per unit as per details given below:

Particulars	Per Unit ₹
Direct material	100
Direct labour	60
Variable overheads	30
Fixed overheads	20
Variable Exp. (Direct)	10
Selling Expenses (20% fixed)	15
Administration Exp. (90% fixed)	10
Distribution Exp. (80% variable)	5
	Total 250

The current selling price is ₹ 300 per unit. At 70% capacity working, material cost per unit increases by 2% and selling price per unit falls by 2%. At 90% capacity working, material cost per unit increases by 5% and selling price per unit falls by 5%. Estimate profits of the factory at 70% and 90% working capacity. **(20)**

3. What is break even analysis? What are its assumptions and limitations? **(20)**

OR

The sales and profit during two years were:

Year	Sales ₹	Profit ₹
2011	1,50,000	20,000
2012	1,70,000	25,000

You are required to calculate:

(i) Break even point

(ii) P/V Ratio

(iii) Sales required to earn profit of ₹ 40,000.

(iv) The profit made when sales are ₹ 2,50,000.

(v) Variable costs of the two periods.

(vi) Margin of safety in 2012. **(20)**

4. Define budget and budgetary control. State its objects and advantages.   **(20)**

OR

The standard material cost to produce a tonne of chemical 'X' is:

   300 kg. of material 'A' at ₹ 10 per kg.

   400 kg. of material 'B' at ₹ 5 per kg.

   500 kg. of material 'C' at ₹ 6 per kg.

During the period, 100 tones of chemical X were produced from the usage of:

   35 tonnes of material 'A' at a cost of ₹ 9,000 per tonne.

   42 tonnes of material 'B' at a cost of ₹ 6,000 per tonne.

   53 tonnes of material 'C' at a cost of ₹ 7,000 per tonne.

Calculate price, usage and mix variances.   **(20)**

5. Write short notes (**any four**):
   1. Limitations of capital investment appraisal.
   2. Types of labour cost variance.
   3. Sales budget.
   4. Profit volume ratio.
   5. Explicit and implicit cost.
   6. Profitability index.   **(20)**

■■■

Time: 3 Hours   **April 2015**   **Max. Marks: 50**

Instructions:

   (1) *All questions are **compulsory**.*

   (2) *Figures to the **right** indicate **full** marks.*

Q.1 Minal Electronics Ltd. is considering the purchase of machine.   **[14]**

Two machine P and Q are available each costing ₹ 3,00,000. In comparing the profitability of machines a discount rate of 10% is to be used. Earnings after taxation are expected to be as follows:

Year	Machine 'P' (₹)	Machine 'Q' (₹)
1	90,000	30,000
2	1,20,000	90,000
3	1,50,000	1,20,000
4	90,000	1,80,000
5	60,000	1,20,000

Indicate which machine would be more profitable under the following methods of ranking investment proposals.

(a) Payback method.

(b) Average Return on investment method.

(c) Net present value method.

The present value of ₹ 1 to be received at the end of each year, at 10% p.a. is given below:

Year	Present Value
1	0.909
2	0.826
3	0.751
4	0.683
5	0.621

OR

Explain how the cost of capital is determined in respect of the following.

(a) Cost of Preference Shares.

(b) Cost of Equity Shares.

(c) Cost of Debt / Debentures.

Q.2 From the following forecasts of income and expenditure, prepare a Cash Budget for the period from June 2014 to August 2014.   **[14]**

Months	Sales (₹)	Purchases (₹)	Wages (₹)	Manu-facturing Expenses	Selling Expenses
April 2014	1,50,000	1,20,000	15,000	20% of wages	5% of Total Sales
May 2014	2,40,000	1,50,000	15,000	20% of wages	5% of Total Sales
June 2014	1,80,000	2,10,000	18,000	20% of wages	5% of Total Sales
July 2014	2,10,000	1,20,000	18,000	20% of wages	5% of Total Sales
Aug. 2014	1,80,000	90,000	21,000	20% of wages	5% of Total Sales

Additional information:

(a) 1/5th of the sales are on cash basis.

(b) 50% of the credit sales are recovered in the next month, whereas 50% are recovered after two months.

(c) Cash sales are made at 5% cash discounts.

(d) All purchase are credit purchase and the due amount is paid after two months.

(e) Wages are paid 15 days in arrears.

(f) Manufacturing expenses and selling expenses are paid in the same month.

(g) A machine costing ₹ 1,80,000 is to be purchased in the month of July 2014. 50% payment is to be made in the same month and the remaining amount is to be paid in three equal installments along with interest @ 18% p.a.

(h) As on 1st June, 2014 cash balance is 1,09,800.

OR

What is Break - Even Analysis? State the assumptions, advantages and limitations of Break - Even Analysis.

Q.3 (a) State the advantages and limitations of Standard costing.   [7]

OR

(b) The following particulars are obtained from the records of a factory manufacturing product X & Y.

Particulars	Product X (Per Unit) ₹	Product Y (Per Unit) ₹
Selling Price	300	600
Material Cost @ ₹ 10 per Kg.	60	150
Wages ₹ 3 per hour	90	180
Variable overheads	30	60
Total Fixed cost ₹ 15,000		

State which product is better to be produced and why in the following cases :

(i)   If total sales in unit is key factor.

(ii) If total sales in value is key factor.

(iii) If raw material is in short supply.

(iv) If labour hours is the limiting factor.

(v) If raw material available is 6000 kgs. And maximum sale of each product is 750 units.

(c) Differentiate between Fixed Budget and Flexible Budget.   [7]

OR

(d) The standard material cost to produce a tonne of chemical Y is:

900 kg. of material A at ₹ 10 per kg.

1200 kg. of material B at ₹ 5 per kg.

1500 kg. of material C at ₹ 6 per kg.

During the period, 100 tonnes of chemical Y were produced from the usage of 105 tones of material A at a cost of ₹ 9,000 per tonne.

105 tones of material A at a cost of ₹ 9,000 per tonne.

126 tones of material B at a cost of ₹ 6,000 per tonne.

159 tones of material C at a cost of ₹ 7,000 per tonne.

Calculate price, usage and mix variances.

Q.4 Write Short Notes :   [8]

(a) Implicit Cost and Explicit Cost.

(b) Master Budget.

(c) Profitability Index.

(d) Key Factor.

■■■

www.ingramcontent.com/pod-product-compliance
Lightning Source LLC
Chambersburg PA
CBHW081326090726
47907CB00010B/2388